KICK-ASS

KICK-ASS: THE NEW GIRL, VOL. 2. First printing. APRIL 2019. Published by Image Comics, Inc. Office of publication: 2701 NW Vaughn St., Suite 780, Portland, OR 97210. Copyright © 2010, 2011, 2012, 2013, and 2019 Dave and Eggsy Ltd and John S Romita. All rights reserved. Contains material originally published in single magazine form as KICK-ASS #7-12. "KICK-ASS", the KICK-ASS logos, and the likenesses of all characters and institutions herein are trademarks of Dave and Eggsy Ltd and John S Romita, unless otherwise noted. "Image" and the Image Comics logos are registered trademarks of Image Comics, Inc. No part of this publication may be reproduced or transmitted, in any form or by any means (except for short excerpts for journalistic or review purposes), without the express written permission of Dave and Eggsy Ltd and John S Romita, or Image Comics, Inc. All names, characters, events, and locales in this publication are entirely fictional. Any resemblance to actual persons (living or dead), events, or places, without satirical intent, is coincidental. Printed in the USA. For information regarding the CPSIA on this printed material call: 203-595-3636. For international rights, contact: lucy@markmillarltd.com ISBN: 978-1-5343-1064-3.

STEVE NILES
WRITER

MARCELO FRUSIN
ARTIST

SUNNY GHO
COLORIST

JOHN WORKMAN
LETTERER

MELINA MIKULIC
DESIGN AND PRODUCTION

RACHAEL FULTON
EDITOR

HIT-GIRL and **KICK-ASS** created by **MARK MILLAR** and **JOHN ROMITA JR.**

ONE

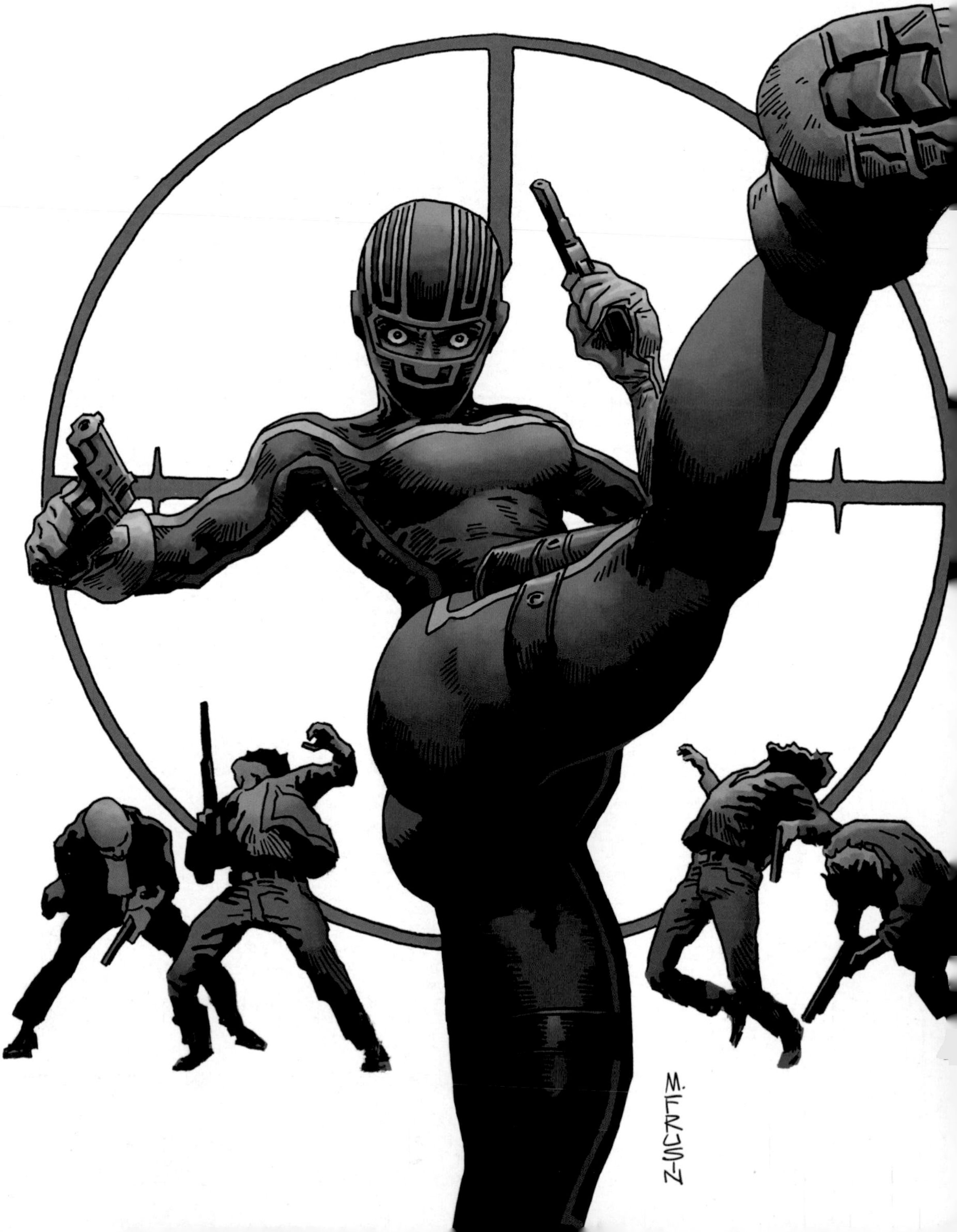

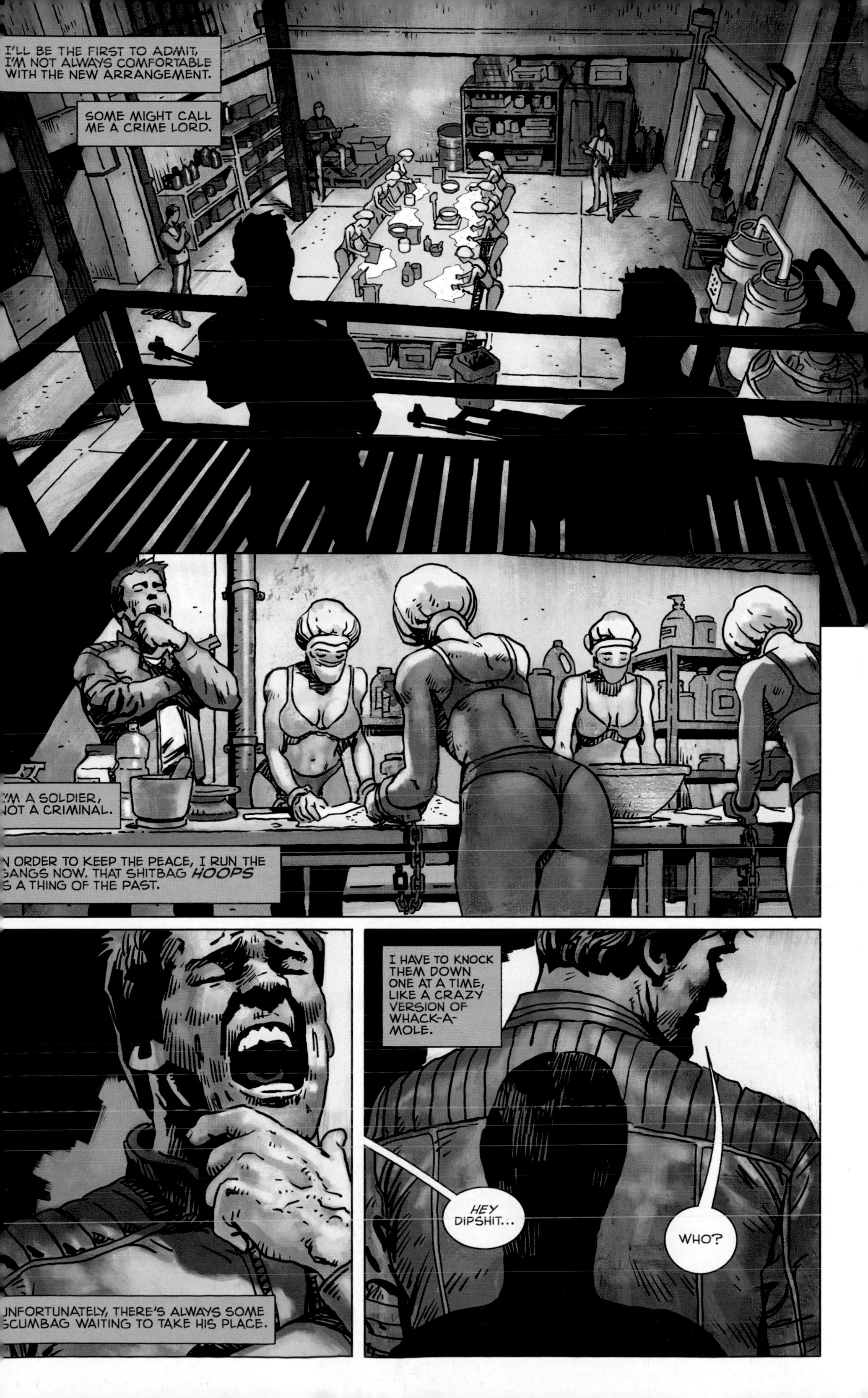

I'LL BE THE FIRST TO ADMIT, I'M NOT ALWAYS COMFORTABLE WITH THE NEW ARRANGEMENT.
SOME MIGHT CALL ME A CRIME LORD.
'M A SOLDIER, NOT A CRIMINAL.
N ORDER TO KEEP THE PEACE, I RUN THE GANGS NOW. THAT SHITBAG HOOPS S A THING OF THE PAST.
UNFORTUNATELY, THERE'S ALWAYS SOME SCUMBAG WAITING TO TAKE HIS PLACE.
I HAVE TO KNOCK THEM DOWN ONE AT A TIME, LIKE A CRAZY VERSION OF WHACK-A-MOLE.
HEY DIPSHIT...
WHO?

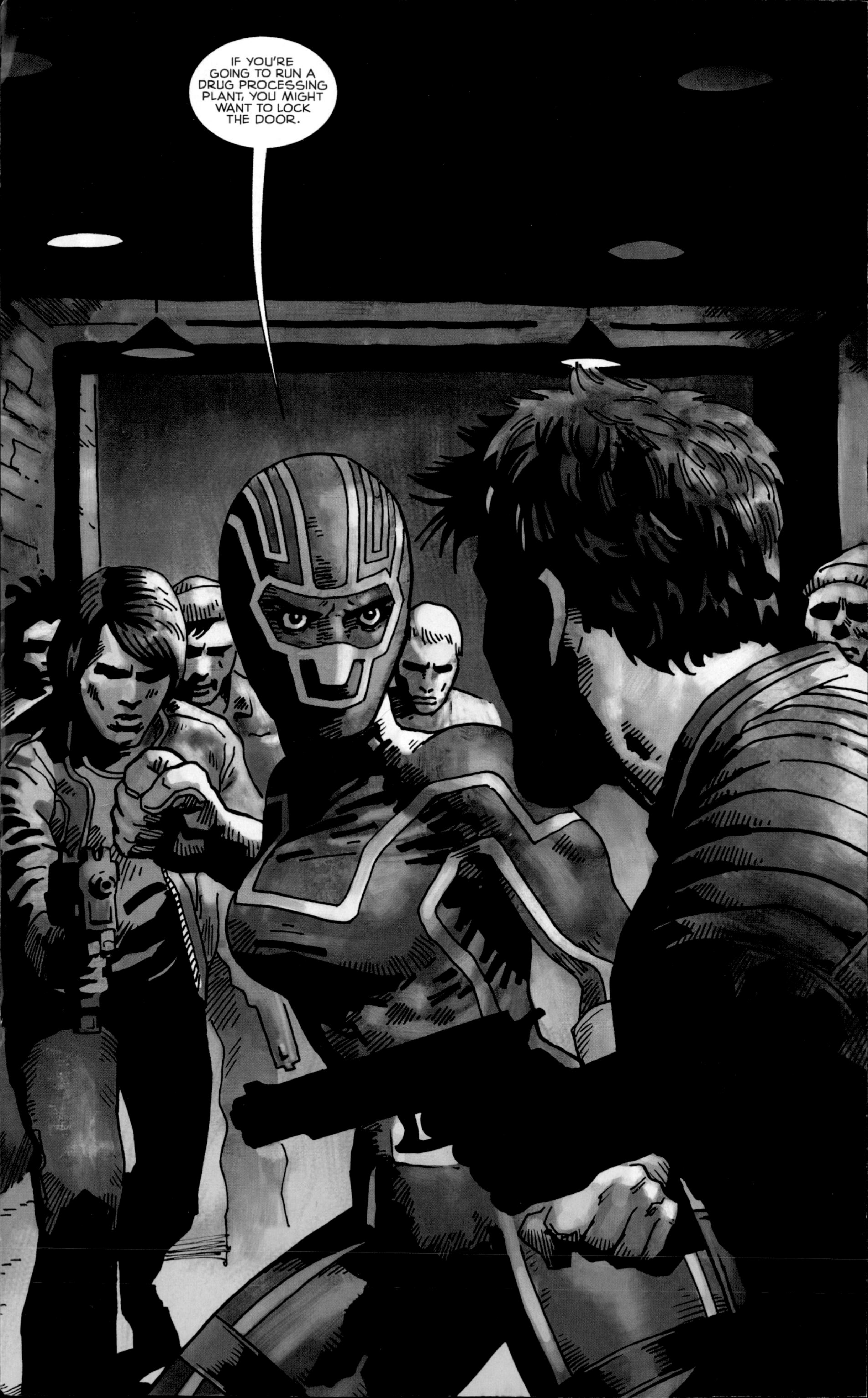
IF YOU'RE GOING TO RUN A DRUG PROCESSING PLANT, YOU MIGHT WANT TO LOCK THE DOOR.

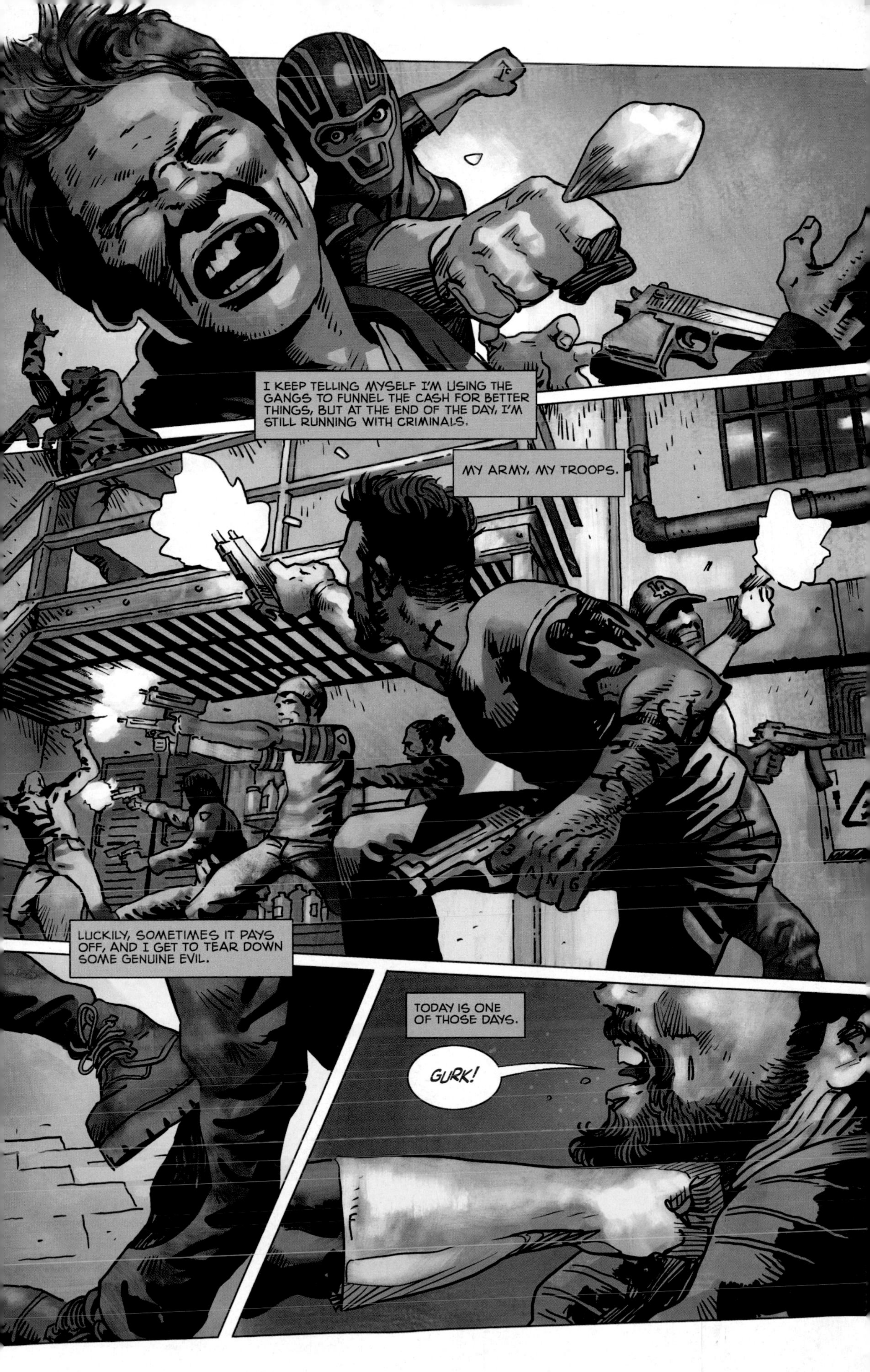
I KEEP TELLING MYSELF I'M USING THE GANGS TO FUNNEL THE CASH FOR BETTER THINGS, BUT AT THE END OF THE DAY, I'M STILL RUNNING WITH CRIMINALS.
MY ARMY, MY TROOPS.
LUCKILY, SOMETIMES IT PAYS OFF, AND I GET TO TEAR DOWN SOME GENUINE EVIL.
TODAY IS ONE OF THOSE DAYS.
GURK!

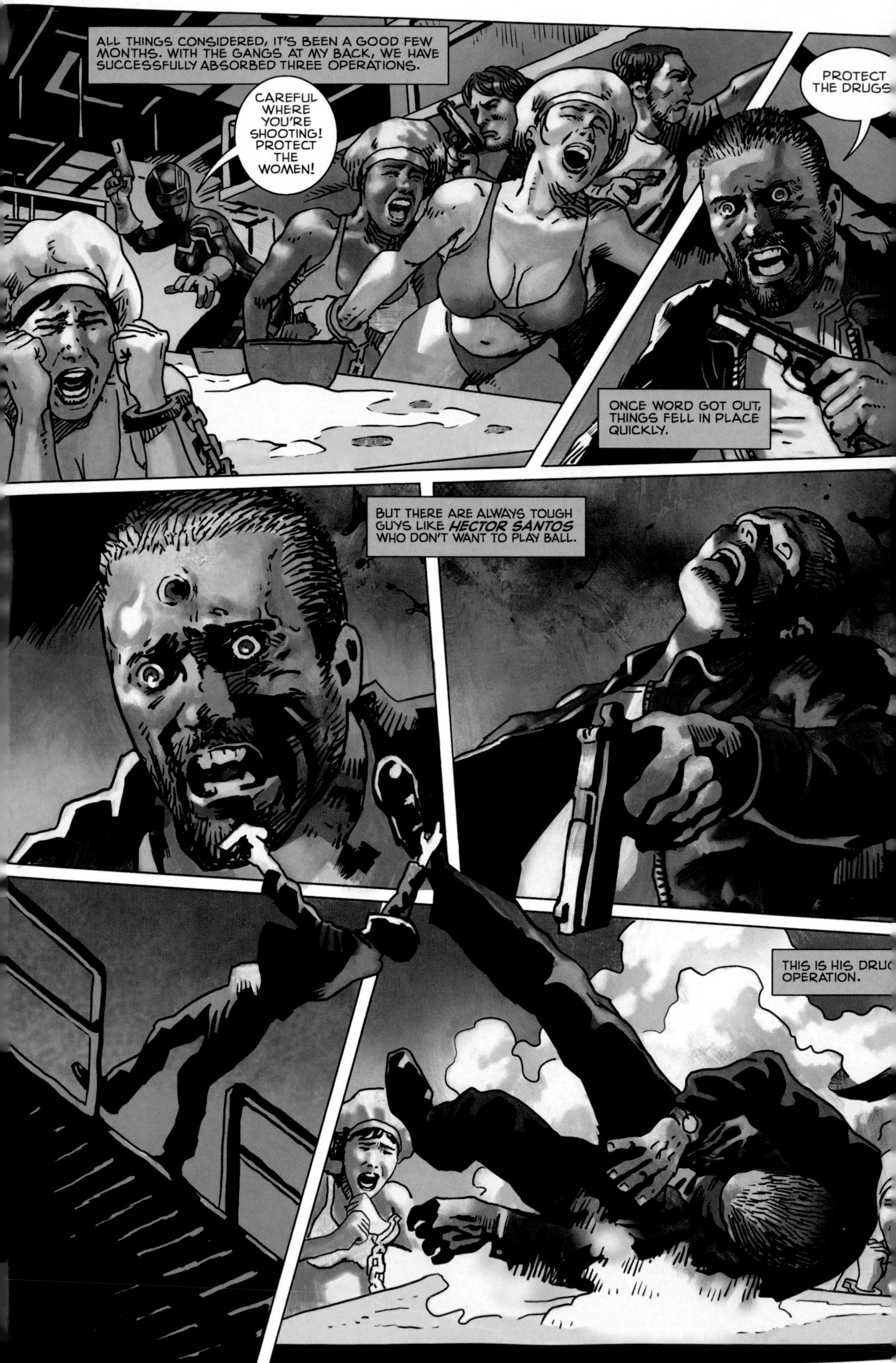
ALL THINGS CONSIDERED, IT'S BEEN A GOOD FEW MONTHS. WITH THE GANGS AT MY BACK, WE HAVE SUCCESSFULLY ABSORBED THREE OPERATIONS.
CAREFUL WHERE YOU'RE SHOOTING! PROTECT THE WOMEN!
PROTECT THE DRUGS
ONCE WORD GOT OUT, THINGS FELL IN PLACE QUICKLY.
BUT THERE ARE ALWAYS TOUGH GUYS LIKE *HECTOR SANTOS* WHO DON'T WANT TO PLAY BALL.
THIS IS HIS DRU OPERATION.

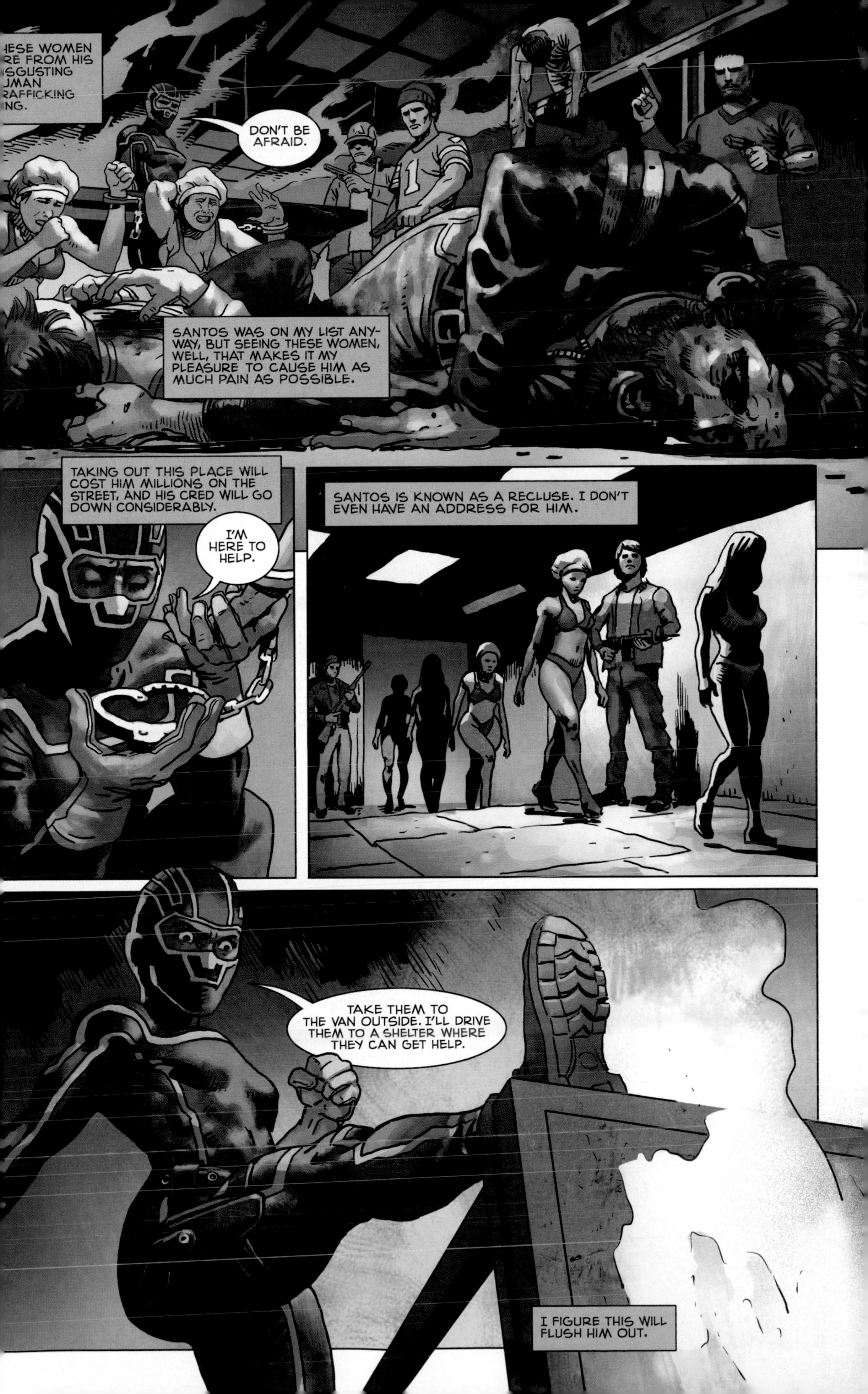
HESE WOMEN
RE FROM HIS
SGUSTING
JMAN
RAFFICKING
NG.
DON'T BE AFRAID.
SANTOS WAS ON MY LIST ANYWAY, BUT SEEING THESE WOMEN, WELL, THAT MAKES IT MY PLEASURE TO CAUSE HIM AS MUCH PAIN AS POSSIBLE.
TAKING OUT THIS PLACE WILL COST HIM MILLIONS ON THE STREET, AND HIS CRED WILL GO DOWN CONSIDERABLY.
I'M HERE TO HELP.
SANTOS IS KNOWN AS A RECLUSE. I DON'T EVEN HAVE AN ADDRESS FOR HIM.
TAKE THEM TO THE VAN OUTSIDE. I'LL DRIVE THEM TO A SHELTER WHERE THEY CAN GET HELP.
I FIGURE THIS WILL FLUSH HIM OUT.

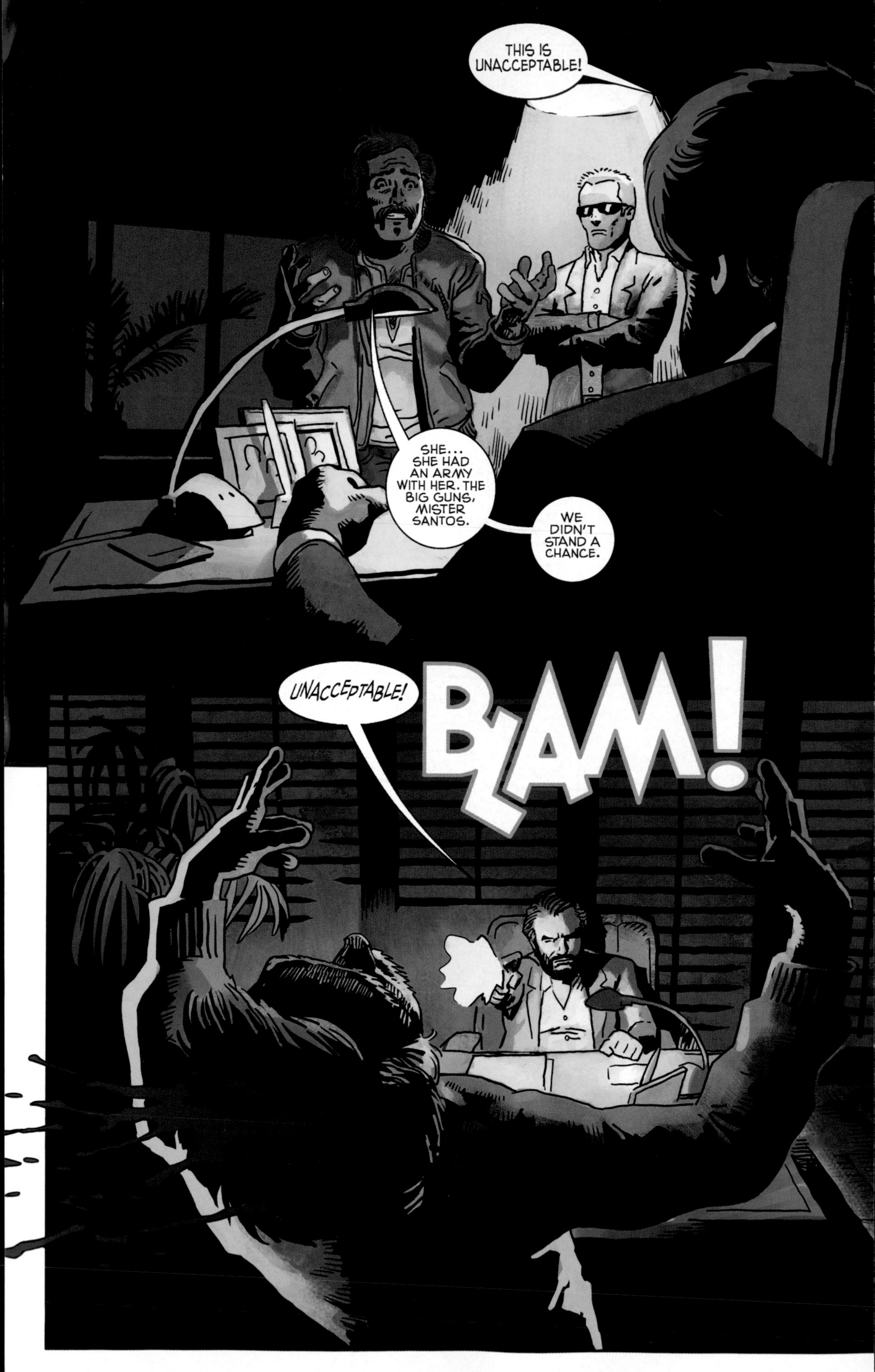
THIS IS UNACCEPTABLE!
SHE... SHE HAD AN ARMY WITH HER. THE BIG GUNS, MISTER SANTOS.
WE DIDN'T STAND A CHANCE.
UNACCEPTABLE!
BLAM!

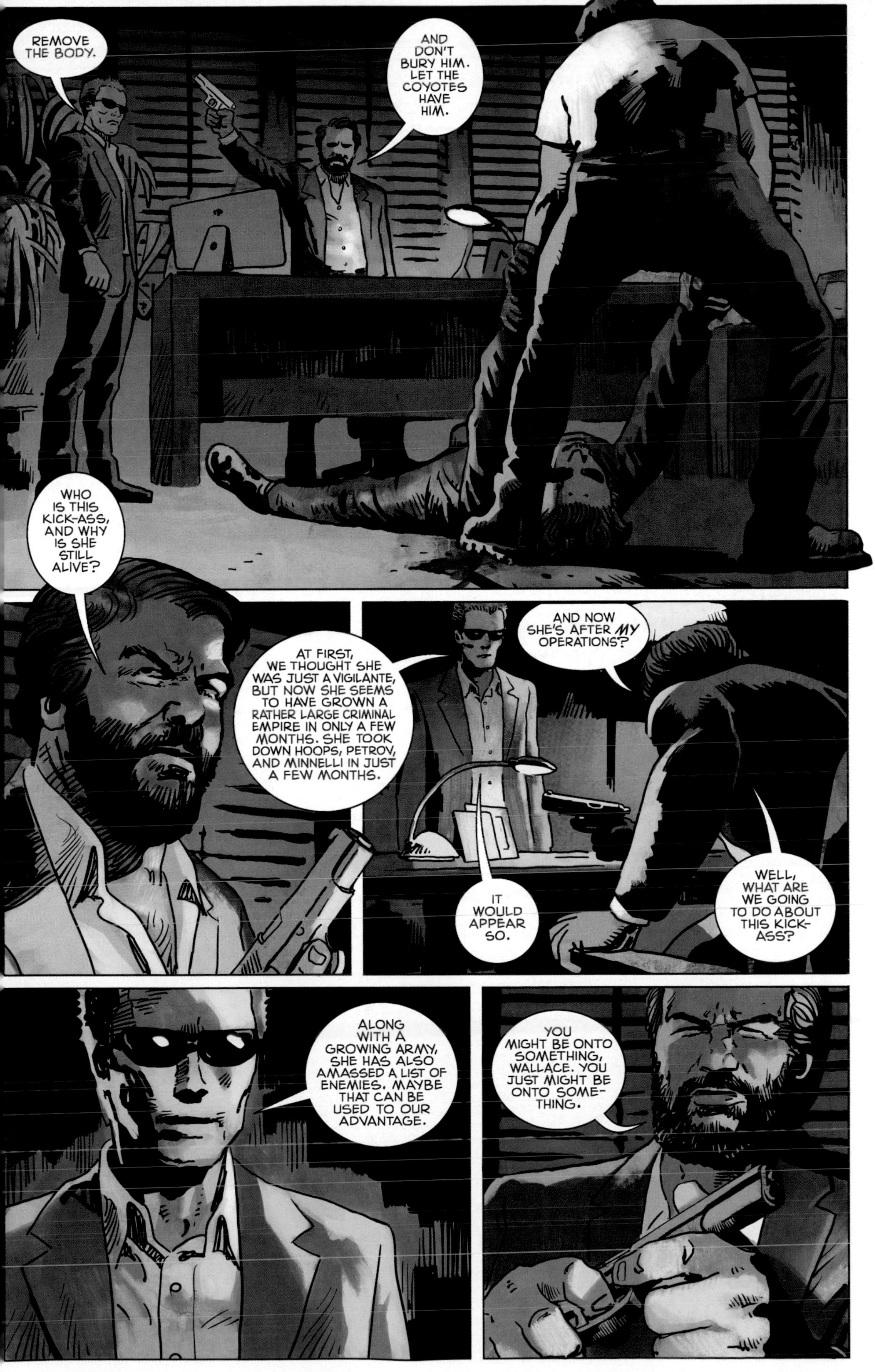
REMOVE THE BODY.
AND DON'T BURY HIM. LET THE COYOTES HAVE HIM.
WHO IS THIS KICK-ASS, AND WHY IS SHE STILL ALIVE?
AT FIRST, WE THOUGHT SHE WAS JUST A VIGILANTE, BUT NOW SHE SEEMS TO HAVE GROWN A RATHER LARGE CRIMINAL EMPIRE IN ONLY A FEW MONTHS. SHE TOOK DOWN HOOPS, PETROV, AND MINNELLI IN JUST A FEW MONTHS.
AND NOW SHE'S AFTER *MY* OPERATIONS?
IT WOULD APPEAR SO.
WELL, WHAT ARE WE GOING TO DO ABOUT THIS KICK-ASS?
ALONG WITH A GROWING ARMY, SHE HAS ALSO AMASSED A LIST OF ENEMIES. MAYBE THAT CAN BE USED TO OUR ADVANTAGE.
YOU MIGHT BE ONTO SOMETHING, WALLACE. YOU JUST MIGHT BE ONTO SOME-THING.

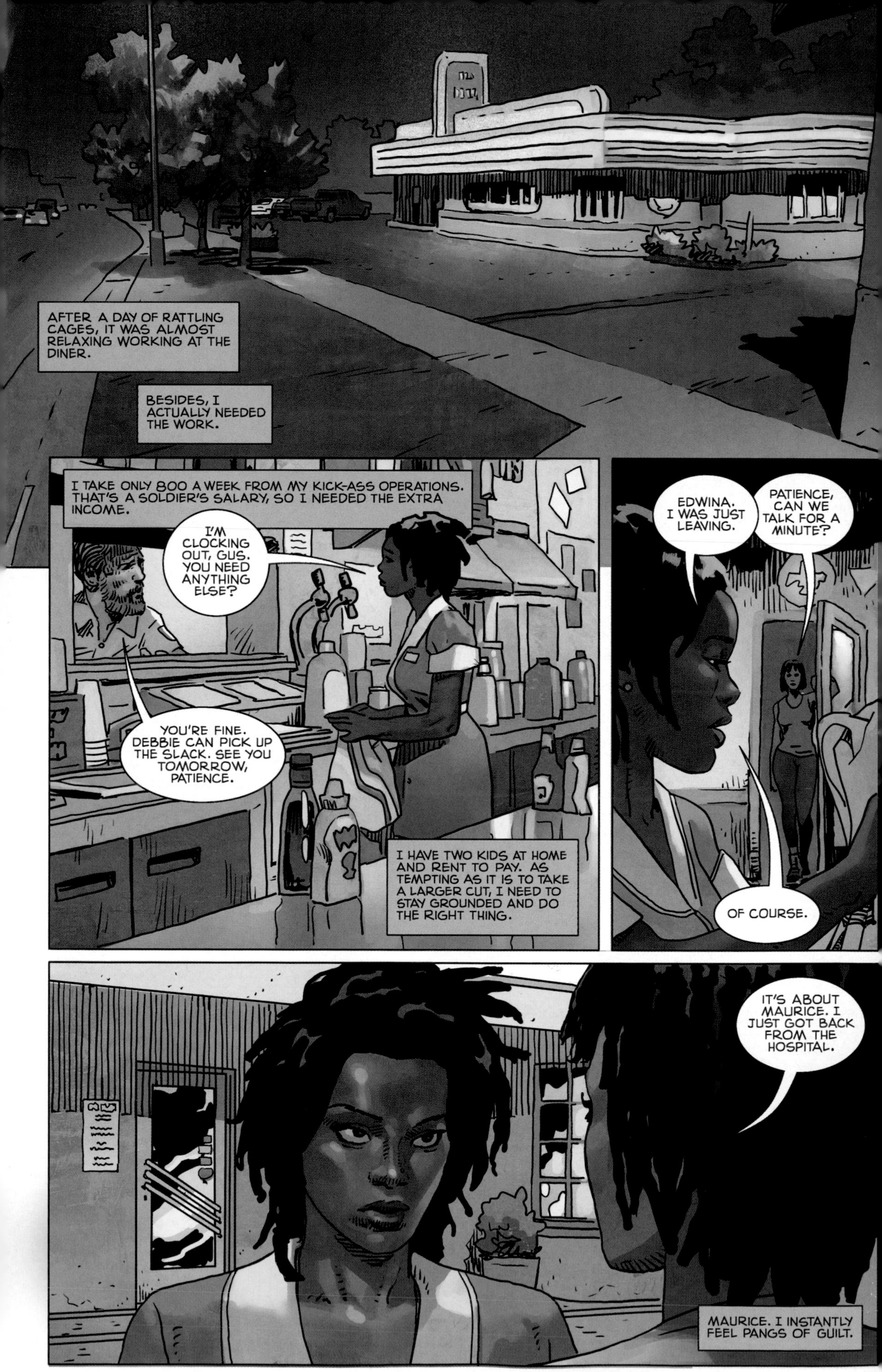
AFTER A DAY OF RATTLING CAGES, IT WAS ALMOST RELAXING WORKING AT THE DINER.
BESIDES, I ACTUALLY NEEDED THE WORK.
I TAKE ONLY 800 A WEEK FROM MY KICK-ASS OPERATIONS. THAT'S A SOLDIER'S SALARY, SO I NEEDED THE EXTRA INCOME.
I'M CLOCKING OUT, GUS. YOU NEED ANYTHING ELSE?
YOU'RE FINE. DEBBIE CAN PICK UP THE SLACK. SEE YOU TOMORROW, PATIENCE.
I HAVE TWO KIDS AT HOME AND RENT TO PAY. AS TEMPTING AS IT IS TO TAKE A LARGER CUT, I NEED TO STAY GROUNDED AND DO THE RIGHT THING.
PATIENCE, CAN WE TALK FOR A MINUTE?
EDWINA. I WAS JUST LEAVING.
OF COURSE.
IT'S ABOUT MAURICE. I JUST GOT BACK FROM THE HOSPITAL.
MAURICE. I INSTANTLY FEEL PANGS OF GUILT.

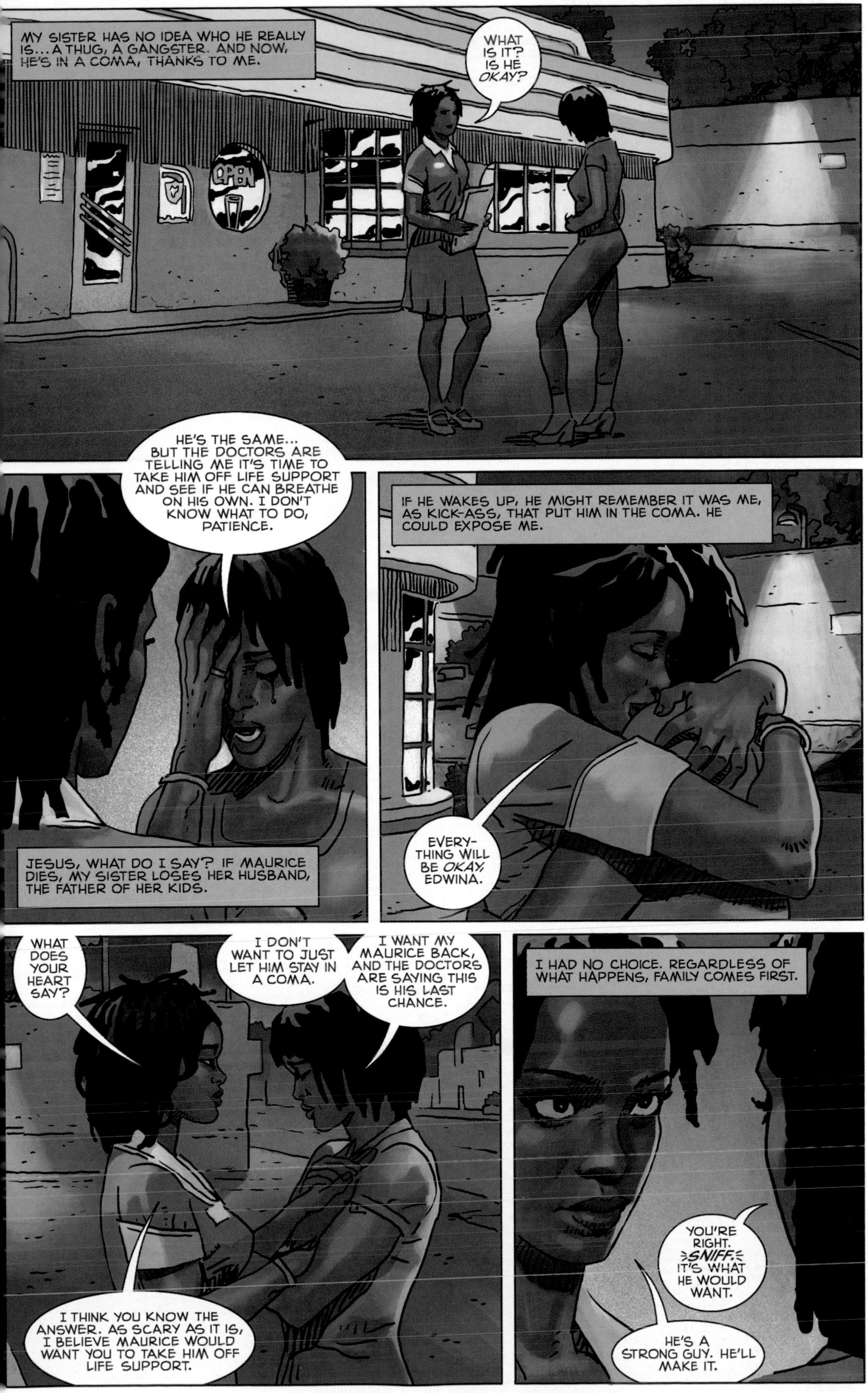
MY SISTER HAS NO IDEA WHO HE REALLY IS... A THUG, A GANGSTER. AND NOW, HE'S IN A COMA, THANKS TO ME.
WHAT IS IT? IS HE *OKAY?*
OPEN
HE'S THE SAME... BUT THE DOCTORS ARE TELLING ME IT'S TIME TO TAKE HIM OFF LIFE SUPPORT AND SEE IF HE CAN BREATHE ON HIS OWN. I DON'T KNOW WHAT TO DO, PATIENCE.
JESUS, WHAT DO I SAY? IF MAURICE DIES, MY SISTER LOSES HER HUSBAND, THE FATHER OF HER KIDS.
IF HE WAKES UP, HE MIGHT REMEMBER IT WAS ME, AS KICK-ASS, THAT PUT HIM IN THE COMA. HE COULD EXPOSE ME.
EVERY-THING WILL BE *OKAY,* EDWINA.
WHAT DOES YOUR HEART SAY?
I DON'T WANT TO JUST LET HIM STAY IN A COMA.
I WANT MY MAURICE BACK, AND THE DOCTORS ARE SAYING THIS IS HIS LAST CHANCE.
I THINK YOU KNOW THE ANSWER. AS SCARY AS IT IS, I BELIEVE MAURICE WOULD WANT YOU TO TAKE HIM OFF LIFE SUPPORT.
I HAD NO CHOICE. REGARDLESS OF WHAT HAPPENS, FAMILY COMES FIRST.
YOU'RE RIGHT. *SNIFF.* IT'S WHAT HE WOULD WANT.
HE'S A STRONG GUY. HE'LL MAKE IT.

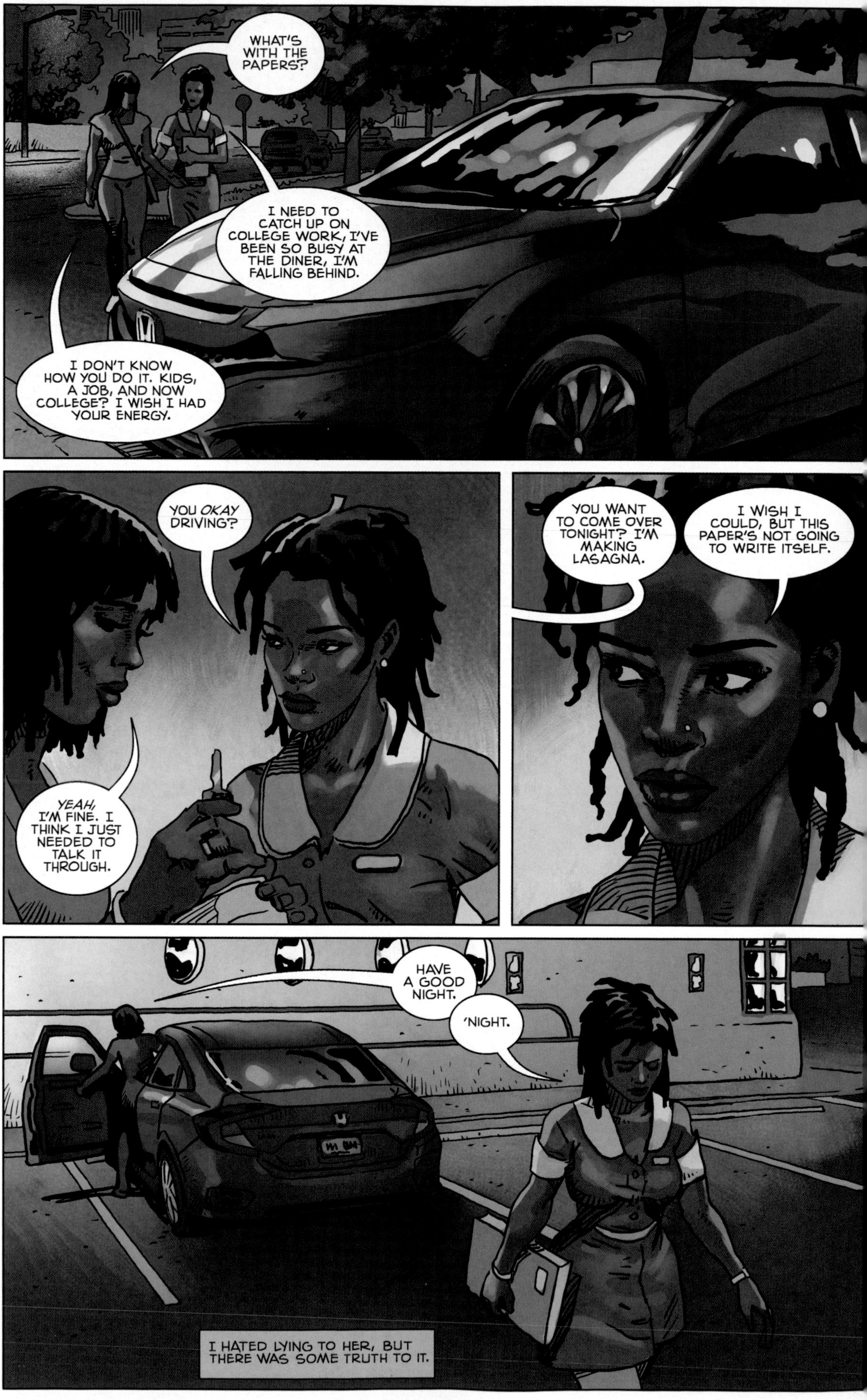
WHAT'S WITH THE PAPERS?
I NEED TO CATCH UP ON COLLEGE WORK, I'VE BEEN SO BUSY AT THE DINER, I'M FALLING BEHIND.
I DON'T KNOW HOW YOU DO IT. KIDS, A JOB, AND NOW COLLEGE? I WISH I HAD YOUR ENERGY.
YOU *OKAY* DRIVING?
YEAH, I'M FINE. I THINK I JUST NEEDED TO TALK IT THROUGH.
YOU WANT TO COME OVER TONIGHT? I'M MAKING LASAGNA.
I WISH I COULD, BUT THIS PAPER'S NOT GOING TO WRITE ITSELF.
HAVE A GOOD NIGHT.
'NIGHT.
I HATED LYING TO HER, BUT THERE WAS SOME TRUTH TO IT.

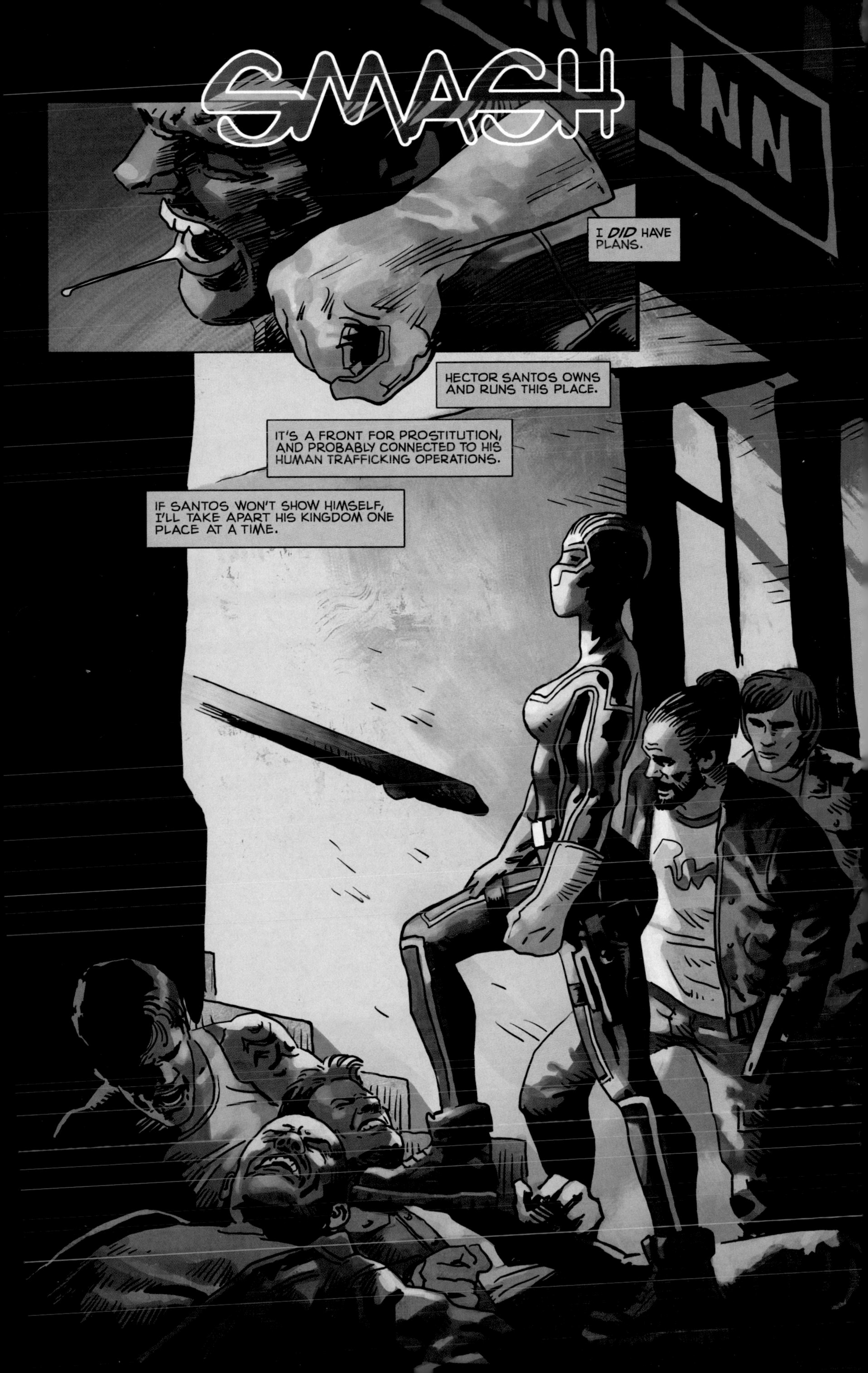
SMACK
INN
I DID HAVE PLANS.
HECTOR SANTOS OWNS AND RUNS THIS PLACE.
IT'S A FRONT FOR PROSTITUTION, AND PROBABLY CONNECTED TO HIS HUMAN TRAFFICKING OPERATIONS.
IF SANTOS WON'T SHOW HIMSELF, I'LL TAKE APART HIS KINGDOM ONE PLACE AT A TIME.

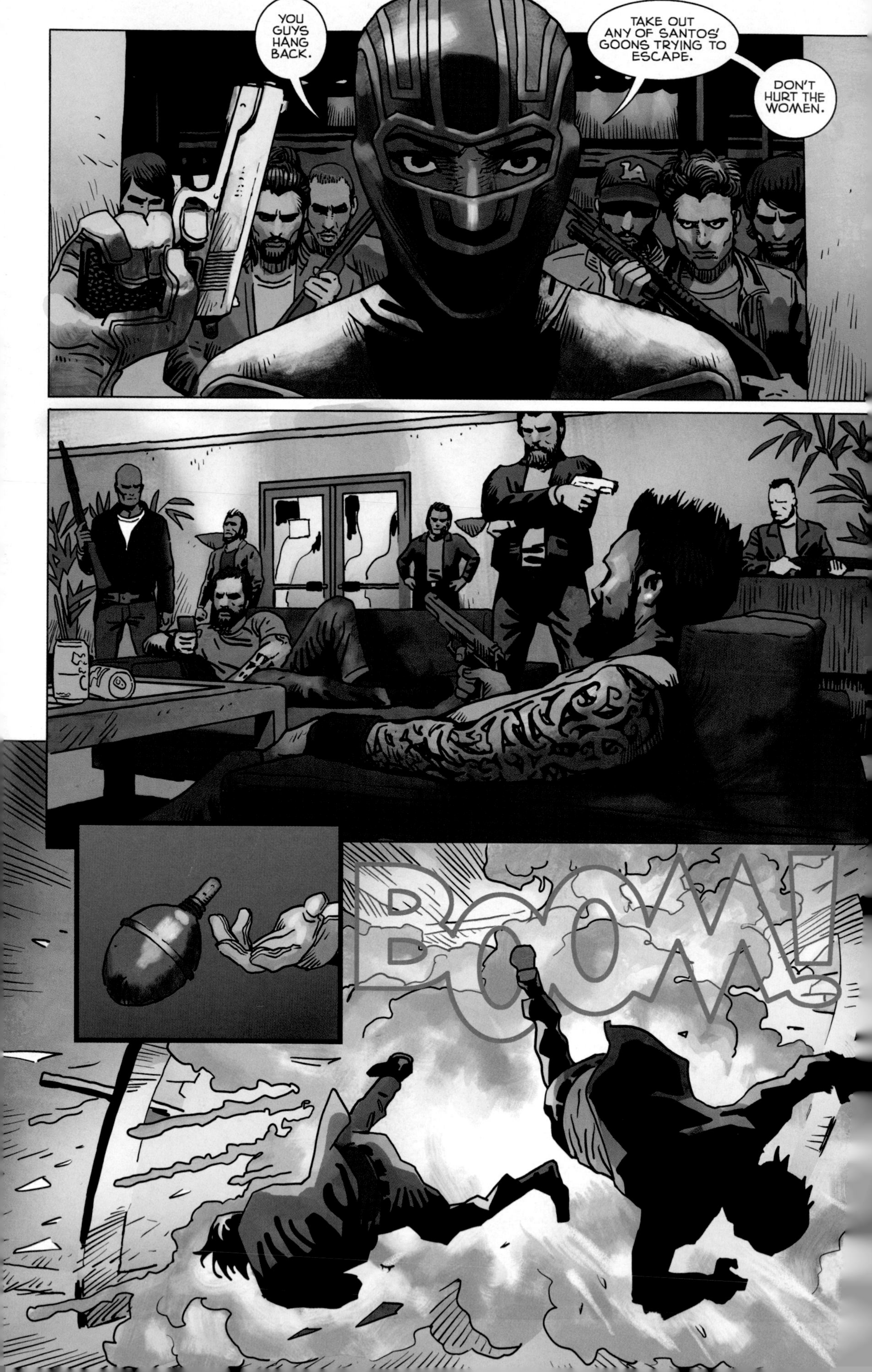
YOU GUYS HANG BACK.
TAKE OUT ANY OF SANTOS' GOONS TRYING TO ESCAPE.
DON'T HURT THE WOMEN.
BOOM!

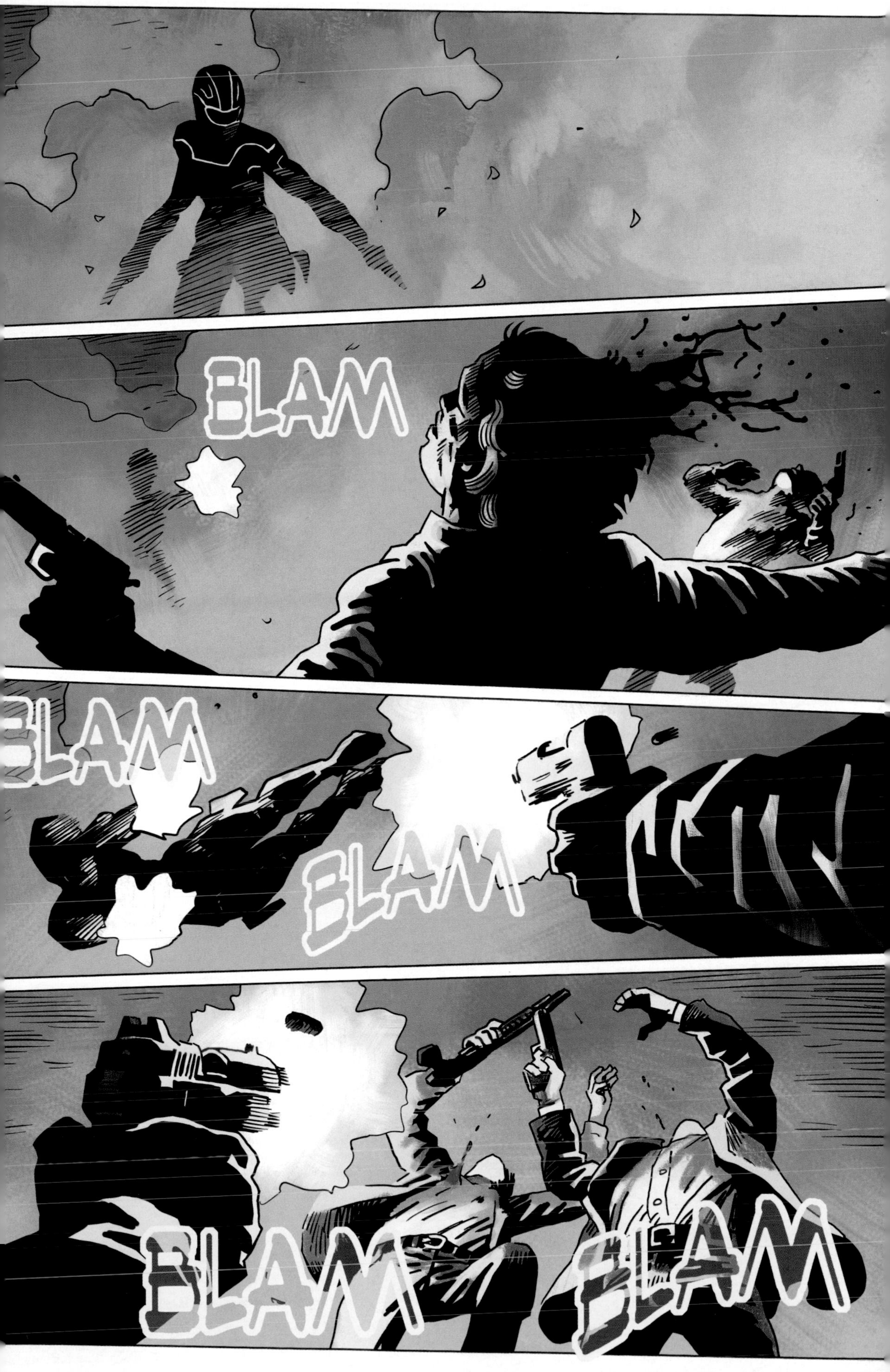
BLAM
BLAM
BLAM
BLAM
BLAM

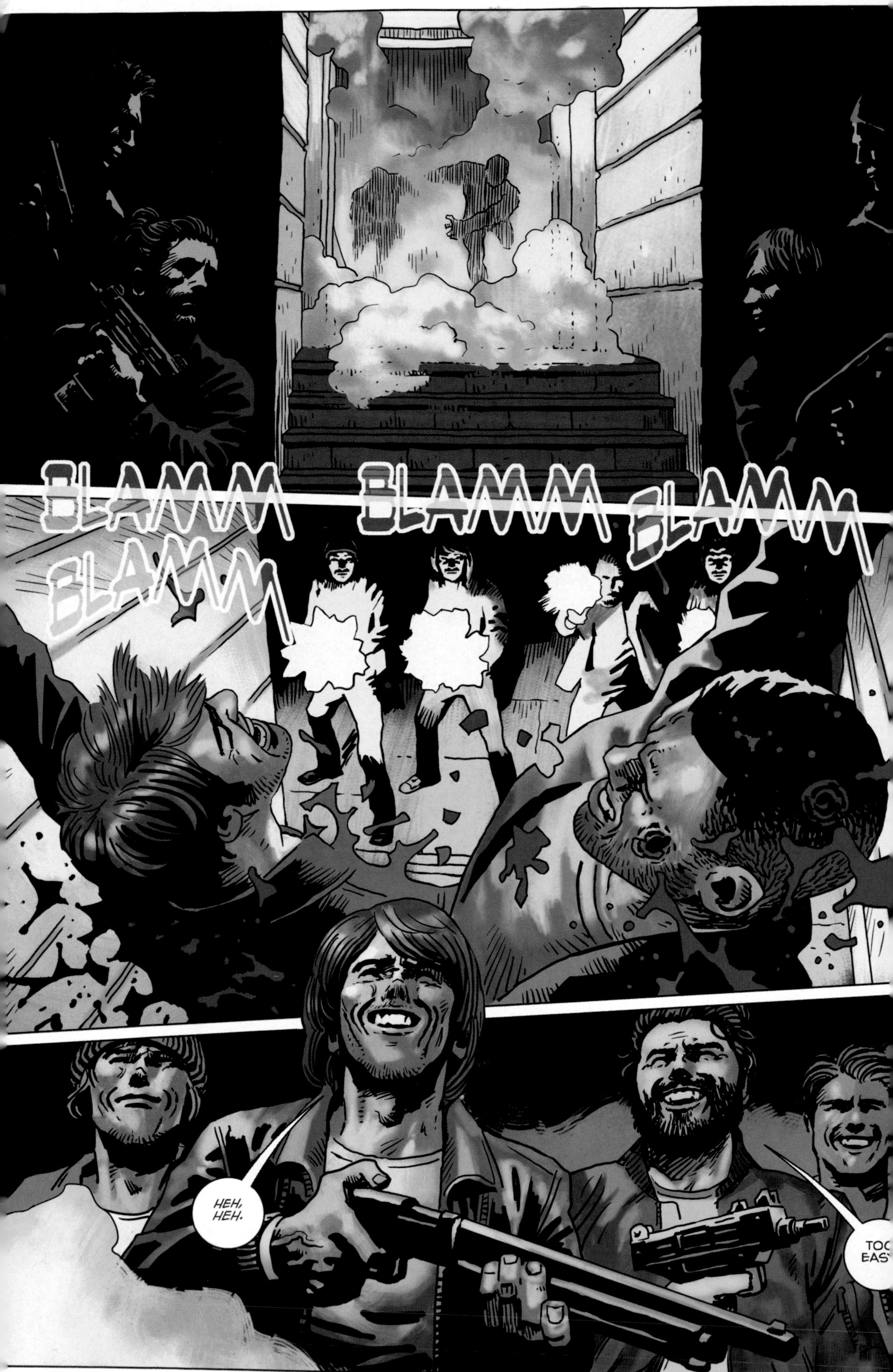
BLAMM
BLAMM
BLAMM
BLAMM
HEH, HEH.
TOO EASY

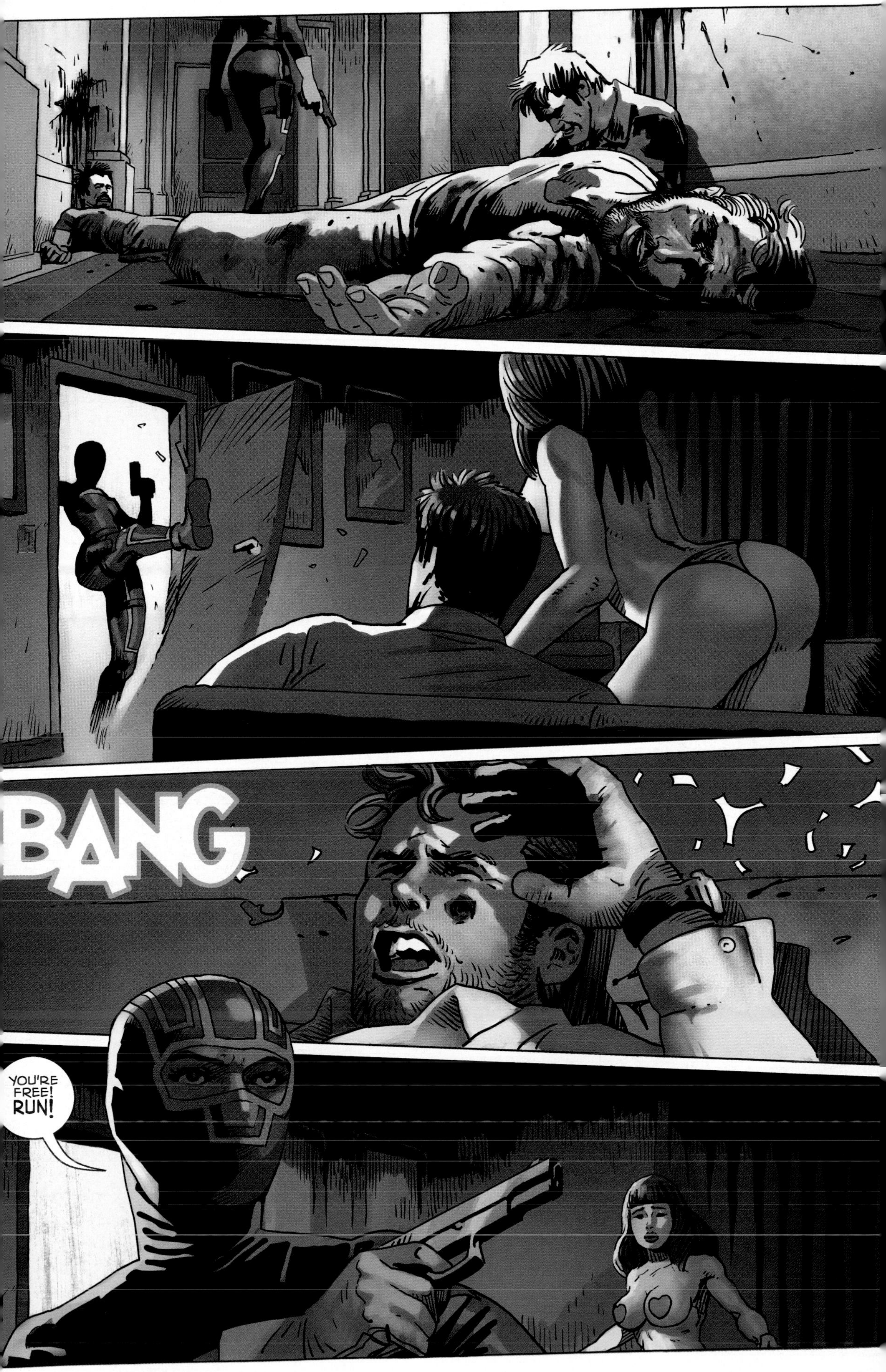
BANG
YOU'RE FREE! RUN!

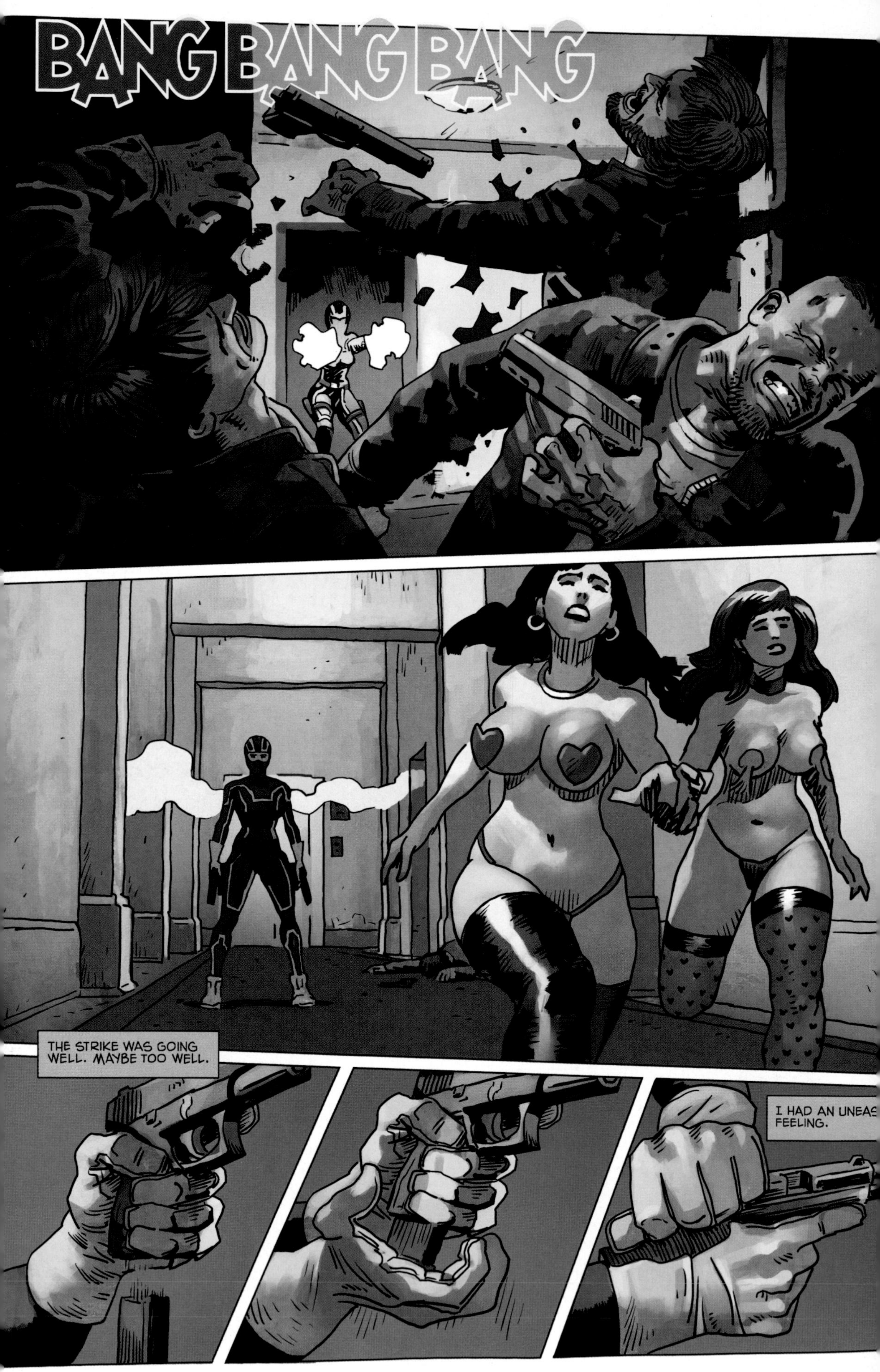
BANG BANG BANG
THE STRIKE WAS GOING WELL. MAYBE TOO WELL.
I HAD AN UNEAS FEELING.

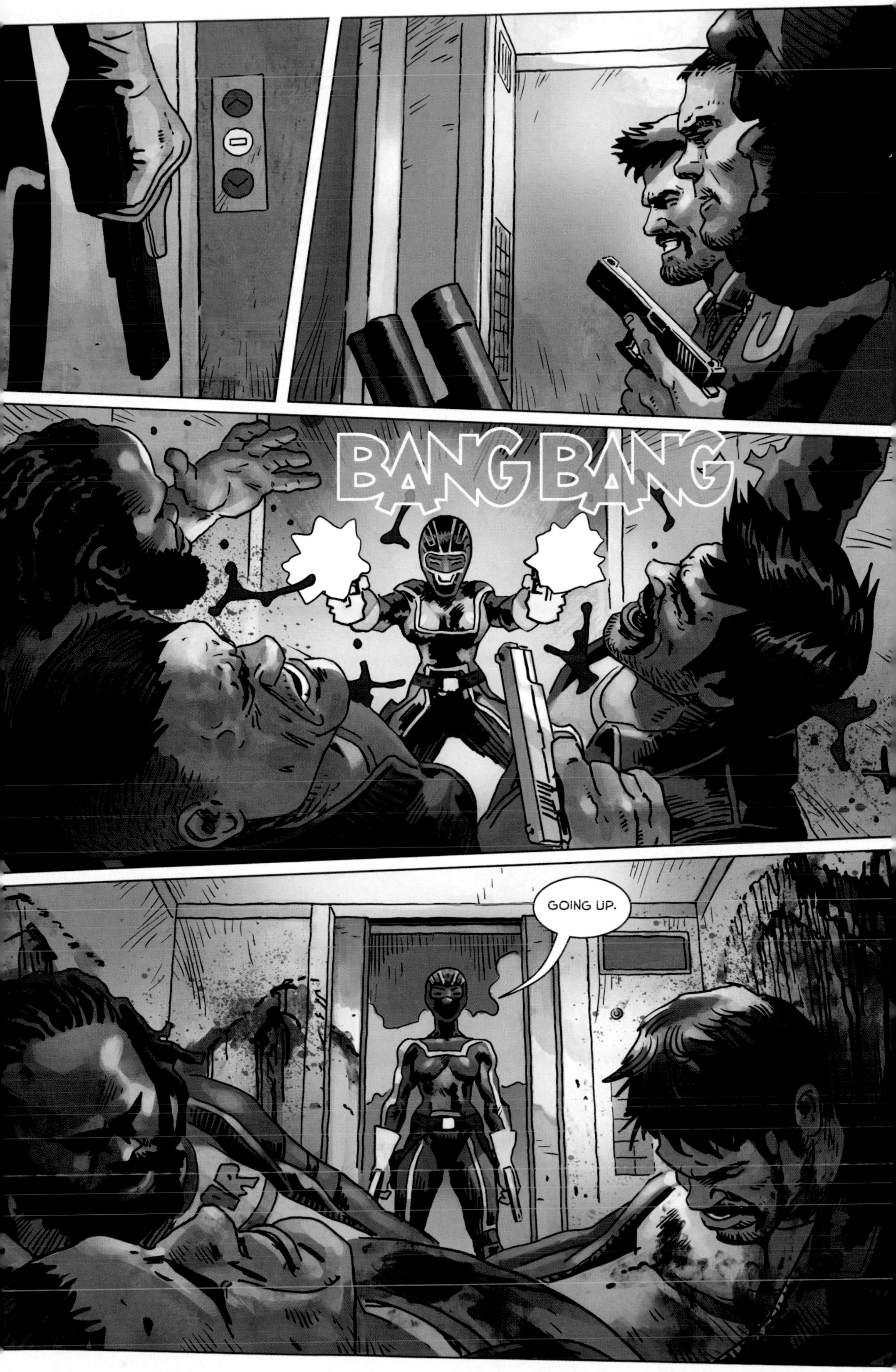
BANG BANG
GOING UP.

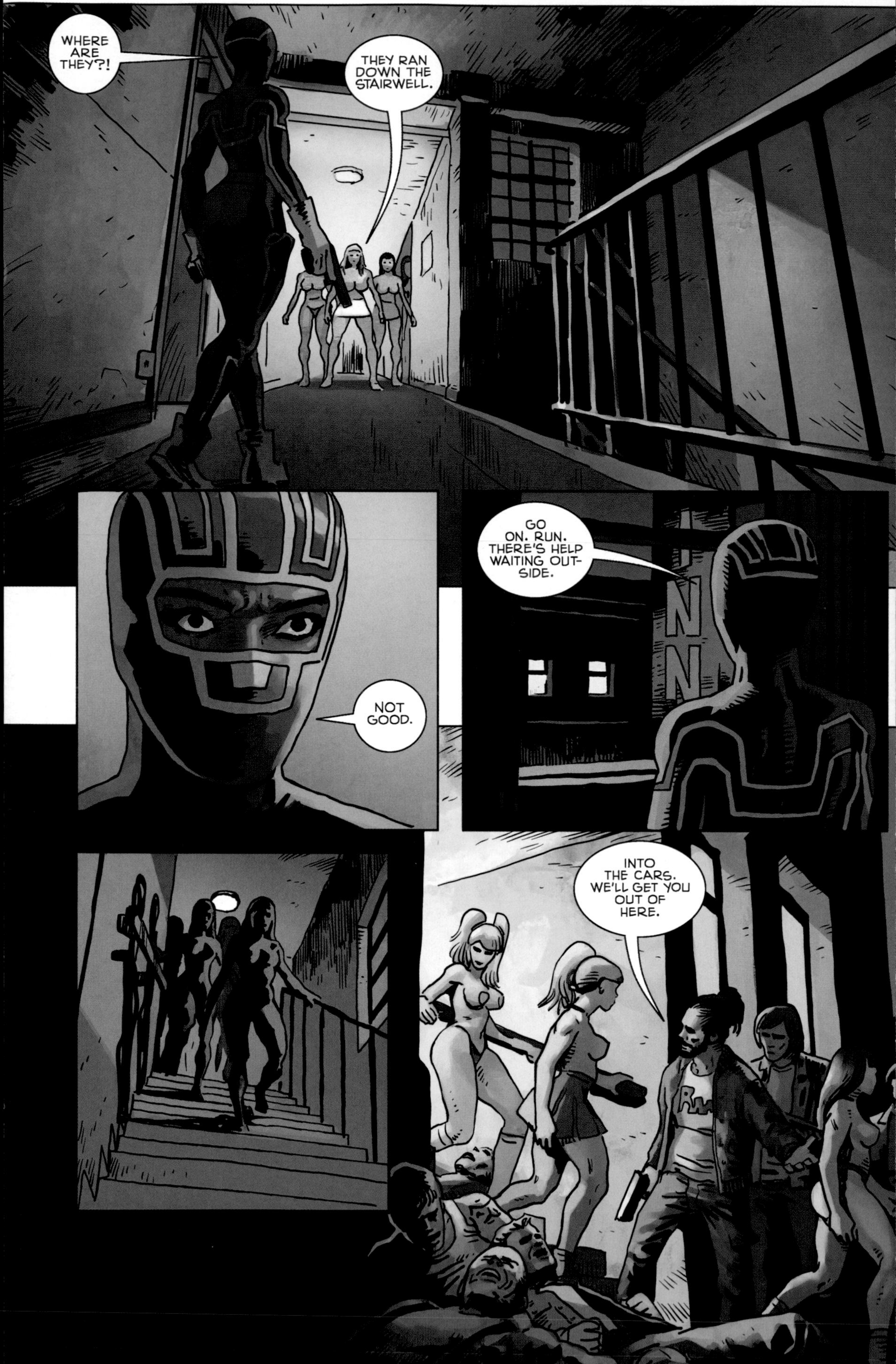
WHERE ARE THEY?!
THEY RAN DOWN THE STAIRWELL.
NOT GOOD.
GO ON. RUN. THERE'S HELP WAITING OUT-SIDE.
INTO THE CARS. WE'LL GET YOU OUT OF HERE.

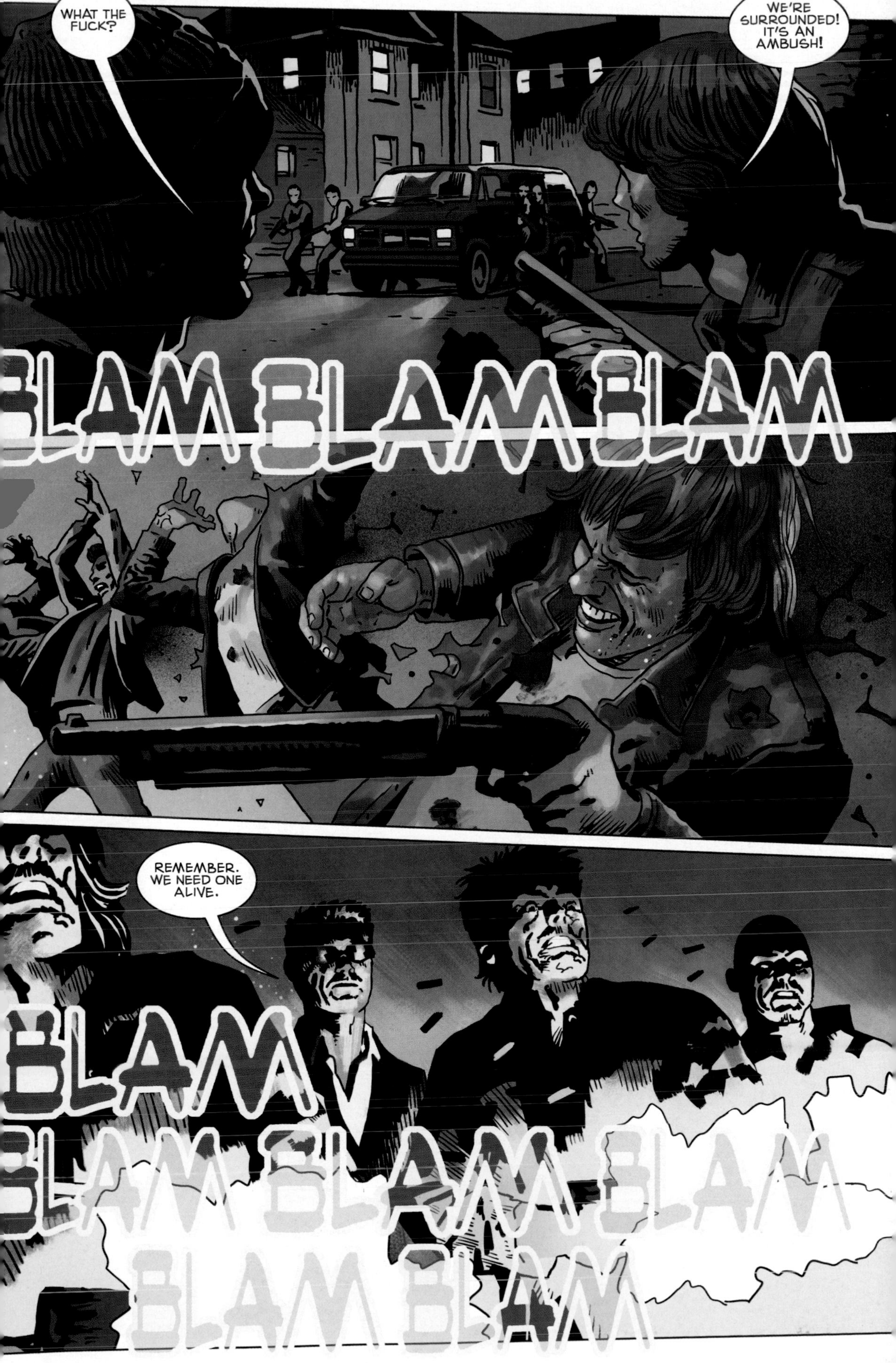
WHAT THE FUCK?
WE'RE SURROUNDED! IT'S AN AMBUSH!
BLAM BLAM BLAM
REMEMBER. WE NEED ONE ALIVE.
BLAM
BLAM BLAM BLAM
BLAM BLAM

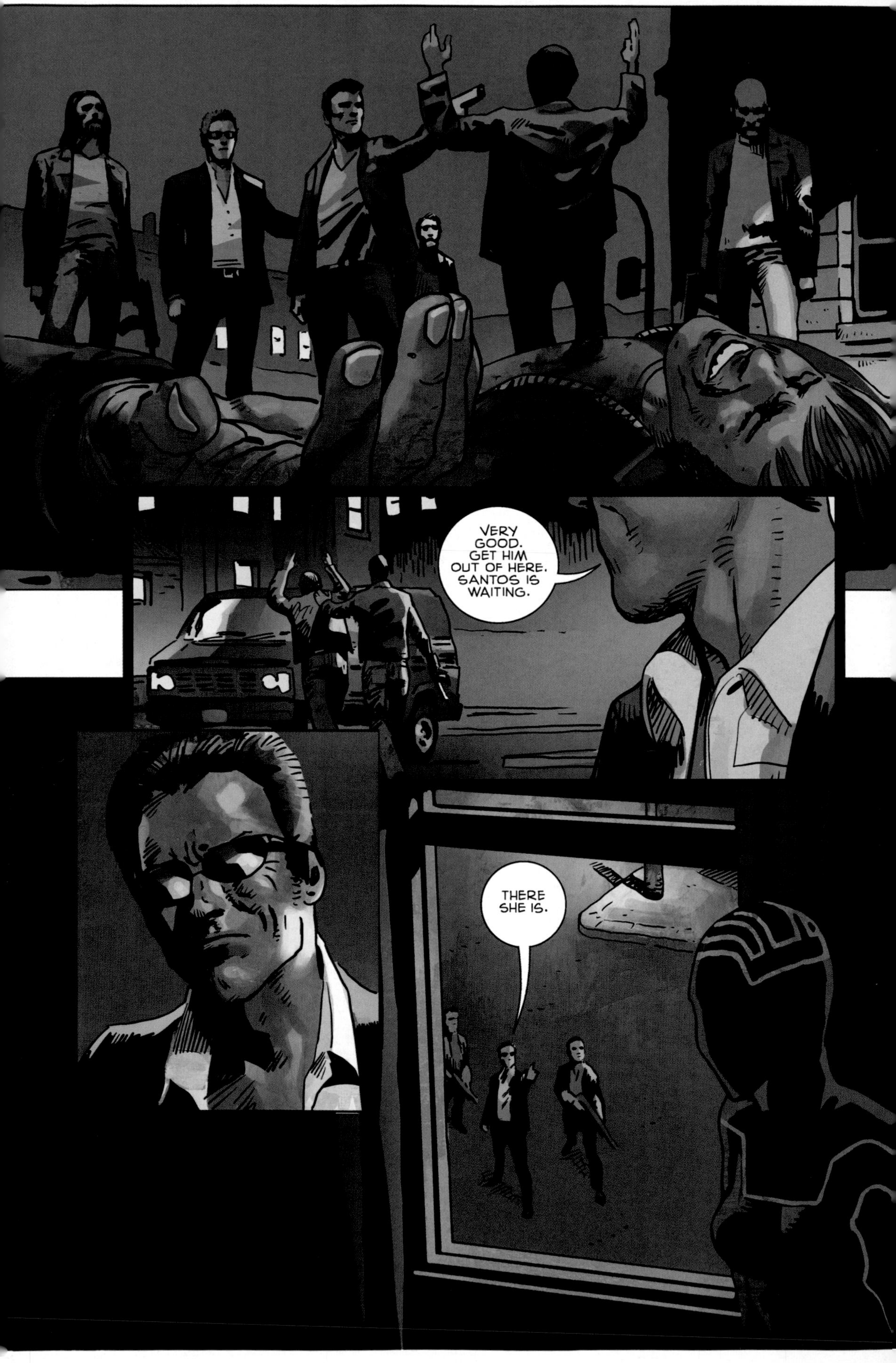
VERY GOOD. GET HIM OUT OF HERE. SANTOS IS WAITING.
THERE SHE IS.

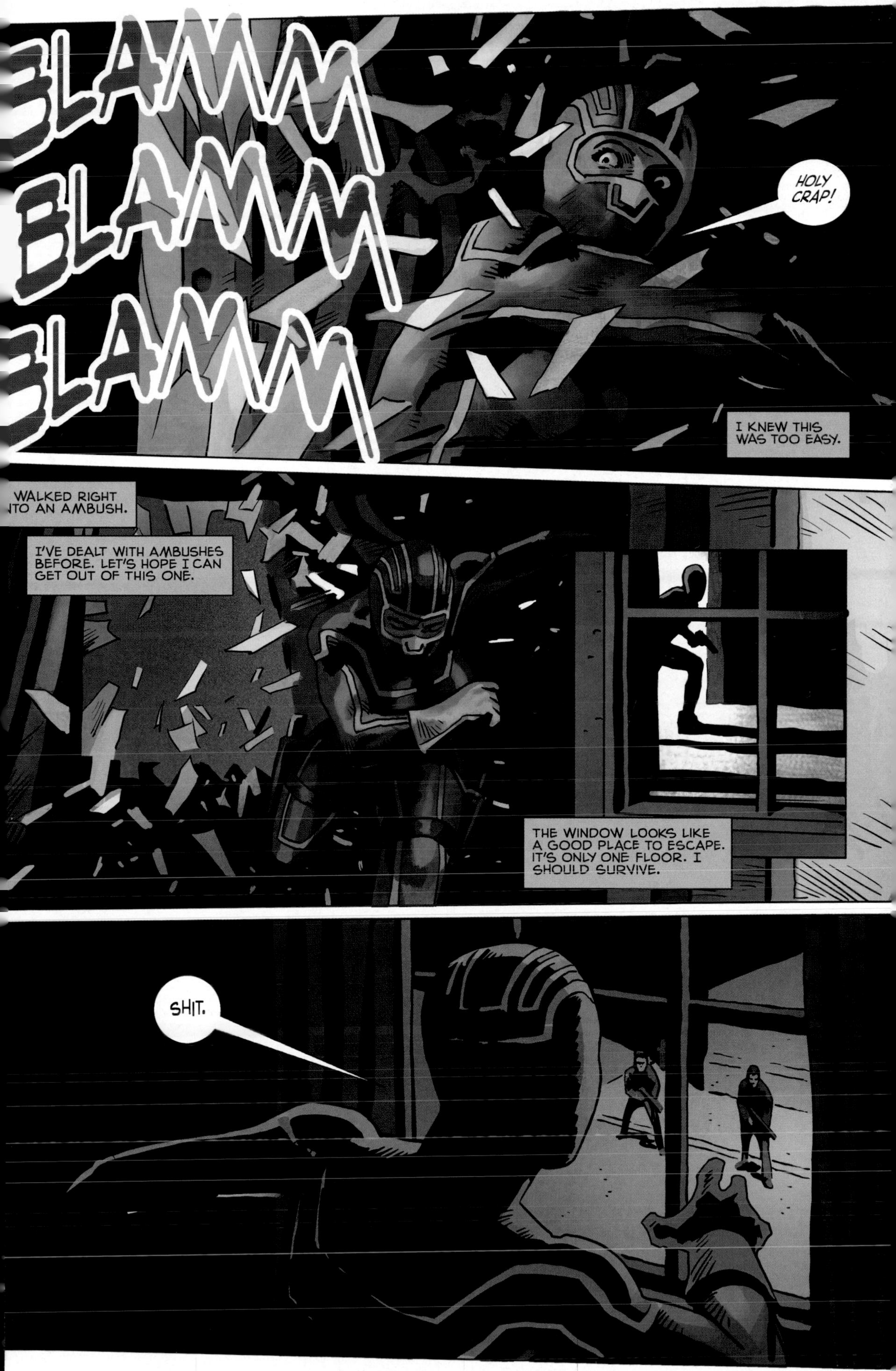
BLAMM BLAMM BLAMM
HOLY CRAP!
I KNEW THIS WAS TOO EASY.
WALKED RIGHT INTO AN AMBUSH.
I'VE DEALT WITH AMBUSHES BEFORE. LET'S HOPE I CAN GET OUT OF THIS ONE.
THE WINDOW LOOKS LIKE A GOOD PLACE TO ESCAPE. IT'S ONLY ONE FLOOR. I SHOULD SURVIVE.
SHIT.

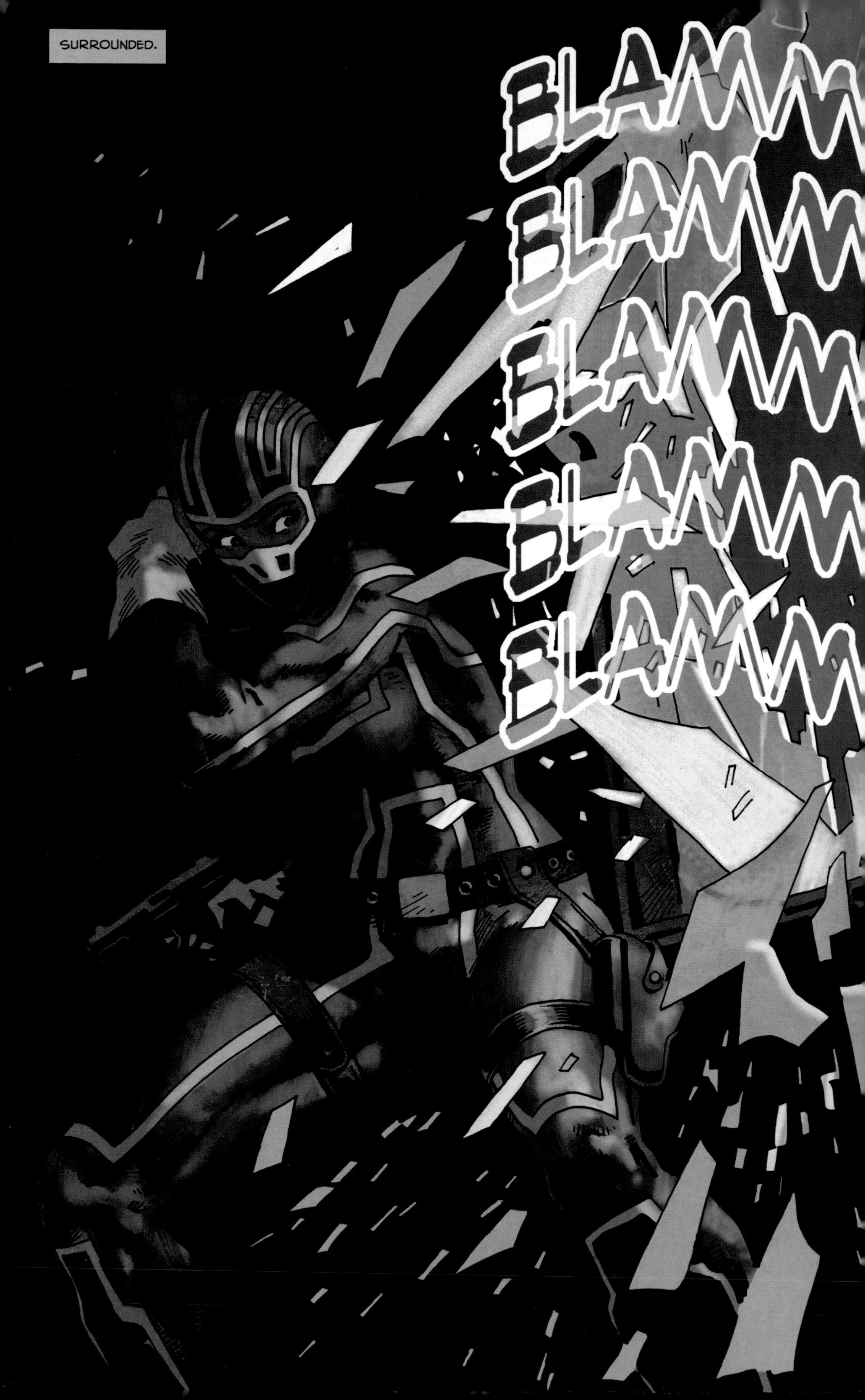
SURROUNDED.
BLAMM
BLAMM
BLAMM
BLAMM
BLAMM

TWO

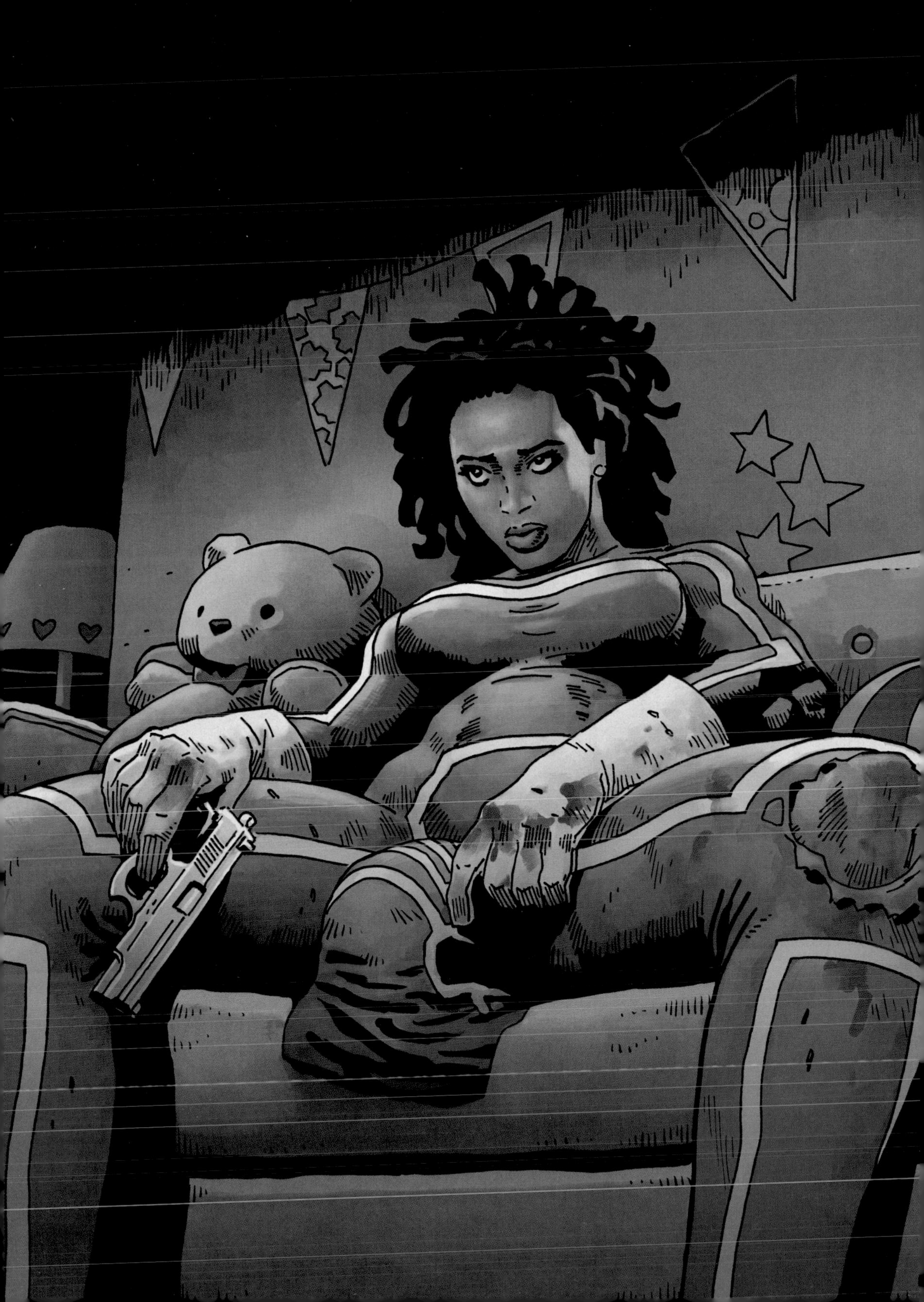

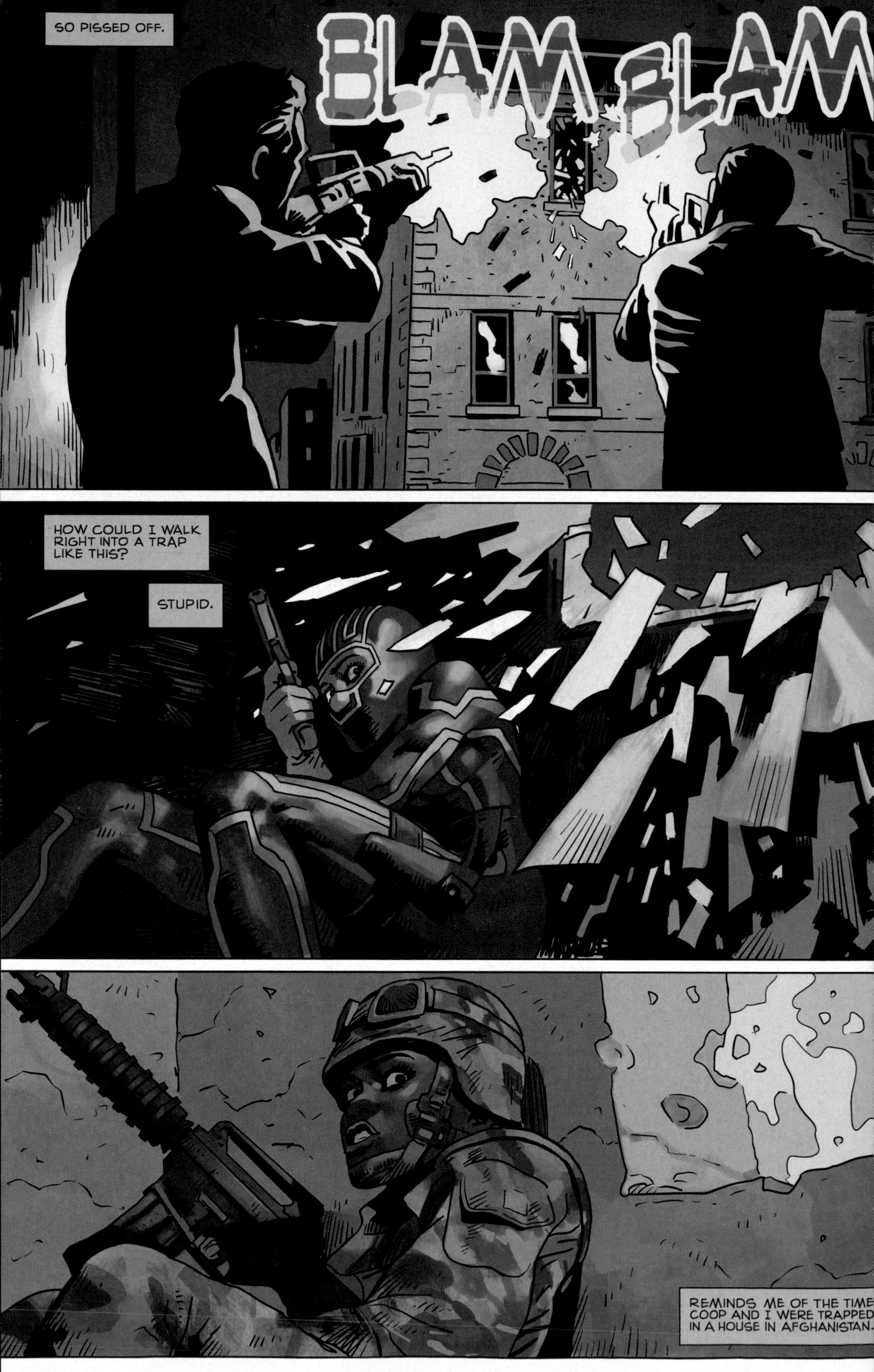
SO PISSED OFF.
BLAM BLAM
HOW COULD I WALK RIGHT INTO A TRAP LIKE THIS?
STUPID.
REMINDS ME OF THE TIME COOP AND I WERE TRAPPED IN A HOUSE IN AFGHANISTAN.

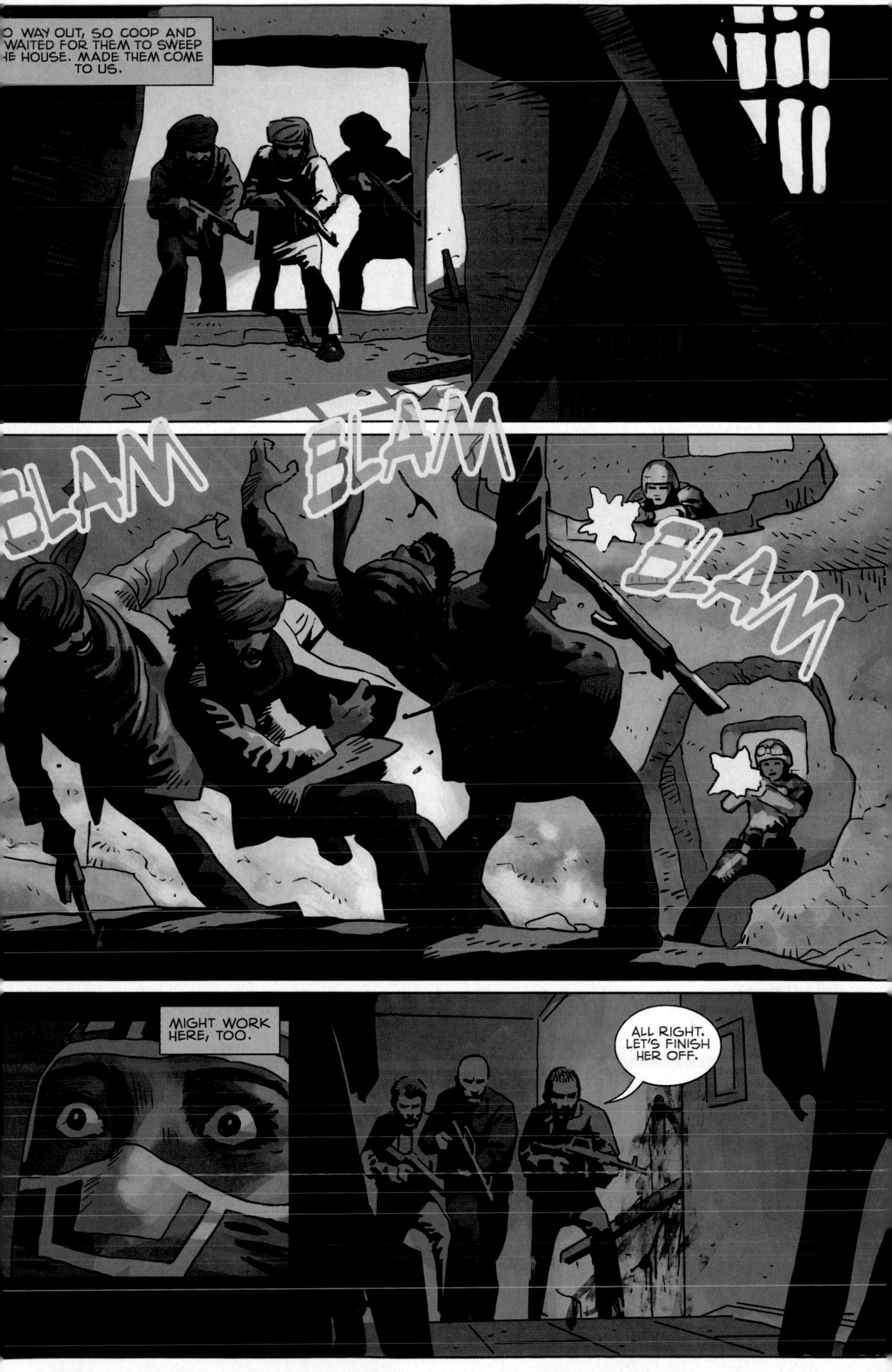
O WAY OUT, SO COOP AND
WAITED FOR THEM TO SWEEP
HE HOUSE. MADE THEM COME
TO US.
BLAM
BLAM
BLAM
MIGHT WORK HERE, TOO.
ALL RIGHT. LET'S FINISH HER OFF.

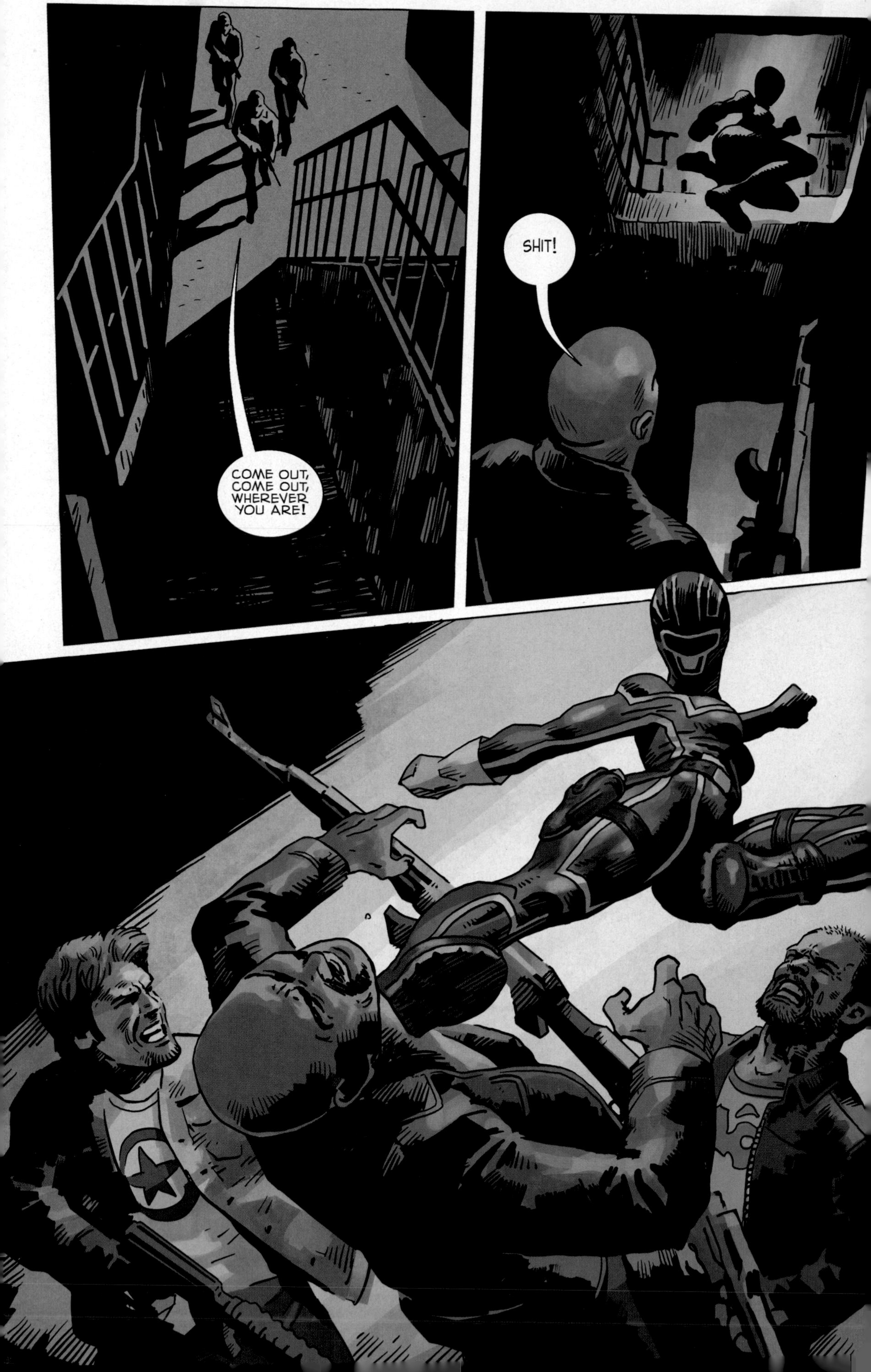
COME OUT, COME OUT, WHEREVER YOU ARE!
SHIT!

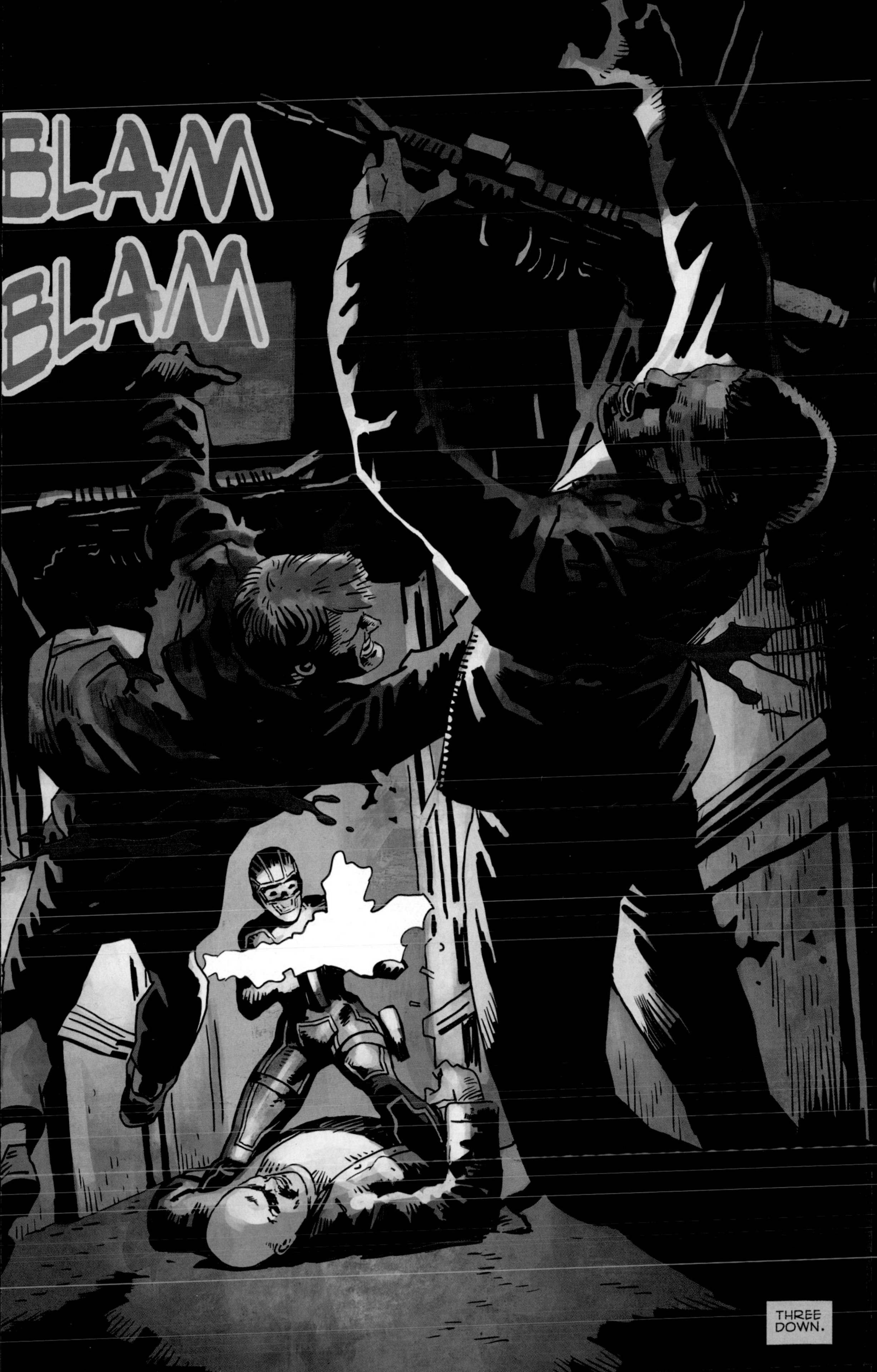
BLAM
BLAM
THREE DOWN.

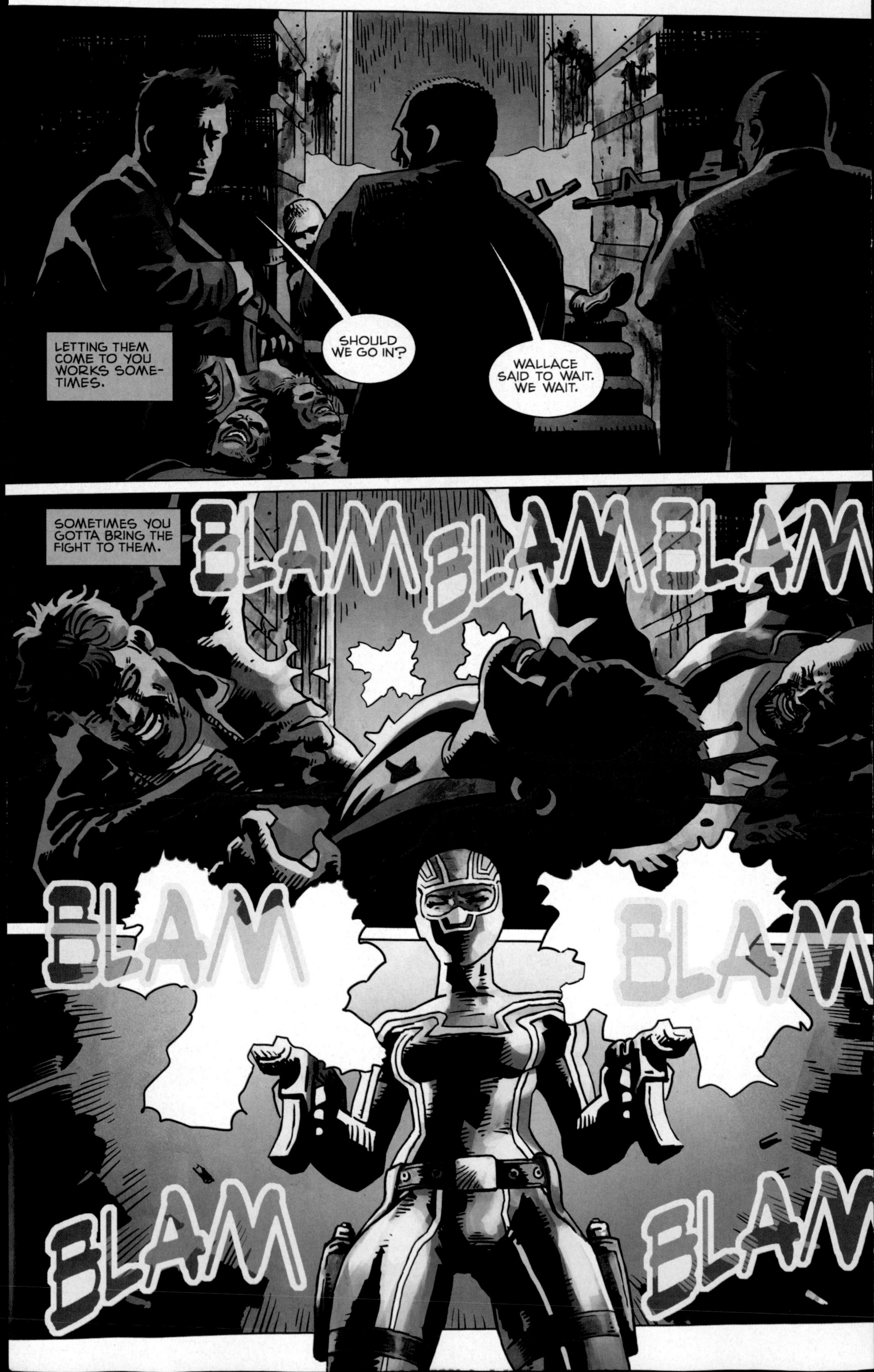
LETTING THEM COME TO YOU WORKS SOME- TIMES.
SHOULD WE GO IN?
WALLACE SAID TO WAIT. WE WAIT.
SOMETIMES YOU GOTTA BRING THE FIGHT TO THEM.
BLAM BLAM BLAM
BLAM BLAM
BLAM BLAM

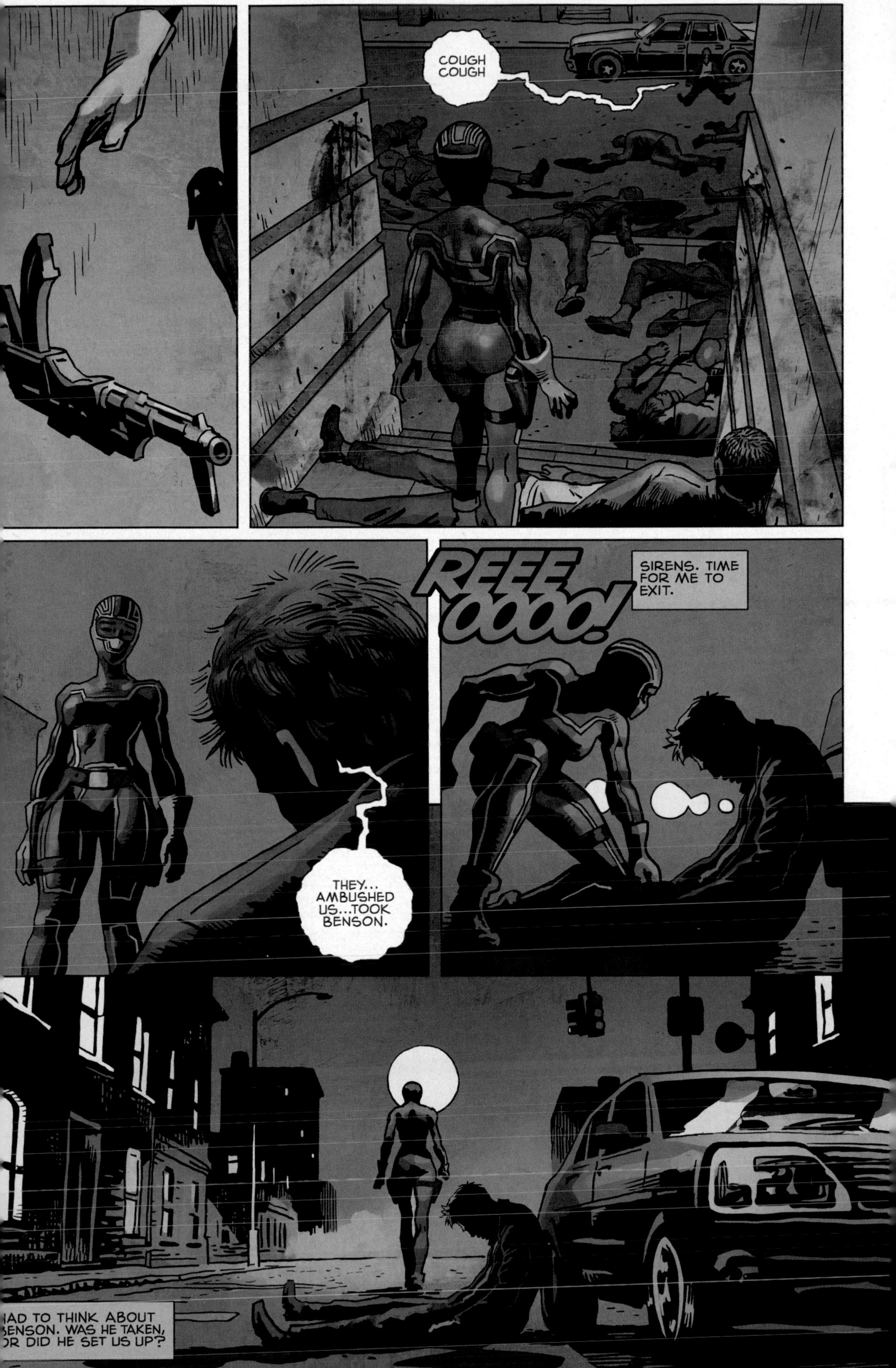
COUGH COUGH
REEE OOOO!
SIRENS. TIME FOR ME TO EXIT.
THEY... AMBUSHED US...TOOK BENSON.
HAD TO THINK ABOUT BENSON. WAS HE TAKEN, OR DID HE SET US UP?

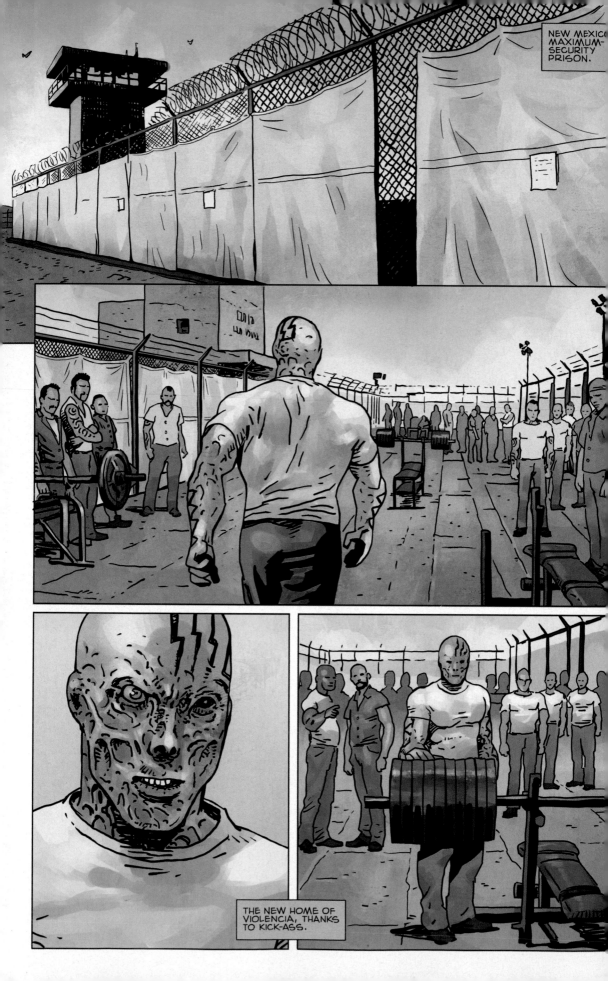

NEW MEXICO MAXIMUM-SECURITY PRISON.

THE NEW HOME OF VIOLENCIA, THANKS TO KICK-ASS.

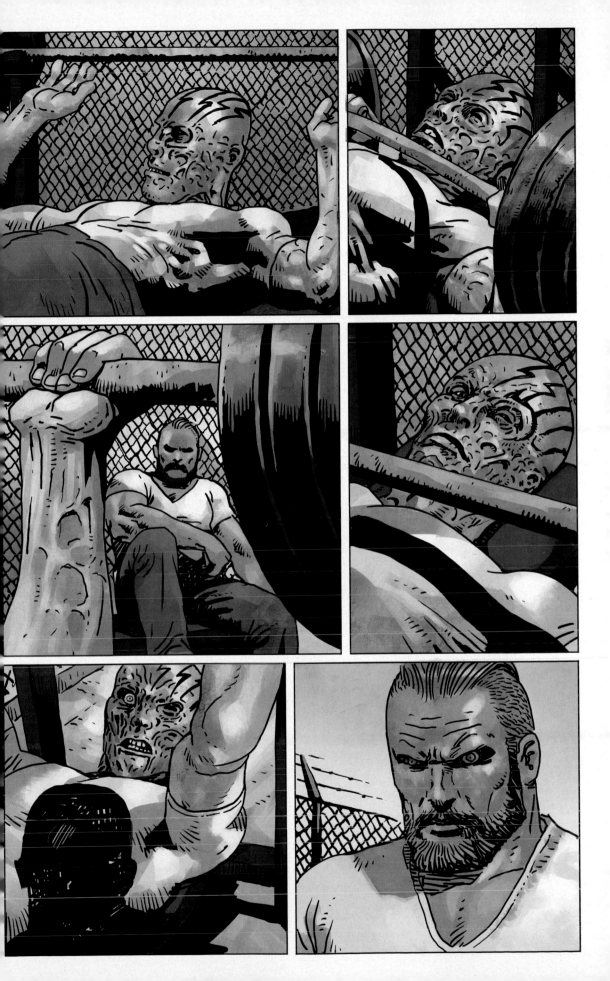

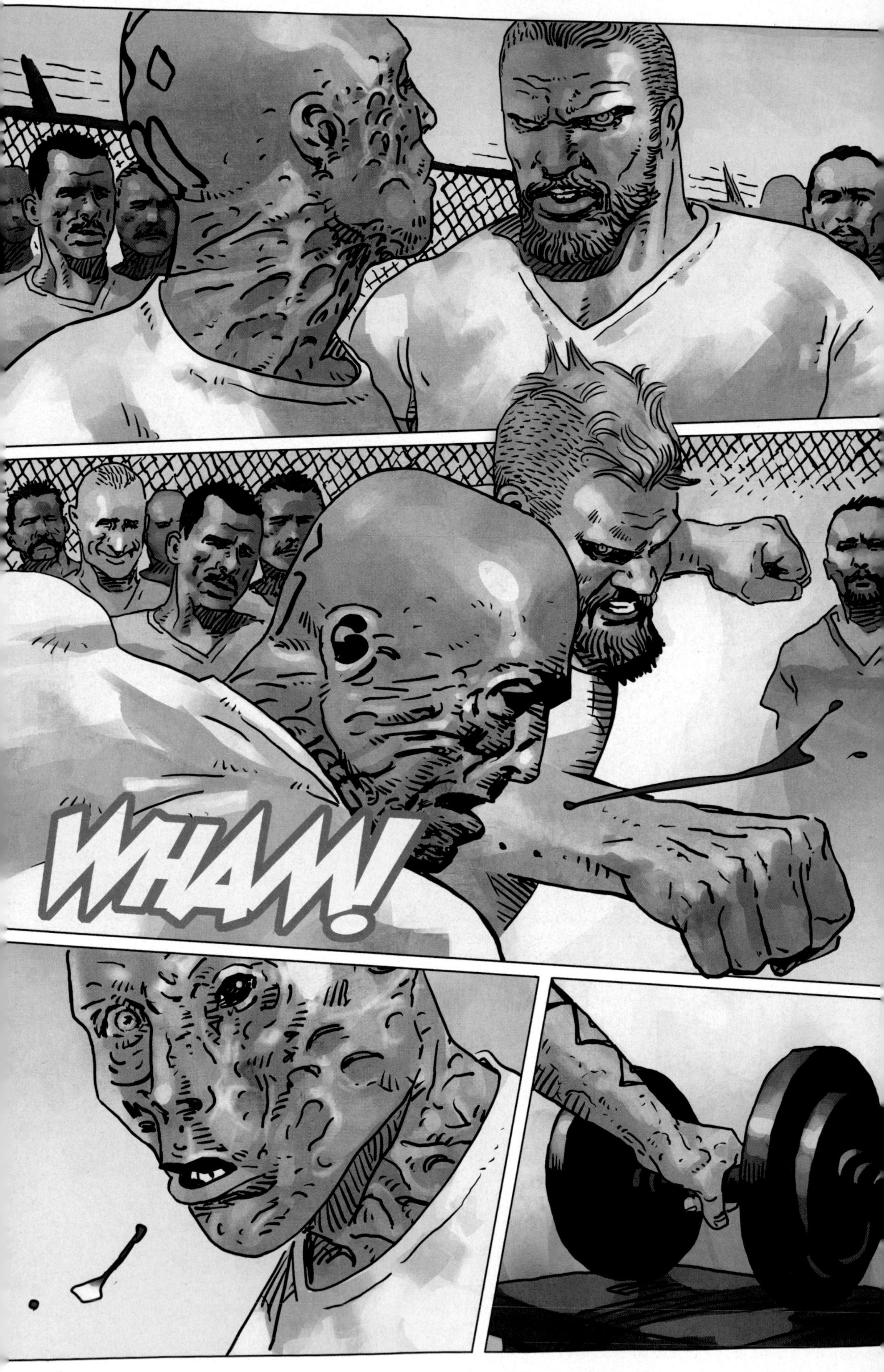
WHAM!

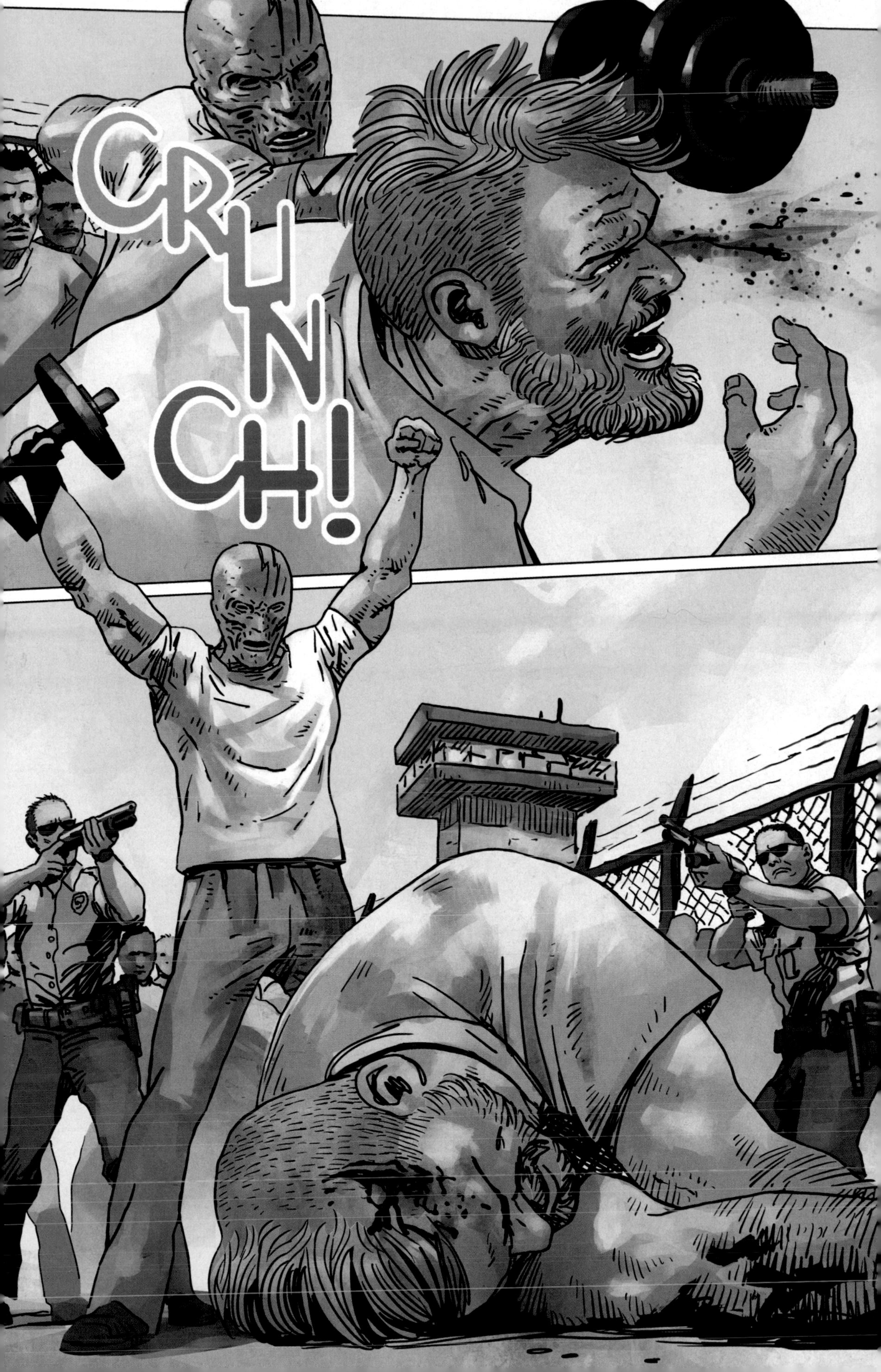
CRUNCH!

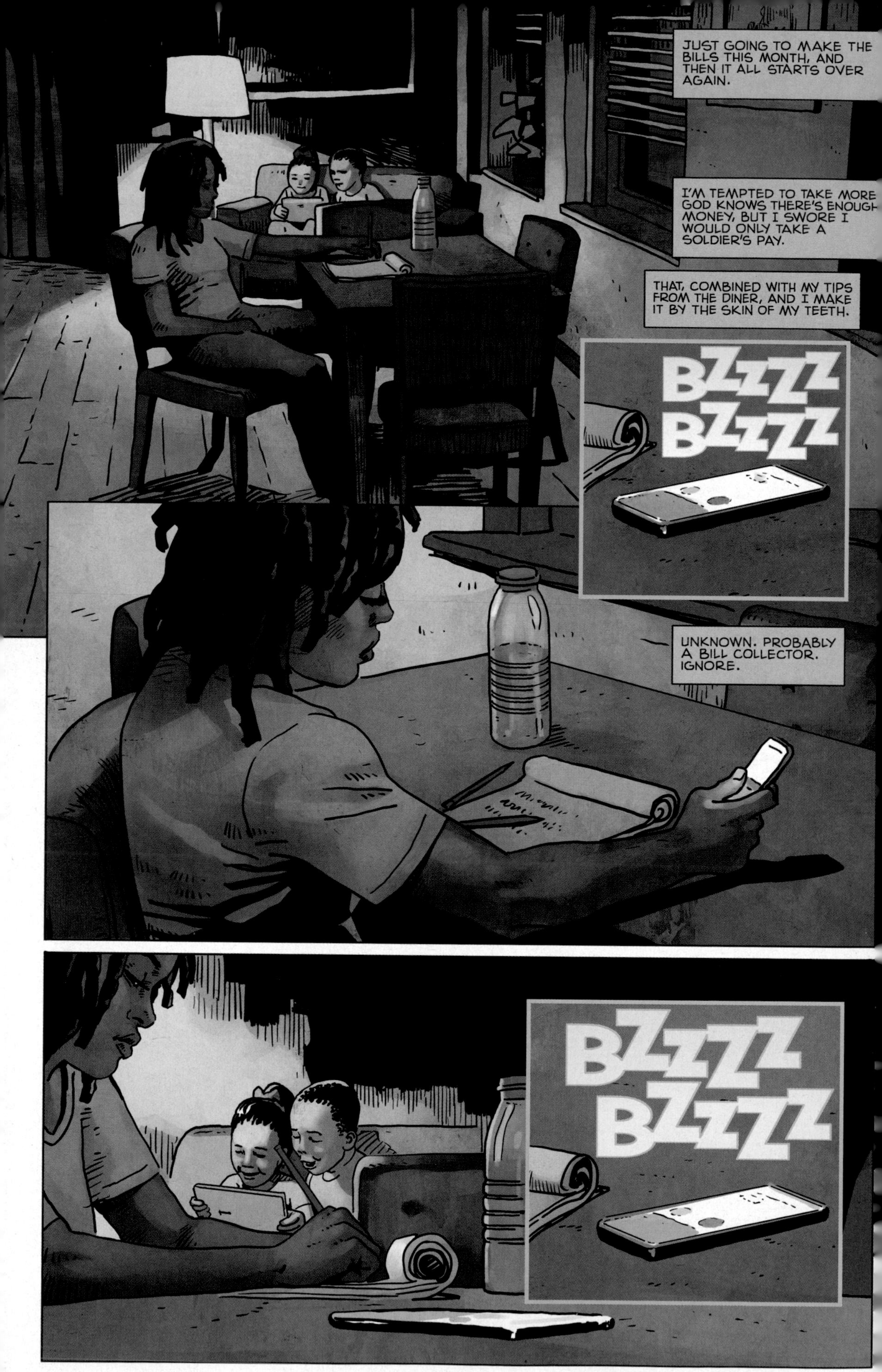
JUST GOING TO MAKE THE BILLS THIS MONTH, AND THEN IT ALL STARTS OVER AGAIN.
I'M TEMPTED TO TAKE MORE. GOD KNOWS THERE'S ENOUGH MONEY, BUT I SWORE I WOULD ONLY TAKE A SOLDIER'S PAY.
THAT, COMBINED WITH MY TIPS FROM THE DINER, AND I MAKE IT BY THE SKIN OF MY TEETH.
BZZZZ BZZZZ
UNKNOWN. PROBABLY A BILL COLLECTOR. IGNORE.
BZZZZ BZZZZ

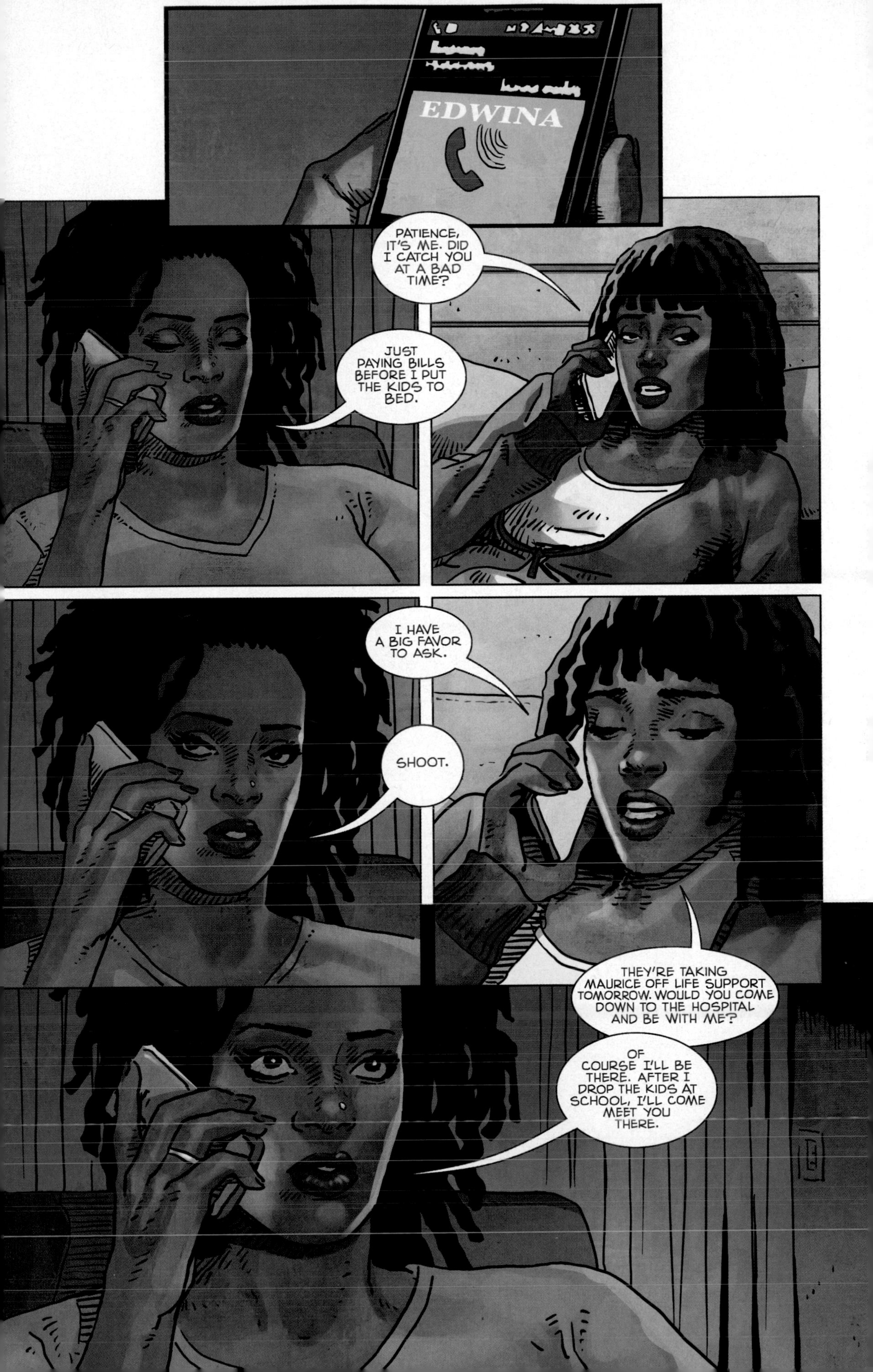
EDWINA
PATIENCE, IT'S ME. DID I CATCH YOU AT A BAD TIME?
JUST PAYING BILLS BEFORE I PUT THE KIDS TO BED.
I HAVE A BIG FAVOR TO ASK.
SHOOT.
THEY'RE TAKING MAURICE OFF LIFE SUPPORT TOMORROW. WOULD YOU COME DOWN TO THE HOSPITAL AND BE WITH ME?
OF COURSE I'LL BE THERE. AFTER I DROP THE KIDS AT SCHOOL, I'LL COME MEET YOU THERE.

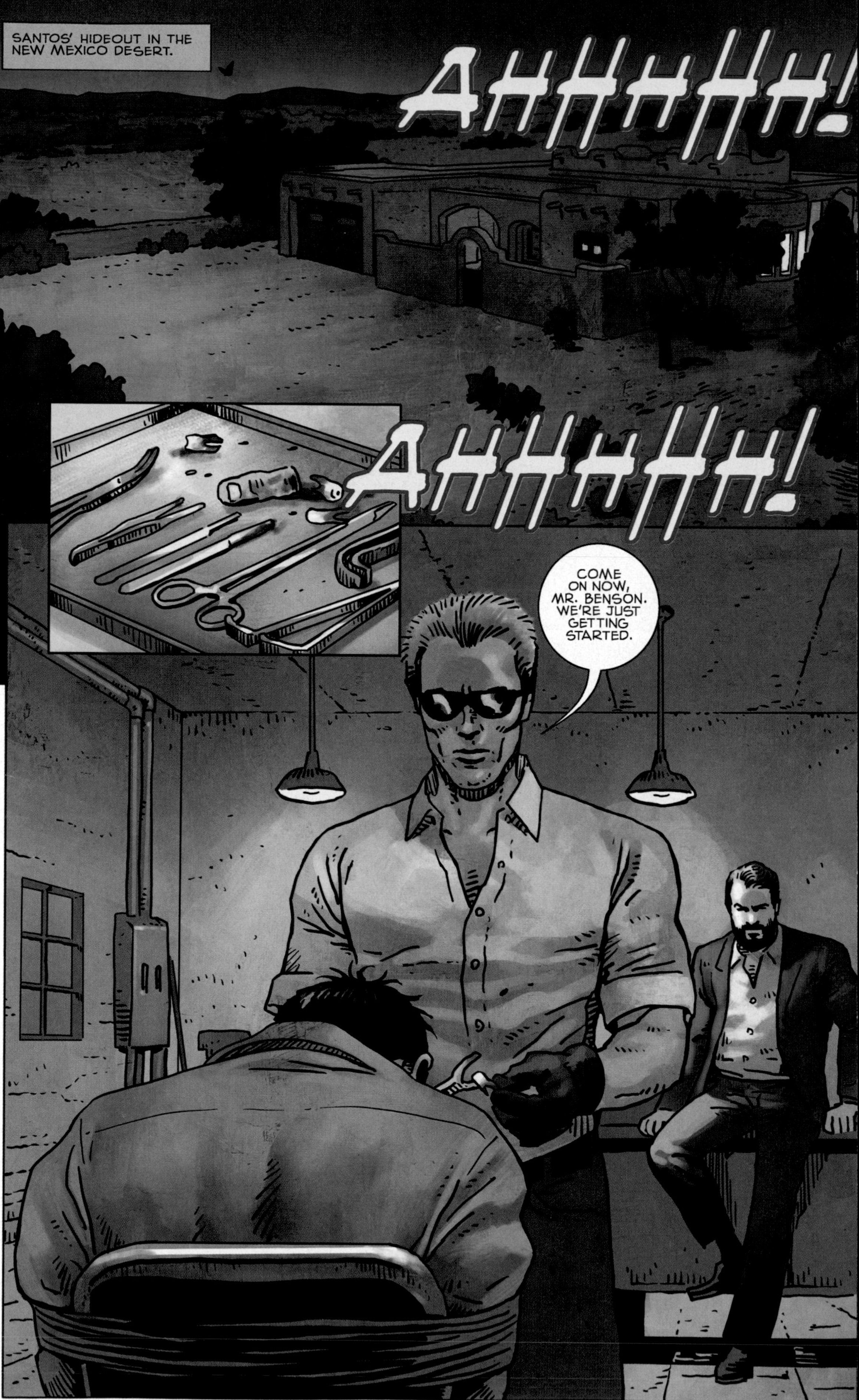
SANTOS' HIDEOUT IN THE NEW MEXICO DESERT.
AHHHHH!
AHHHHH!
COME ON NOW, MR. BENSON. WE'RE JUST GETTING STARTED.

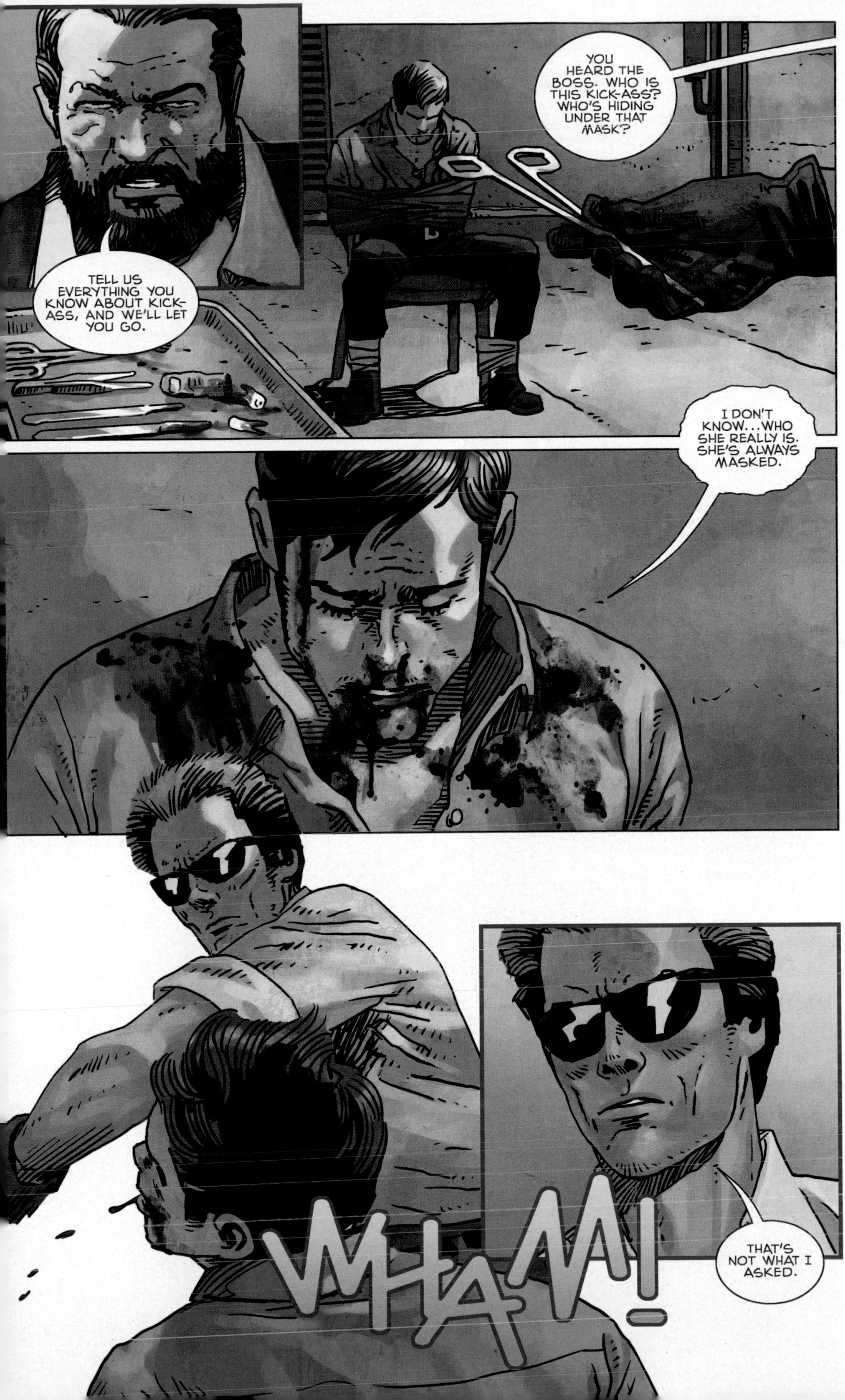
TELL US EVERYTHING YOU KNOW ABOUT KICK-ASS, AND WE'LL LET YOU GO.
YOU HEARD THE BOSS. WHO IS THIS KICK-ASS? WHO'S HIDING UNDER THAT MASK?
I DON'T KNOW...WHO SHE REALLY IS. SHE'S ALWAYS MASKED.
WHAM!
THAT'S NOT WHAT I ASKED.

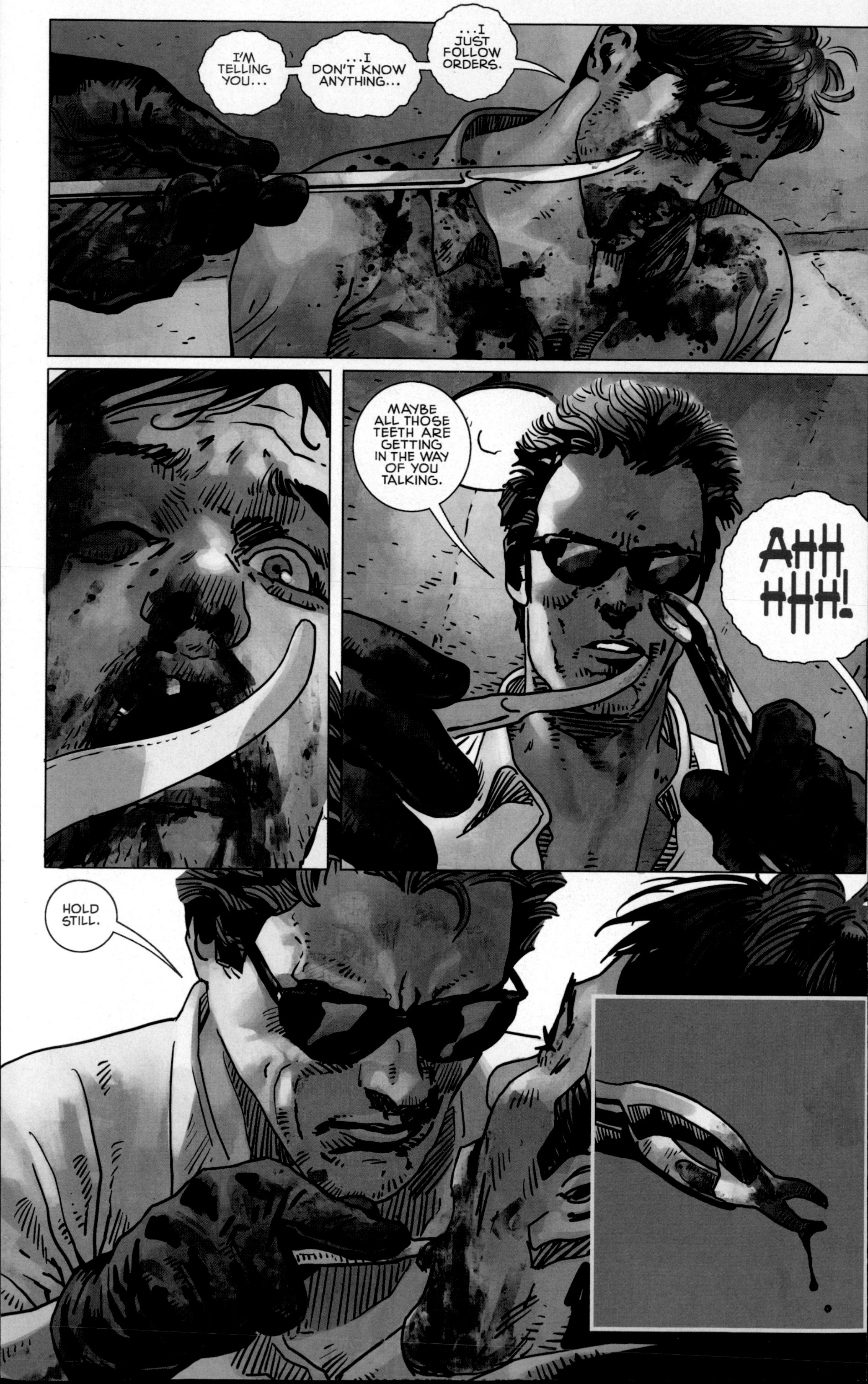
I'M TELLING YOU...
...I DON'T KNOW ANYTHING...
...I JUST FOLLOW ORDERS.
MAYBE ALL THOSE TEETH ARE GETTING IN THE WAY OF YOU TALKING.
AHHHHH!
HOLD STILL.

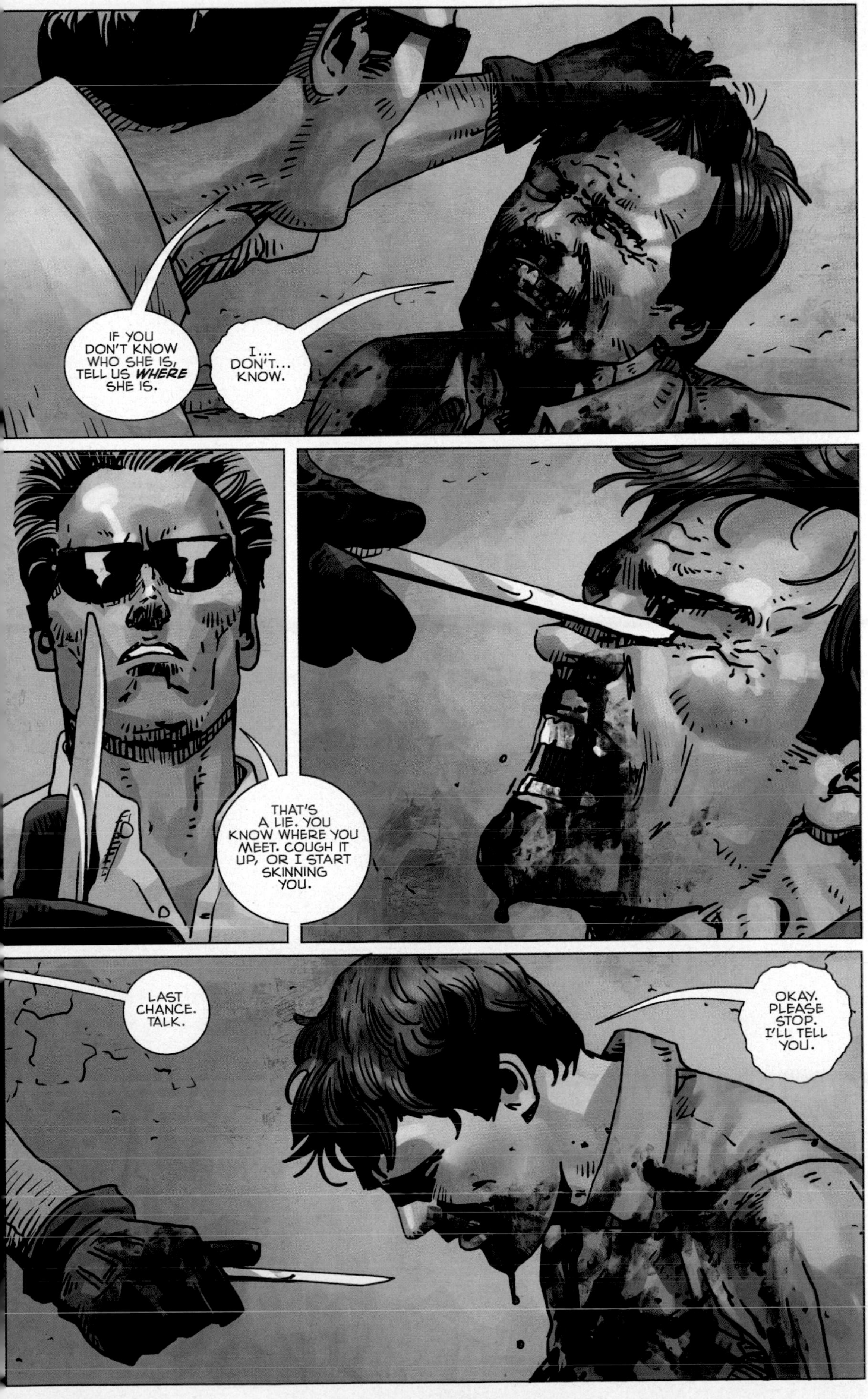
IF YOU DON'T KNOW WHO SHE IS, TELL US *WHERE* SHE IS.
I... DON'T... KNOW.
THAT'S A LIE. YOU KNOW WHERE YOU MEET. COUGH IT UP, OR I START SKINNING YOU.
LAST CHANCE. TALK.
OKAY. PLEASE STOP. I'LL TELL YOU.

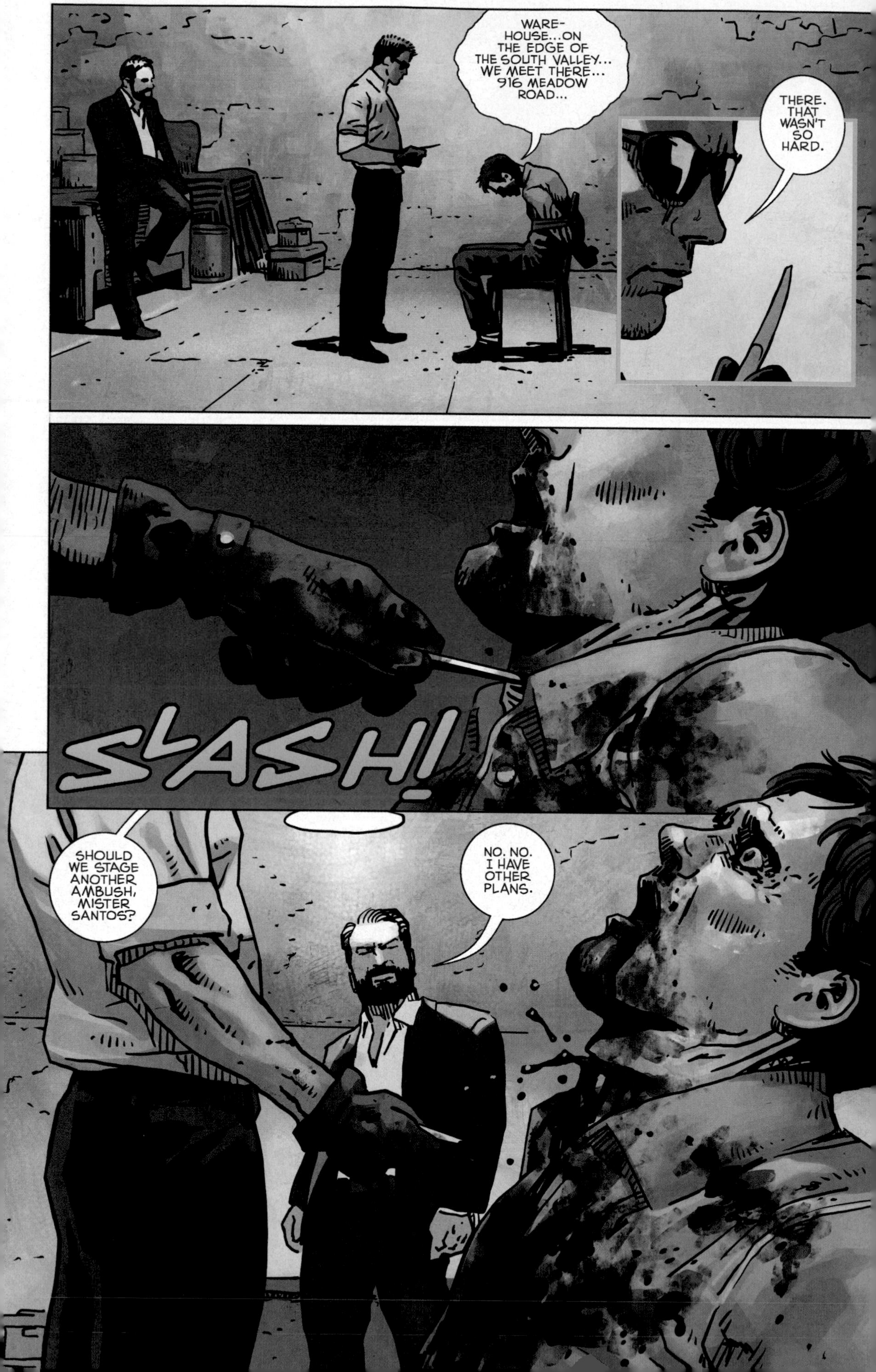
WARE-HOUSE...ON THE EDGE OF THE SOUTH VALLEY... WE MEET THERE... 916 MEADOW ROAD...
THERE. THAT WASN'T SO HARD.
SLASH!
SHOULD WE STAGE ANOTHER AMBUSH, MISTER SANTOS?
NO. NO. I HAVE OTHER PLANS.

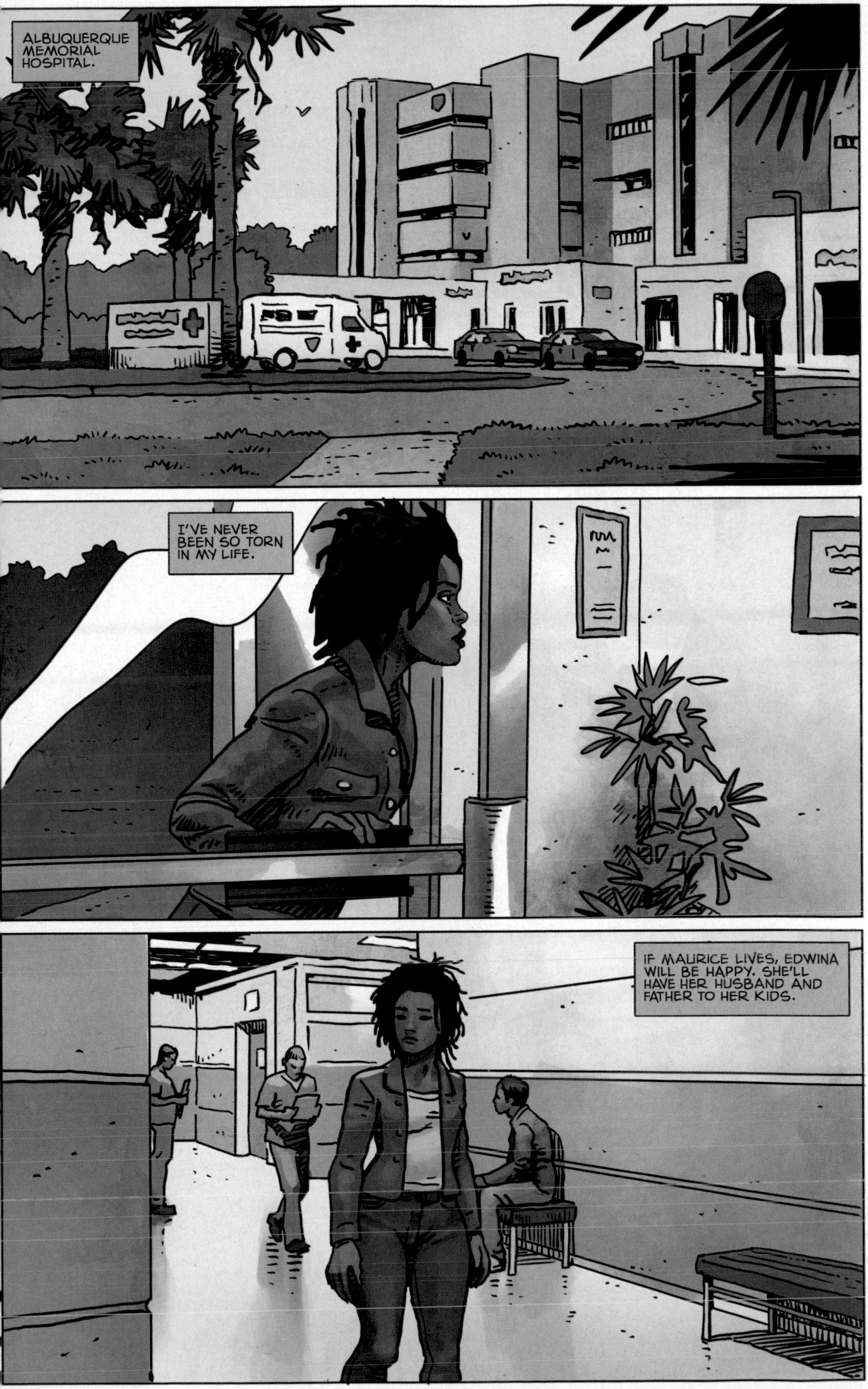
ALBUQUERQUE MEMORIAL HOSPITAL.
I'VE NEVER BEEN SO TORN IN MY LIFE.
IF MAURICE LIVES, EDWINA WILL BE HAPPY. SHE'LL HAVE HER HUSBAND AND FATHER TO HER KIDS.

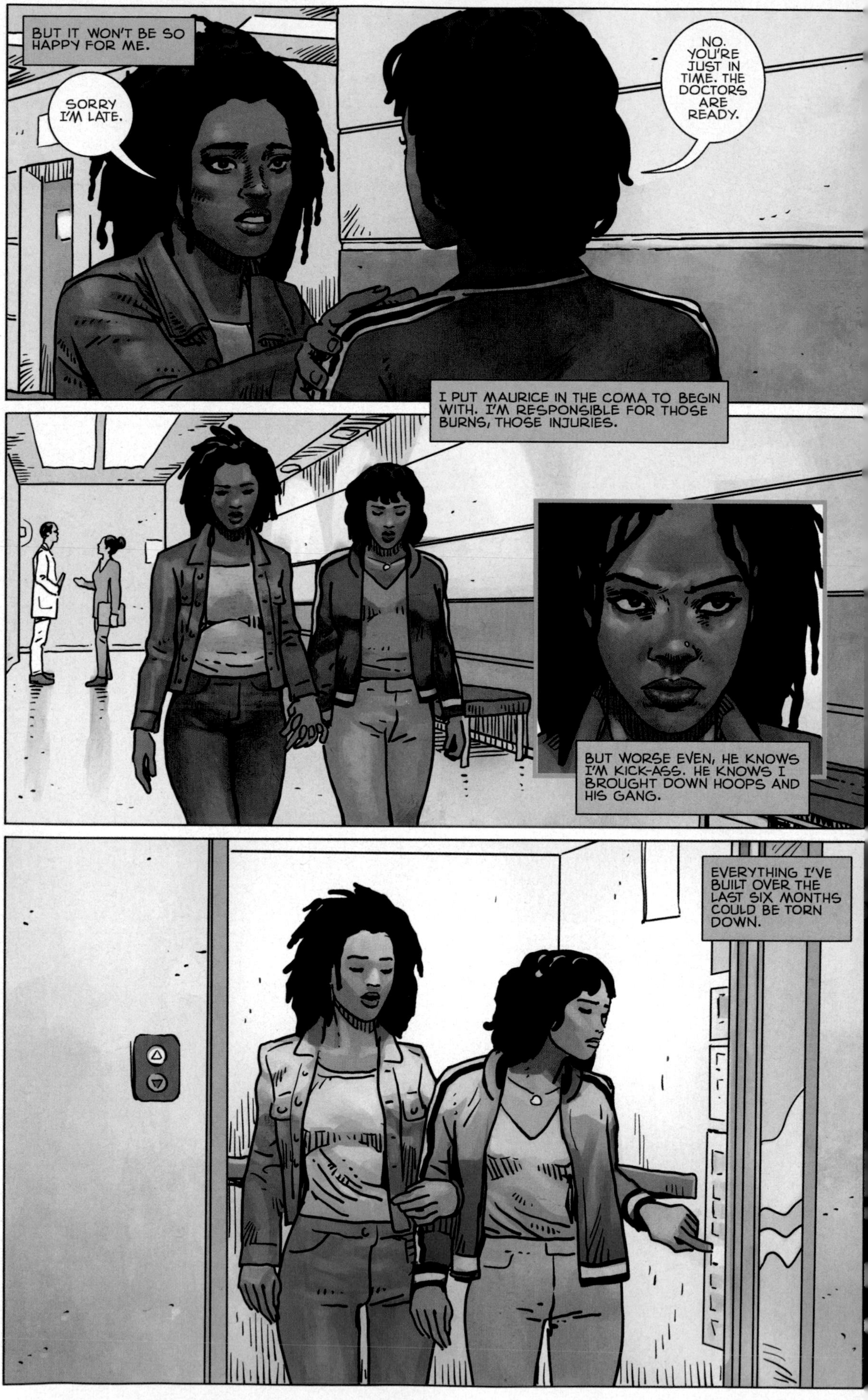
BUT IT WON'T BE SO HAPPY FOR ME.
SORRY I'M LATE.
NO. YOU'RE JUST IN TIME. THE DOCTORS ARE READY.
I PUT MAURICE IN THE COMA TO BEGIN WITH. I'M RESPONSIBLE FOR THOSE BURNS, THOSE INJURIES.
BUT WORSE EVEN, HE KNOWS I'M KICK-ASS. HE KNOWS I BROUGHT DOWN HOOPS AND HIS GANG.
EVERYTHING I'VE BUILT OVER THE LAST SIX MONTHS COULD BE TORN DOWN.

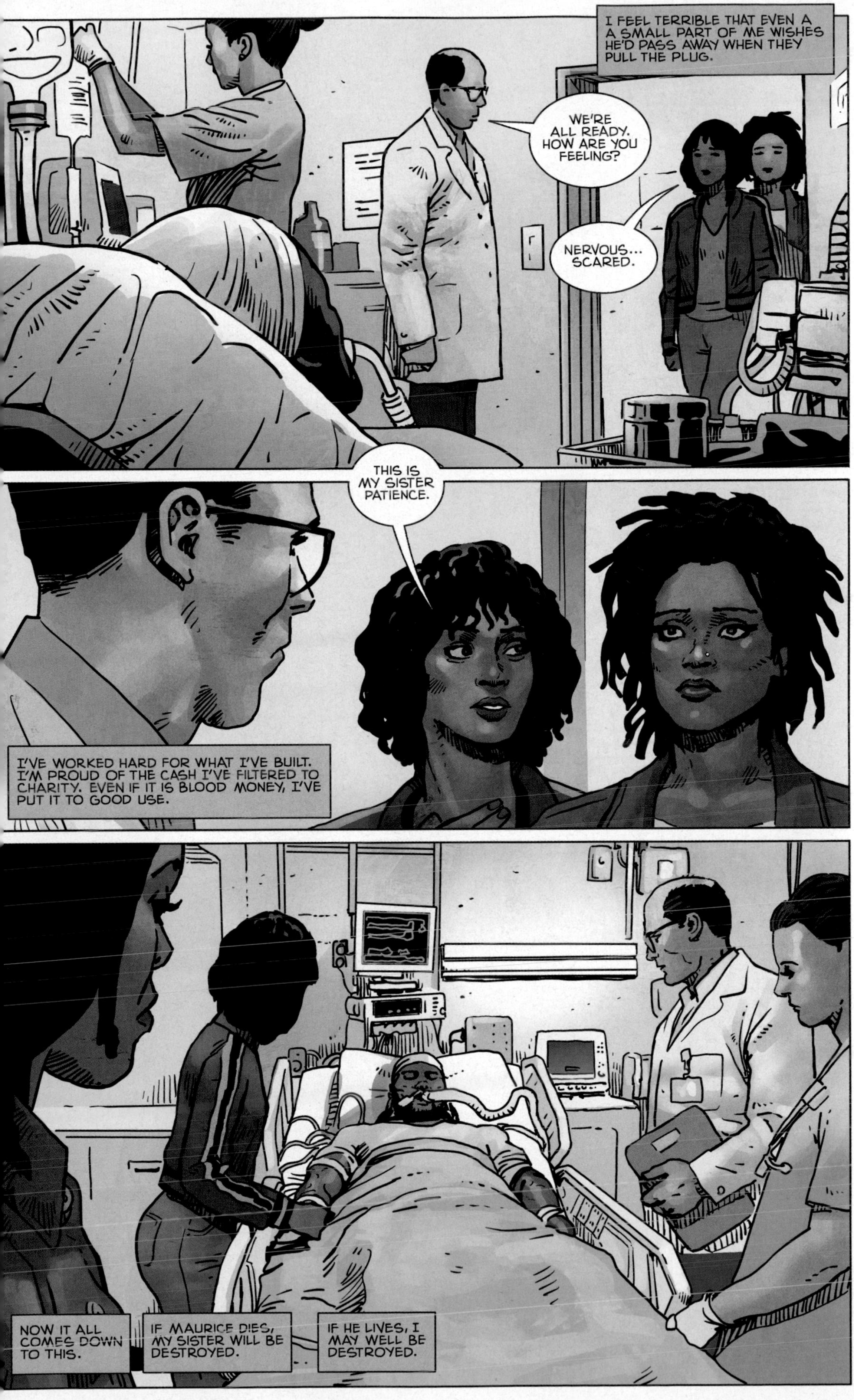
I FEEL TERRIBLE THAT EVEN A A SMALL PART OF ME WISHES HE'D PASS AWAY WHEN THEY PULL THE PLUG.
WE'RE ALL READY. HOW ARE YOU FEELING?
NERVOUS... SCARED.
THIS IS MY SISTER PATIENCE.
I'VE WORKED HARD FOR WHAT I'VE BUILT. I'M PROUD OF THE CASH I'VE FILTERED TO CHARITY. EVEN IF IT IS BLOOD MONEY, I'VE PUT IT TO GOOD USE.
NOW IT ALL COMES DOWN TO THIS.
IF MAURICE DIES, MY SISTER WILL BE DESTROYED.
IF HE LIVES, I MAY WELL BE DESTROYED.

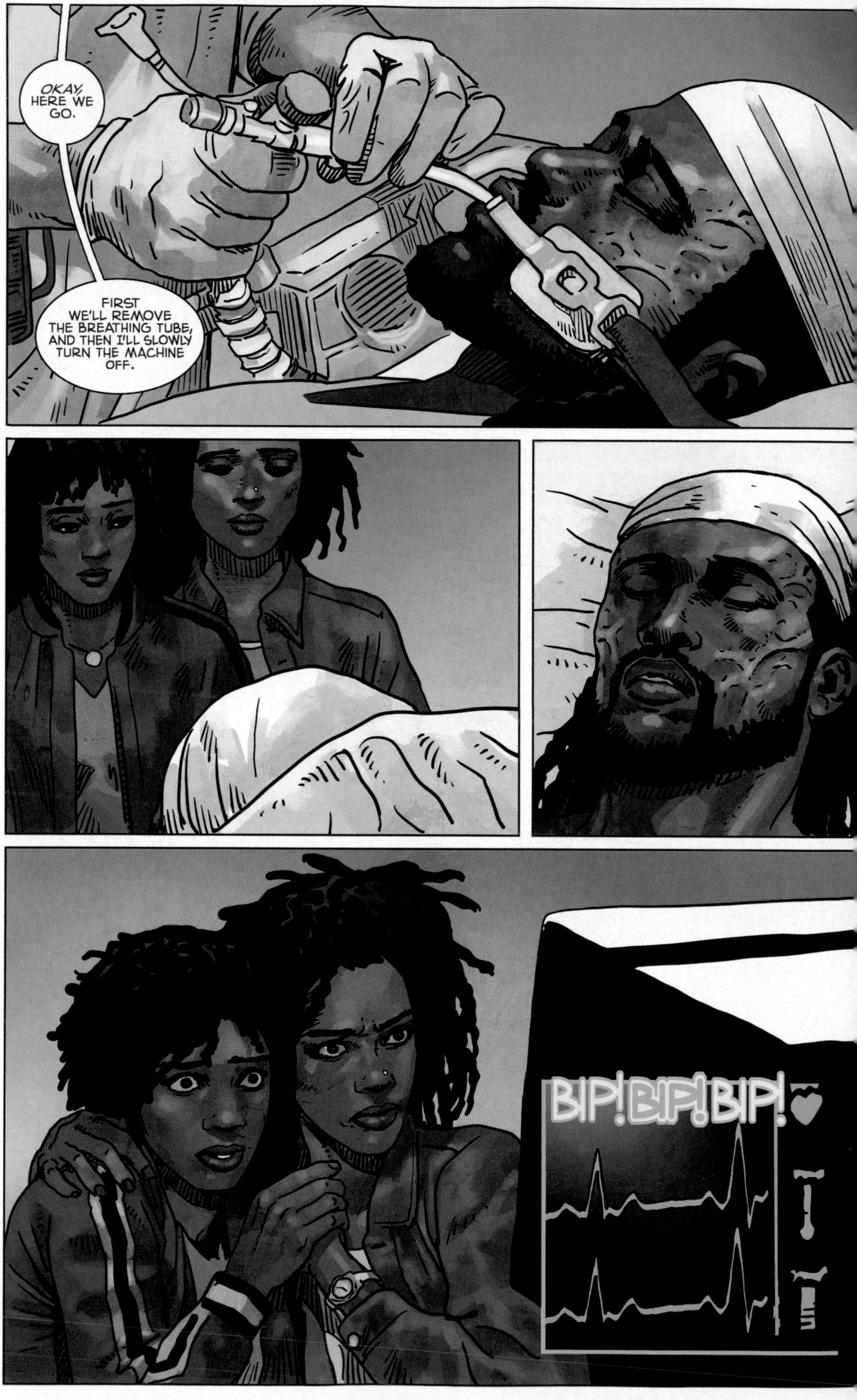
OKAY, HERE WE GO.
FIRST WE'LL REMOVE THE BREATHING TUBE, AND THEN I'LL SLOWLY TURN THE MACHINE OFF.
BIP! BIP! BIP!

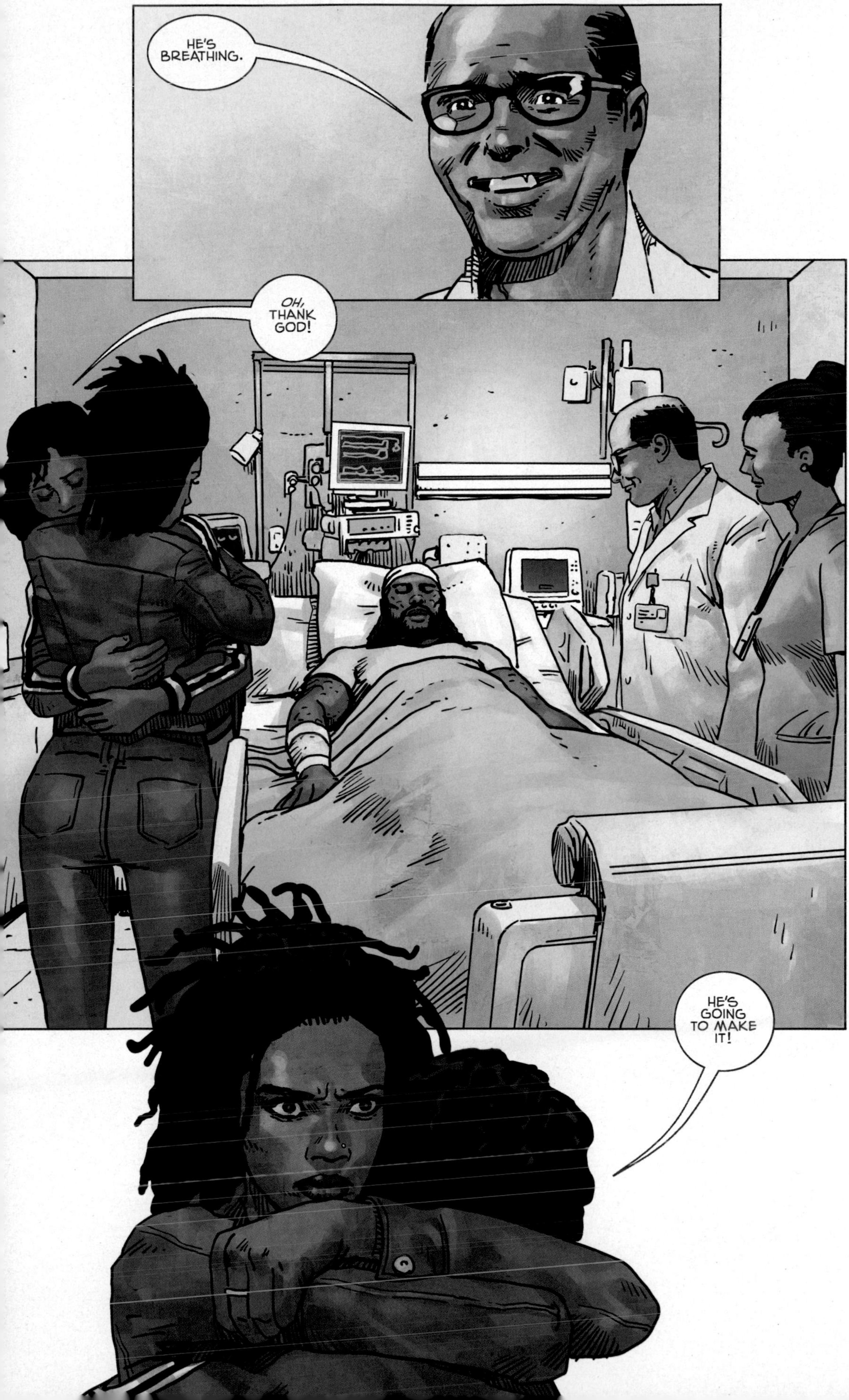
HE'S BREATHING.
OH, THANK GOD!
HE'S GOING TO MAKE IT!

THREE

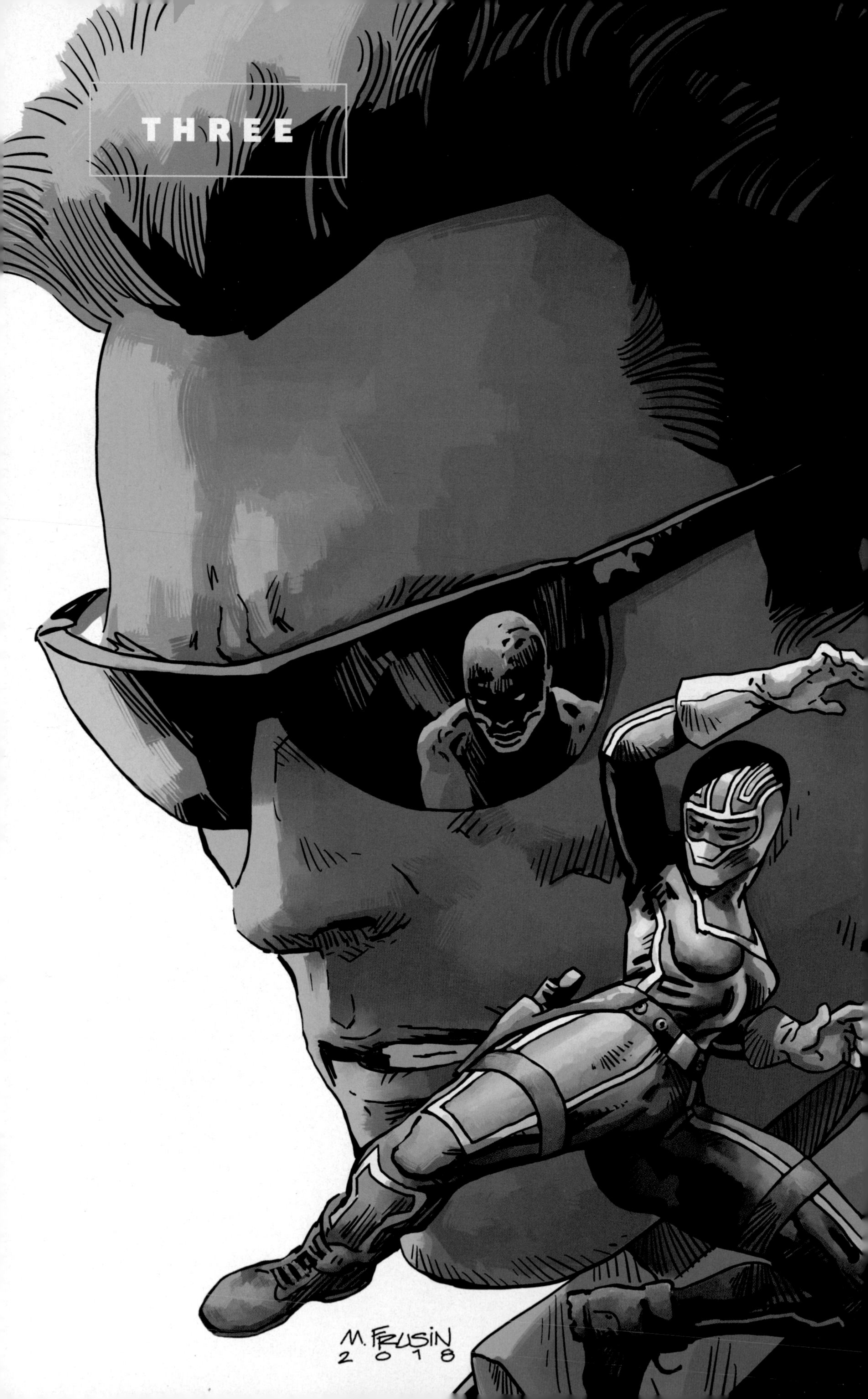
M. FRUSIN
2018

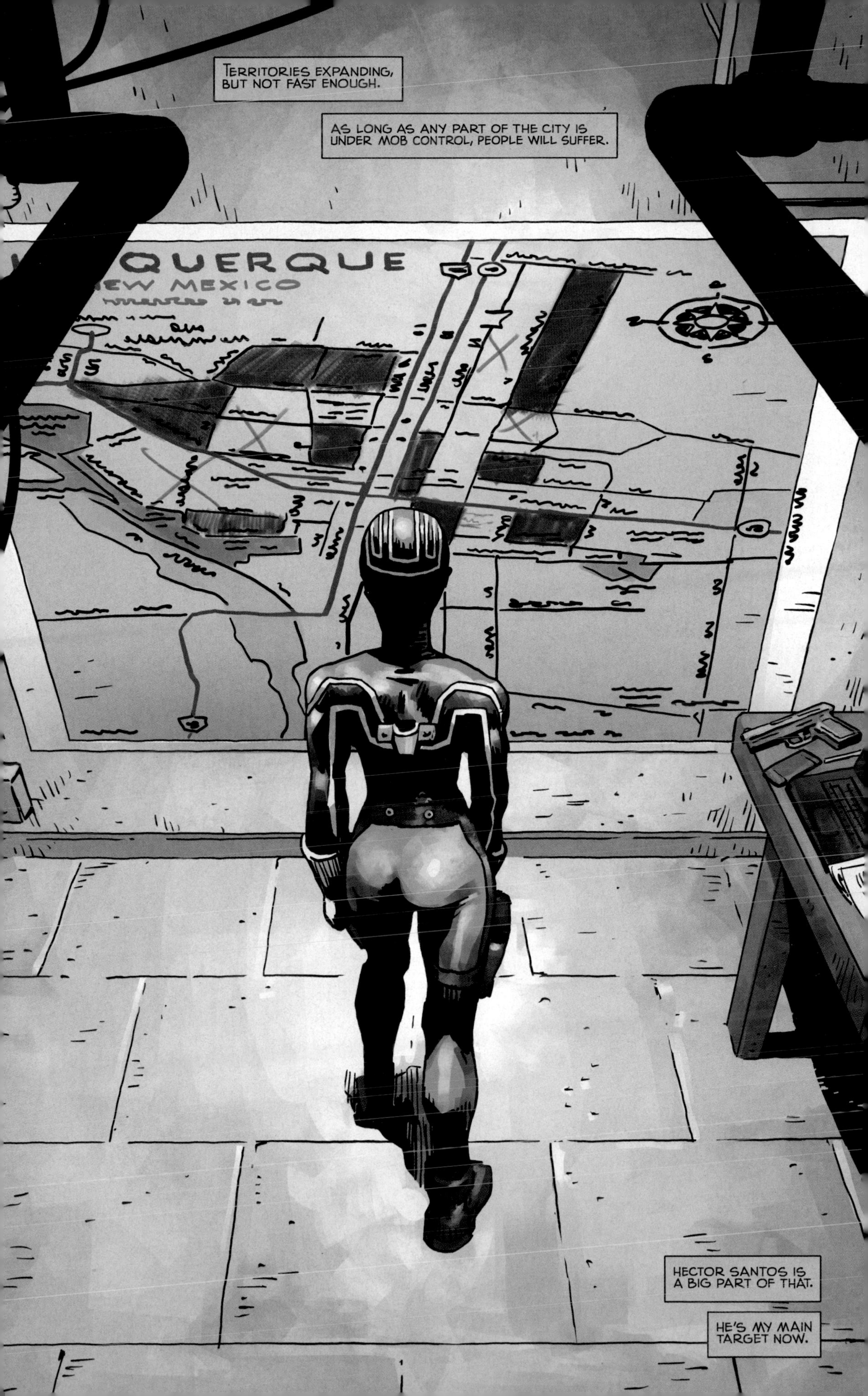
TERRITORIES EXPANDING, BUT NOT FAST ENOUGH.
AS LONG AS ANY PART OF THE CITY IS UNDER MOB CONTROL, PEOPLE WILL SUFFER.
QUERQUE
EW MEXICO
HECTOR SANTOS IS A BIG PART OF THAT.
HE'S MY MAIN TARGET NOW.

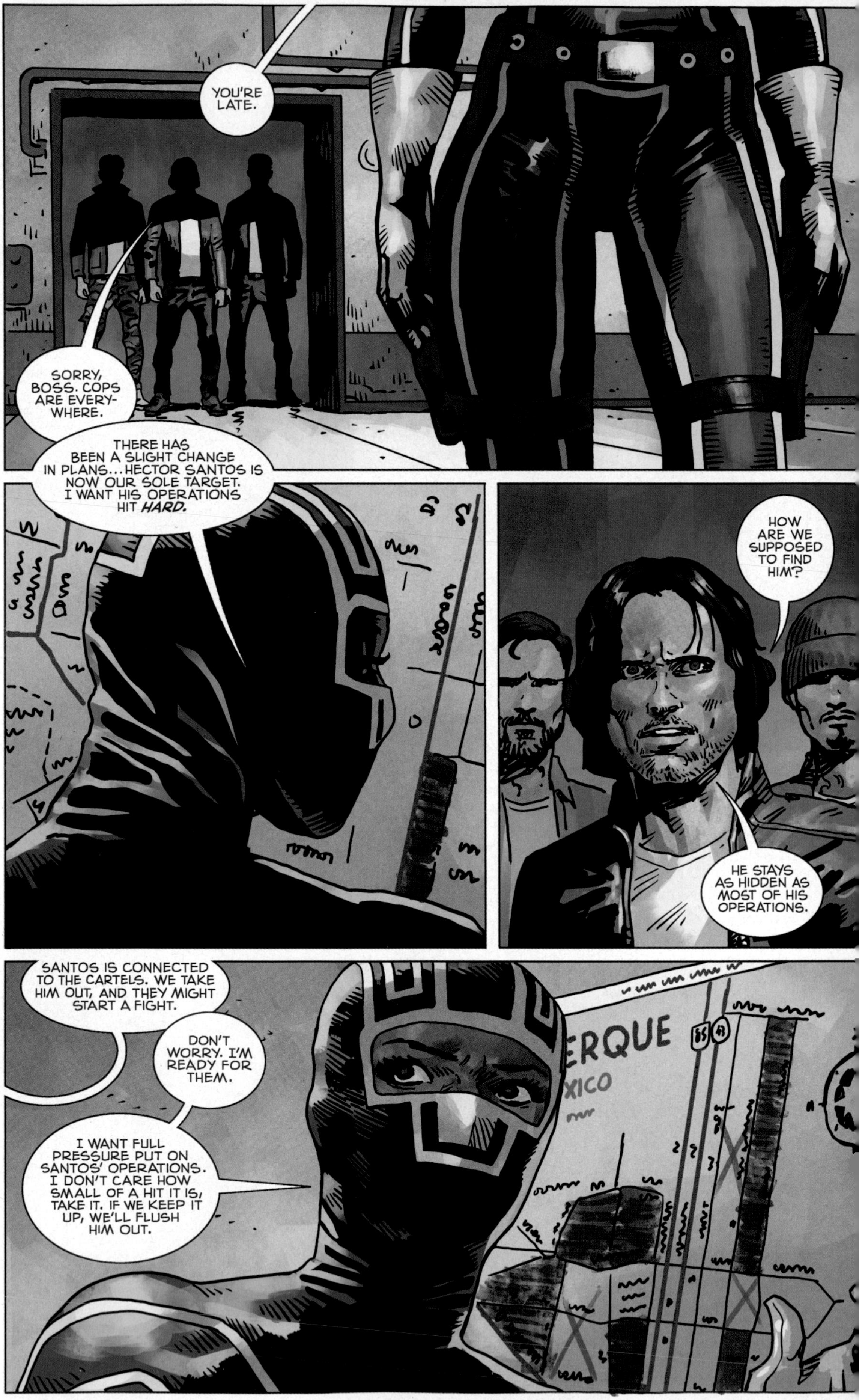
YOU'RE LATE.
SORRY, BOSS. COPS ARE EVERY-WHERE.
THERE HAS BEEN A SLIGHT CHANGE IN PLANS... HECTOR SANTOS IS NOW OUR SOLE TARGET. I WANT HIS OPERATIONS HIT HARD.
HOW ARE WE SUPPOSED TO FIND HIM?
HE STAYS AS HIDDEN AS MOST OF HIS OPERATIONS.
SANTOS IS CONNECTED TO THE CARTELS. WE TAKE HIM OUT, AND THEY MIGHT START A FIGHT.
DON'T WORRY. I'M READY FOR THEM.
I WANT FULL PRESSURE PUT ON SANTOS' OPERATIONS. I DON'T CARE HOW SMALL OF A HIT IT IS, TAKE IT. IF WE KEEP IT UP, WE'LL FLUSH HIM OUT.
ERQUE
XICO

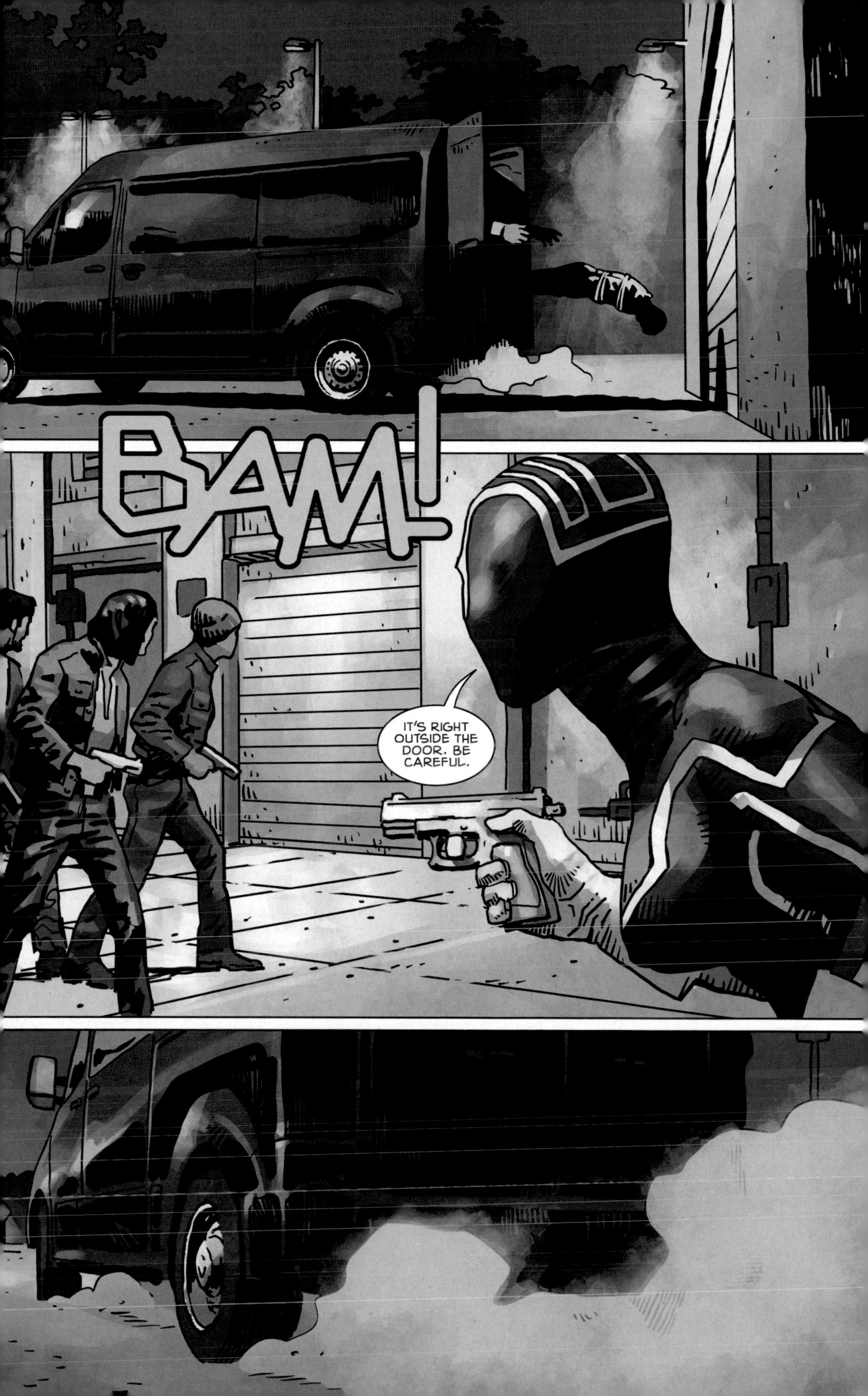
BAM!
IT'S RIGHT OUTSIDE THE DOOR. BE CAREFUL.

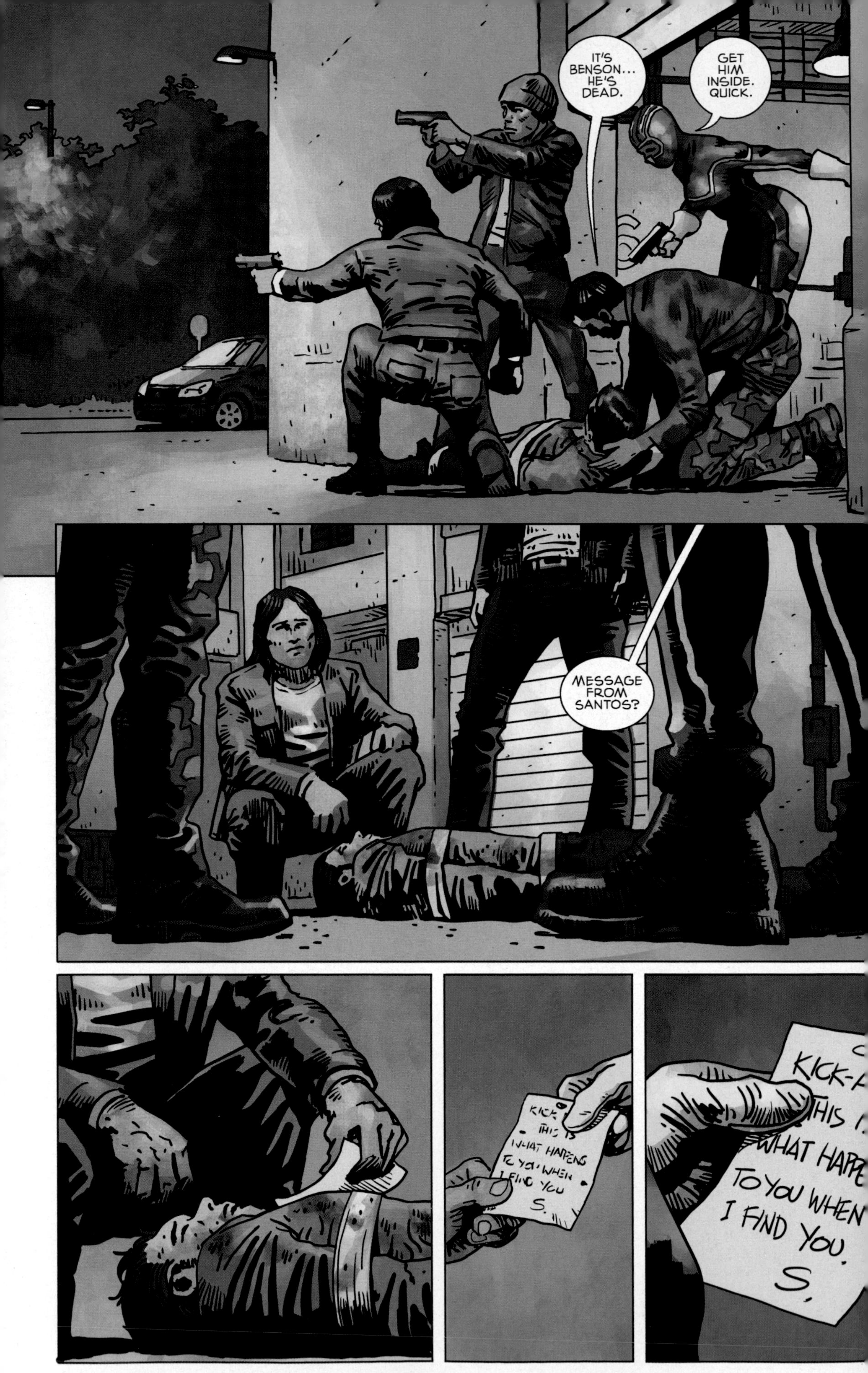
IT'S BENSON... HE'S DEAD.
GET HIM INSIDE. QUICK.
MESSAGE FROM SANTOS?
KICK-
THIS IS
WHAT HAPPENS
TO YOU WHEN
I FIND YOU
S.
TO YOU WHEN
I FIND YOU.
S.

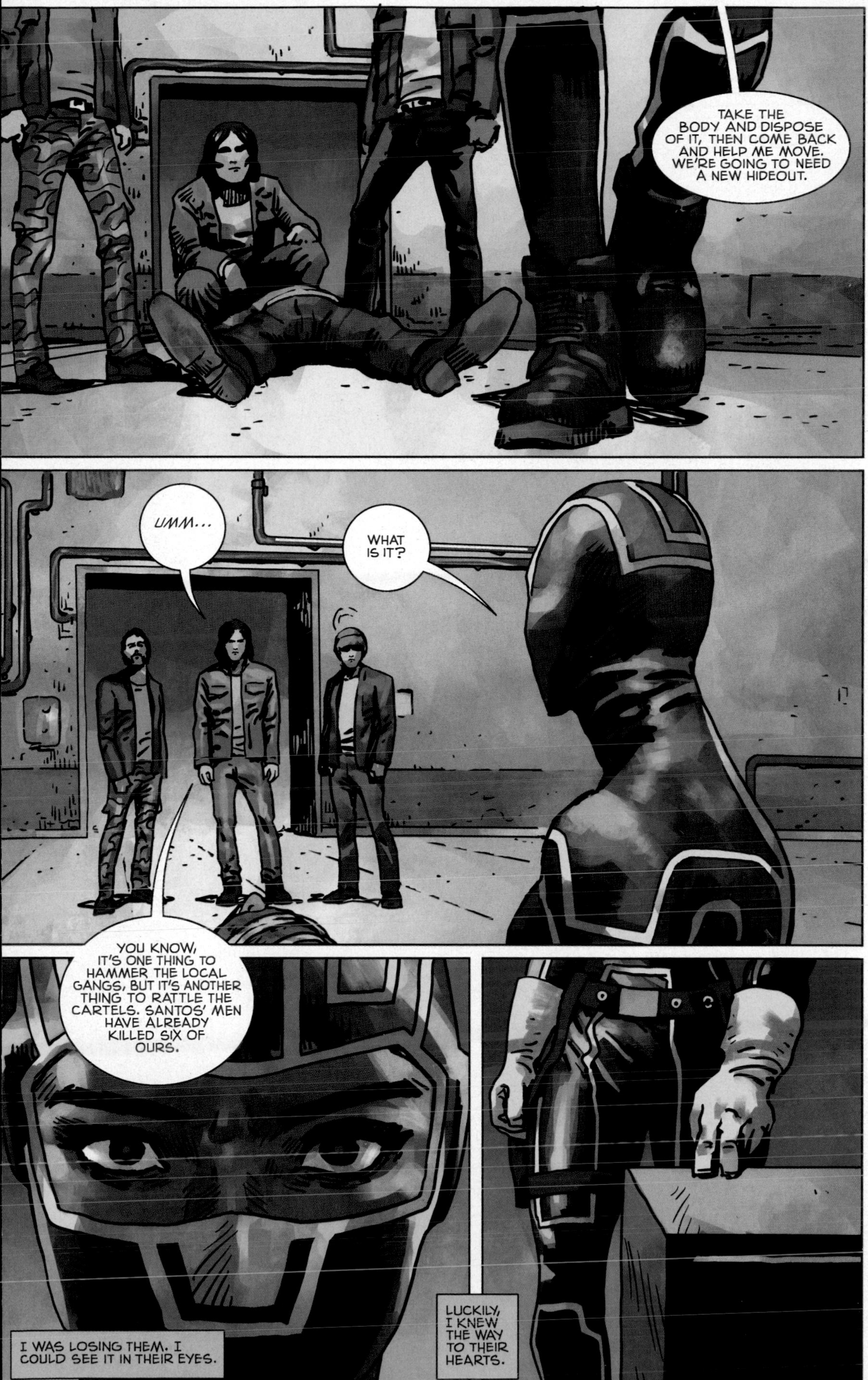
TAKE THE BODY AND DISPOSE OF IT, THEN COME BACK AND HELP ME MOVE. WE'RE GOING TO NEED A NEW HIDEOUT.
UMM...
WHAT IS IT?
YOU KNOW, IT'S ONE THING TO HAMMER THE LOCAL GANGS, BUT IT'S ANOTHER THING TO RATTLE THE CARTELS. SANTOS' MEN HAVE ALREADY KILLED SIX OF OURS.
I WAS LOSING THEM. I COULD SEE IT IN THEIR EYES.
LUCKILY, I KNEW THE WAY TO THEIR HEARTS.

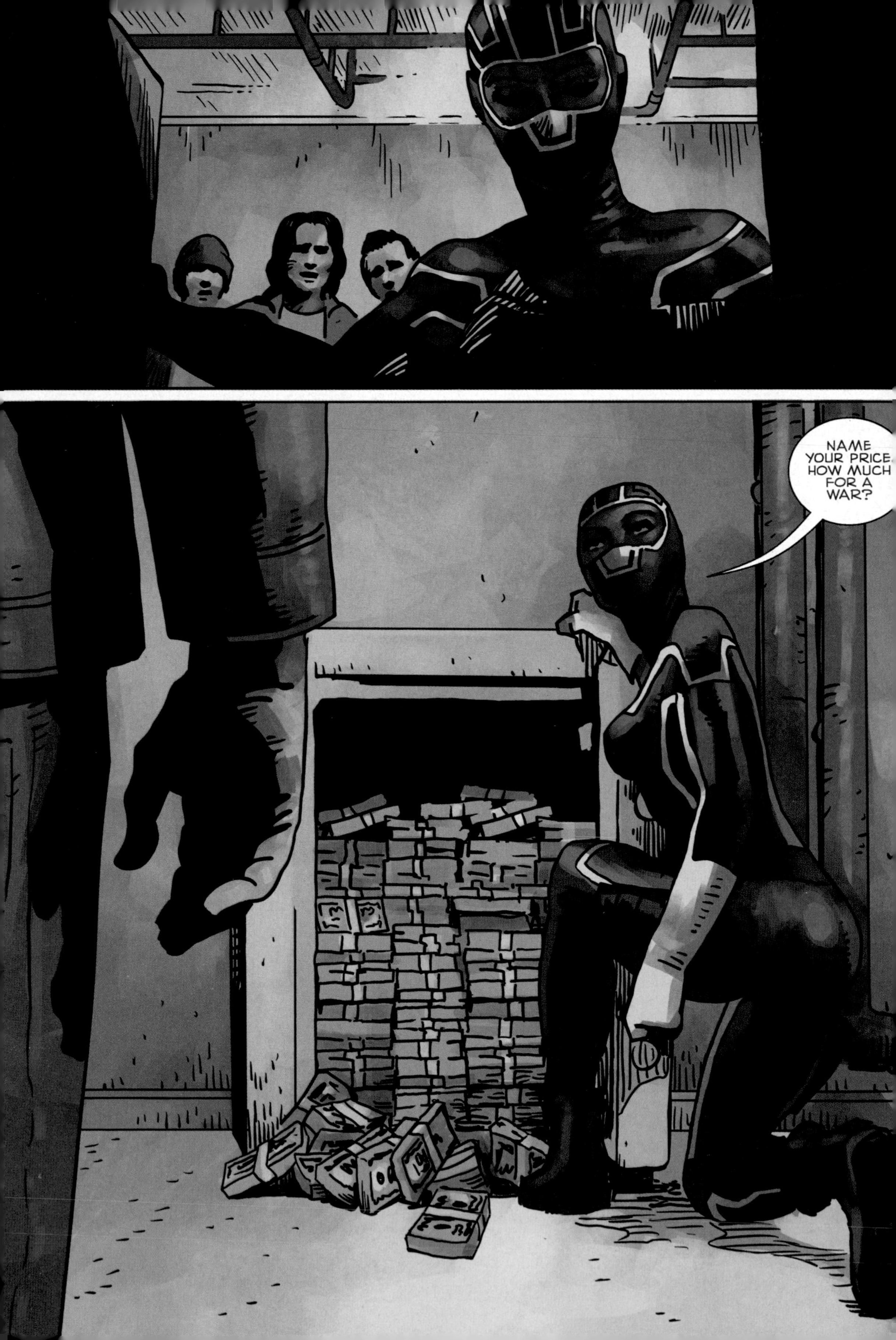
NAME YOUR PRICE. HOW MUCH FOR A WAR?

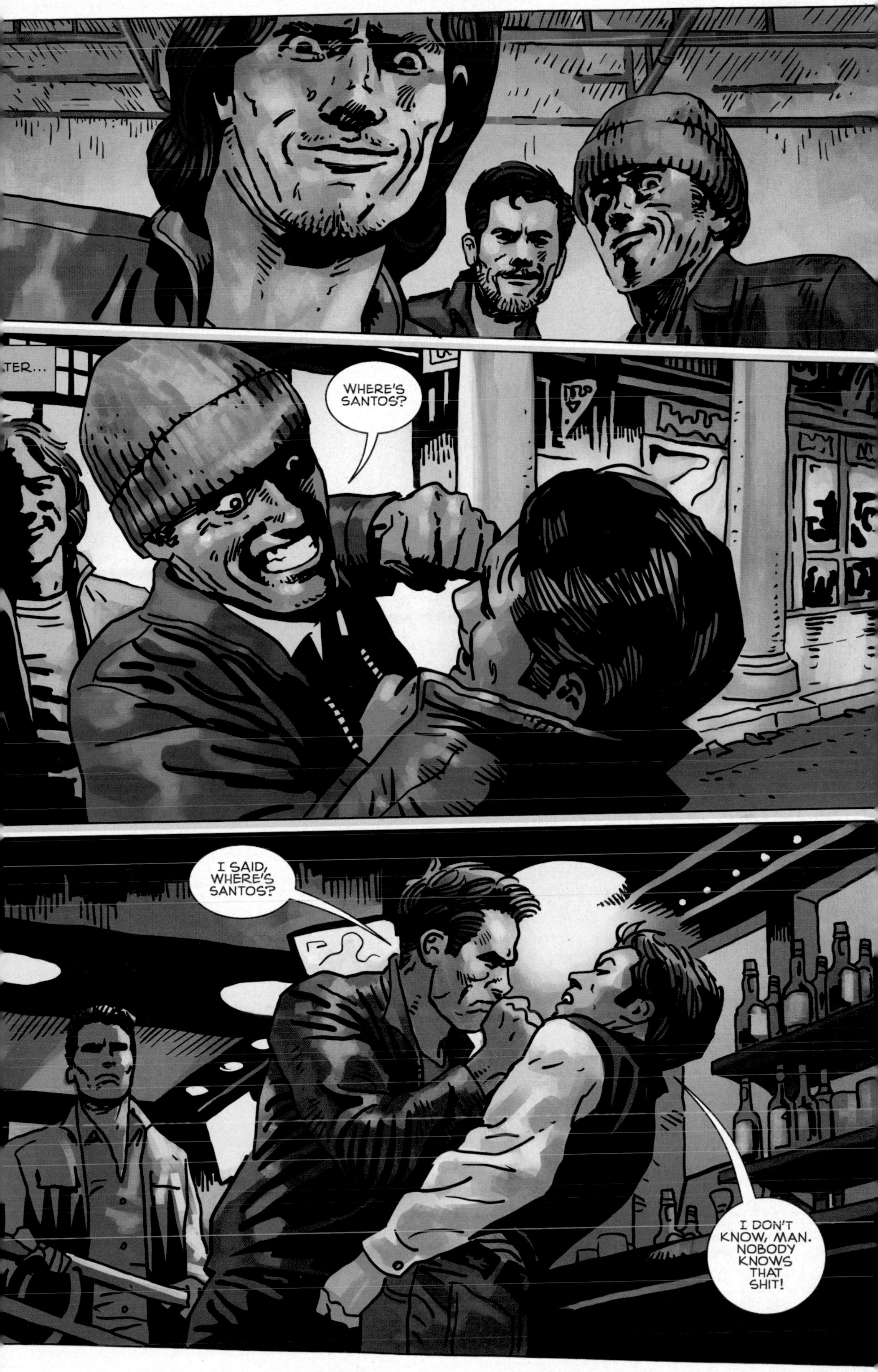
TER...
WHERE'S SANTOS?
I SAID, WHERE'S SANTOS?
I DON'T KNOW, MAN. NOBODY KNOWS THAT SHIT!

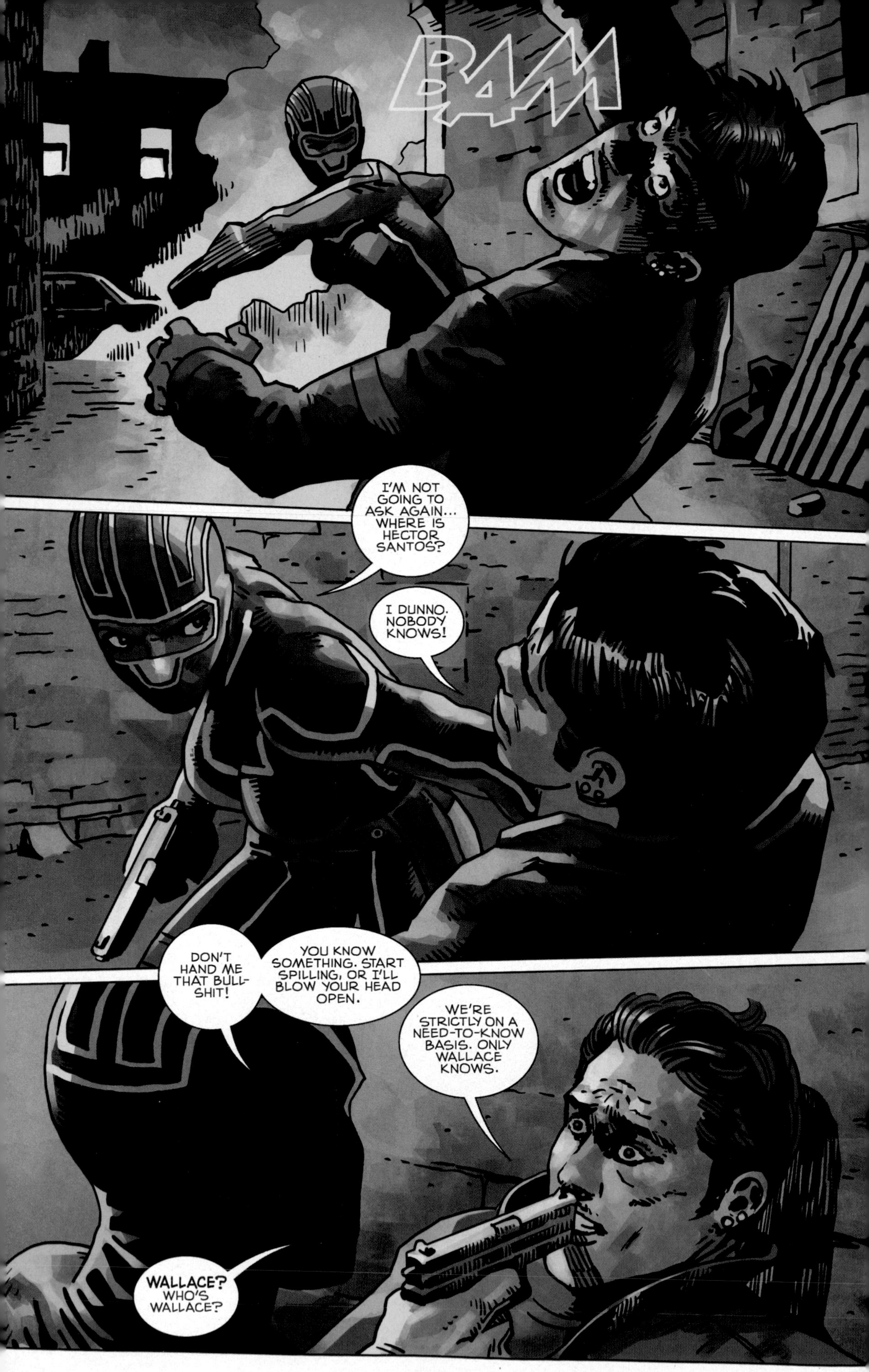
BAM
I'M NOT GOING TO ASK AGAIN... WHERE IS HECTOR SANTOS?
I DUNNO. NOBODY KNOWS!
DON'T HAND ME THAT BULL-SHIT!
YOU KNOW SOMETHING. START SPILLING, OR I'LL BLOW YOUR HEAD OPEN.
WE'RE STRICTLY ON A NEED-TO-KNOW BASIS. ONLY WALLACE KNOWS.
WALLACE? WHO'S WALLACE?

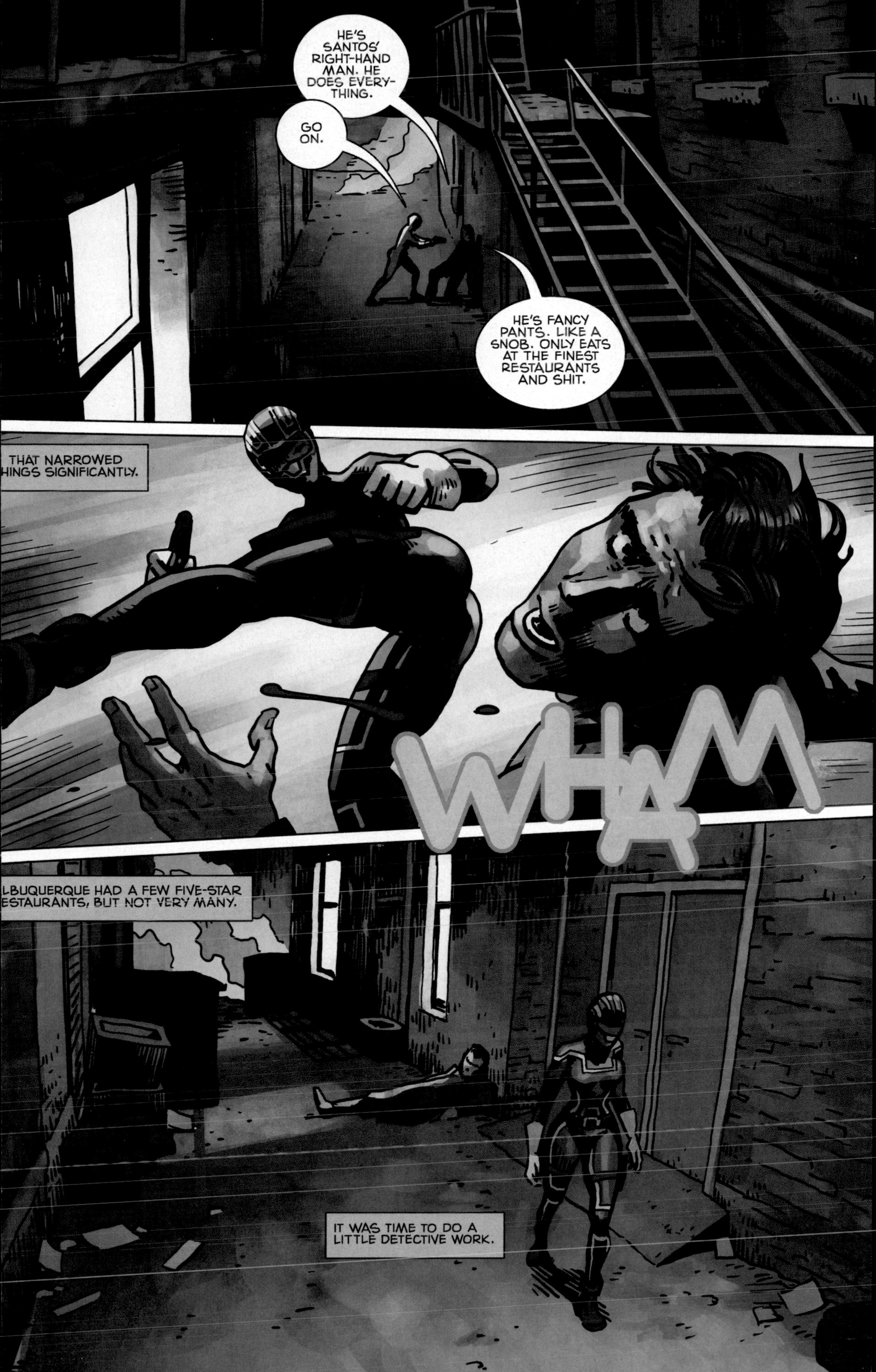
HE'S SANTOS' RIGHT-HAND MAN. HE DOES EVERY-THING.
GO ON.
HE'S FANCY PANTS. LIKE A SNOB. ONLY EATS AT THE FINEST RESTAURANTS AND SHIT.
THAT NARROWED HINGS SIGNIFICANTLY.
WHAM
LBUQUERQUE HAD A FEW FIVE-STAR ESTAURANTS, BUT NOT VERY MANY.
IT WAS TIME TO DO A LITTLE DETECTIVE WORK.

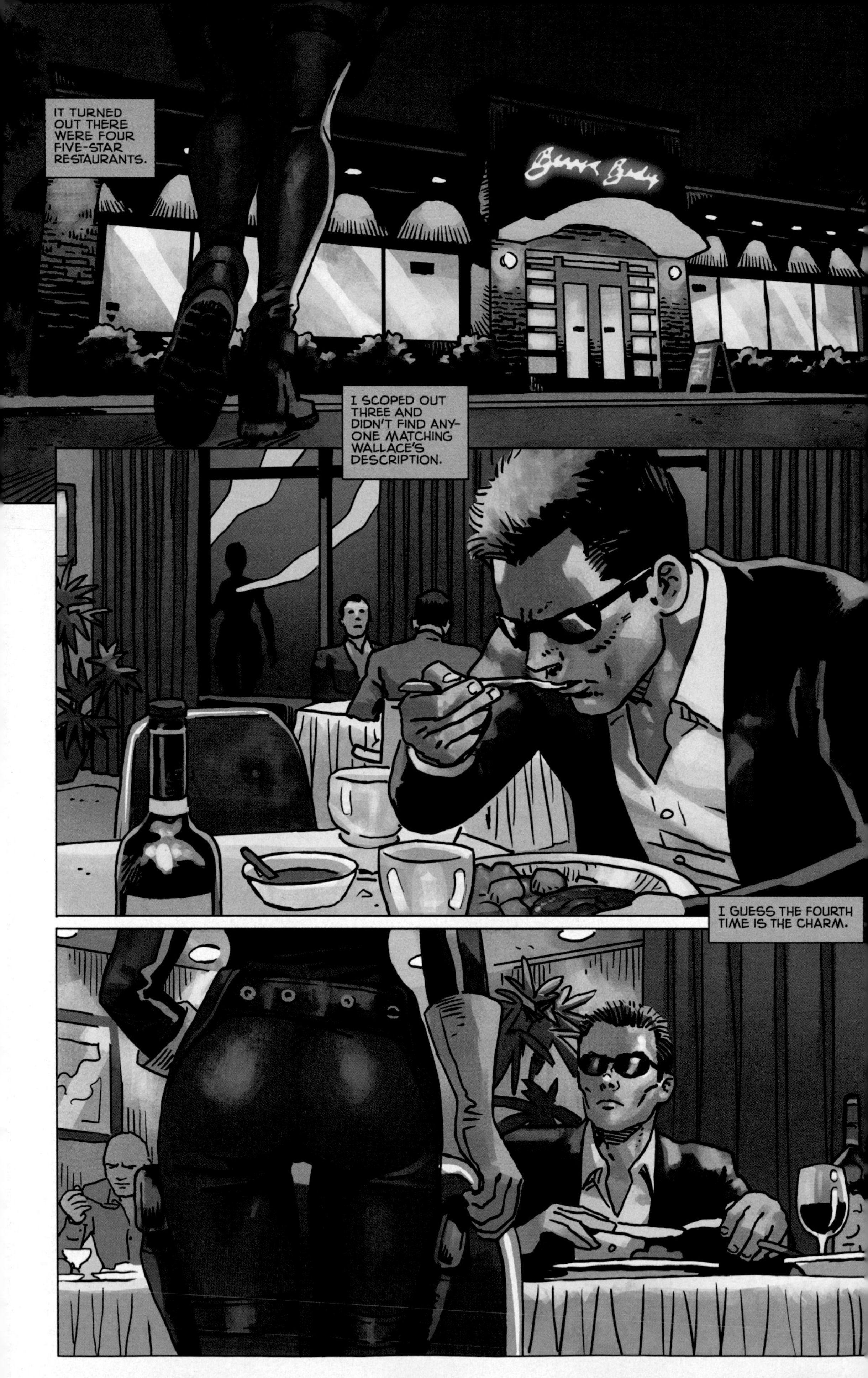
IT TURNED OUT THERE WERE FOUR FIVE-STAR RESTAURANTS.
I SCOPED OUT THREE AND DIDN'T FIND ANY-ONE MATCHING WALLACE'S DESCRIPTION.
I GUESS THE FOURTH TIME IS THE CHARM.

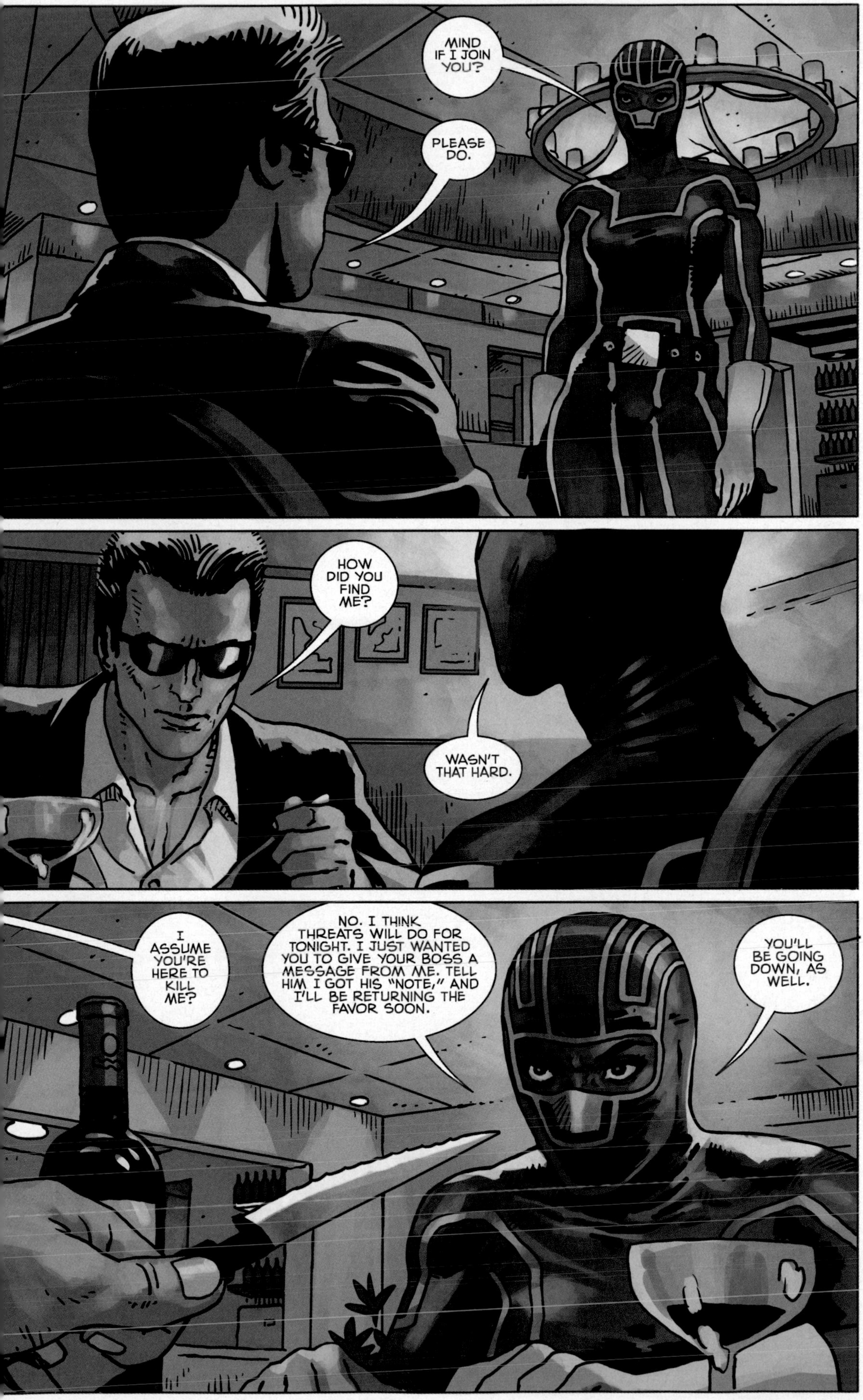
MIND IF I JOIN YOU?
PLEASE DO.
HOW DID YOU FIND ME?
WASN'T THAT HARD.
I ASSUME YOU'RE HERE TO KILL ME?
NO. I THINK THREATS WILL DO FOR TONIGHT. I JUST WANTED YOU TO GIVE YOUR BOSS A MESSAGE FROM ME. TELL HIM I GOT HIS "NOTE," AND I'LL BE RETURNING THE FAVOR SOON.
YOU'LL BE GOING DOWN, AS WELL.

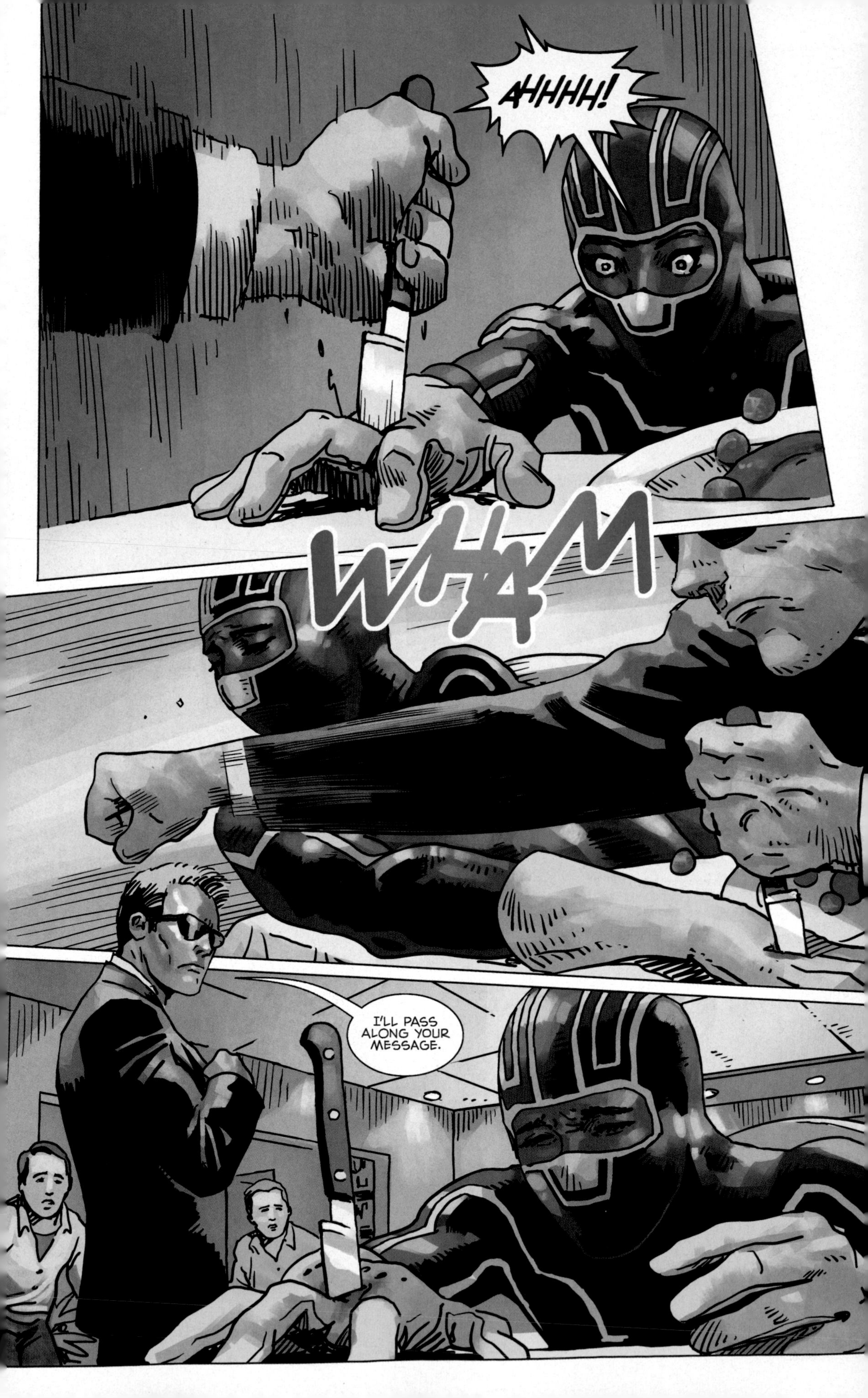
AHHHH!
WHAM
I'LL PASS ALONG YOUR MESSAGE.

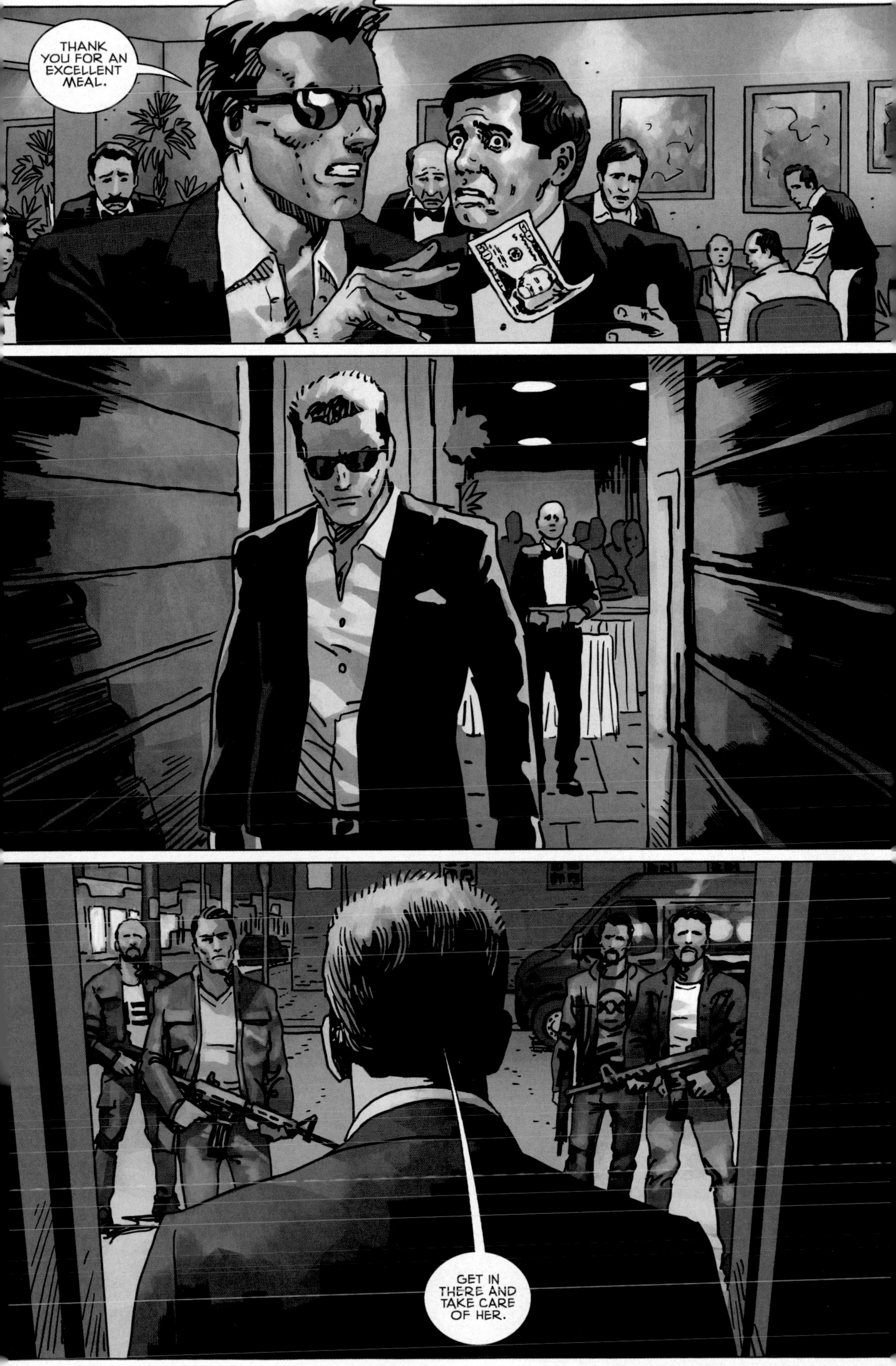
THANK YOU FOR AN EXCELLENT MEAL.
GET IN THERE AND TAKE CARE OF HER.

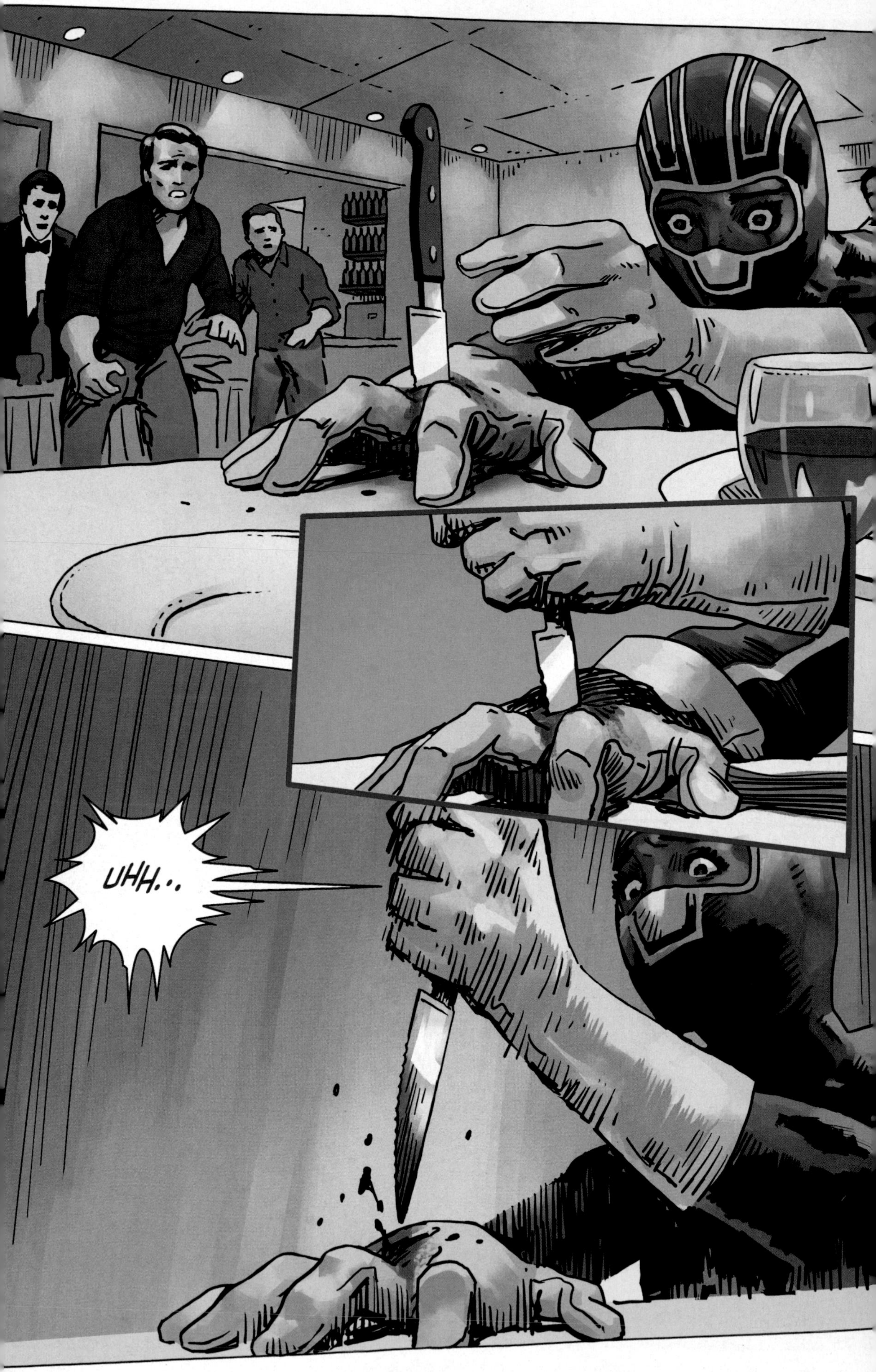
UHH...

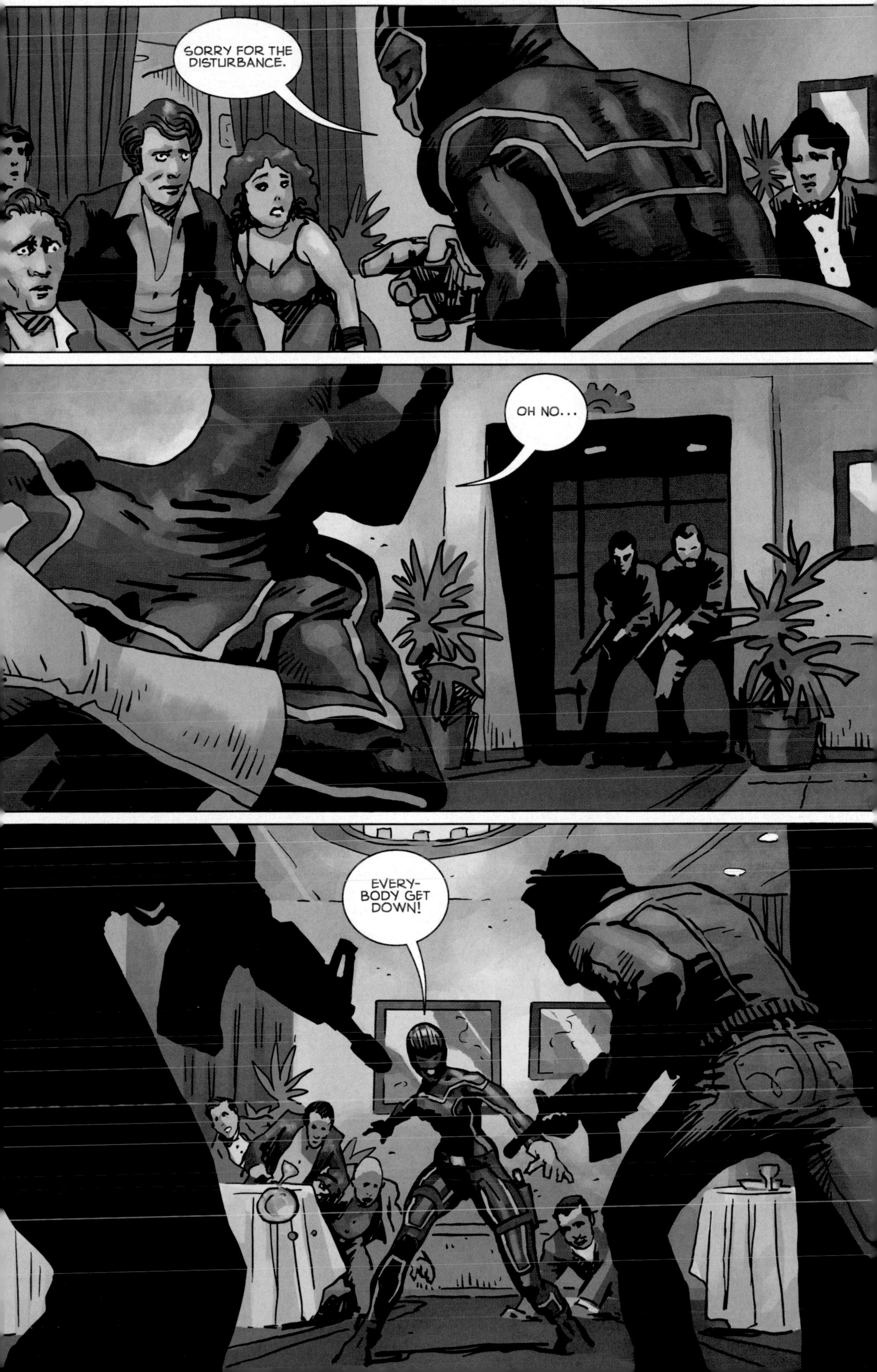
SORRY FOR THE DISTURBANCE.
OH NO...
EVERY-BODY GET DOWN!

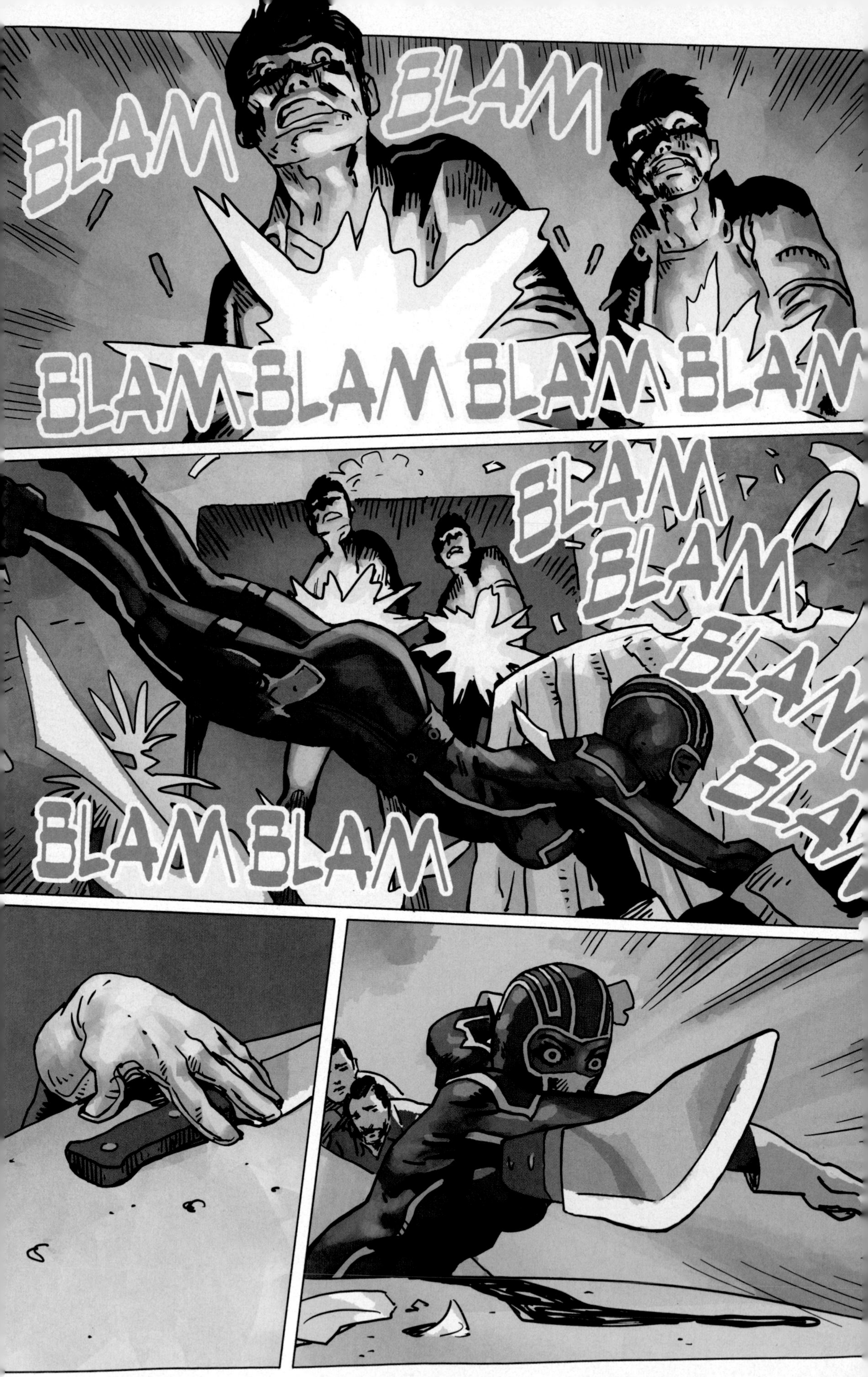
BLAM
BLAM
BLAM BLAM BLAM BLAM
BLAM
BLAM
BLAM
BLAM
BLAM BLAM

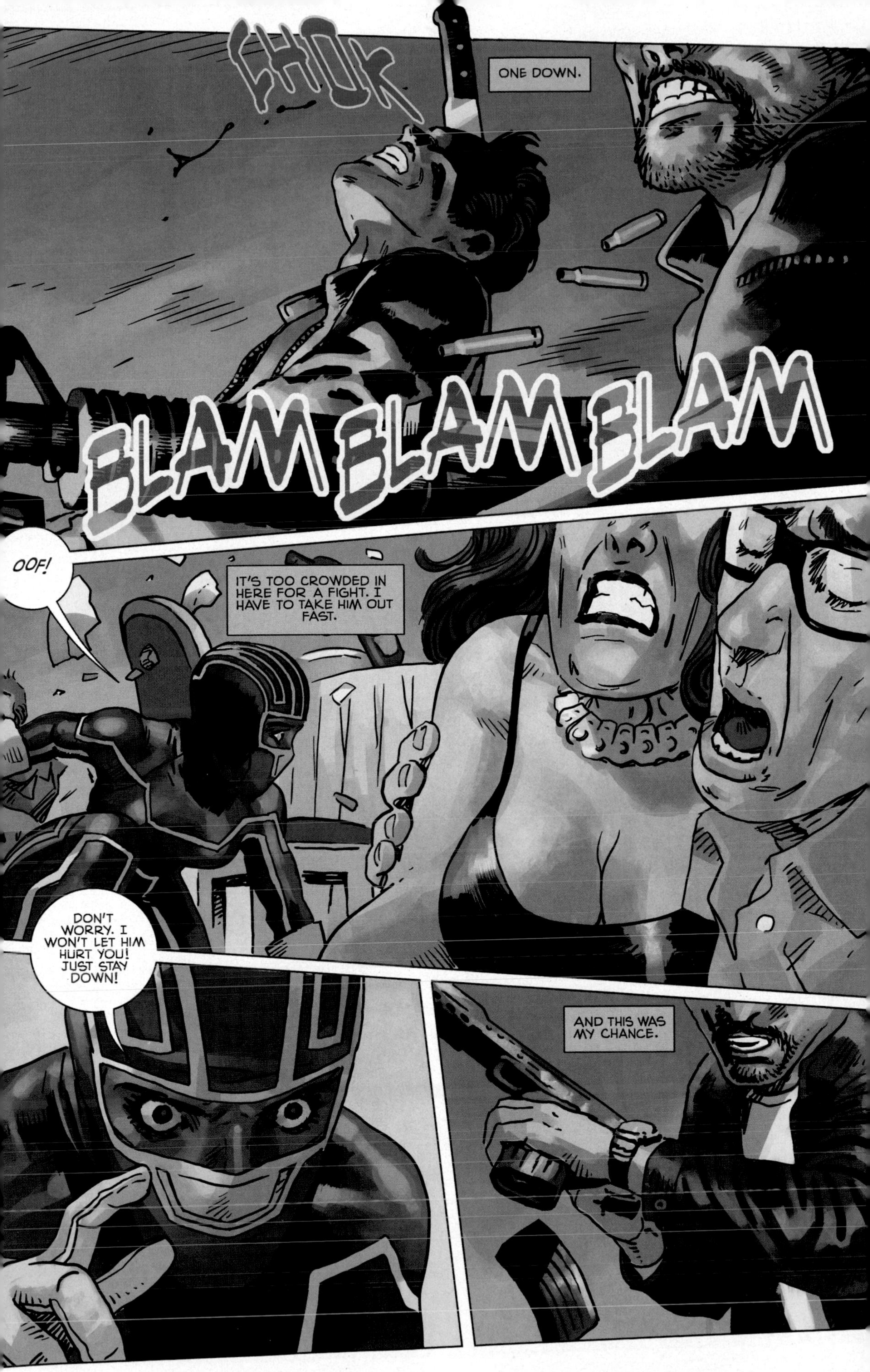
CHOK
ONE DOWN.
BLAM BLAM BLAM
OOF!
IT'S TOO CROWDED IN HERE FOR A FIGHT. I HAVE TO TAKE HIM OUT FAST.
DON'T WORRY. I WON'T LET HIM HURT YOU! JUST STAY DOWN!
AND THIS WAS MY CHANCE.

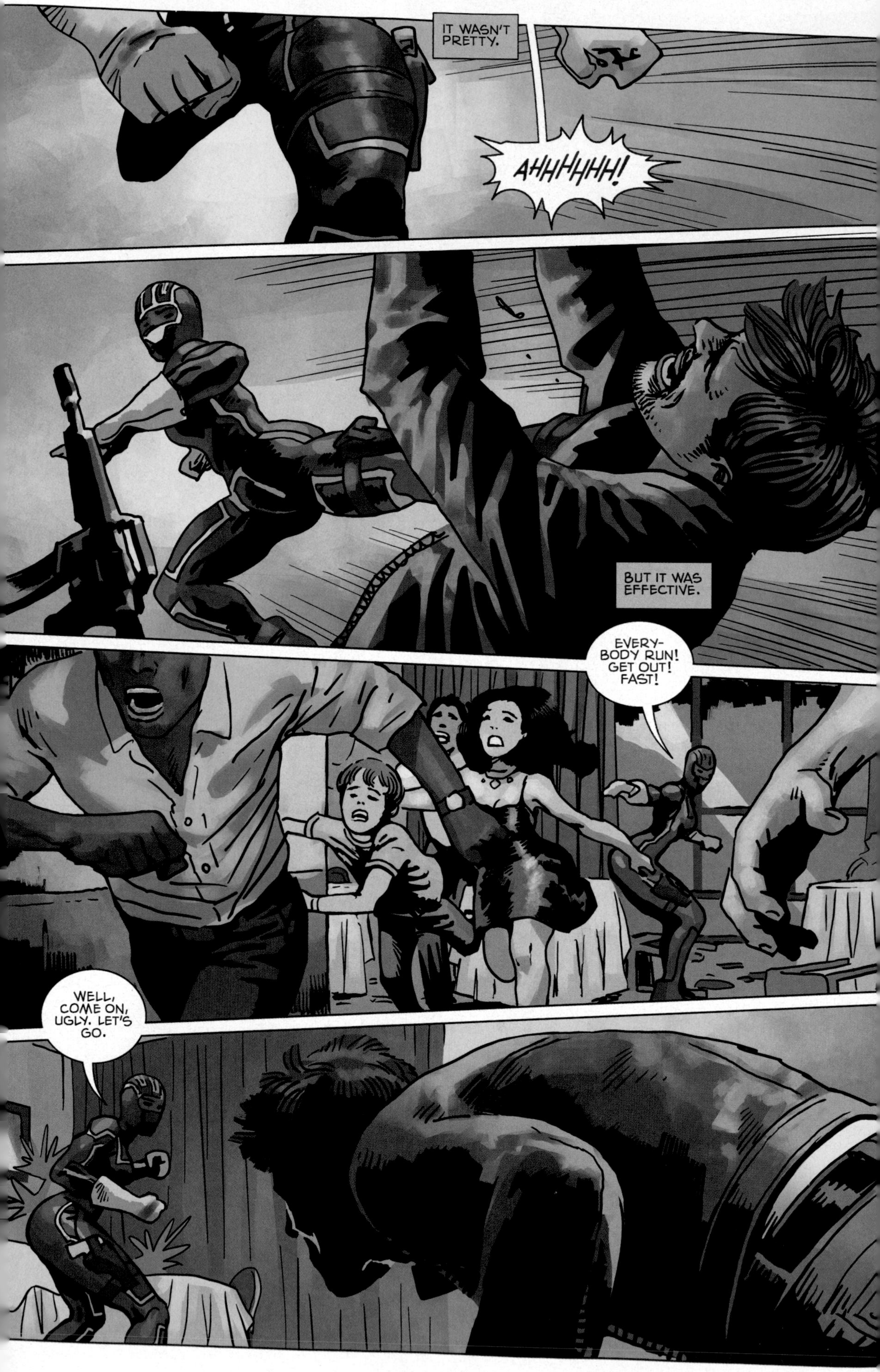
IT WASN'T PRETTY.
AHHHHHH!
BUT IT WAS EFFECTIVE.
EVERY-BODY RUN! GET OUT! FAST!
WELL, COME ON, UGLY. LET'S GO.

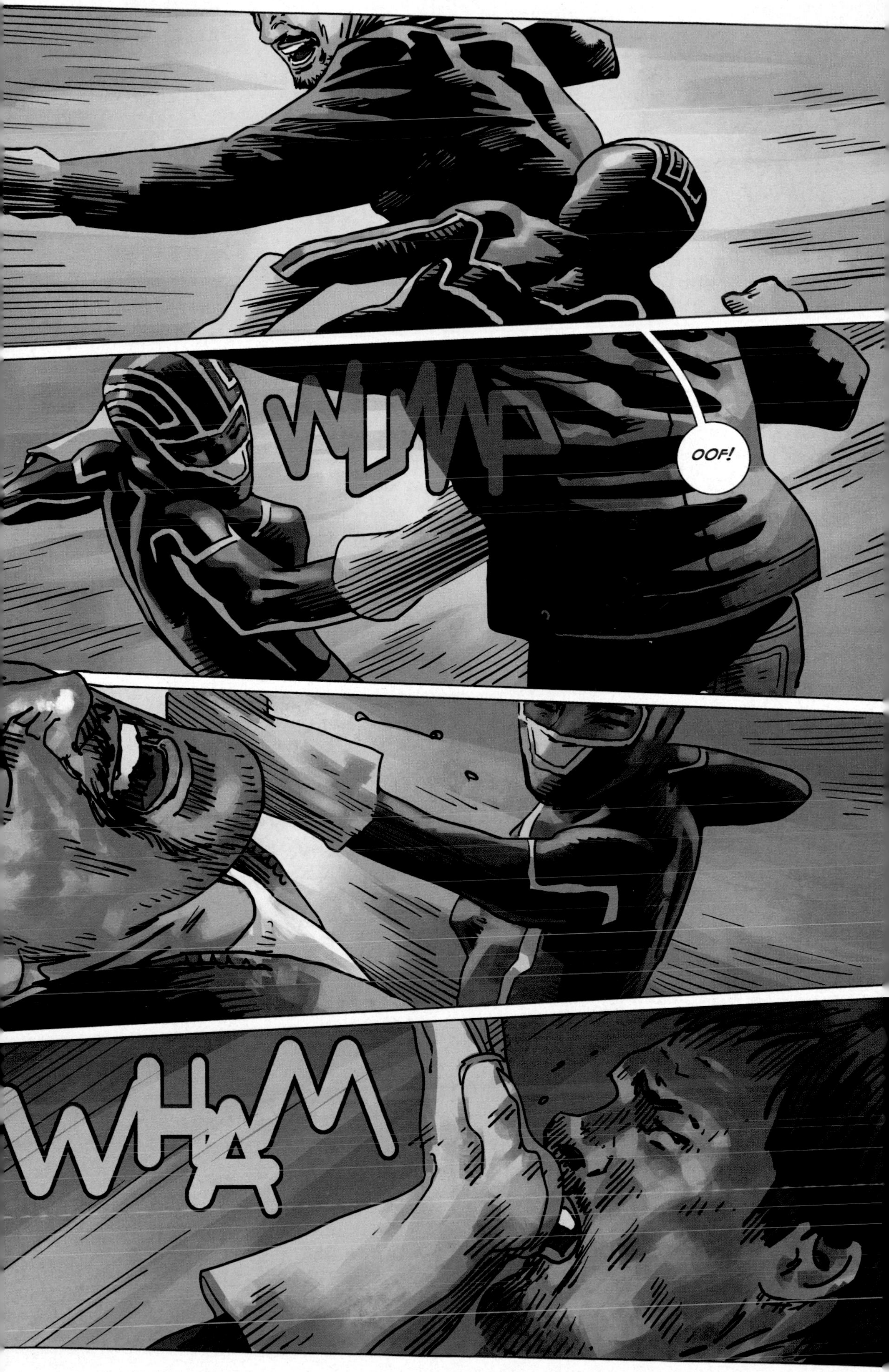
WUMP
OOF!
WHAM

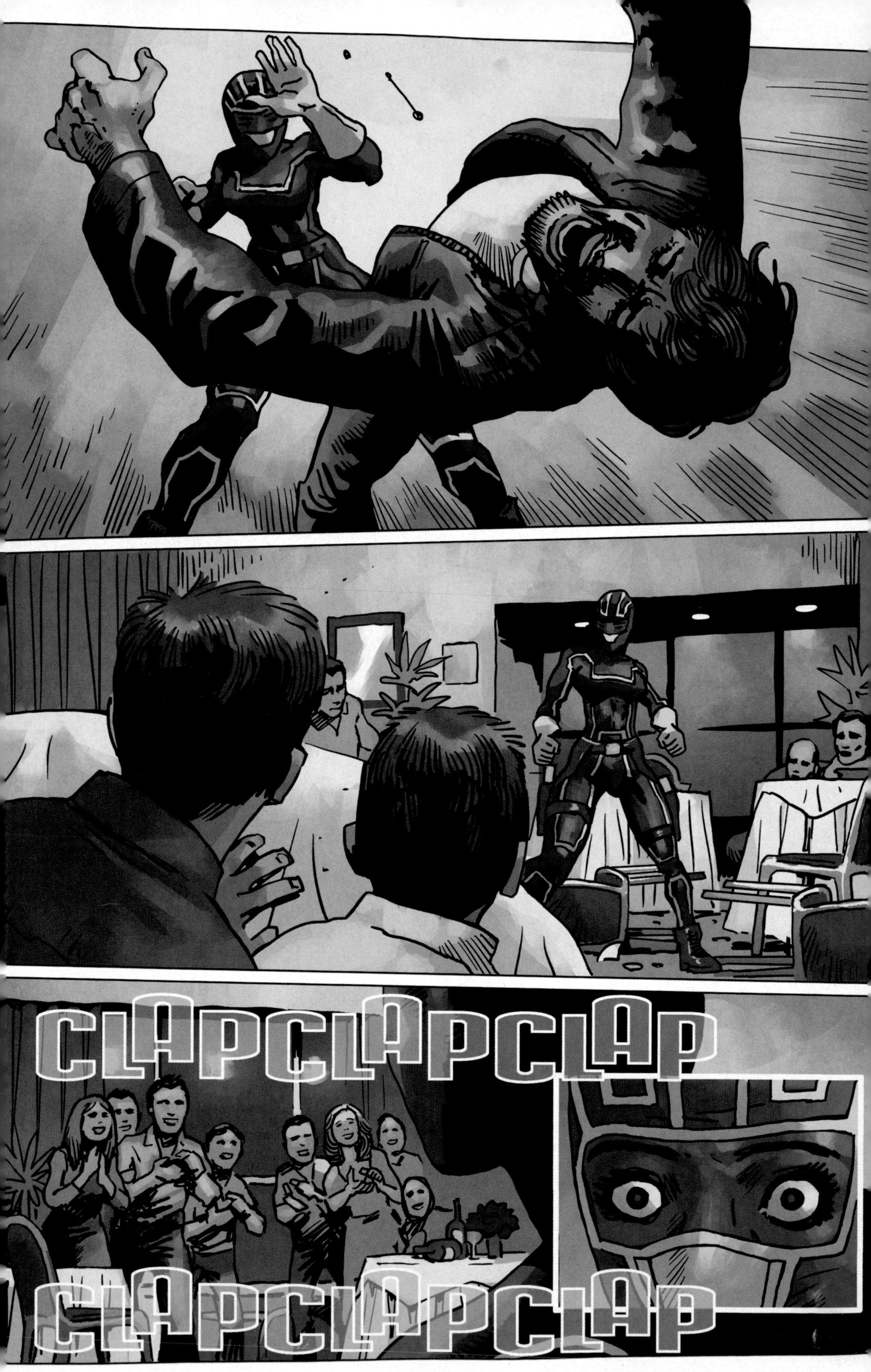
CLAPCLAPCLAP
CLAPCLAPCLAP

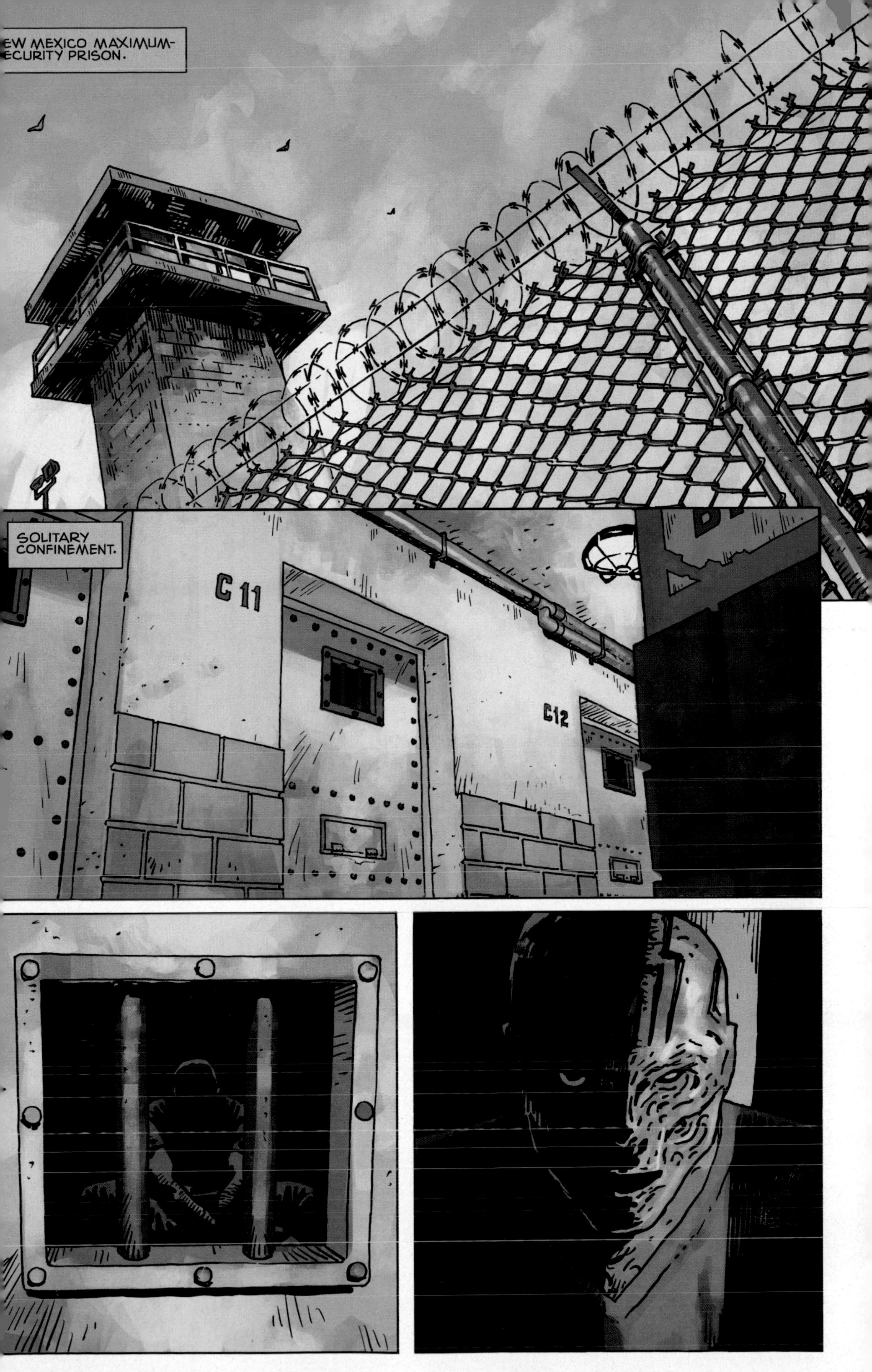
EW MEXICO MAXIMUM-
ECURITY PRISON.
SOLITARY
CONFINEMENT.
C 11
C12

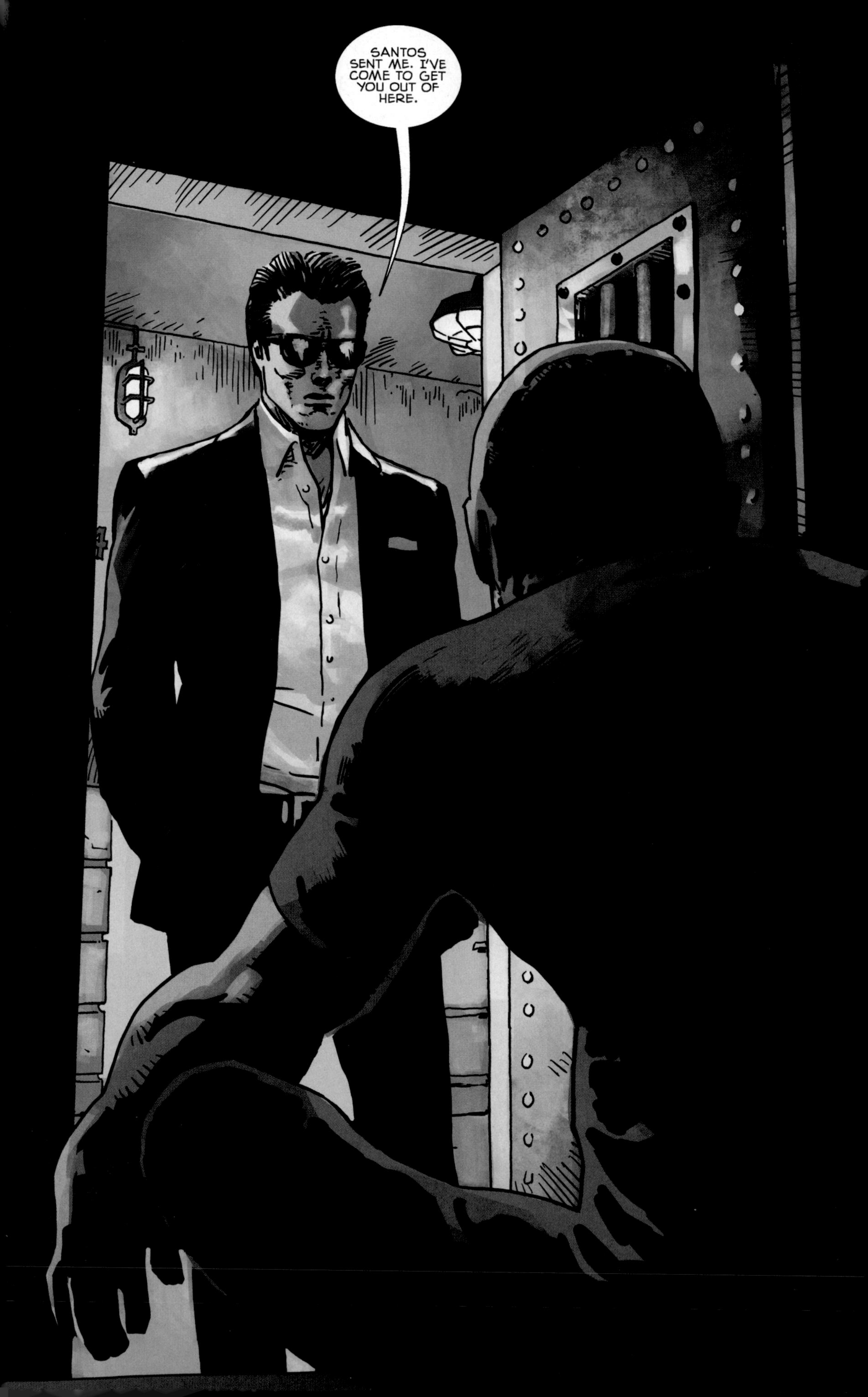
SANTOS SENT ME. I'VE COME TO GET YOU OUT OF HERE.

FOUR

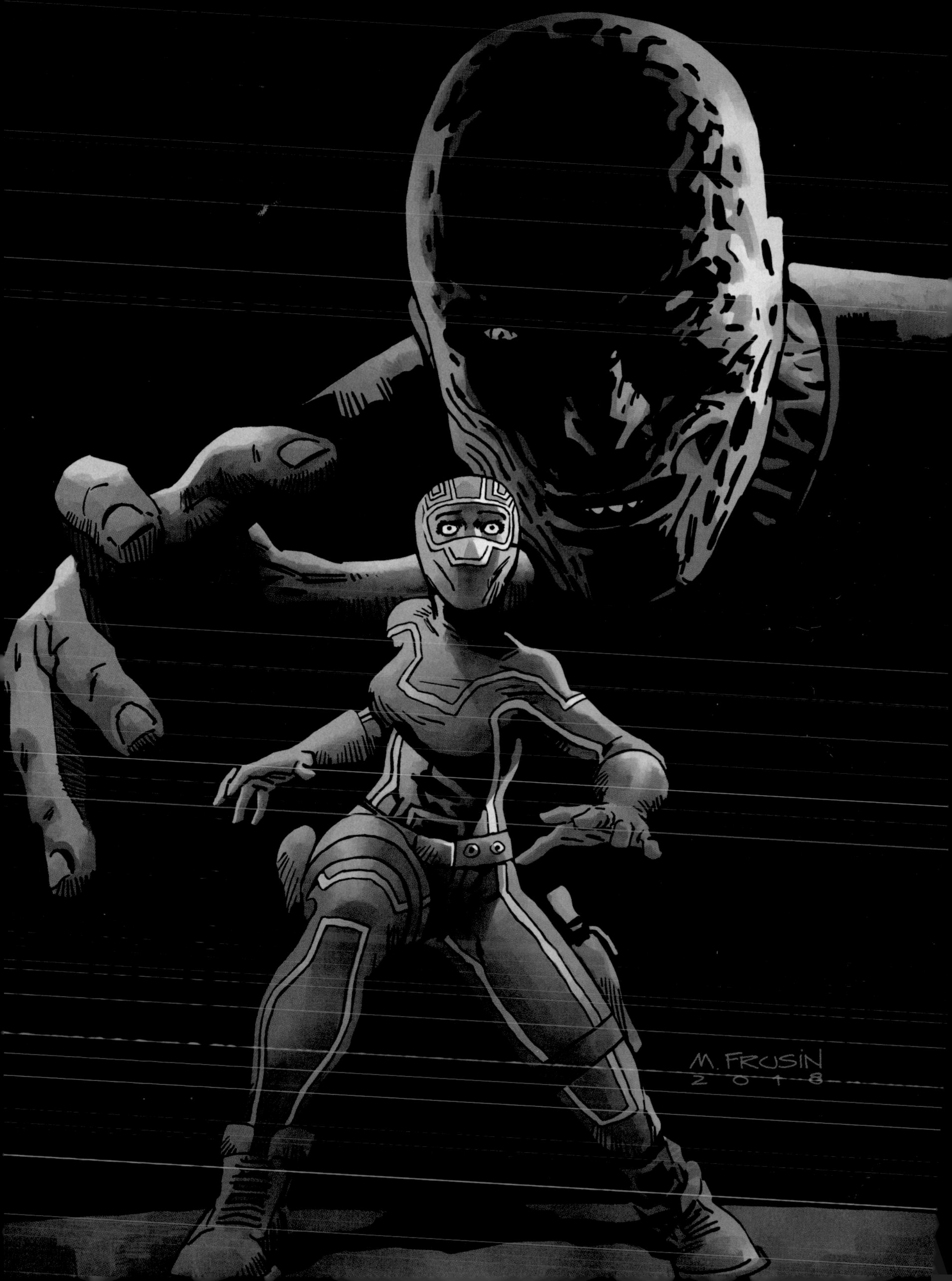
M. FRUSIN
2018

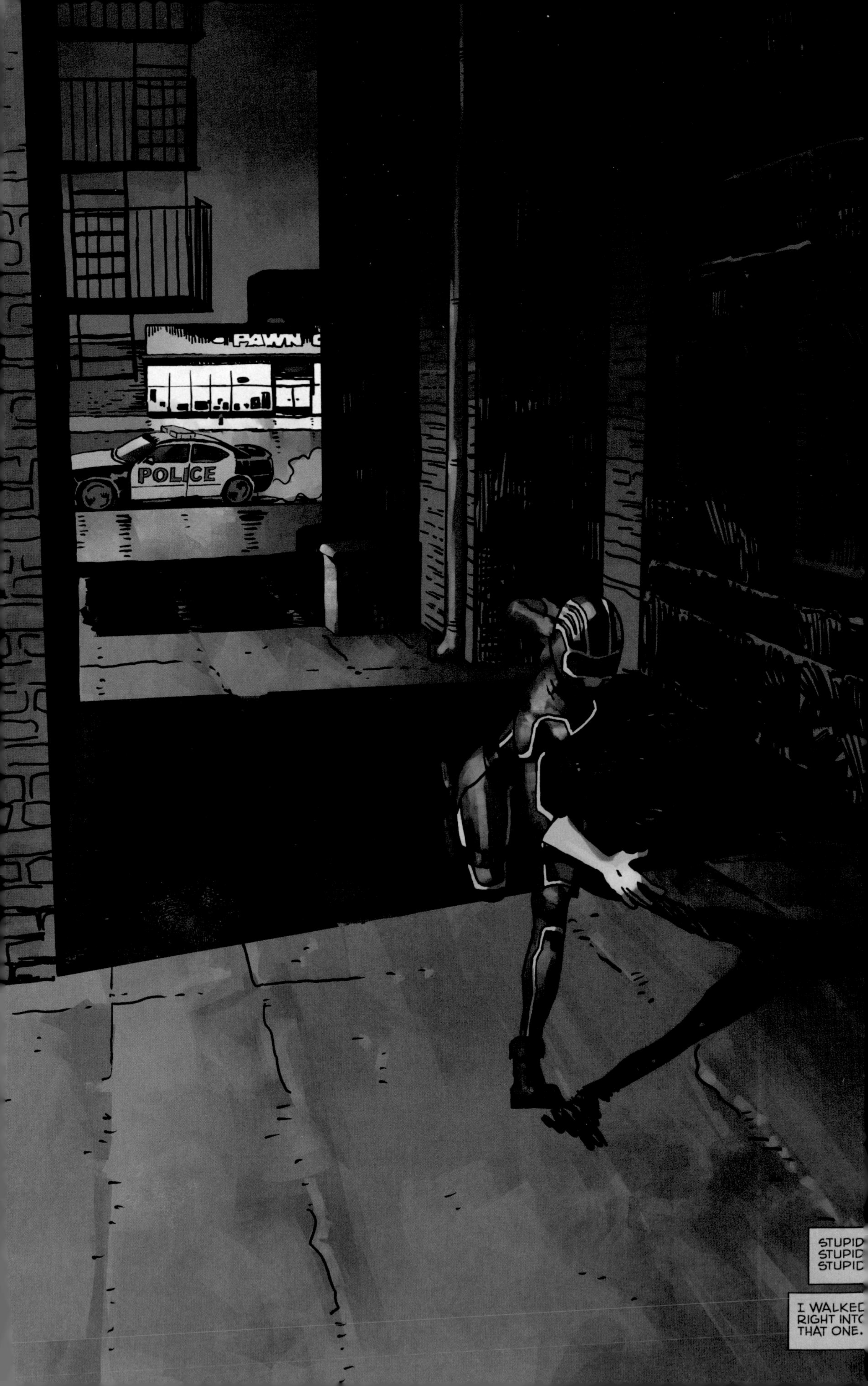
PAWN
POLICE
STUPID
STUPID
STUPID
I WALKED
RIGHT INTO
THAT ONE.

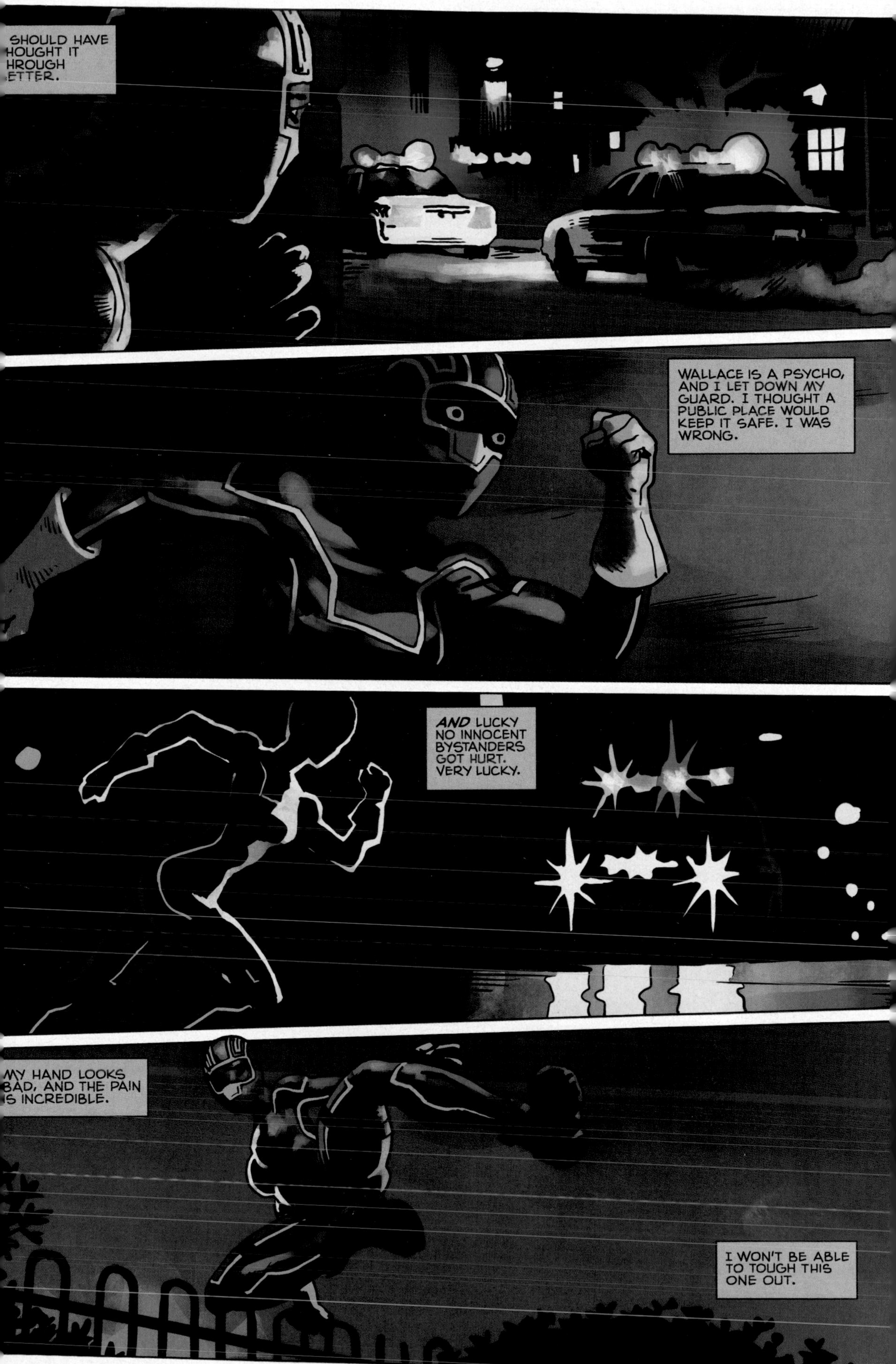
SHOULD HAVE
HOUGHT IT
HROUGH
ETTER.
WALLACE IS A PSYCHO, AND I LET DOWN MY GUARD. I THOUGHT A PUBLIC PLACE WOULD KEEP IT SAFE. I WAS WRONG.
AND LUCKY NO INNOCENT BYSTANDERS GOT HURT. VERY LUCKY.
MY HAND LOOKS BAD, AND THE PAIN IS INCREDIBLE.
I WON'T BE ABLE TO TOUGH THIS ONE OUT.

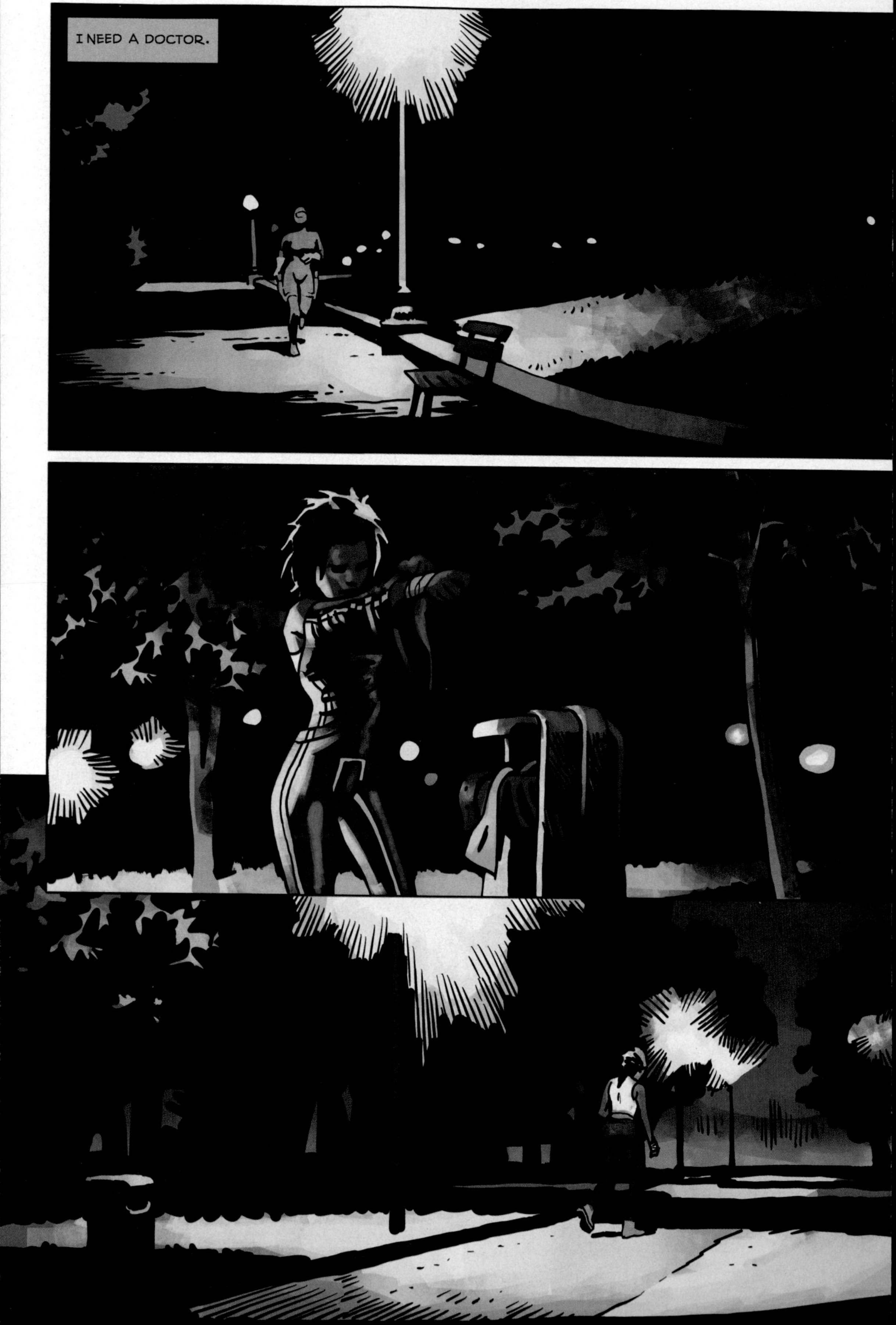
I NEED A DOCTOR.

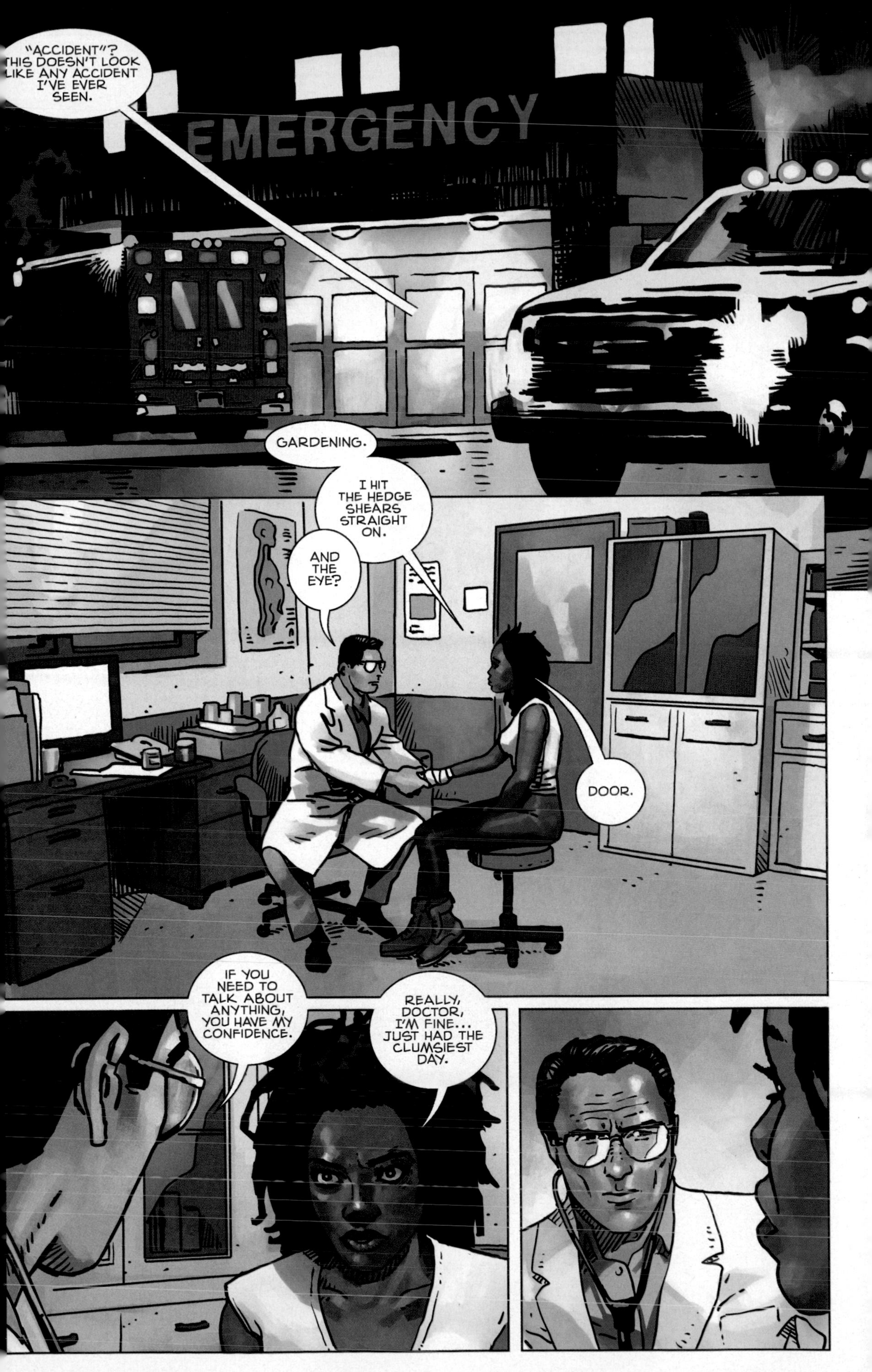
"ACCIDENT"? THIS DOESN'T LOOK LIKE ANY ACCIDENT I'VE EVER SEEN.
EMERGENCY
GARDENING.
I HIT THE HEDGE SHEARS STRAIGHT ON.
AND THE EYE?
DOOR.
IF YOU NEED TO TALK ABOUT ANYTHING, YOU HAVE MY CONFIDENCE.
REALLY, DOCTOR, I'M FINE... JUST HAD THE CLUMSIEST DAY.

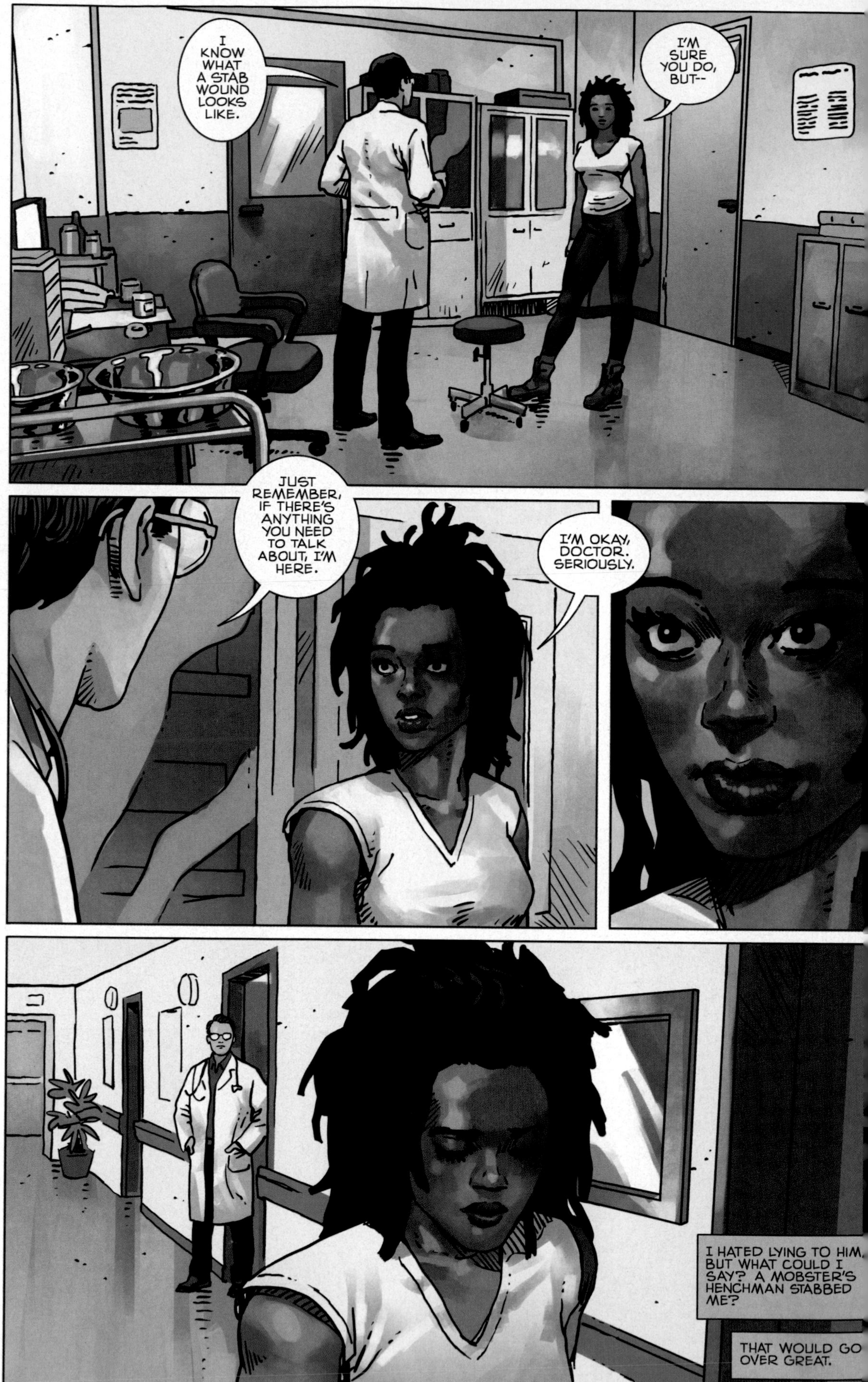
I KNOW WHAT A STAB WOUND LOOKS LIKE.
I'M SURE YOU DO, BUT--
JUST REMEMBER, IF THERE'S ANYTHING YOU NEED TO TALK ABOUT, I'M HERE.
I'M OKAY, DOCTOR. SERIOUSLY.
I HATED LYING TO HIM, BUT WHAT COULD I SAY? A MOBSTER'S HENCHMAN STABBED ME?
THAT WOULD GO OVER GREAT.

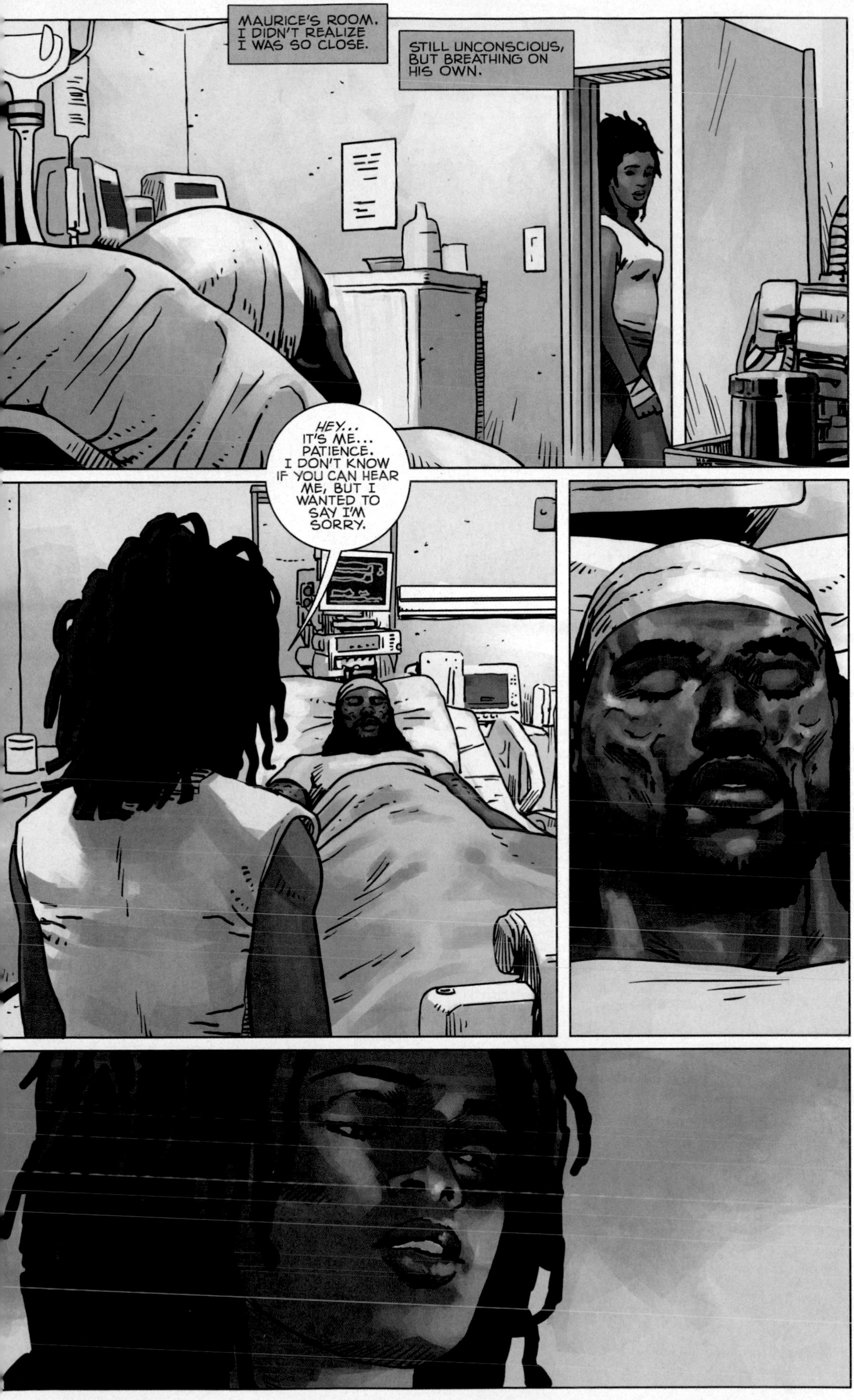
MAURICE'S ROOM. I DIDN'T REALIZE I WAS SO CLOSE.
STILL UNCONSCIOUS, BUT BREATHING ON HIS OWN.
HEY... IT'S ME... PATIENCE. I DON'T KNOW IF YOU CAN HEAR ME, BUT I WANTED TO SAY I'M SORRY.

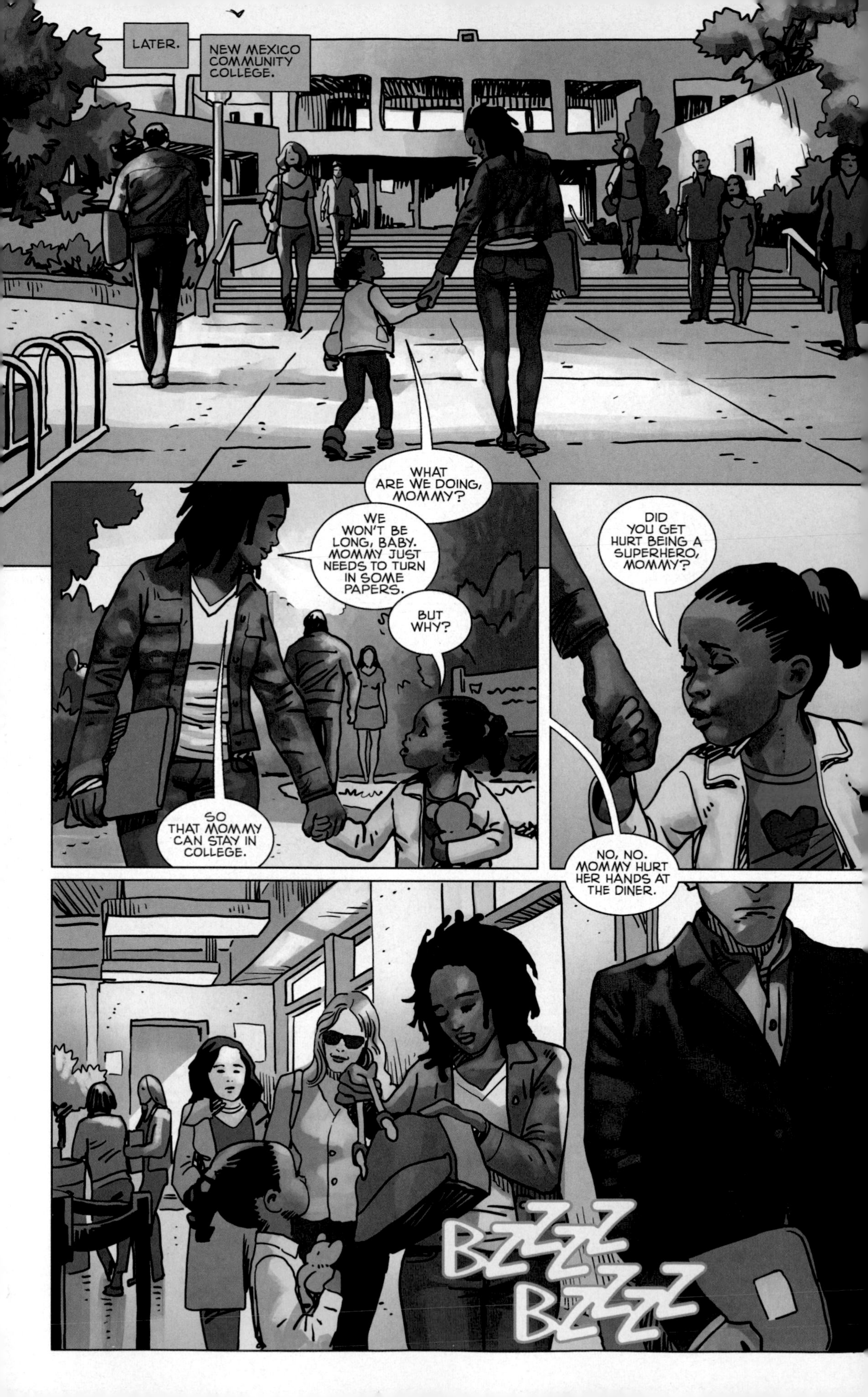
LATER.
NEW MEXICO COMMUNITY COLLEGE.
WHAT ARE WE DOING, MOMMY?
WE WON'T BE LONG, BABY. MOMMY JUST NEEDS TO TURN IN SOME PAPERS.
BUT WHY?
SO THAT MOMMY CAN STAY IN COLLEGE.
DID YOU GET HURT BEING A SUPERHERO, MOMMY?
NO, NO. MOMMY HURT HER HANDS AT THE DINER.
BZZZZ BZZZZ

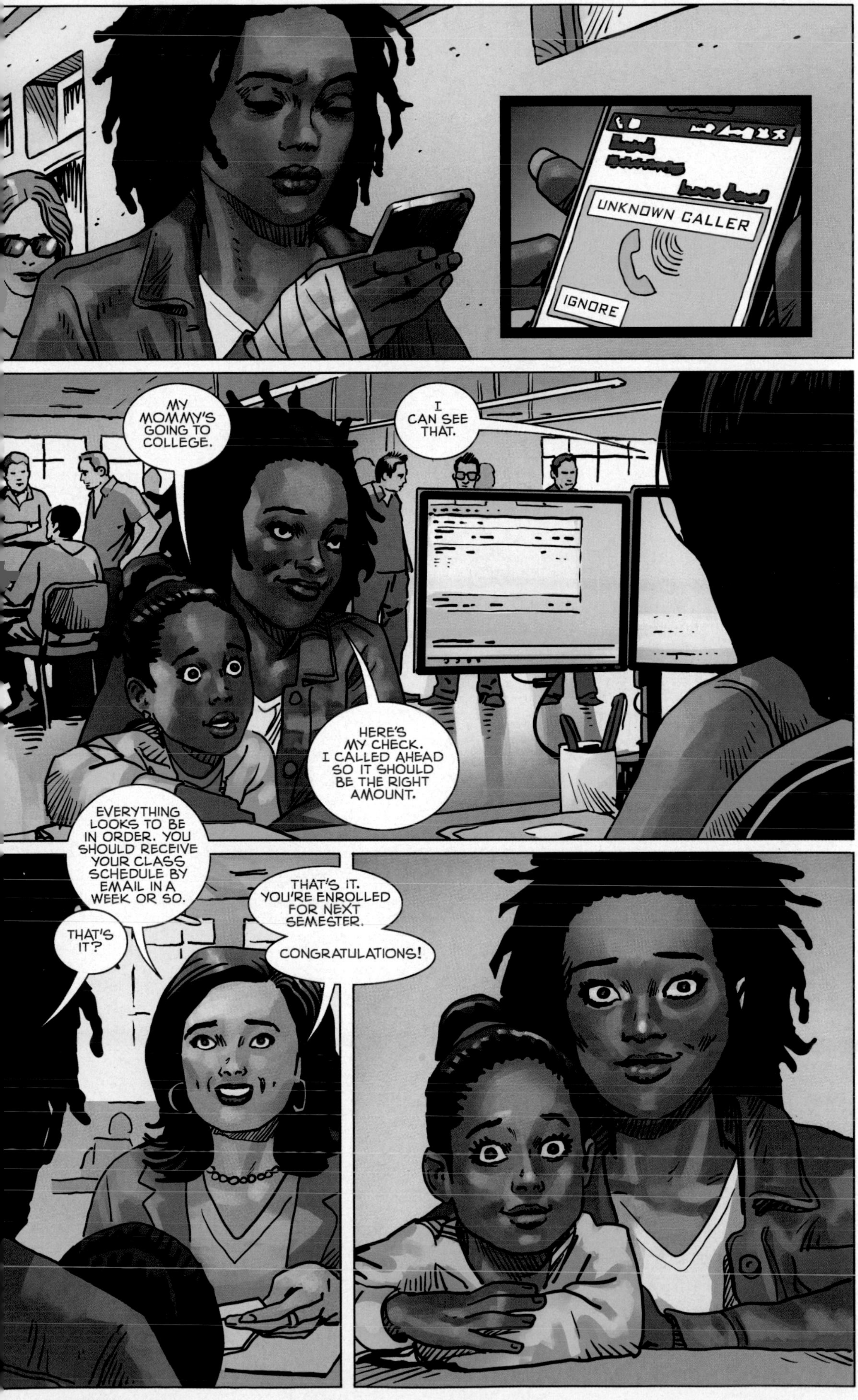
UNKNOWN CALLER
IGNORE
MY MOMMY'S GOING TO COLLEGE.
I CAN SEE THAT.
HERE'S MY CHECK. I CALLED AHEAD SO IT SHOULD BE THE RIGHT AMOUNT.
EVERYTHING LOOKS TO BE IN ORDER. YOU SHOULD RECEIVE YOUR CLASS SCHEDULE BY EMAIL IN A WEEK OR SO.
THAT'S IT?
THAT'S IT. YOU'RE ENROLLED FOR NEXT SEMESTER.
CONGRATULATIONS!

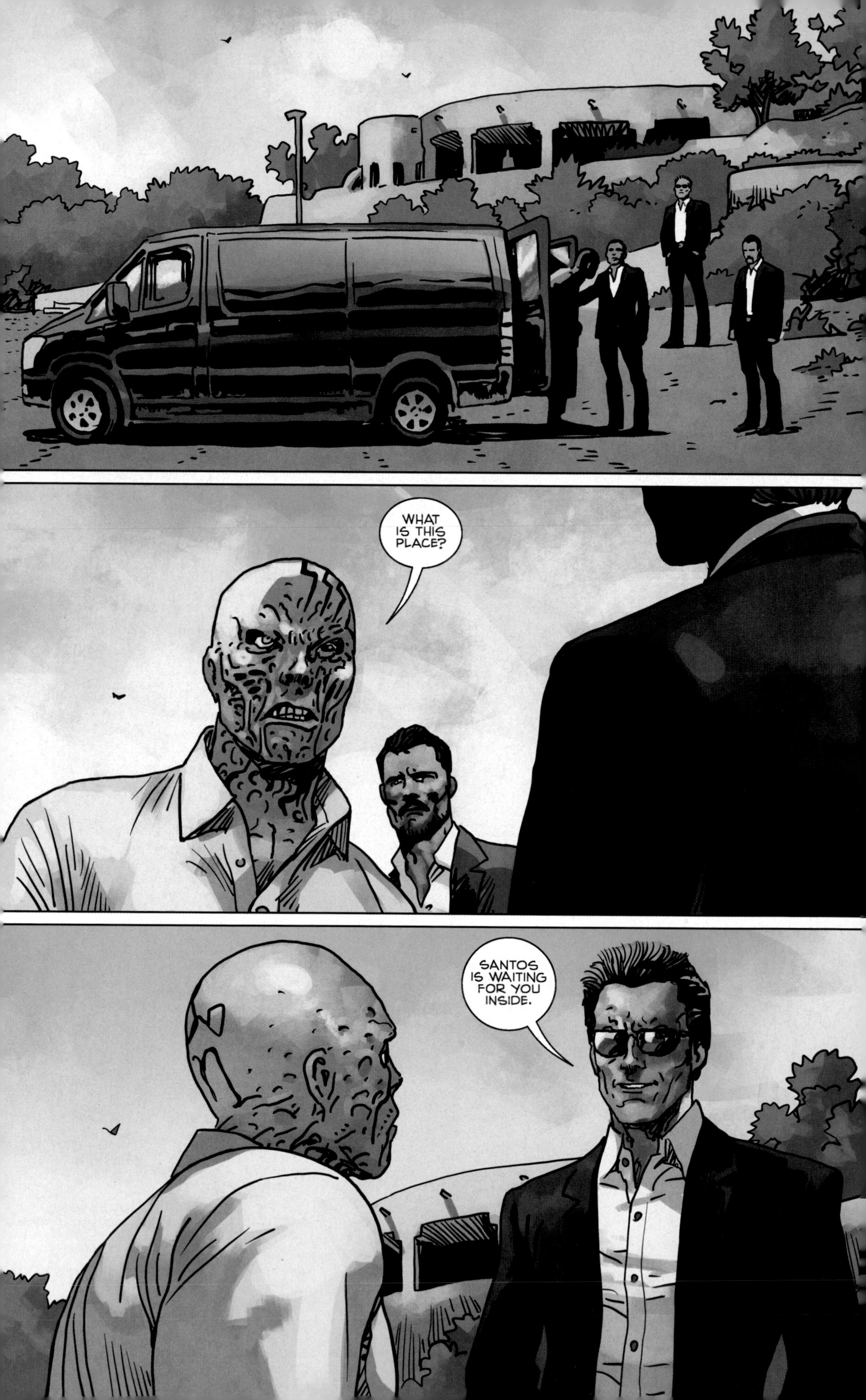
WHAT IS THIS PLACE?
SANTOS IS WAITING FOR YOU INSIDE.

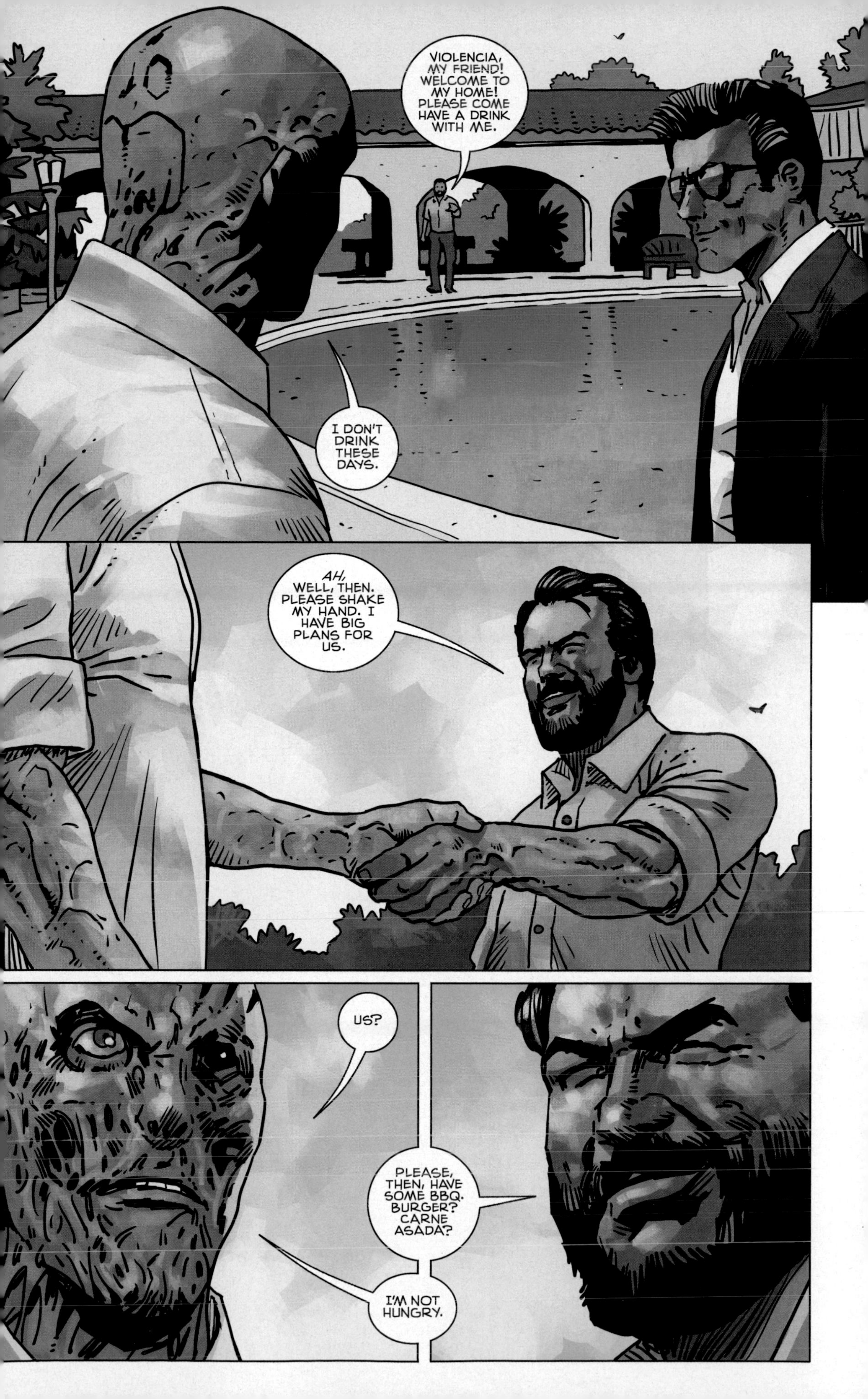
VIOLENCIA, MY FRIEND! WELCOME TO MY HOME! PLEASE COME HAVE A DRINK WITH ME.
I DON'T DRINK THESE DAYS.
AH, WELL, THEN. PLEASE SHAKE MY HAND. I HAVE BIG PLANS FOR US.
US?
PLEASE, THEN, HAVE SOME BBQ. BURGER? CARNE ASADA?
I'M NOT HUNGRY.

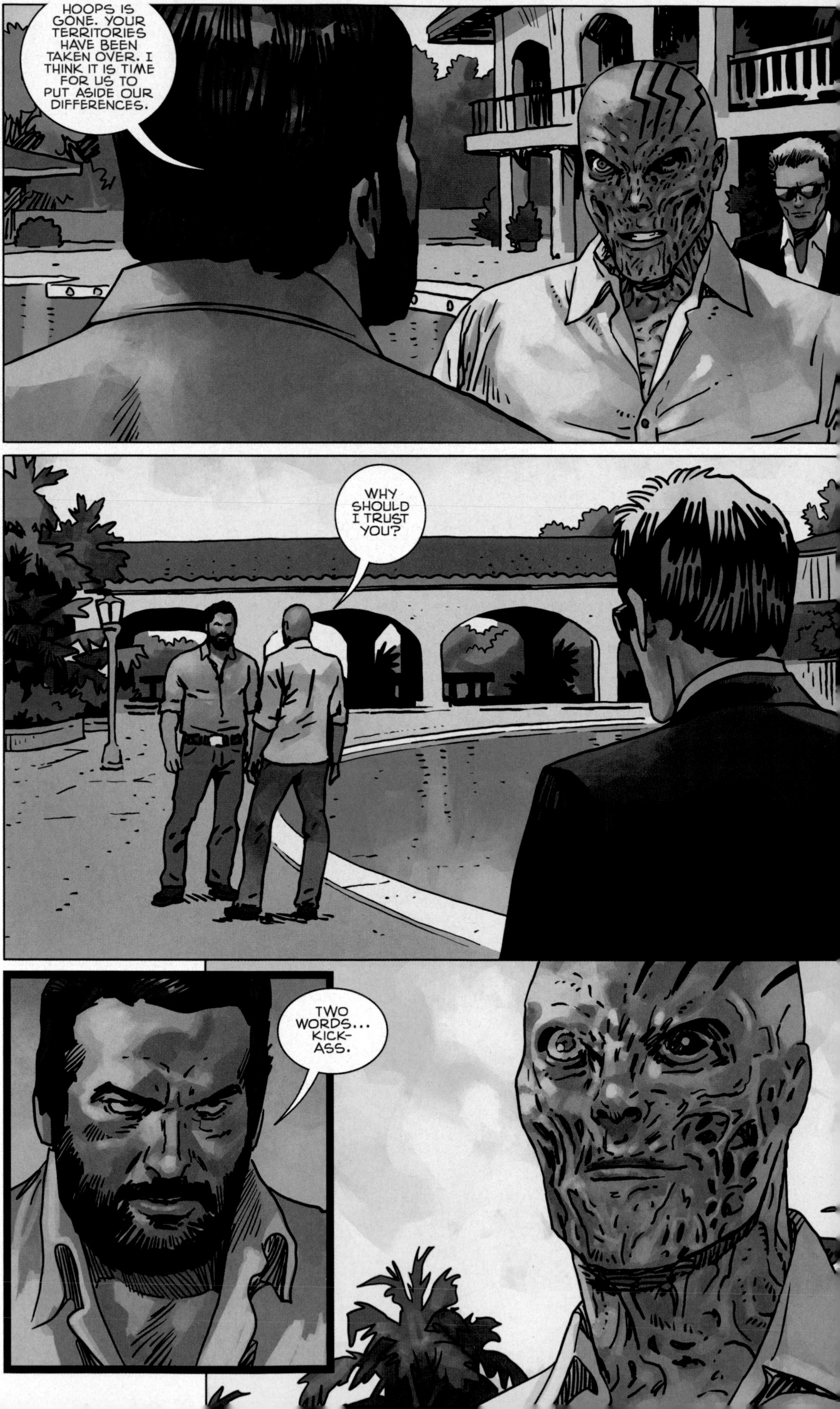
HOOPS IS GONE. YOUR TERRITORIES HAVE BEEN TAKEN OVER. I THINK IT IS TIME FOR US TO PUT ASIDE OUR DIFFERENCES.
WHY SHOULD I TRUST YOU?
TWO WORDS... KICK-ASS.

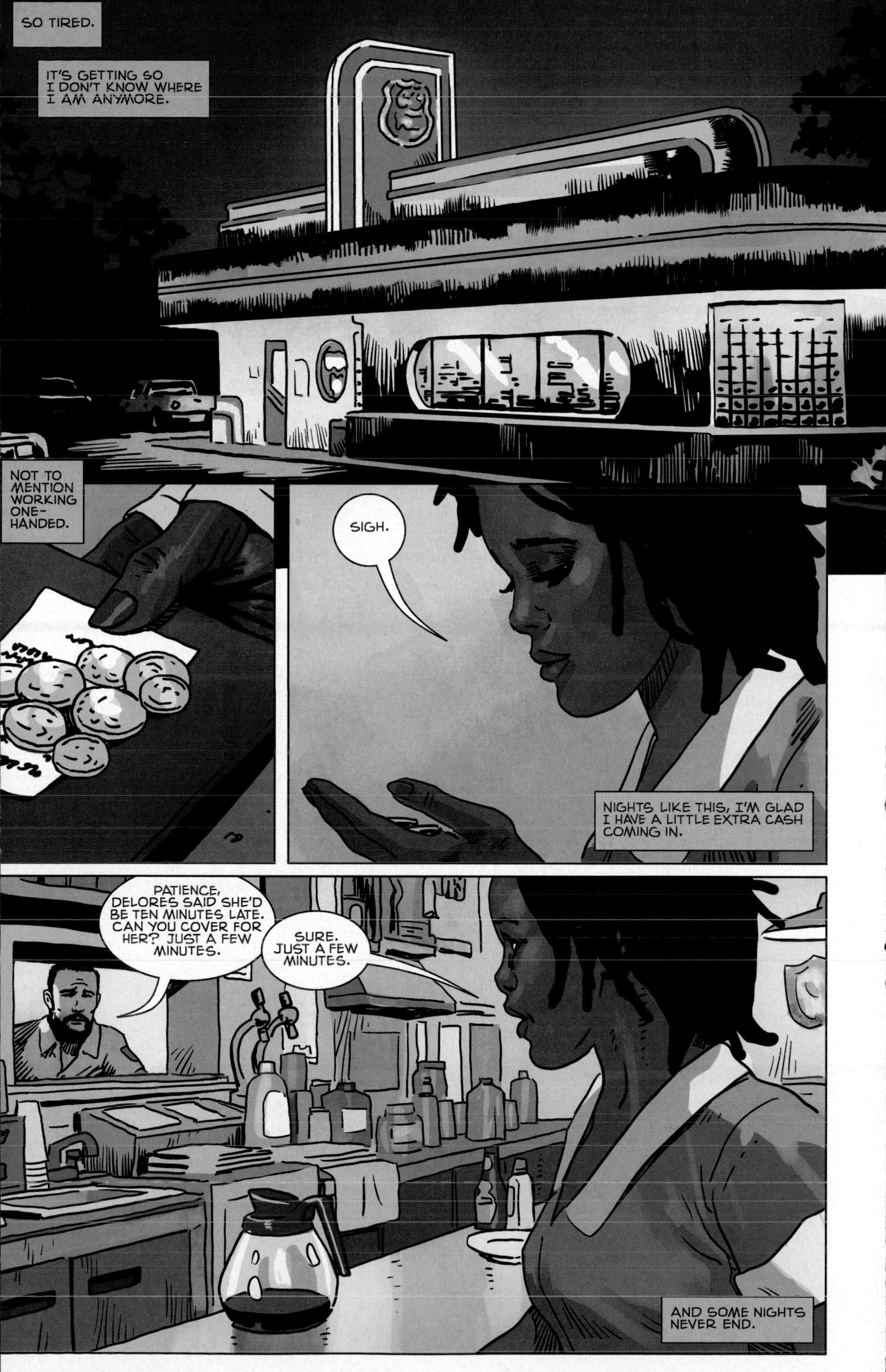

SO TIRED.
IT'S GETTING SO I DON'T KNOW WHERE I AM ANYMORE.
NOT TO MENTION WORKING ONE-HANDED.
SIGH.
NIGHTS LIKE THIS, I'M GLAD I HAVE A LITTLE EXTRA CASH COMING IN.
PATIENCE, DELORES SAID SHE'D BE TEN MINUTES LATE. CAN YOU COVER FOR HER? JUST A FEW MINUTES.
SURE. JUST A FEW MINUTES.
AND SOME NIGHTS NEVER END.

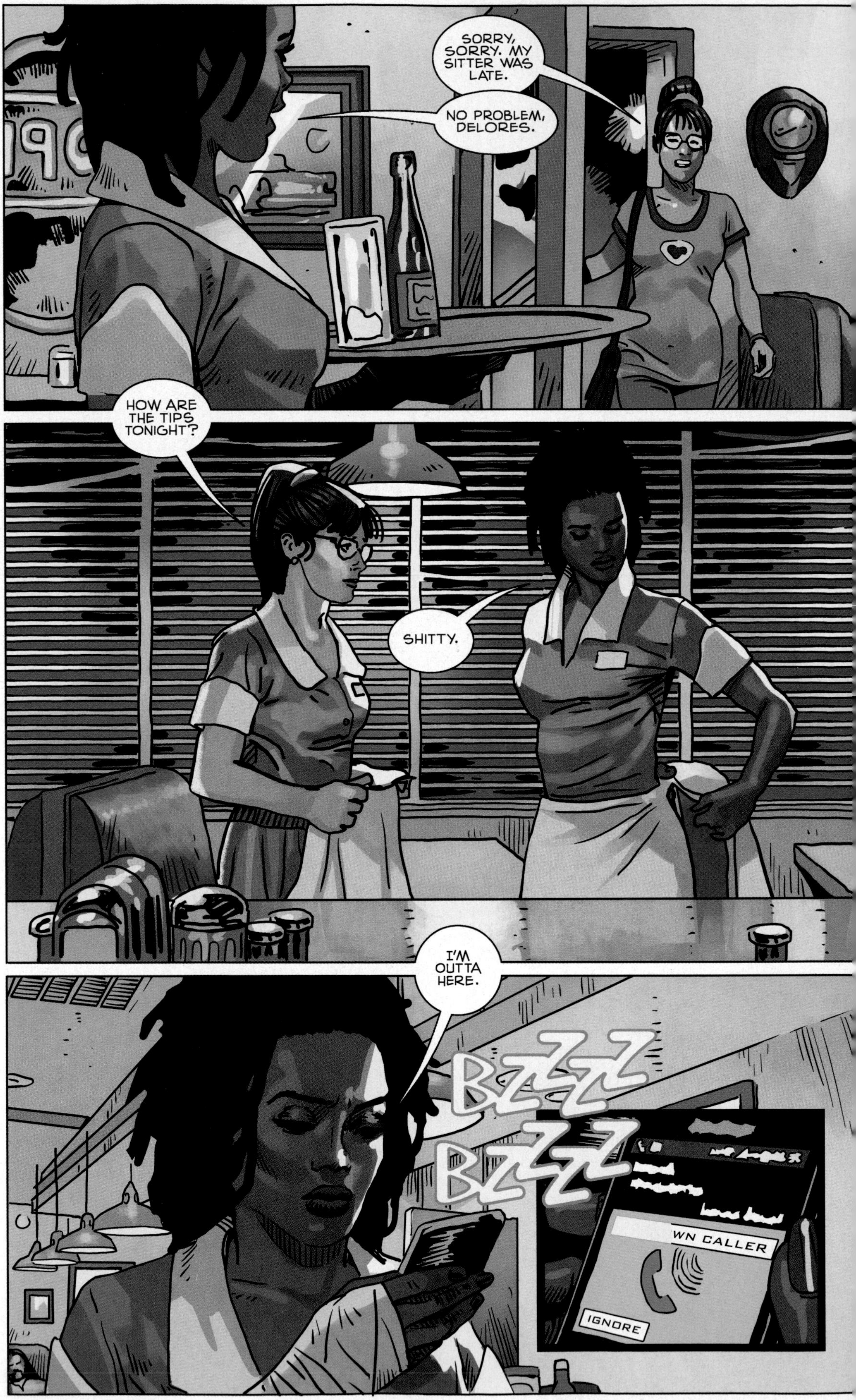
SORRY, SORRY. MY SITTER WAS LATE.
NO PROBLEM, DELORES.
HOW ARE THE TIPS TONIGHT?
SHITTY.
I'M OUTTA HERE.
BZZZ BZZZ
WN CALLER
IGNORE

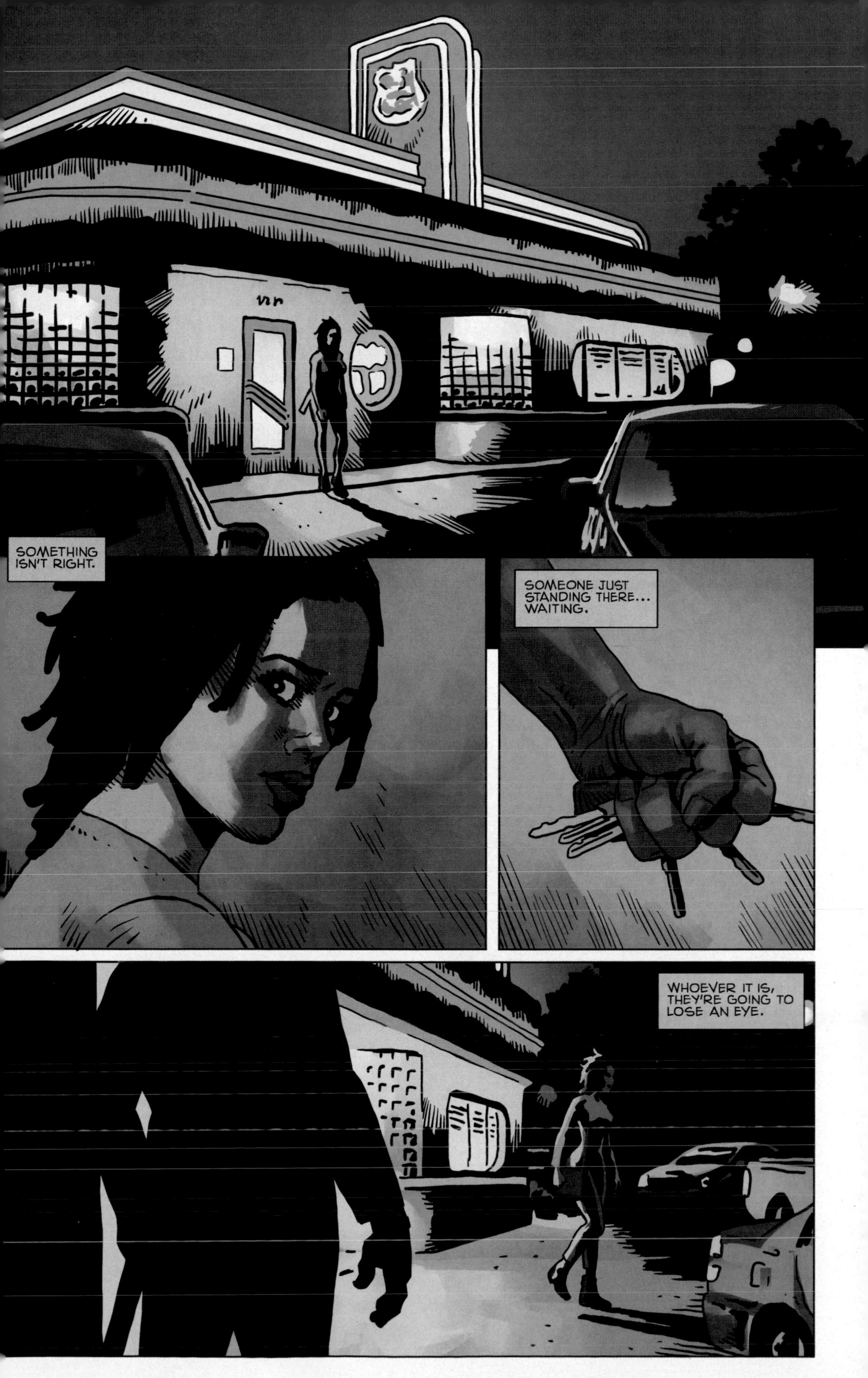
SOMETHING ISN'T RIGHT.
SOMEONE JUST STANDING THERE... WAITING.
WHOEVER IT IS, THEY'RE GOING TO LOSE AN EYE.

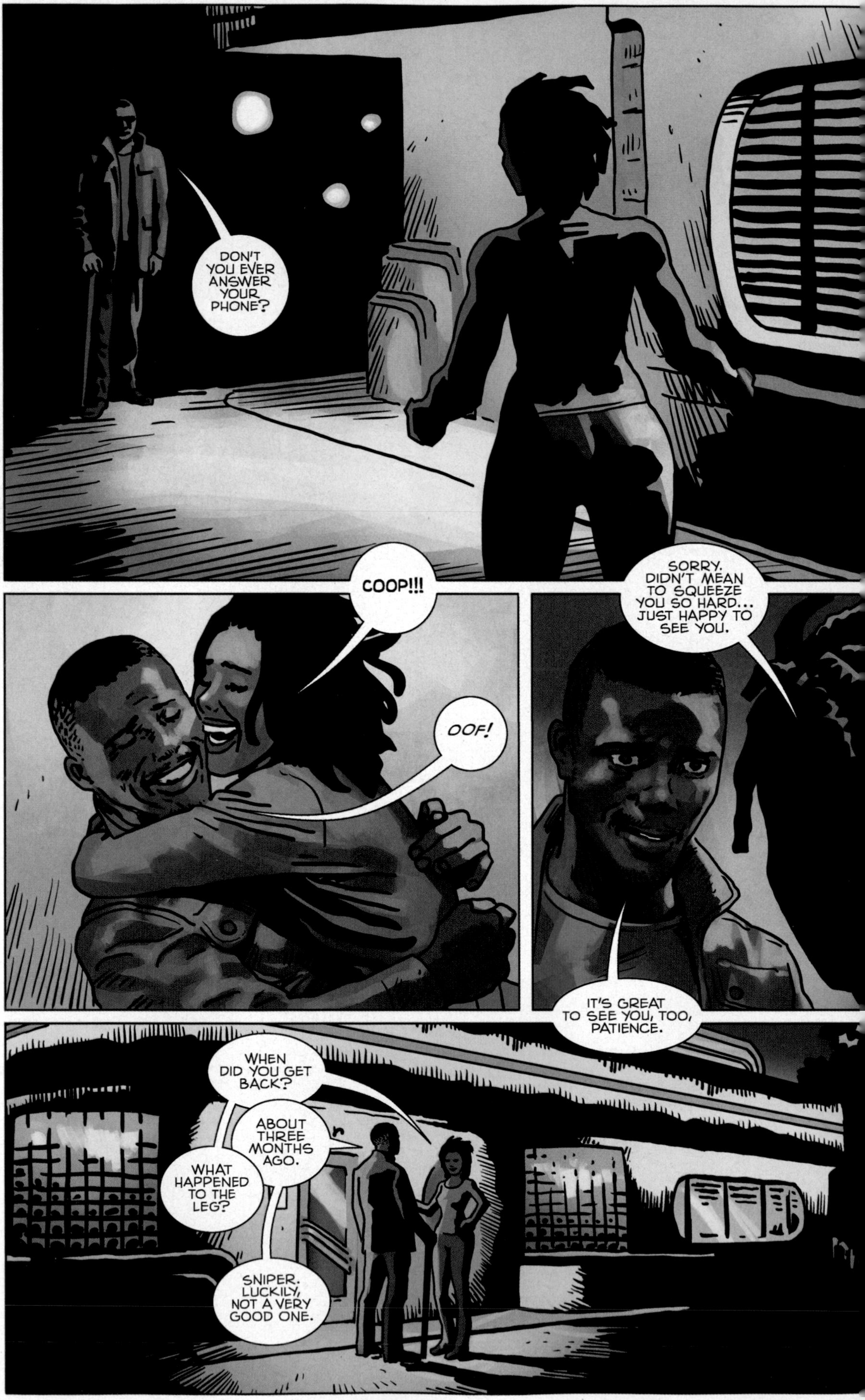
DON'T YOU EVER ANSWER YOUR PHONE?
COOP!!!
OOF!
SORRY. DIDN'T MEAN TO SQUEEZE YOU SO HARD... JUST HAPPY TO SEE YOU.
IT'S GREAT TO SEE YOU, TOO, PATIENCE.
WHEN DID YOU GET BACK?
ABOUT THREE MONTHS AGO.
WHAT HAPPENED TO THE LEG?
SNIPER. LUCKILY, NOT A VERY GOOD ONE.

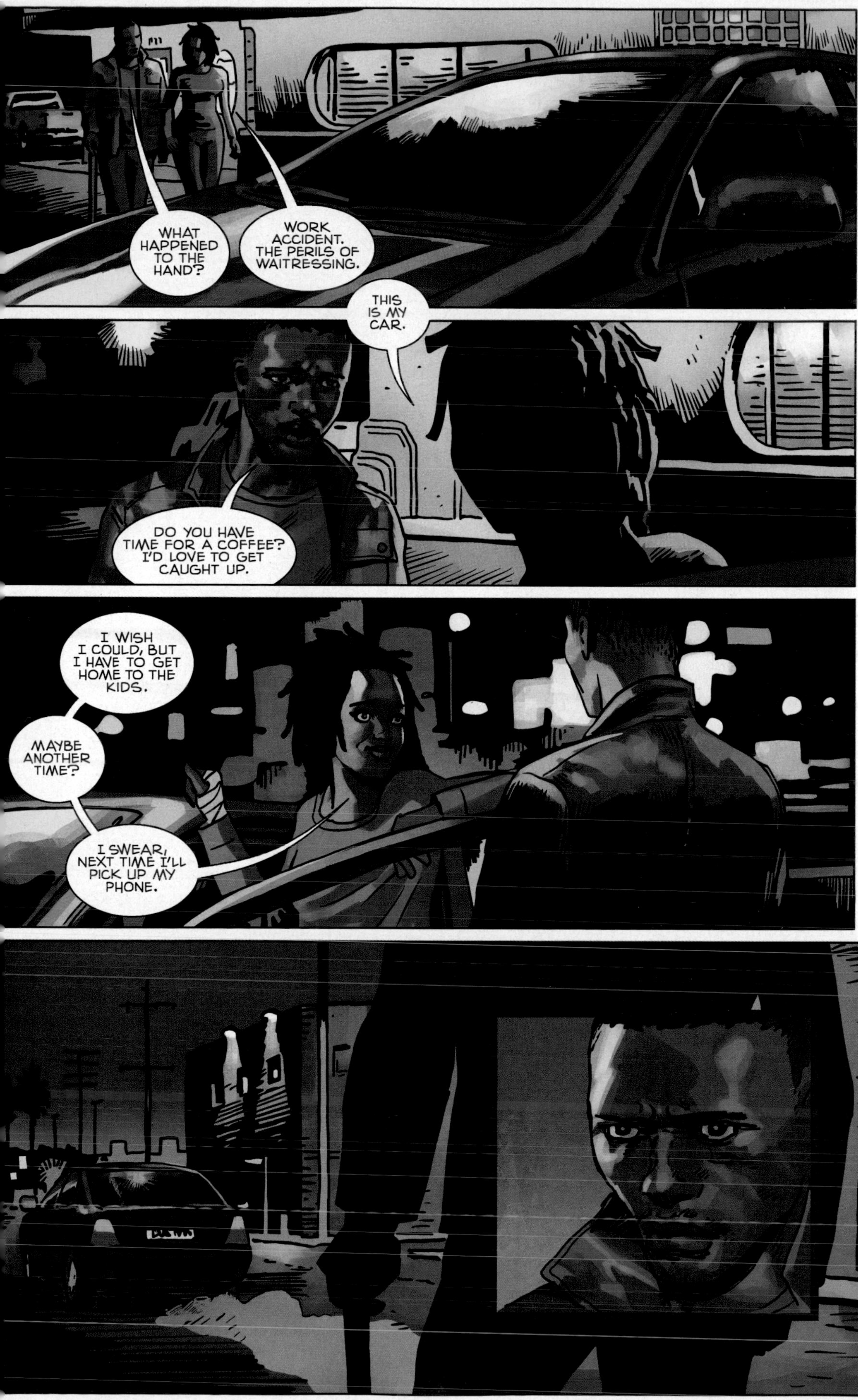
WHAT HAPPENED TO THE HAND?
WORK ACCIDENT. THE PERILS OF WAITRESSING.
THIS IS MY CAR.
DO YOU HAVE TIME FOR A COFFEE? I'D LOVE TO GET CAUGHT UP.
I WISH I COULD, BUT I HAVE TO GET HOME TO THE KIDS.
MAYBE ANOTHER TIME?
I SWEAR, NEXT TIME I'LL PICK UP MY PHONE.

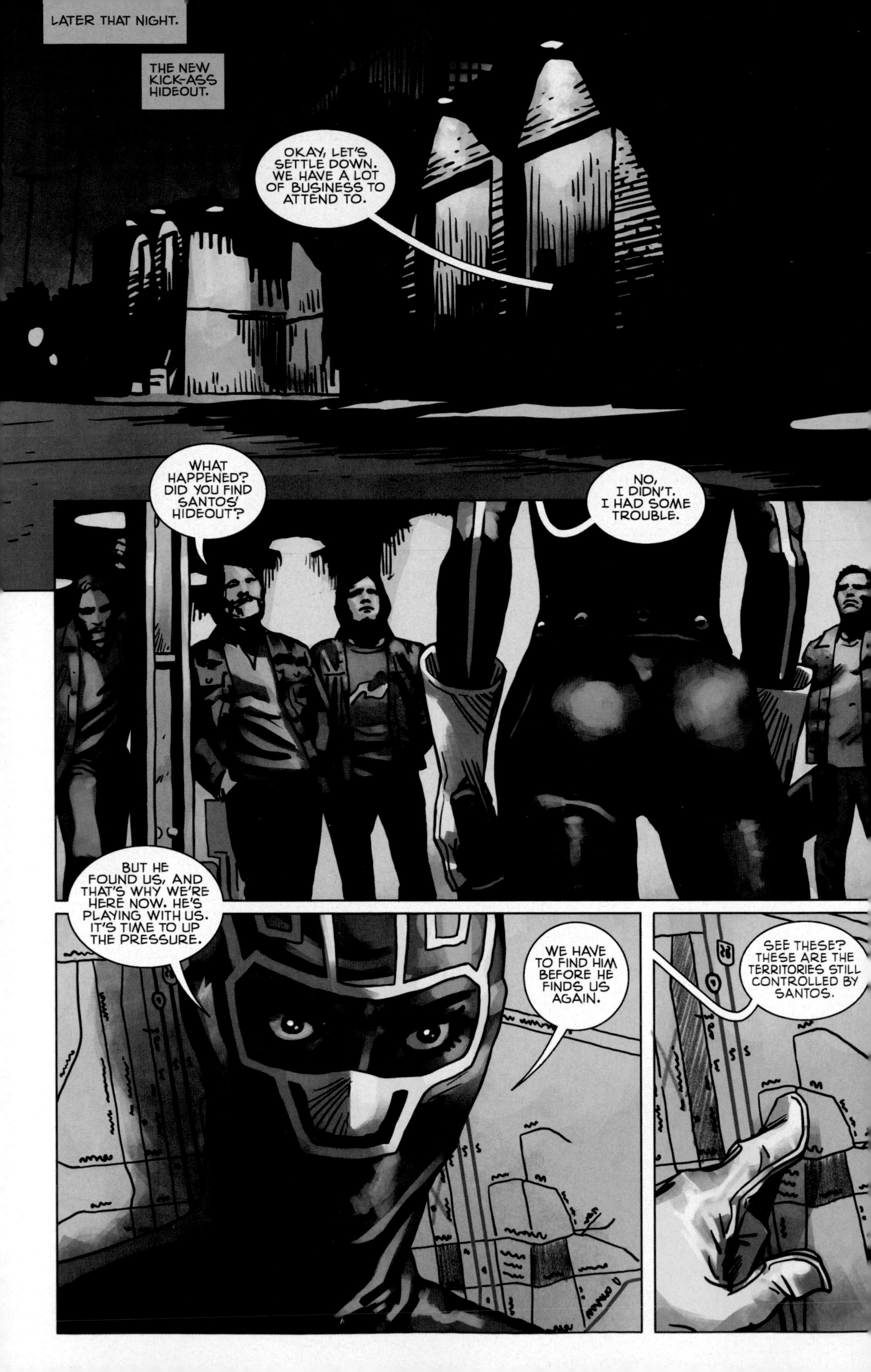
LATER THAT NIGHT.
THE NEW KICK-ASS HIDEOUT.
OKAY, LET'S SETTLE DOWN. WE HAVE A LOT OF BUSINESS TO ATTEND TO.
WHAT HAPPENED? DID YOU FIND SANTOS' HIDEOUT?
NO, I DIDN'T. I HAD SOME TROUBLE.
BUT HE FOUND US, AND THAT'S WHY WE'RE HERE NOW. HE'S PLAYING WITH US. IT'S TIME TO UP THE PRESSURE.
WE HAVE TO FIND HIM BEFORE HE FINDS US AGAIN.
SEE THESE? THESE ARE THE TERRITORIES STILL CONTROLLED BY SANTOS.

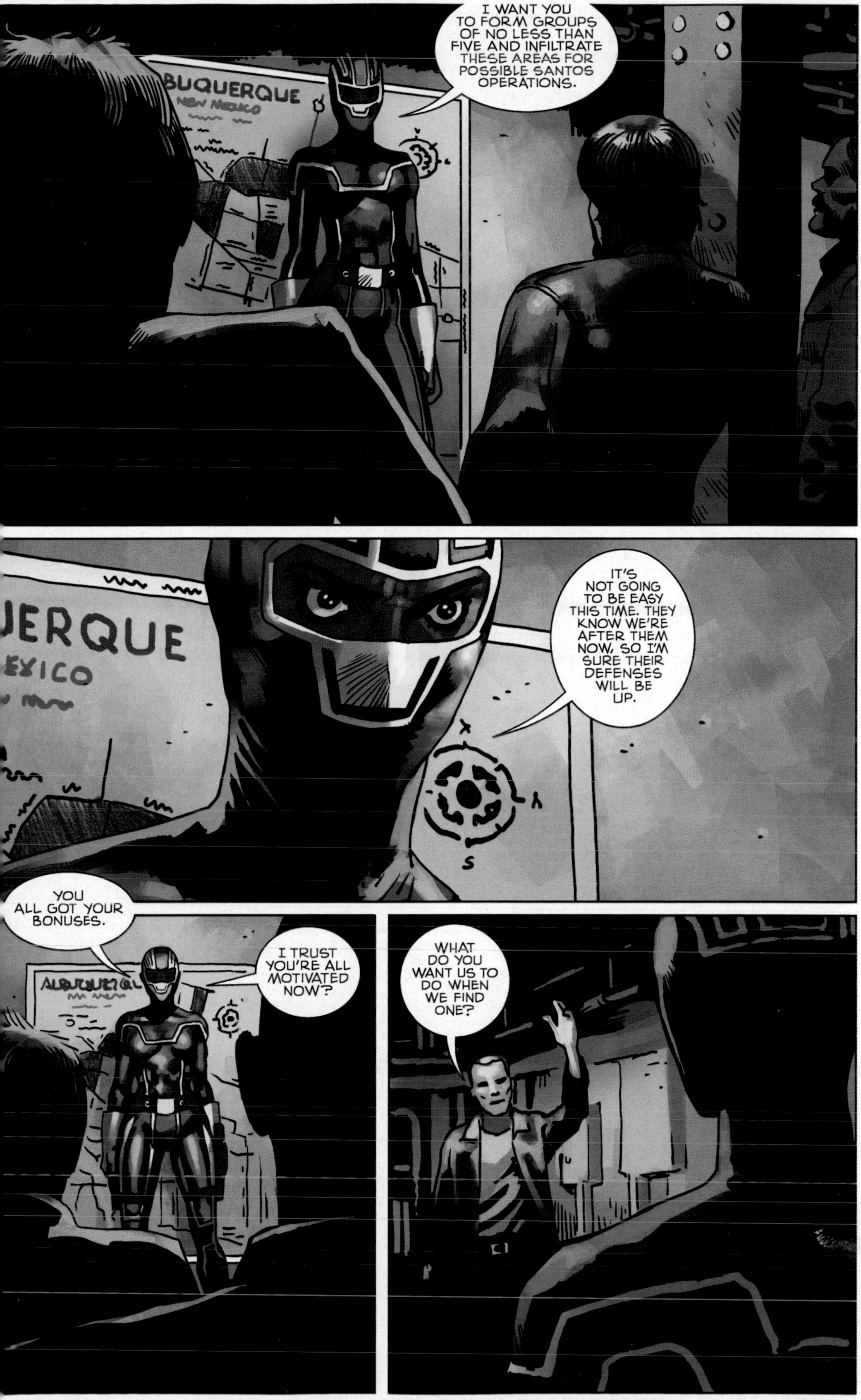
I WANT YOU TO FORM GROUPS OF NO LESS THAN FIVE AND INFILTRATE THESE AREAS FOR POSSIBLE SANTOS OPERATIONS.
BUQUERQUE
NEW MEXICO
IT'S NOT GOING TO BE EASY THIS TIME. THEY KNOW WE'RE AFTER THEM NOW, SO I'M SURE THEIR DEFENSES WILL BE UP.
UERQUE
YOU ALL GOT YOUR BONUSES.
I TRUST YOU'RE ALL MOTIVATED NOW?
WHAT DO YOU WANT US TO DO WHEN WE FIND ONE?

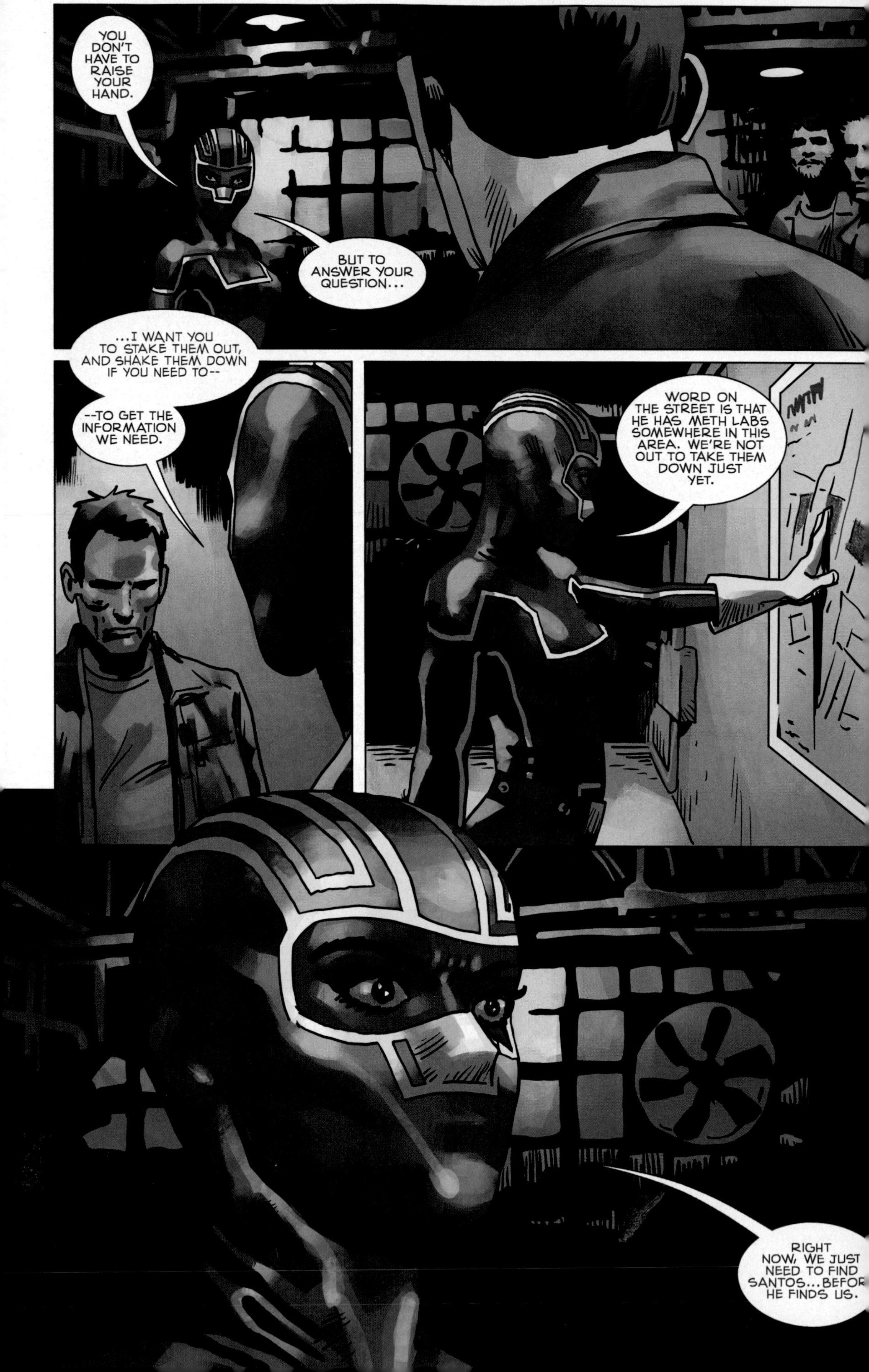
YOU DON'T HAVE TO RAISE YOUR HAND.
BUT TO ANSWER YOUR QUESTION...
...I WANT YOU TO STAKE THEM OUT, AND SHAKE THEM DOWN IF YOU NEED TO--
--TO GET THE INFORMATION WE NEED.
WORD ON THE STREET IS THAT HE HAS METH LABS SOMEWHERE IN THIS AREA. WE'RE NOT OUT TO TAKE THEM DOWN JUST YET.
RIGHT NOW, WE JUST NEED TO FIND SANTOS...BEFOR HE FINDS US.

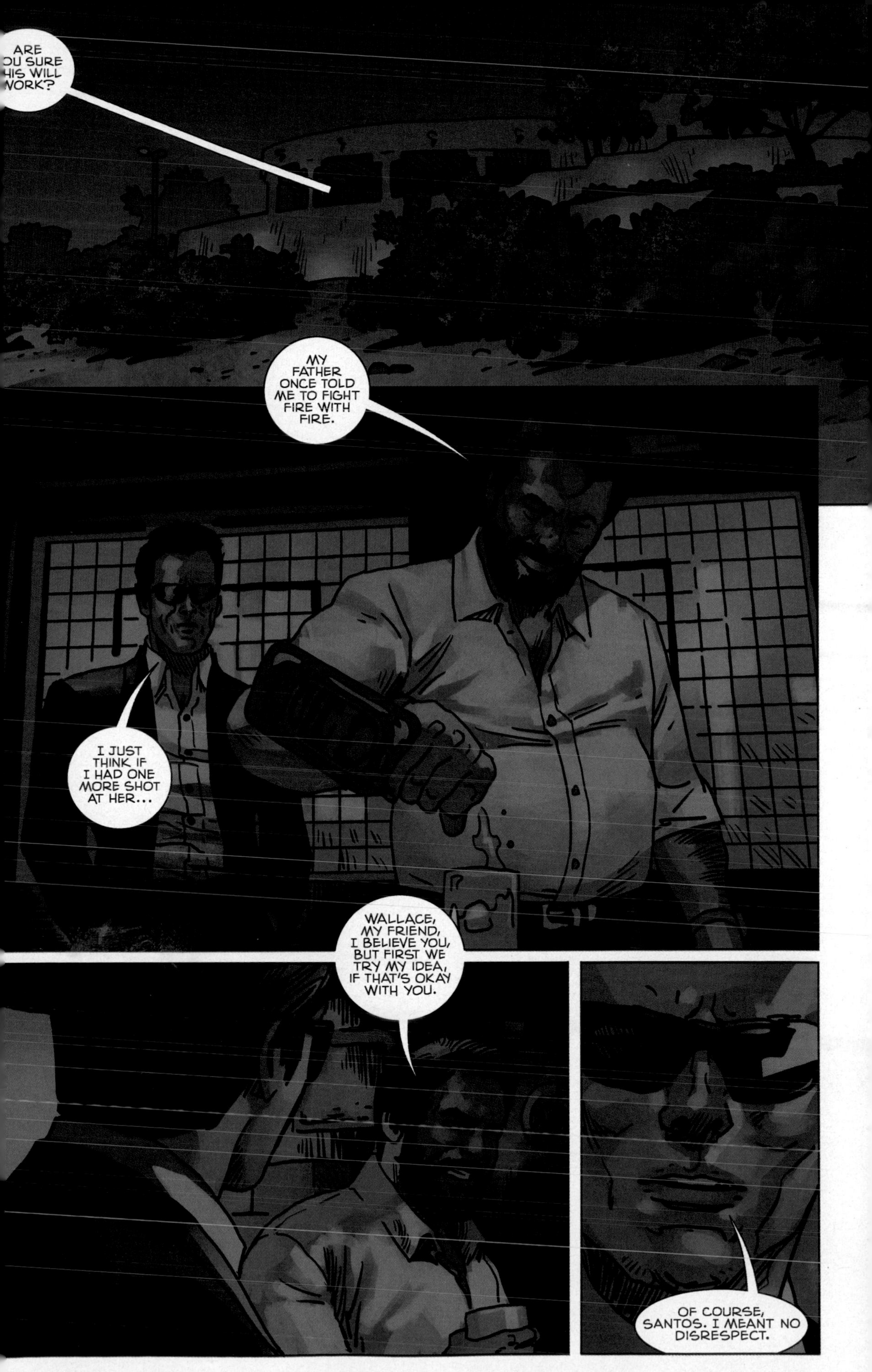
ARE YOU SURE THIS WILL WORK?
MY FATHER ONCE TOLD ME TO FIGHT FIRE WITH FIRE.
I JUST THINK IF I HAD ONE MORE SHOT AT HER...
WALLACE, MY FRIEND, I BELIEVE YOU, BUT FIRST WE TRY MY IDEA, IF THAT'S OKAY WITH YOU.
OF COURSE, SANTOS. I MEANT NO DISRESPECT.

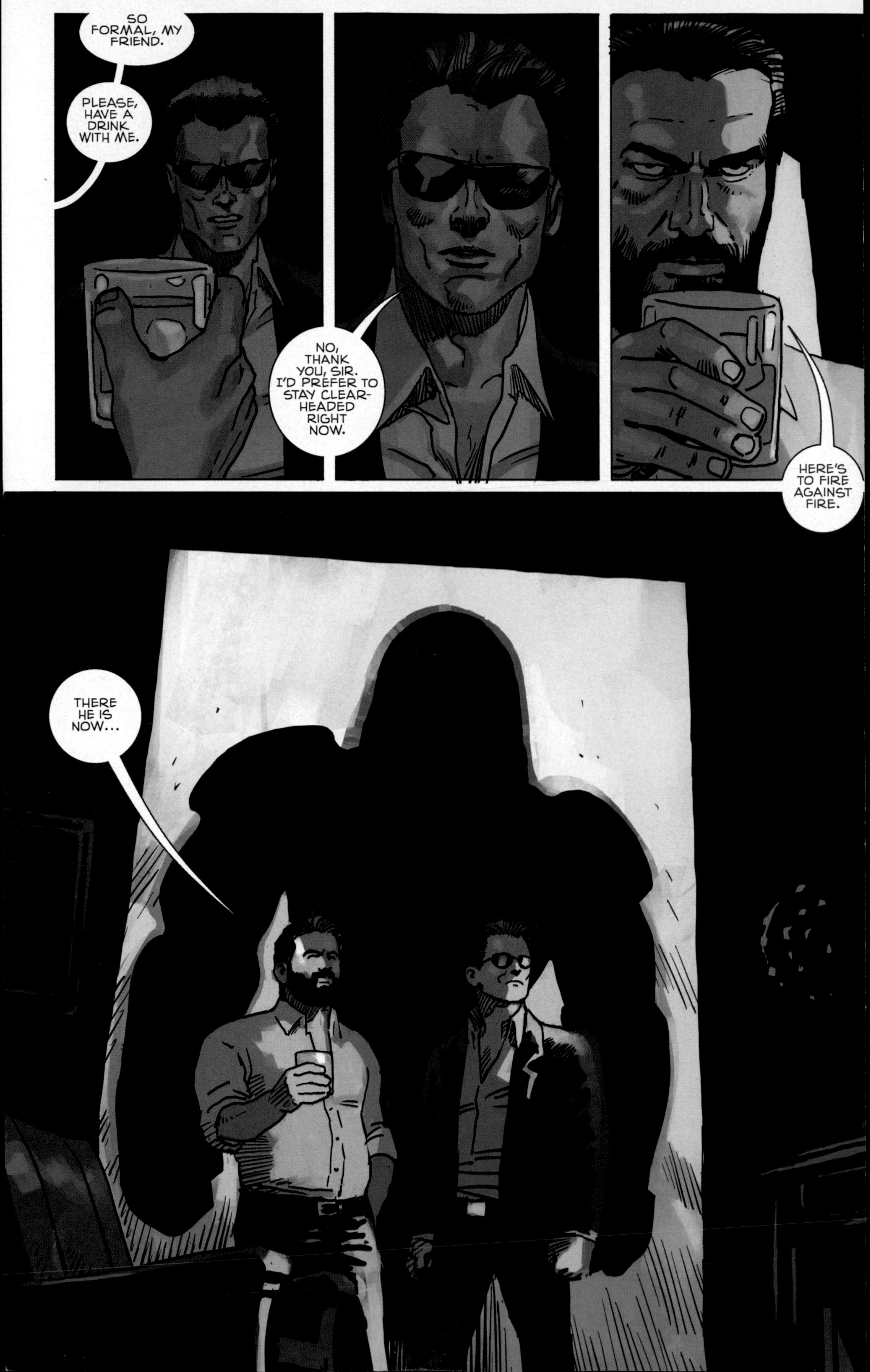
SO FORMAL, MY FRIEND.
PLEASE, HAVE A DRINK WITH ME.
NO, THANK YOU, SIR. I'D PREFER TO STAY CLEAR-HEADED RIGHT NOW.
HERE'S TO FIRE AGAINST FIRE.
THERE HE IS NOW...

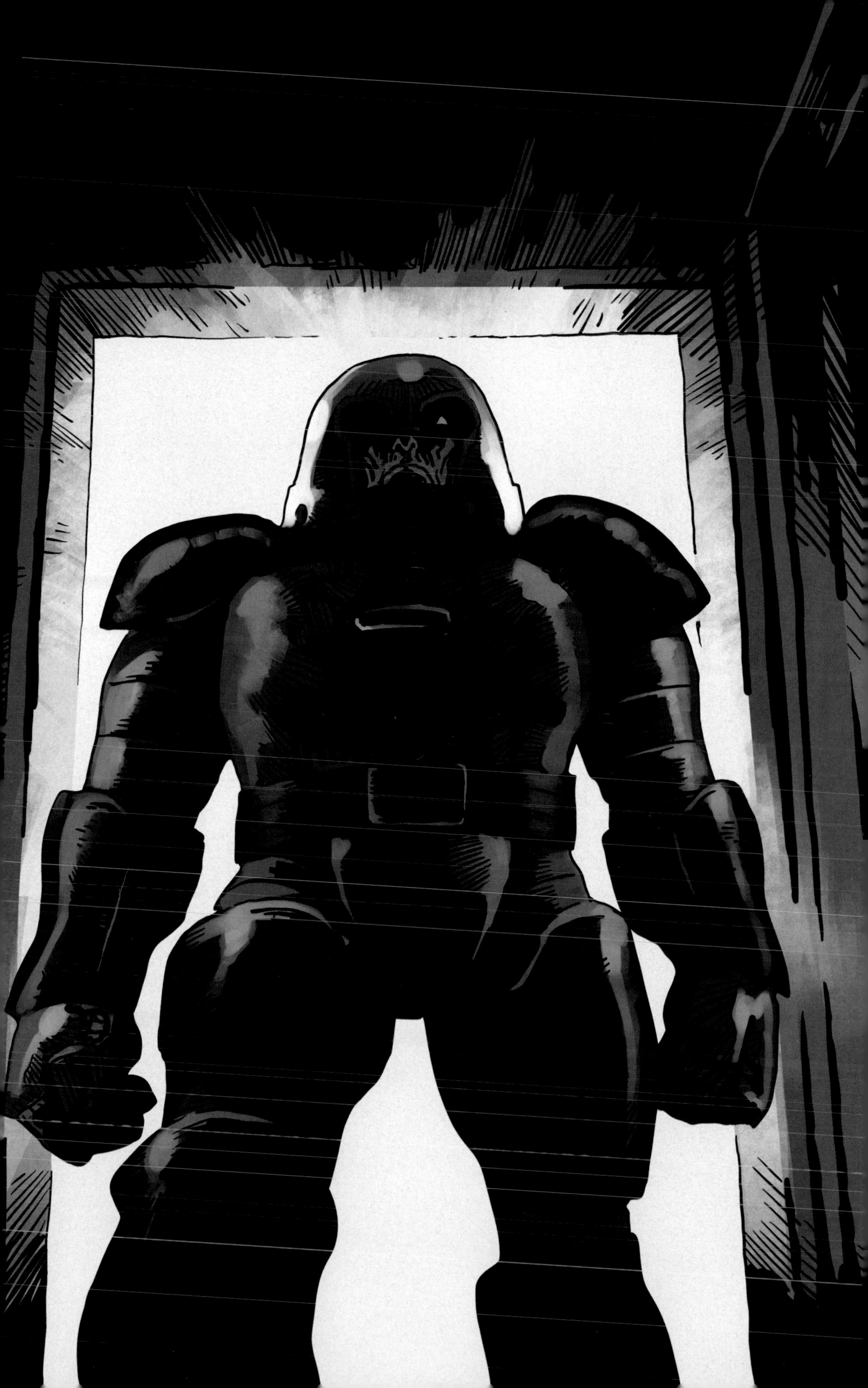

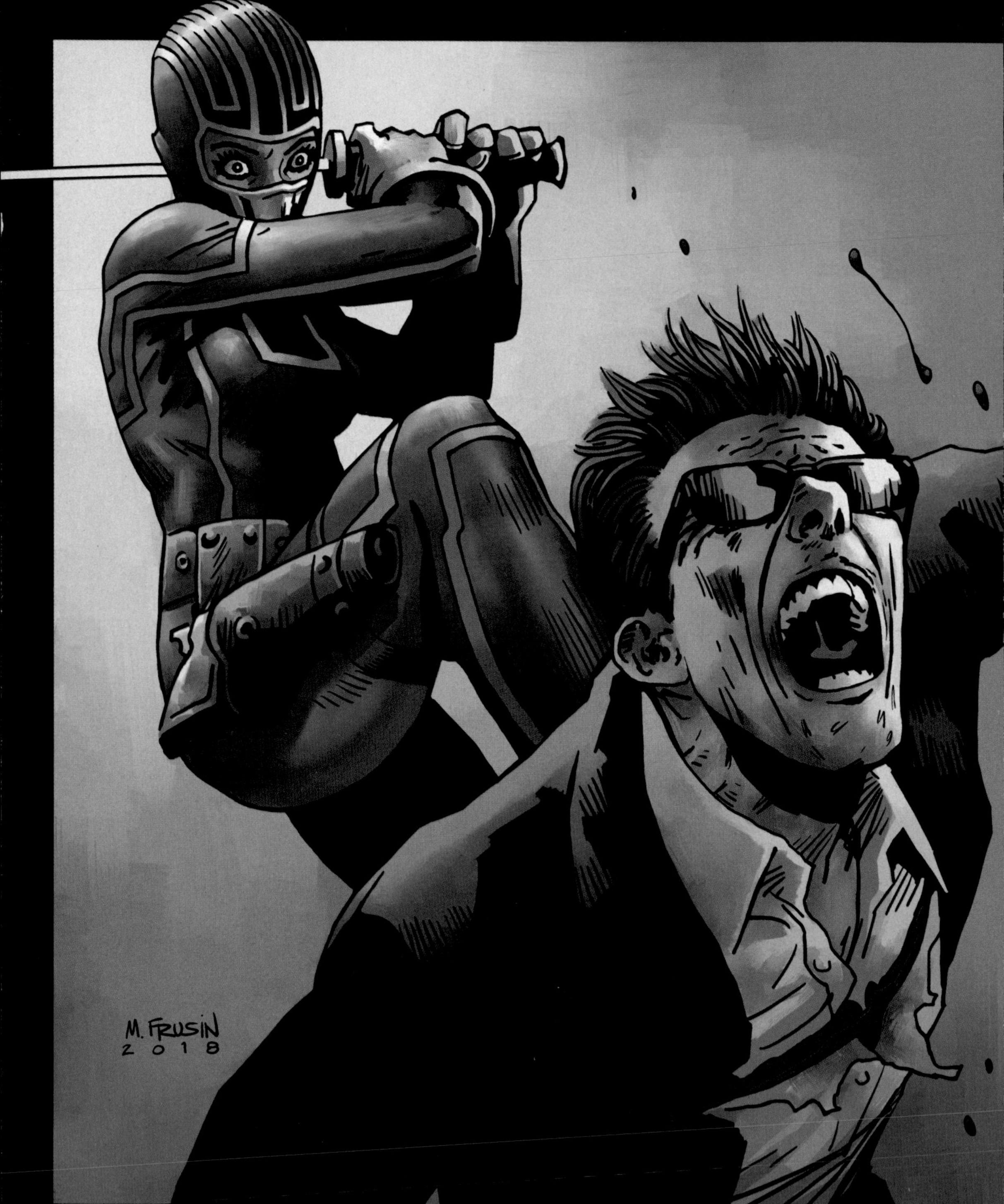
M. FRUSIN
2018

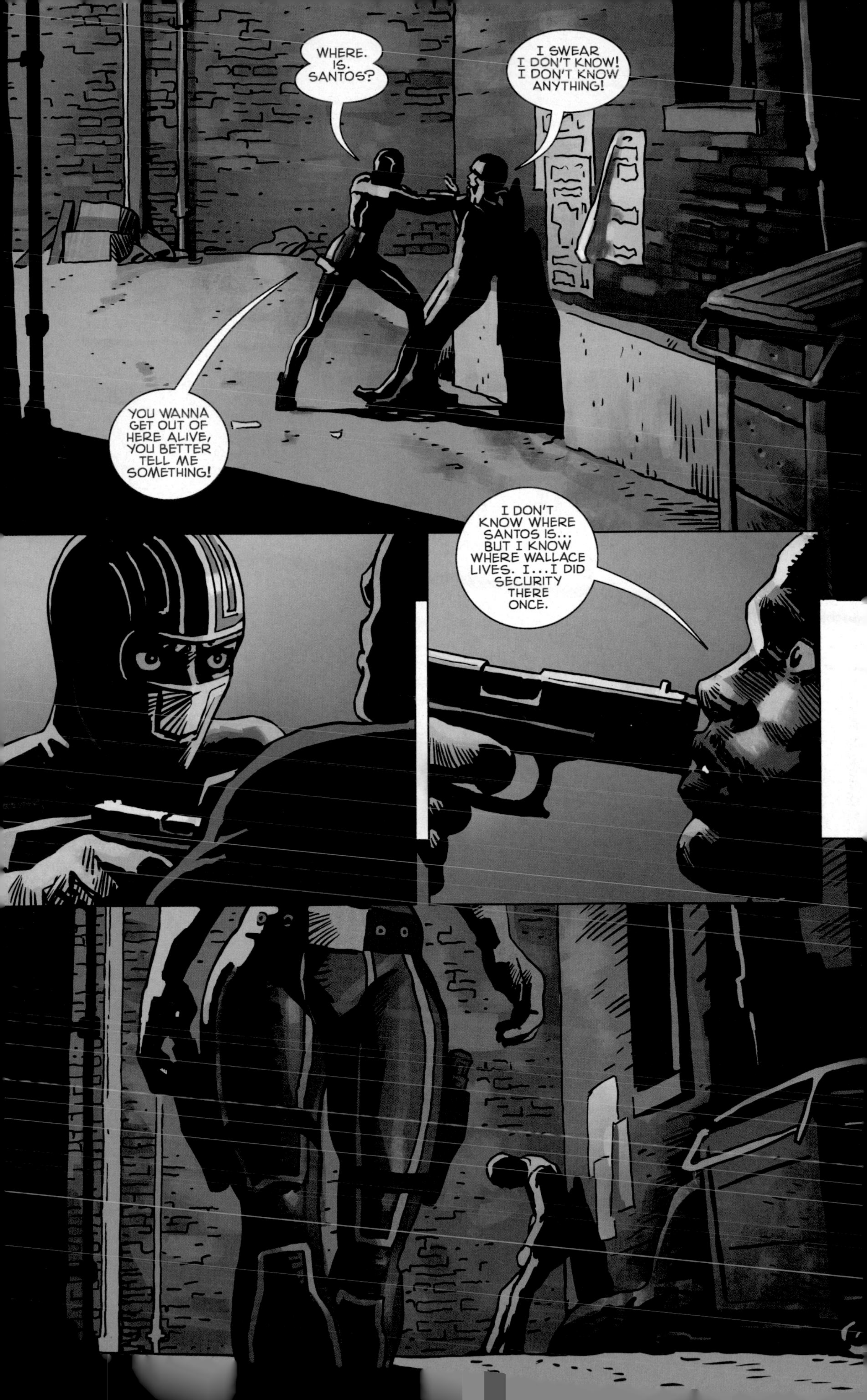
WHERE. IS. SANTOS?
I SWEAR I DON'T KNOW! I DON'T KNOW ANYTHING!
YOU WANNA GET OUT OF HERE ALIVE, YOU BETTER TELL ME SOMETHING!
I DON'T KNOW WHERE SANTOS IS... BUT I KNOW WHERE WALLACE LIVES. I...I DID SECURITY THERE ONCE.

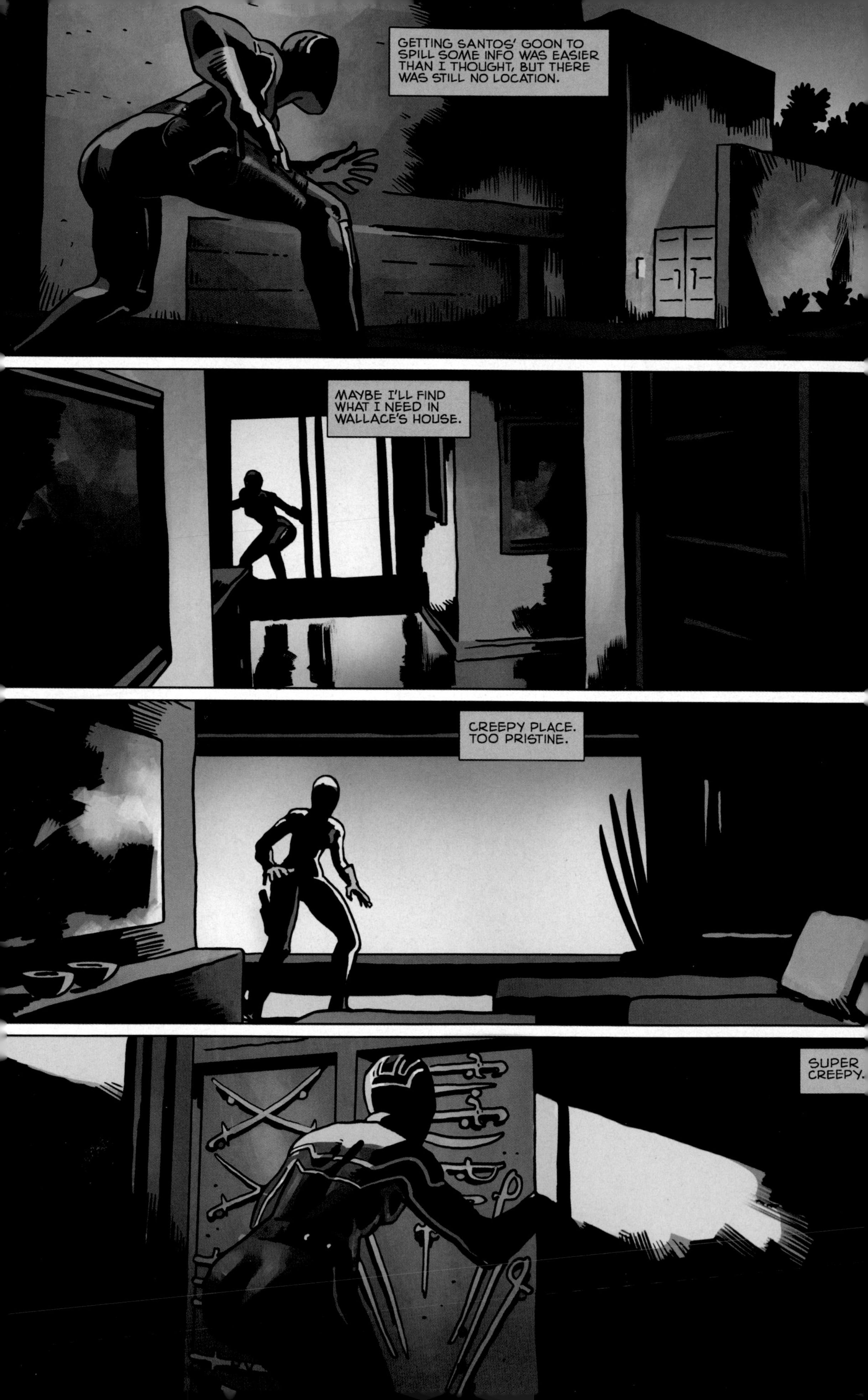
GETTING SANTOS' GOON TO SPILL SOME INFO WAS EASIER THAN I THOUGHT, BUT THERE WAS STILL NO LOCATION.
MAYBE I'LL FIND WHAT I NEED IN WALLACE'S HOUSE.
CREEPY PLACE. TOO PRISTINE.
SUPER CREEPY.

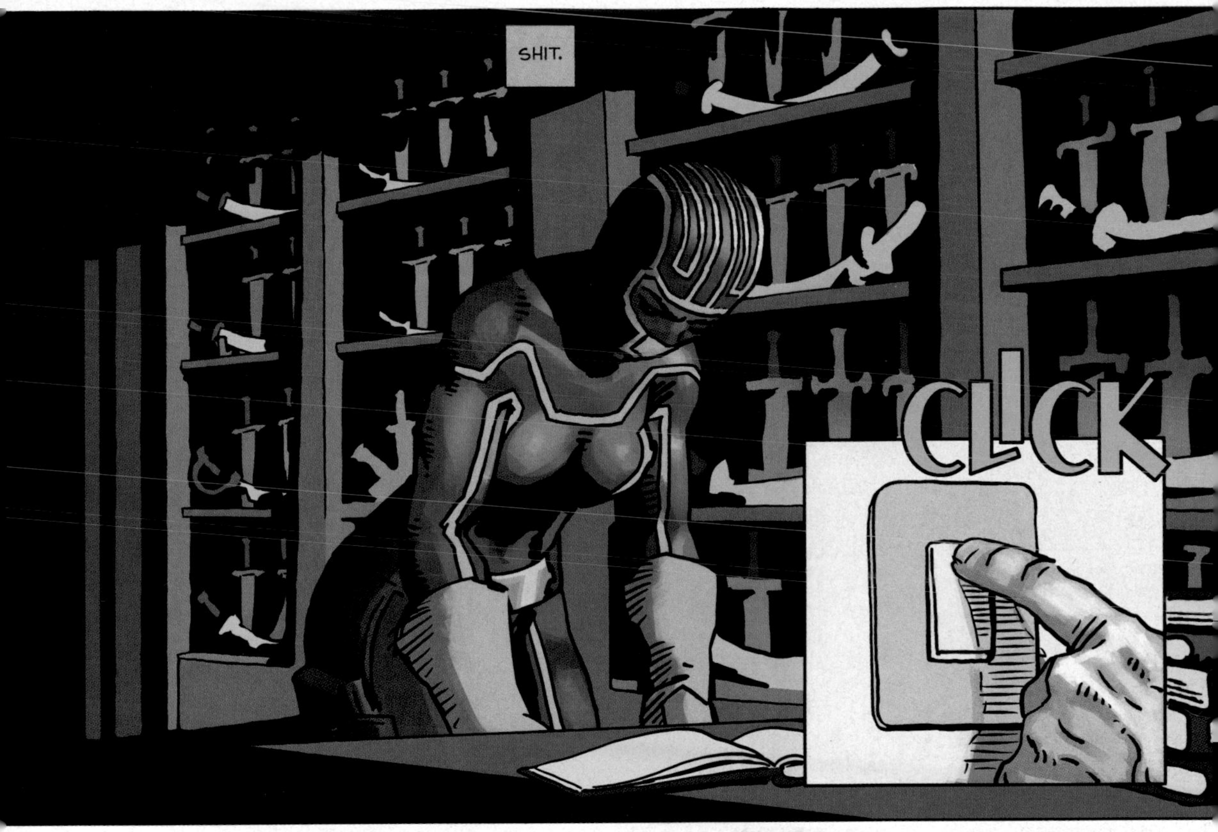
SHIT.
CLICK

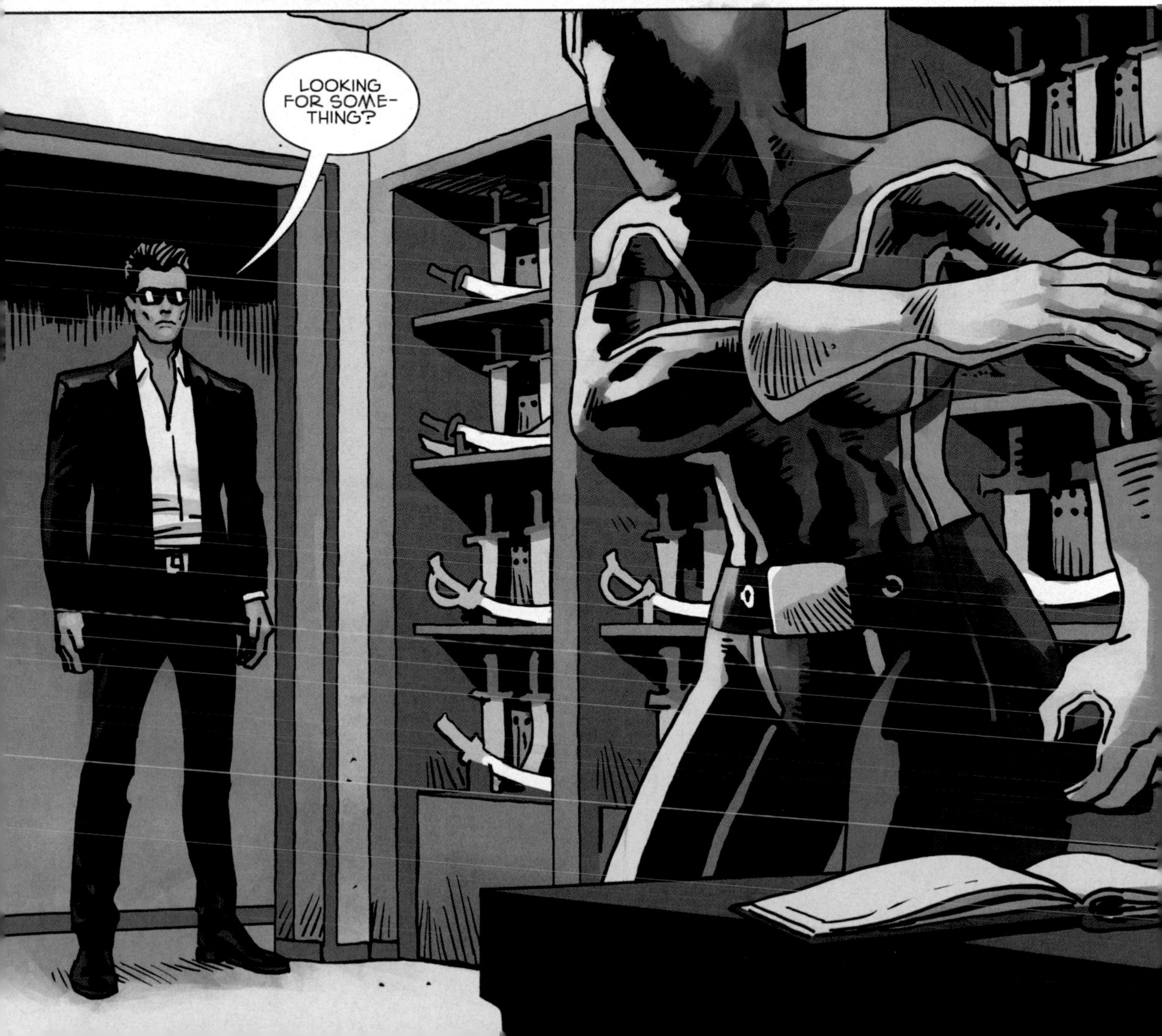
LOOKING FOR SOME- THING?

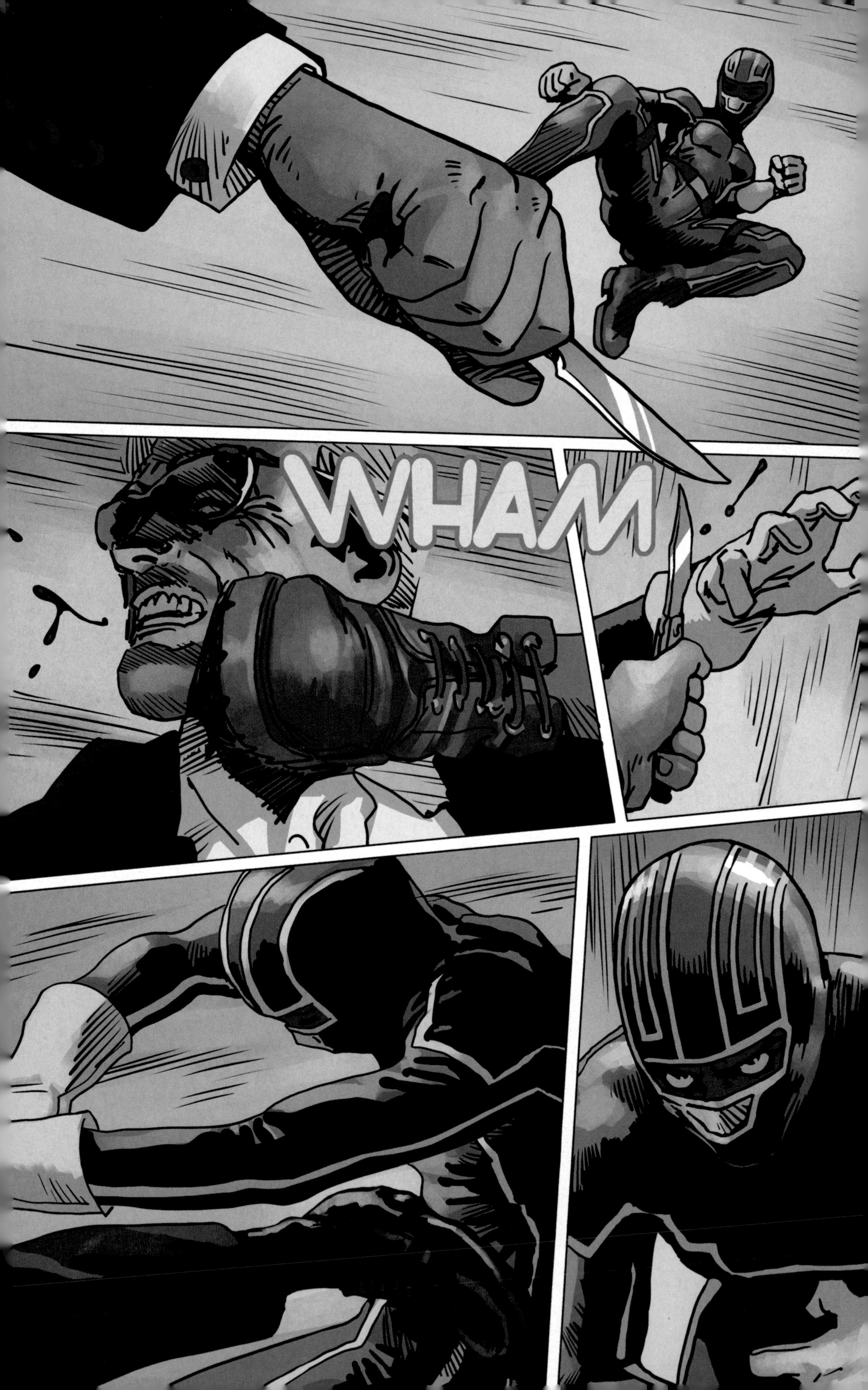
WHAM

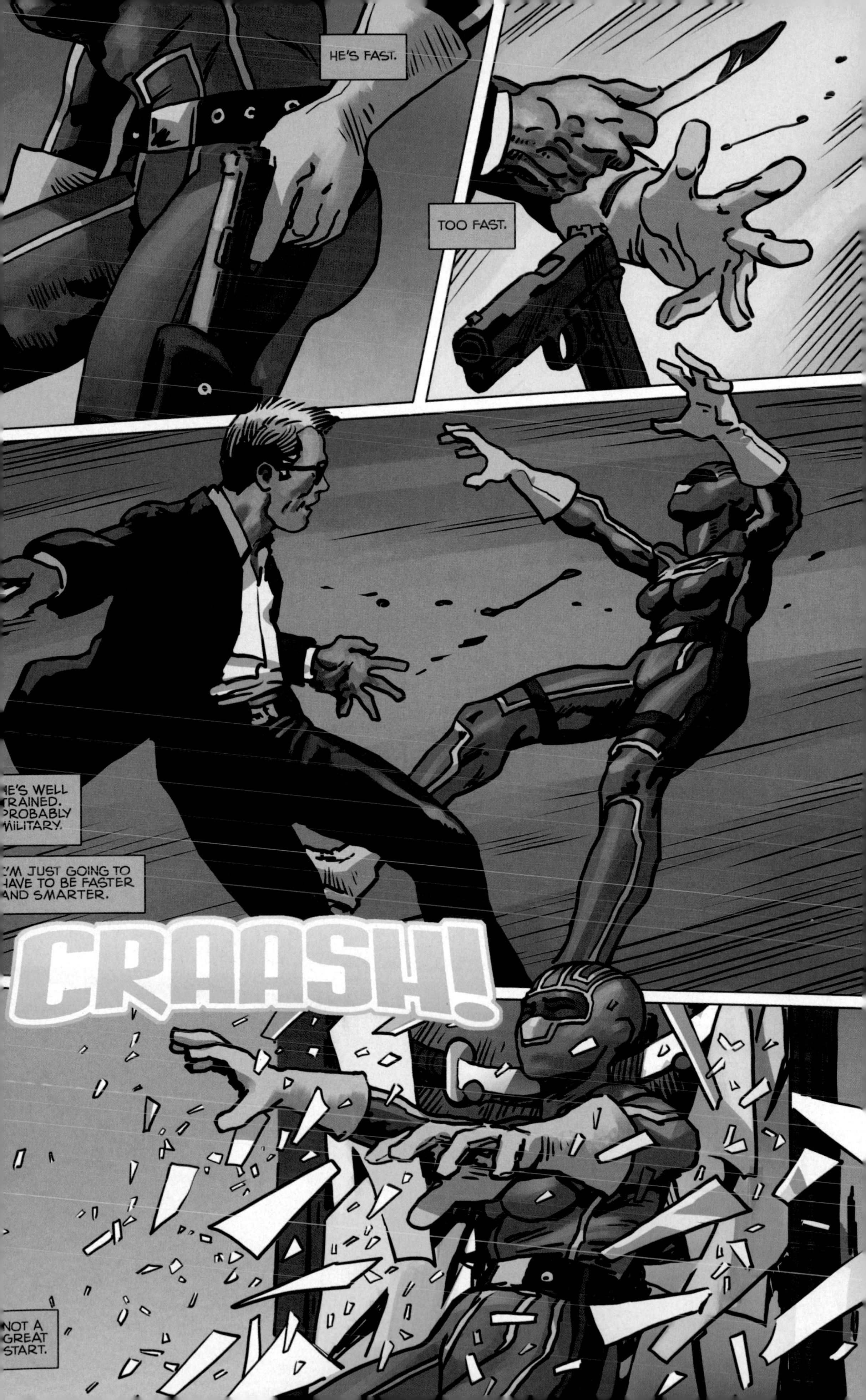

HE'S FAST.
TOO FAST.
HE'S WELL TRAINED. PROBABLY MILITARY.
I'M JUST GOING TO HAVE TO BE FASTER AND SMARTER.
CRAASH!
NOT A GREAT START.

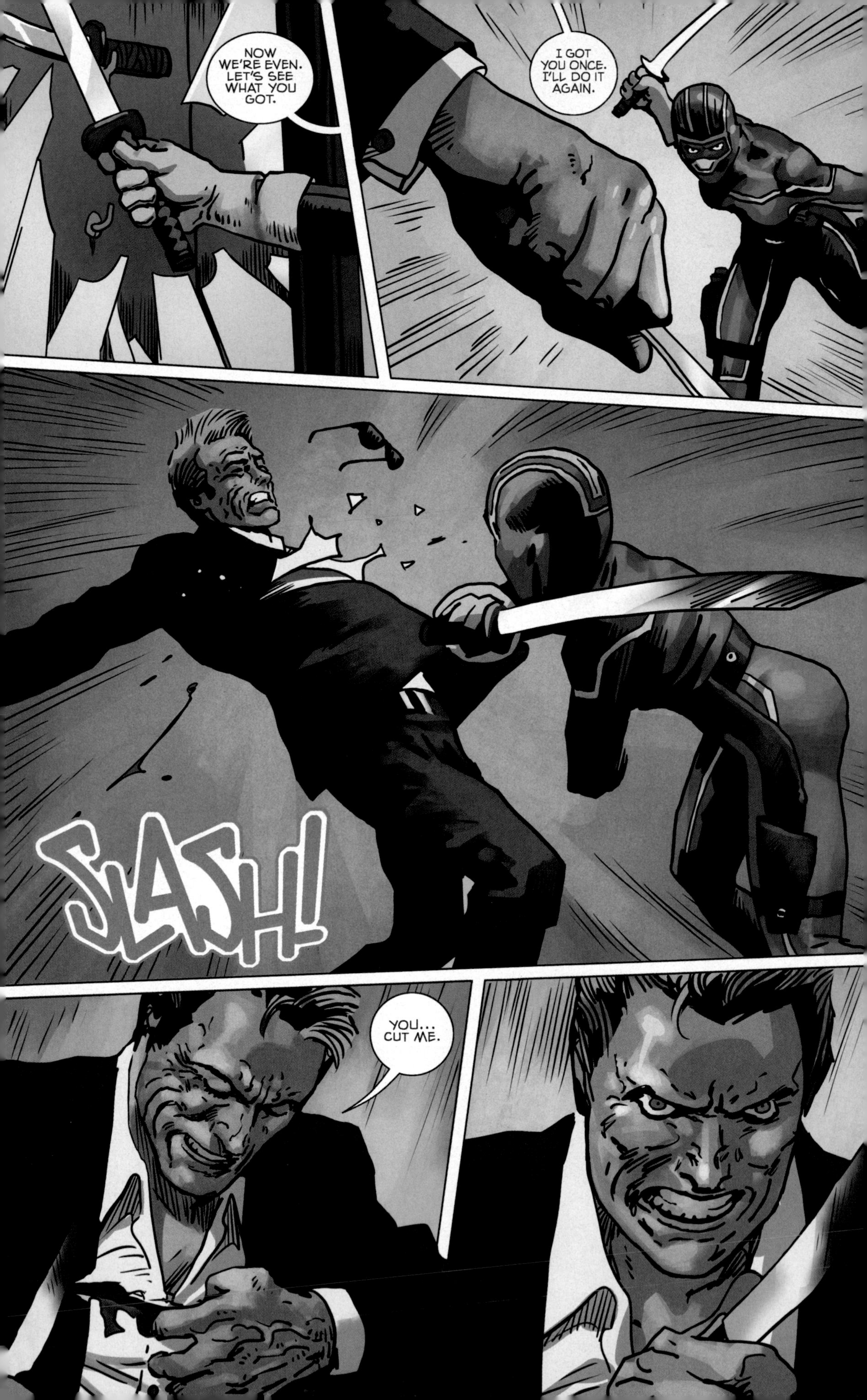
NOW WE'RE EVEN. LET'S SEE WHAT YOU GOT.
I GOT YOU ONCE. I'LL DO IT AGAIN.
SLASH!
YOU... CUT ME.

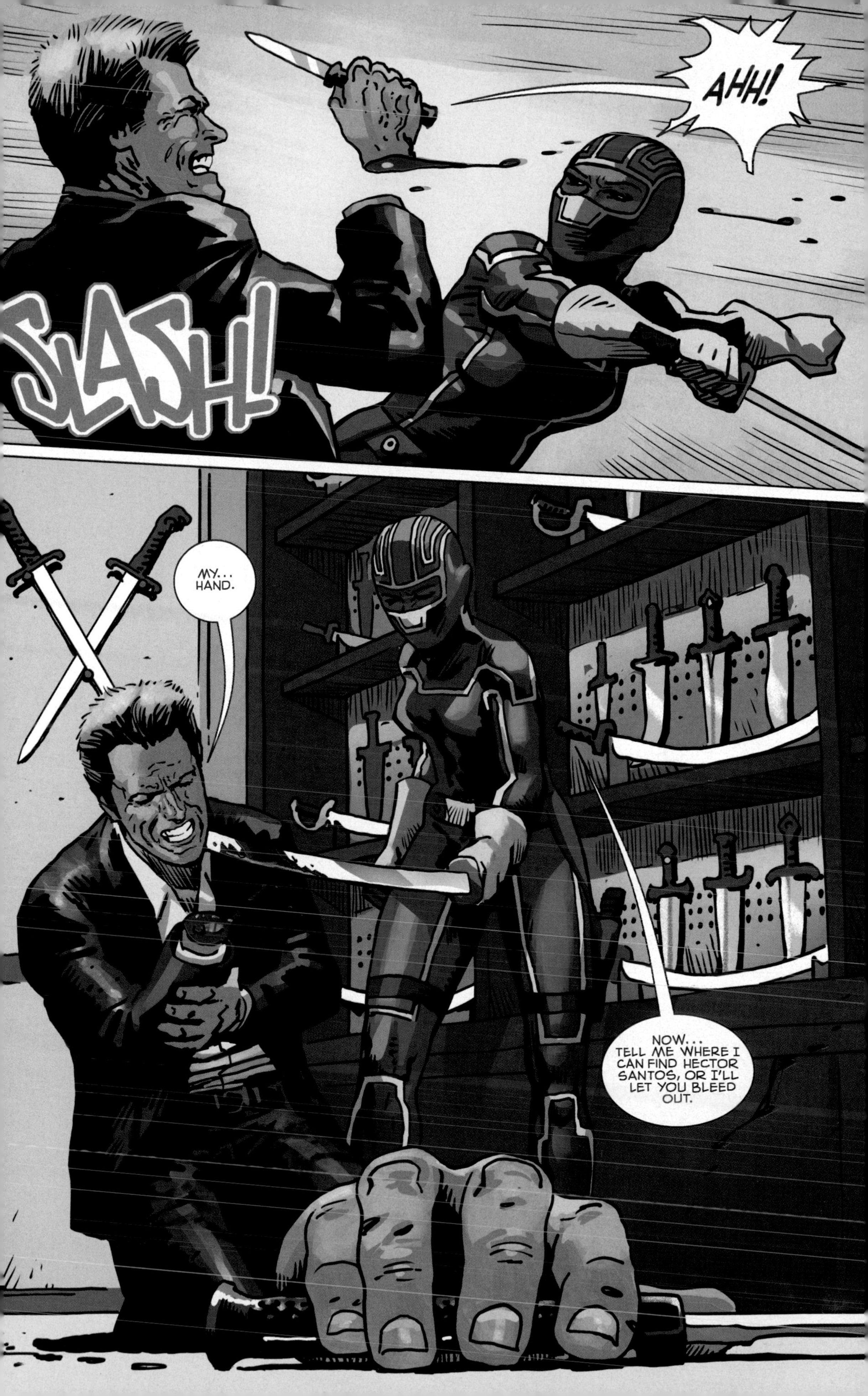
AHH!
SLASH!
MY... HAND.
NOW... TELL ME WHERE I CAN FIND HECTOR SANTOS, OR I'LL LET YOU BLEED OUT.

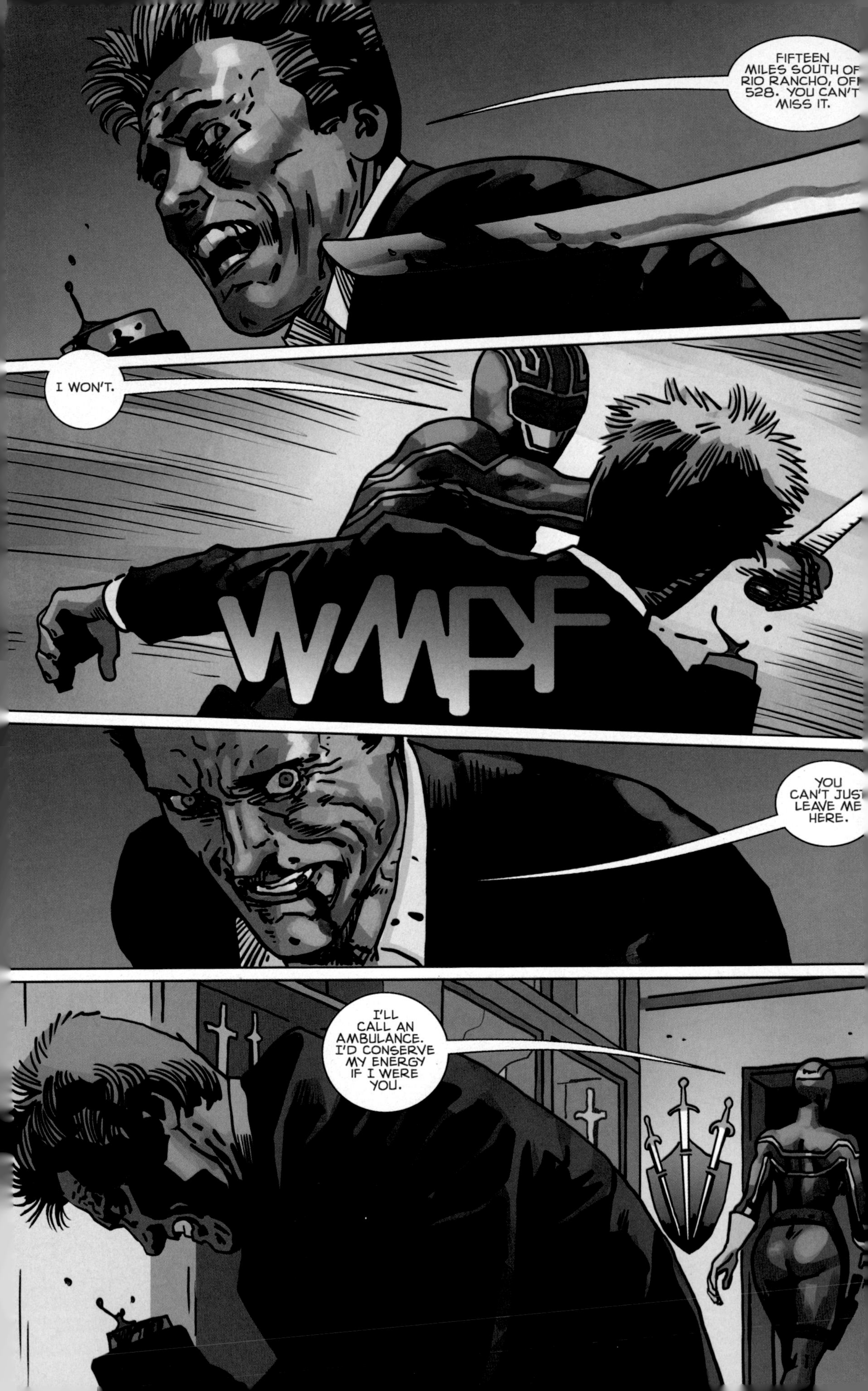
FIFTEEN MILES SOUTH OF RIO RANCHO, OFF 528. YOU CAN'T MISS IT.
I WON'T.
WMPF
YOU CAN'T JUST LEAVE ME HERE.
I'LL CALL AN AMBULANCE. I'D CONSERVE MY ENERGY IF I WERE YOU.

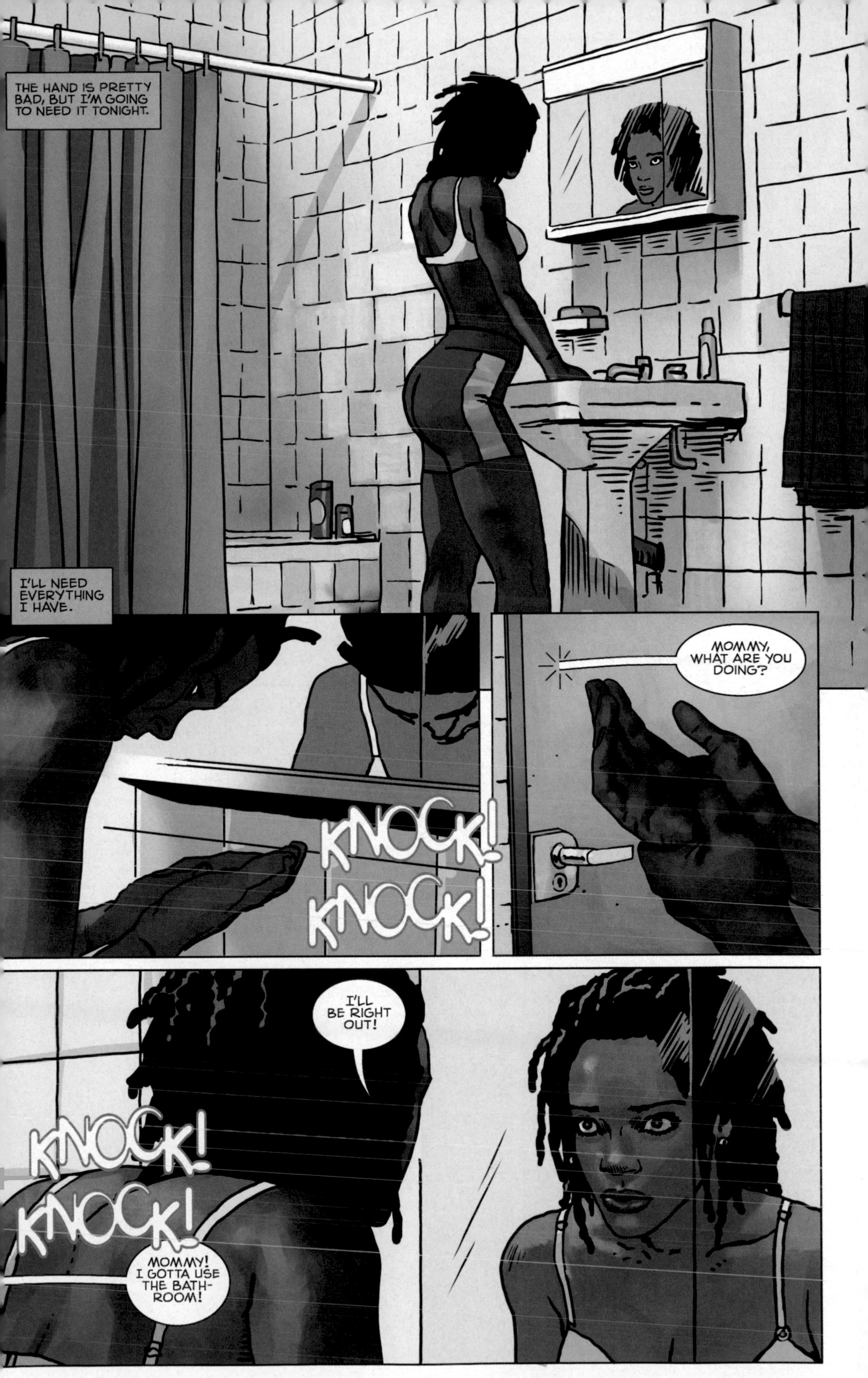
THE HAND IS PRETTY BAD, BUT I'M GOING TO NEED IT TONIGHT.
I'LL NEED EVERYTHING I HAVE.
MOMMY, WHAT ARE YOU DOING?
KNOCK! KNOCK!
I'LL BE RIGHT OUT!
KNOCK! KNOCK!
MOMMY! I GOTTA USE THE BATH-ROOM!

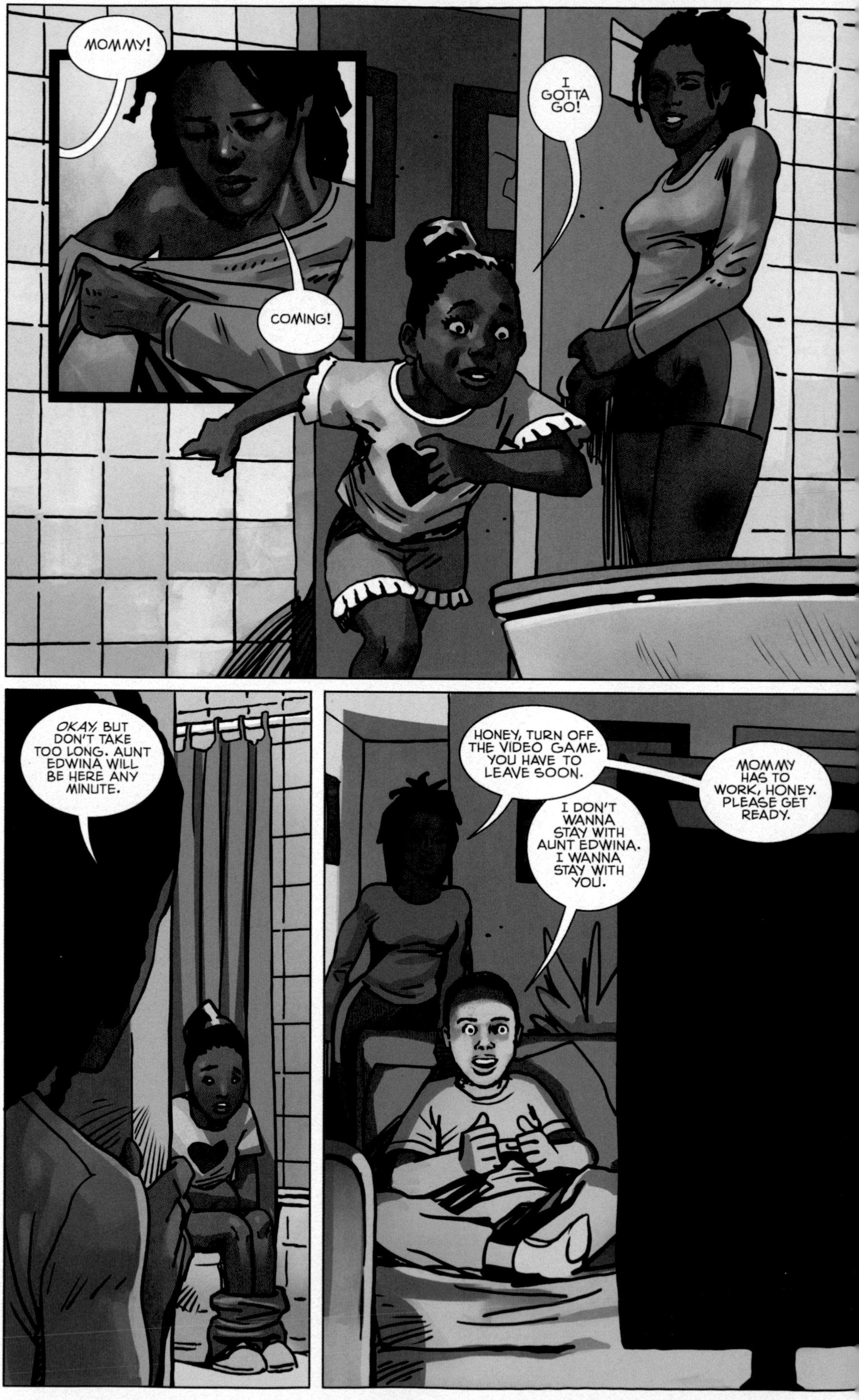
MOMMY!
COMING!
I GOTTA GO!
OKAY, BUT DON'T TAKE TOO LONG. AUNT EDWINA WILL BE HERE ANY MINUTE.
HONEY, TURN OFF THE VIDEO GAME. YOU HAVE TO LEAVE SOON.
I DON'T WANNA STAY WITH AUNT EDWINA. I WANNA STAY WITH YOU.
MOMMY HAS TO WORK, HONEY. PLEASE GET READY.

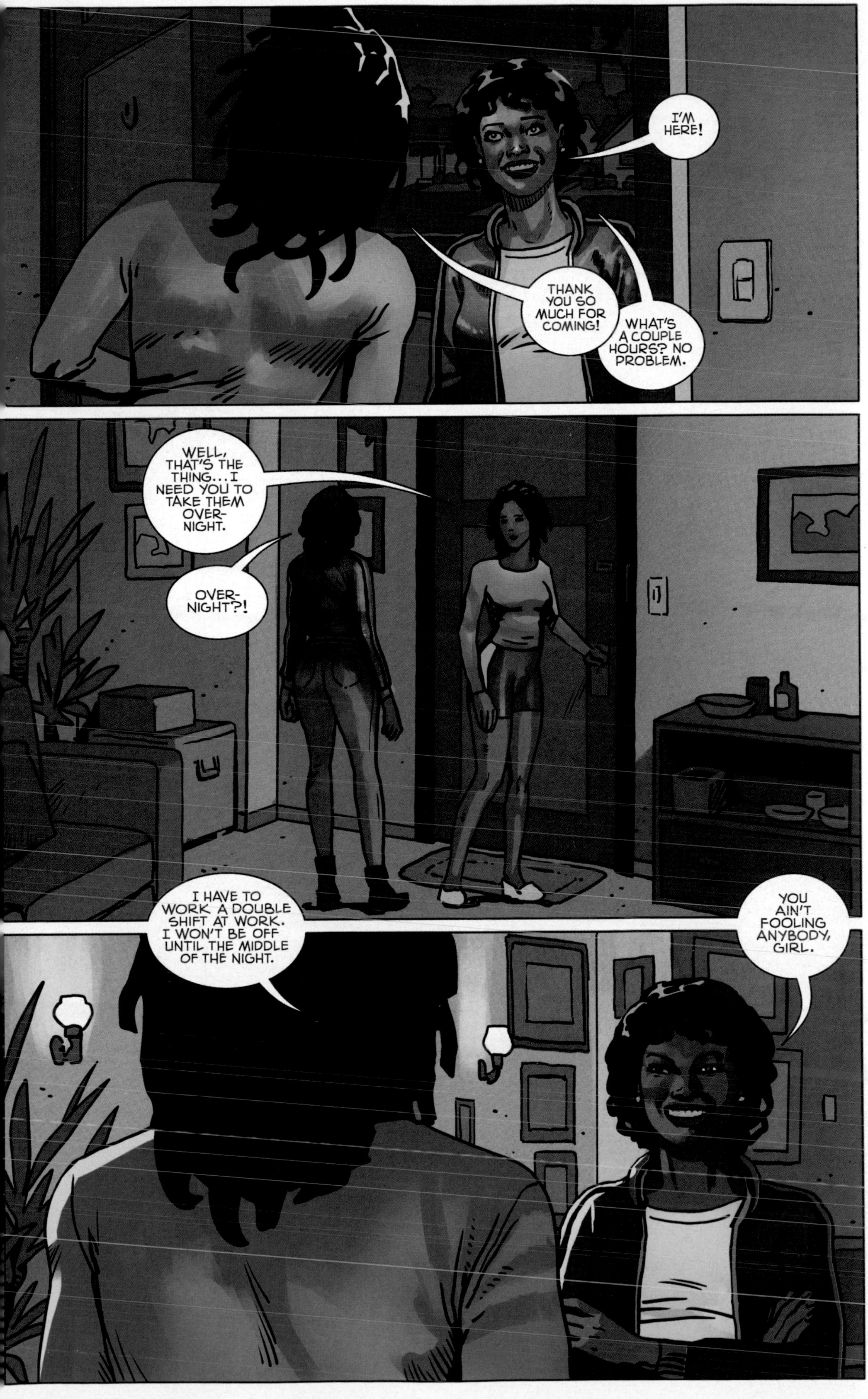
I'M HERE!
THANK YOU SO MUCH FOR COMING!
WHAT'S A COUPLE HOURS? NO PROBLEM.
WELL, THAT'S THE THING... I NEED YOU TO TAKE THEM OVER-NIGHT.
OVER-NIGHT?!
I HAVE TO WORK A DOUBLE SHIFT AT WORK. I WON'T BE OFF UNTIL THE MIDDLE OF THE NIGHT.
YOU AIN'T FOOLING ANYBODY, GIRL.

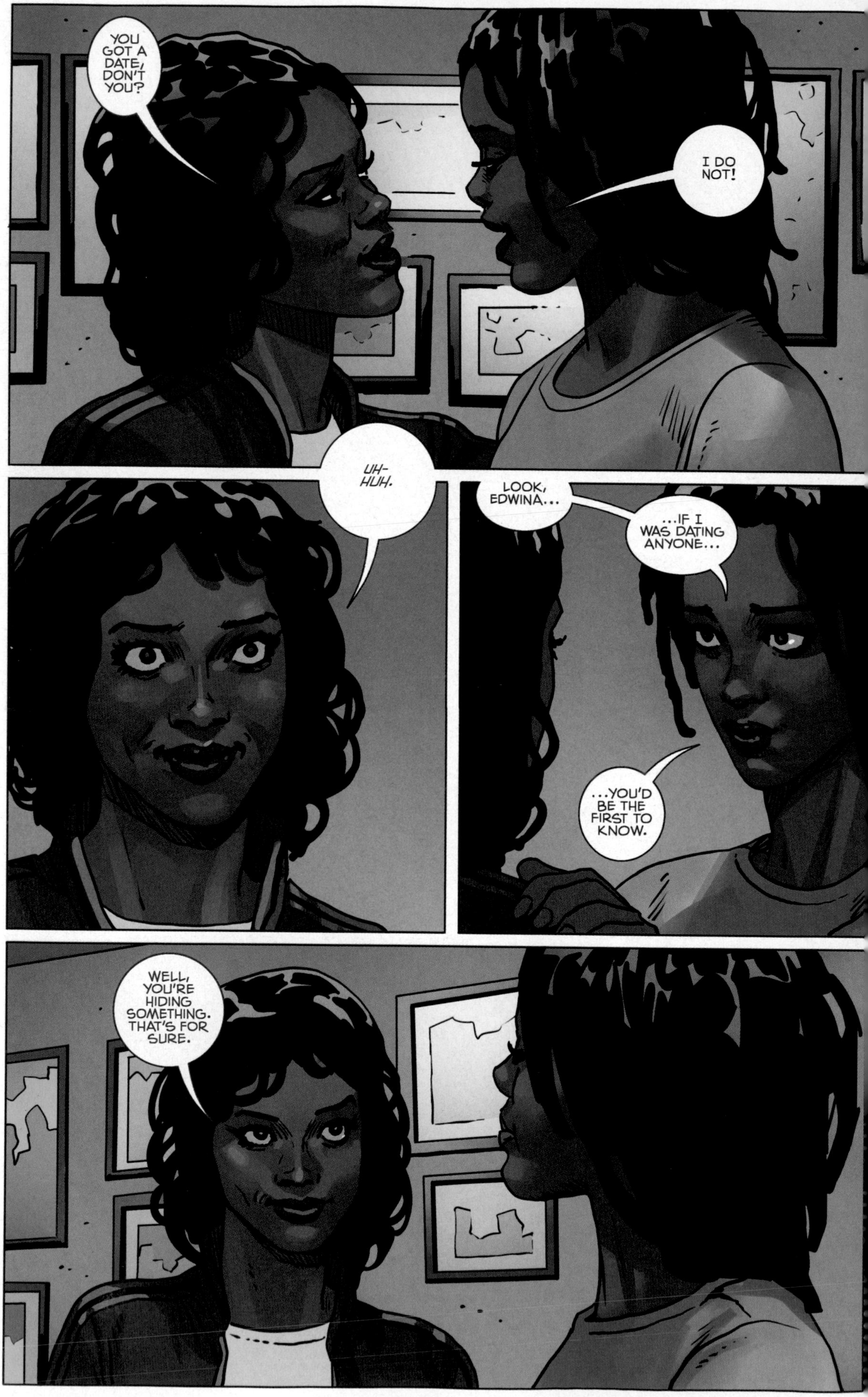
YOU GOT A DATE, DON'T YOU?
I DO NOT!
UH-HUH.
LOOK, EDWINA...
...IF I WAS DATING ANYONE...
...YOU'D BE THE FIRST TO KNOW.
WELL, YOU'RE HIDING SOMETHING. THAT'S FOR SURE.

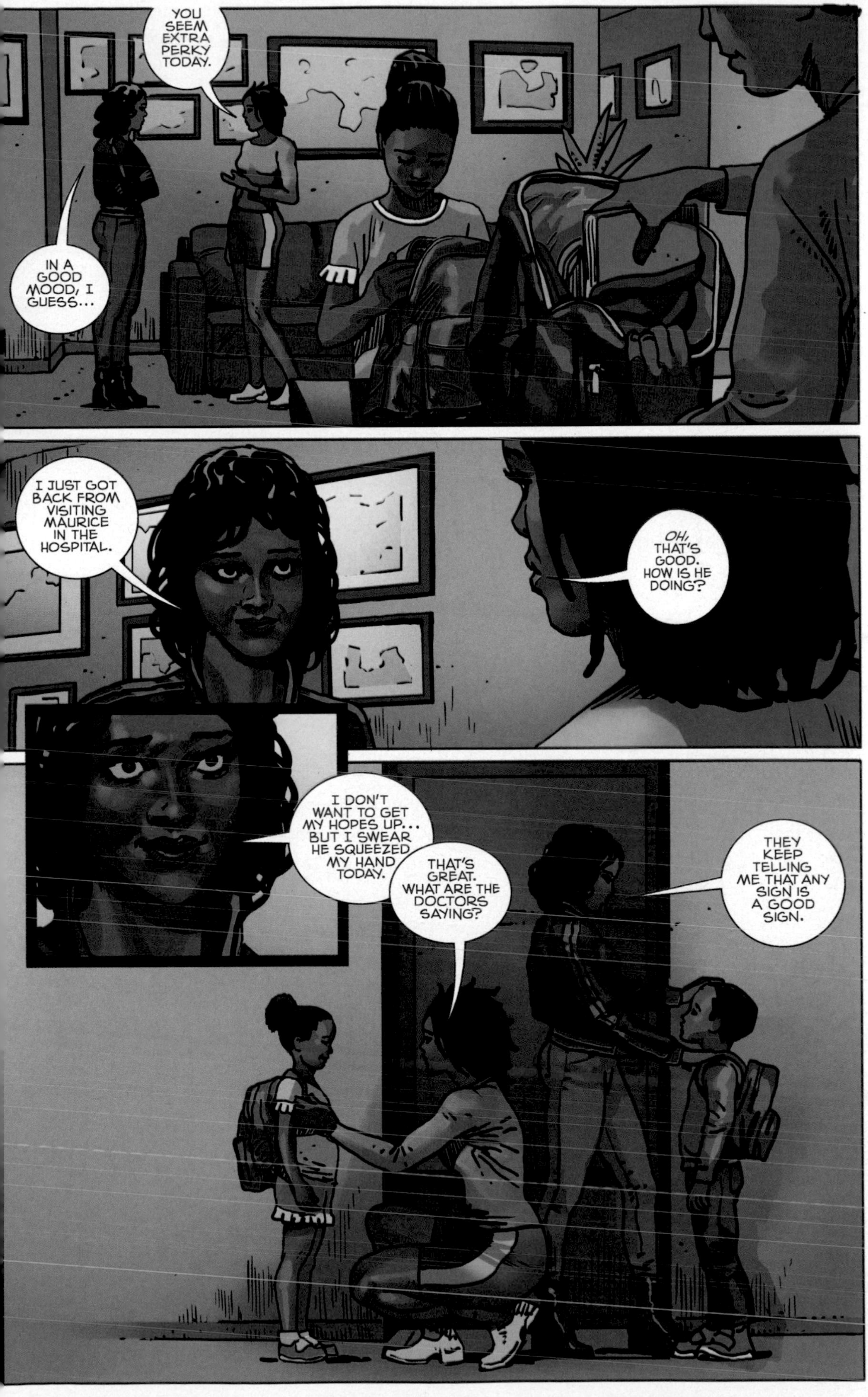

YOU SEEM EXTRA PERKY TODAY.
IN A GOOD MOOD, I GUESS...
I JUST GOT BACK FROM VISITING MAURICE IN THE HOSPITAL.
OH, THAT'S GOOD. HOW IS HE DOING?
I DON'T WANT TO GET MY HOPES UP... BUT I SWEAR HE SQUEEZED MY HAND TODAY.
THAT'S GREAT. WHAT ARE THE DOCTORS SAYING?
THEY KEEP TELLING ME THAT ANY SIGN IS A GOOD SIGN.

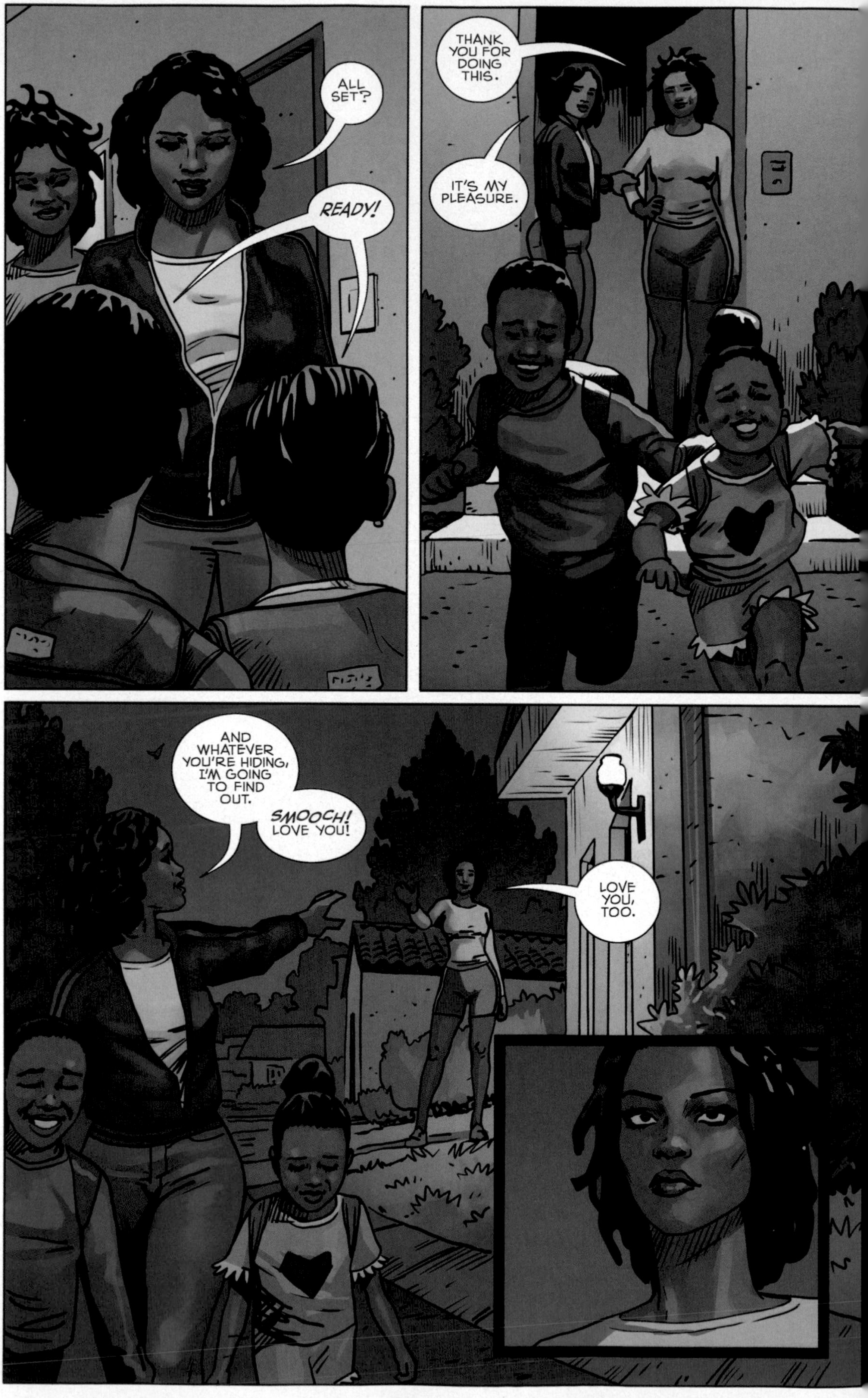
ALL SET?
READY!
THANK YOU FOR DOING THIS.
IT'S MY PLEASURE.
AND WHATEVER YOU'RE HIDING, I'M GOING TO FIND OUT.
SMOOCH! LOVE YOU!
LOVE YOU, TOO.

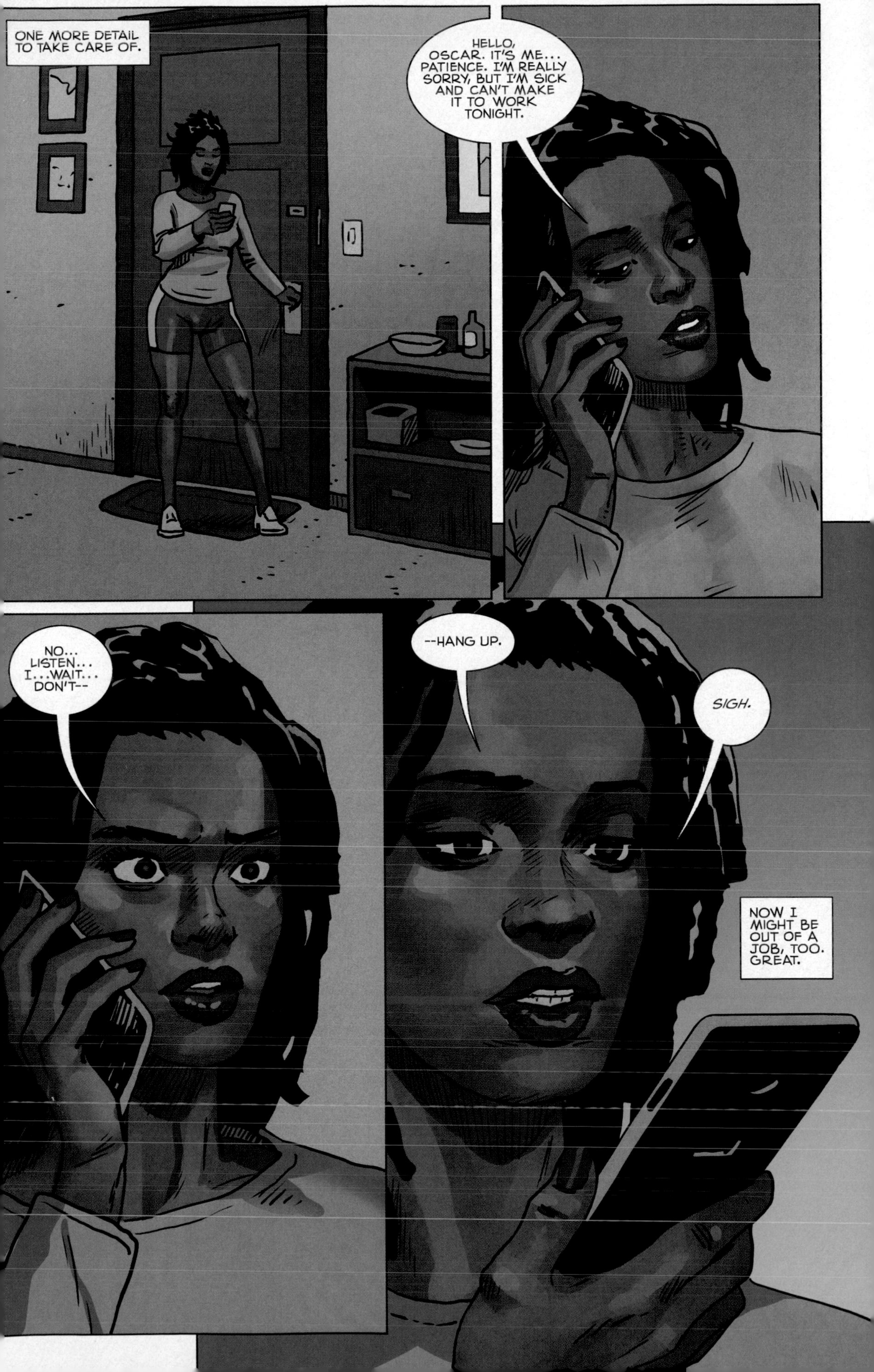
ONE MORE DETAIL TO TAKE CARE OF.
HELLO, OSCAR. IT'S ME... PATIENCE. I'M REALLY SORRY, BUT I'M SICK AND CAN'T MAKE IT TO WORK TONIGHT.
NO... LISTEN... I...WAIT... DON'T--
--HANG UP.
SIGH.
NOW I MIGHT BE OUT OF A JOB, TOO. GREAT.

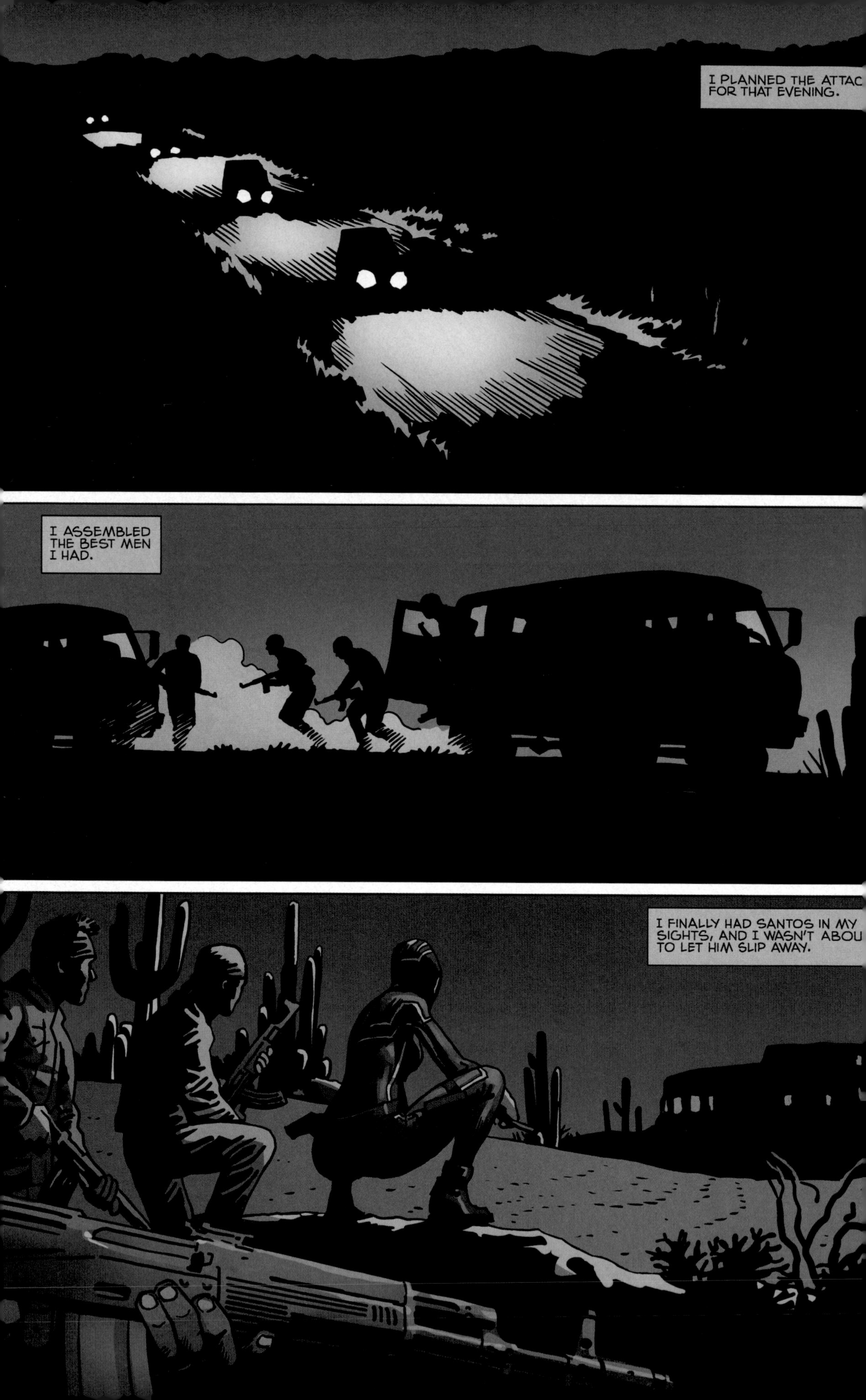
I PLANNED THE ATTAC FOR THAT EVENING.
I ASSEMBLED THE BEST MEN I HAD.
I FINALLY HAD SANTOS IN MY SIGHTS, AND I WASN'T ABOU TO LET HIM SLIP AWAY.

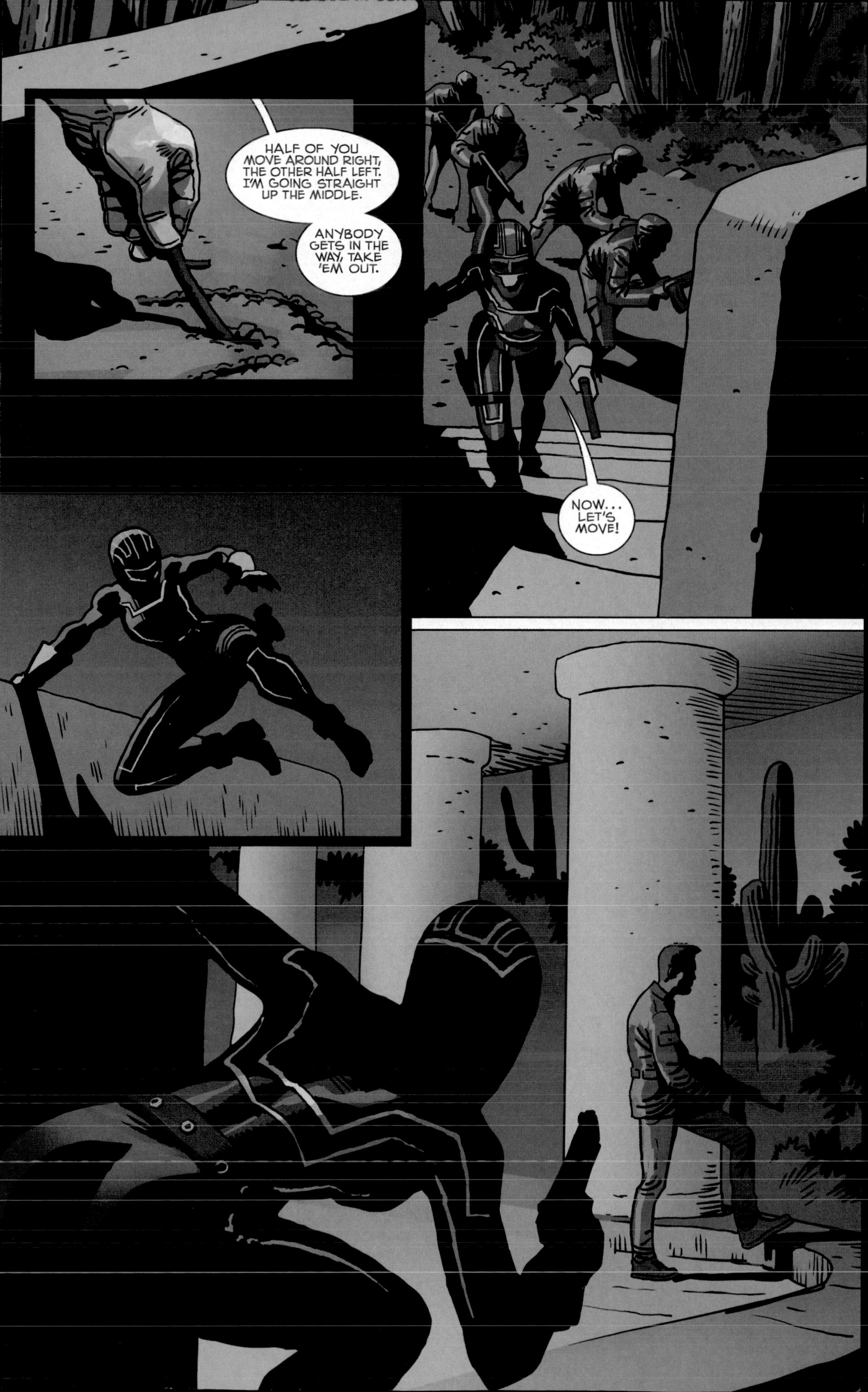
HALF OF YOU MOVE AROUND RIGHT, THE OTHER HALF LEFT. I'M GOING STRAIGHT UP THE MIDDLE.
ANYBODY GETS IN THE WAY, TAKE 'EM OUT.
NOW... LET'S MOVE!

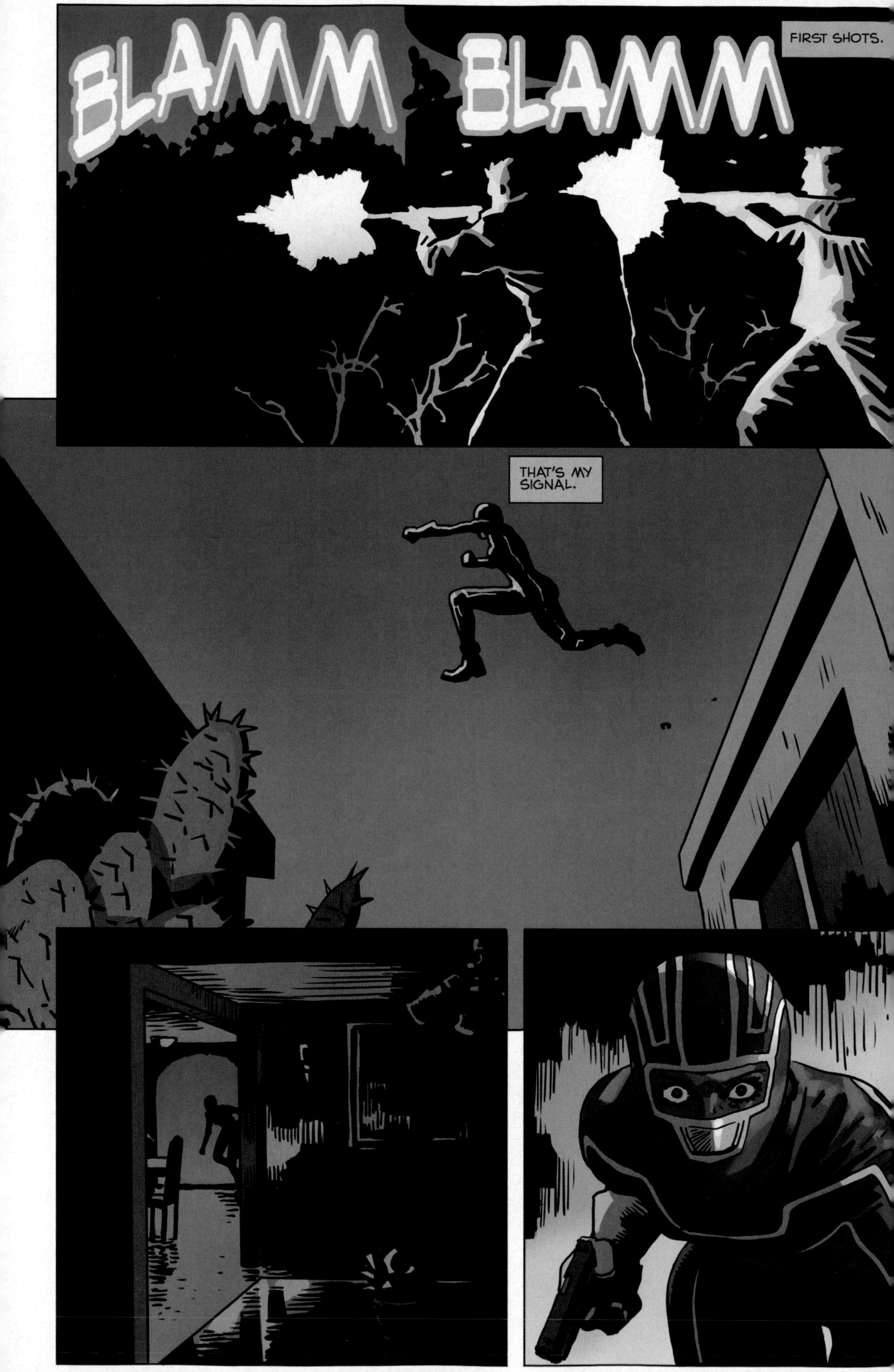

FIRST SHOTS.
BLAMM BLAMM
THAT'S MY SIGNAL.

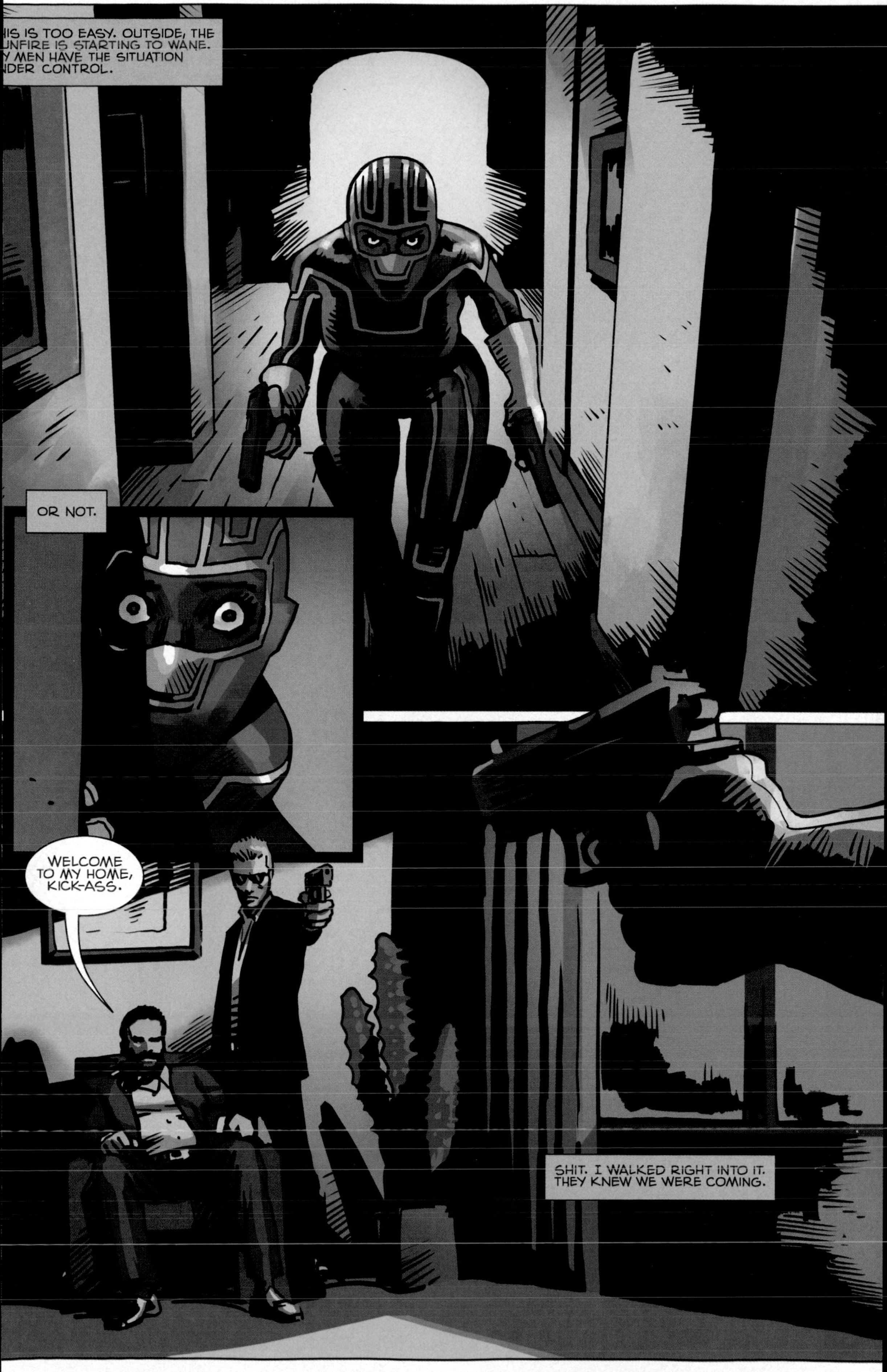
HIS IS TOO EASY. OUTSIDE, THE
UNFIRE IS STARTING TO WANE.
Y MEN HAVE THE SITUATION
NDER CONTROL.
OR NOT.
WELCOME TO MY HOME, KICK-ASS.
SHIT. I WALKED RIGHT INTO IT. THEY KNEW WE WERE COMING.

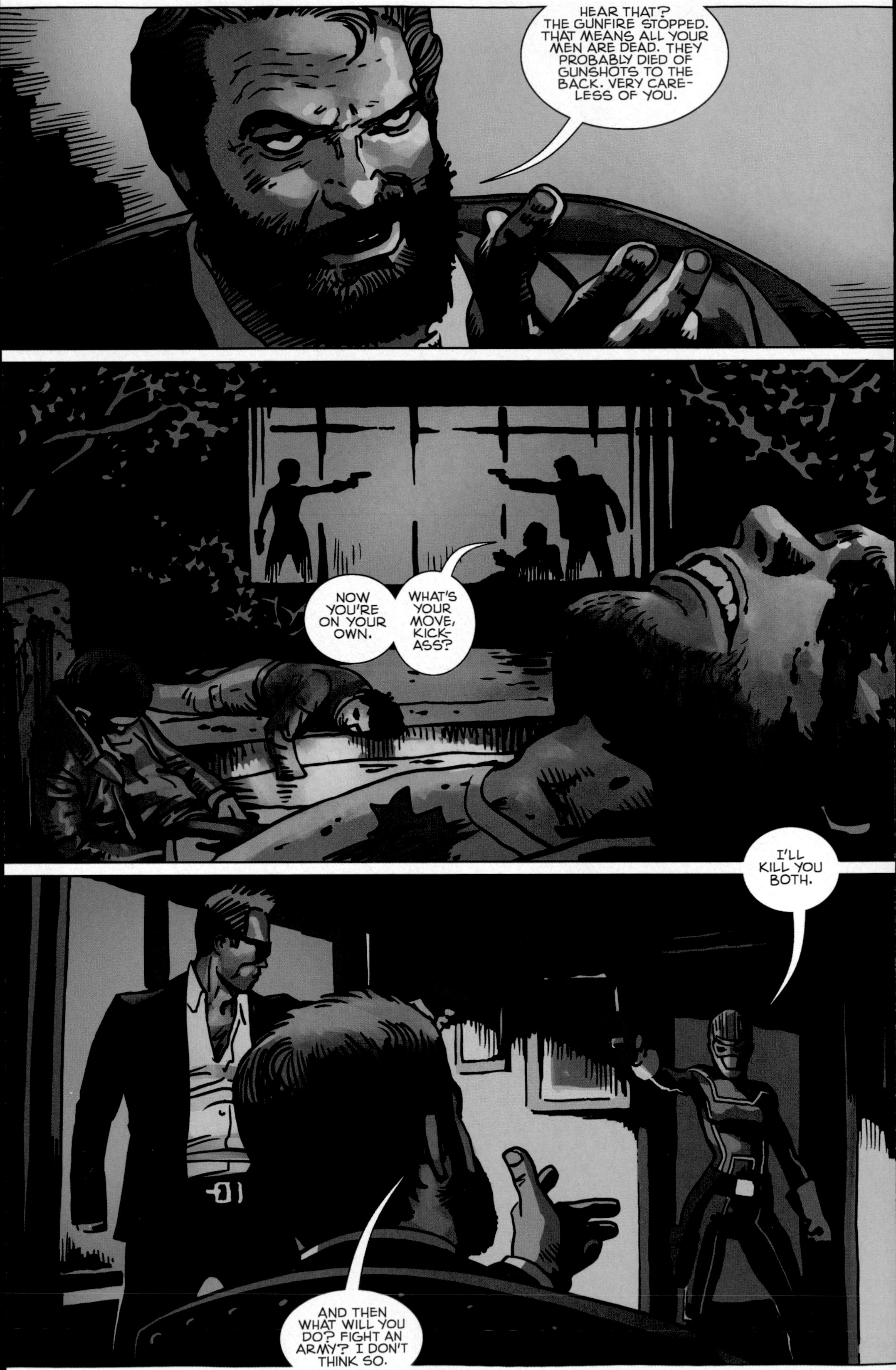
HEAR THAT? THE GUNFIRE STOPPED. THAT MEANS ALL YOUR MEN ARE DEAD. THEY PROBABLY DIED OF GUNSHOTS TO THE BACK. VERY CARELESS OF YOU.
NOW YOU'RE ON YOUR OWN.
WHAT'S YOUR MOVE, KICK-ASS?
I'LL KILL YOU BOTH.
AND THEN WHAT WILL YOU DO? FIGHT AN ARMY? I DON'T THINK SO.

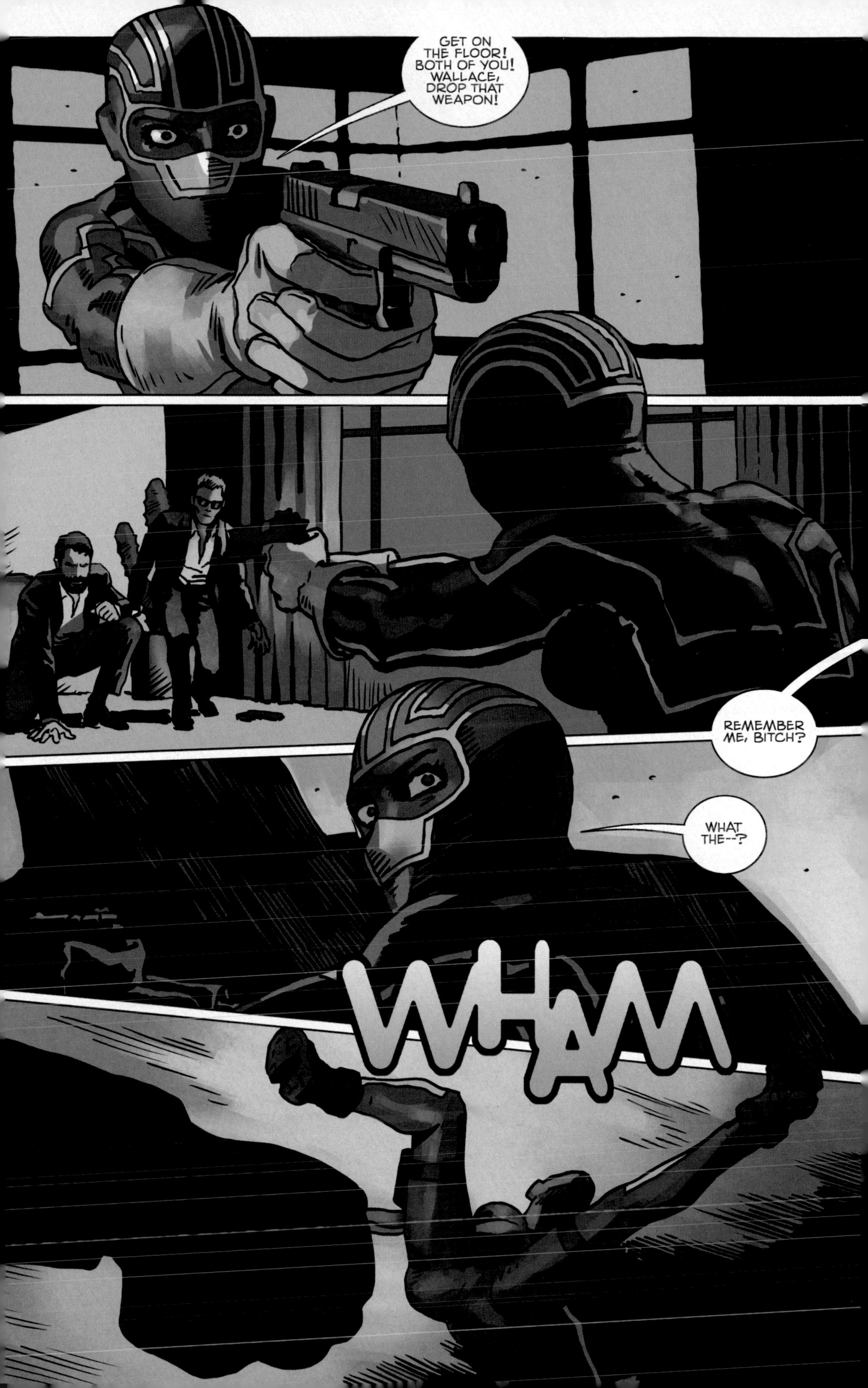
GET ON THE FLOOR! BOTH OF YOU! WALLACE, DROP THAT WEAPON!
REMEMBER ME, BITCH?
WHAT THE--?
WHAM

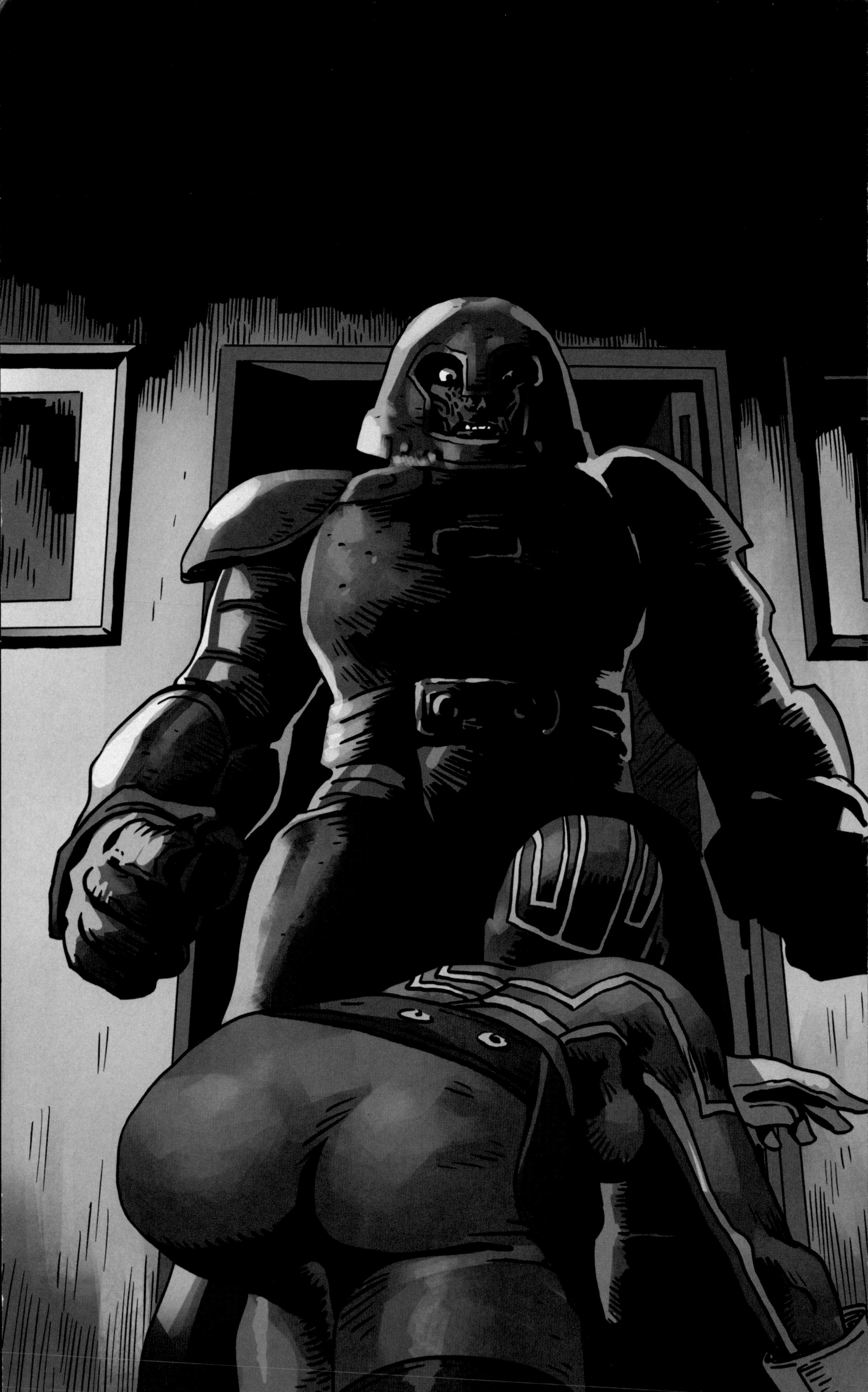

SIX

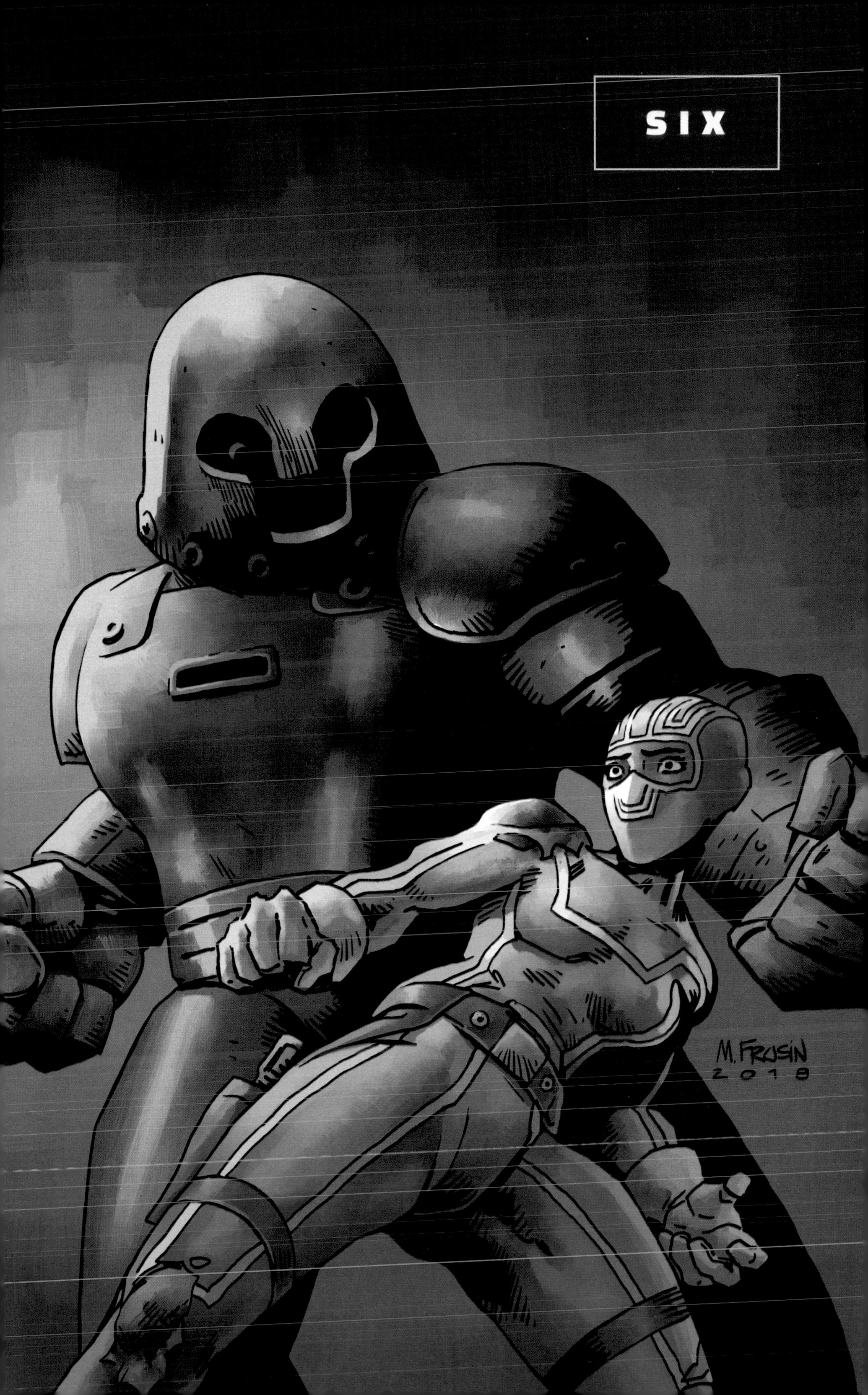
M. FRUSIN
2018

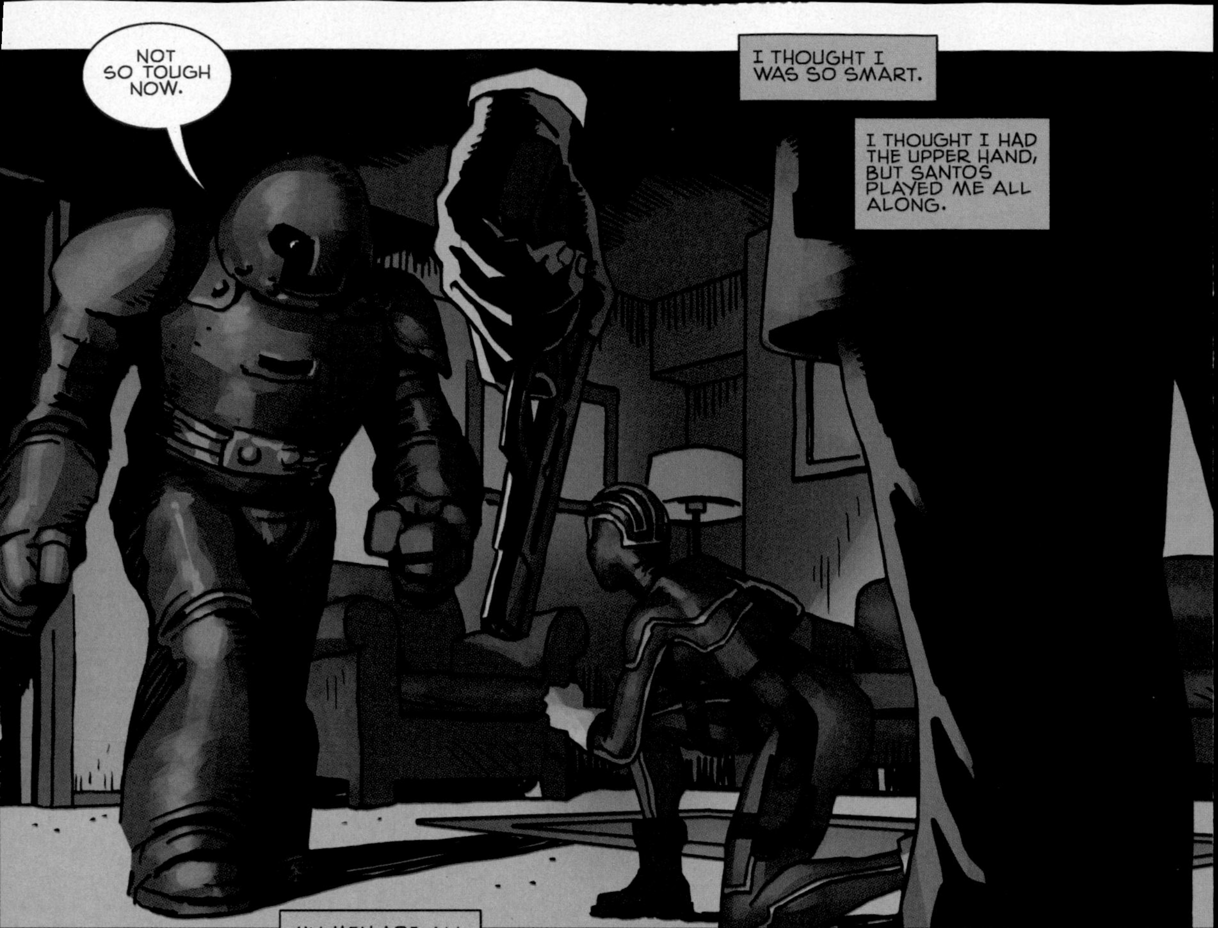
NOT SO TOUGH NOW.
I THOUGHT I WAS SO SMART.
I THOUGHT I HAD THE UPPER HAND, BUT SANTOS PLAYED ME ALL ALONG.

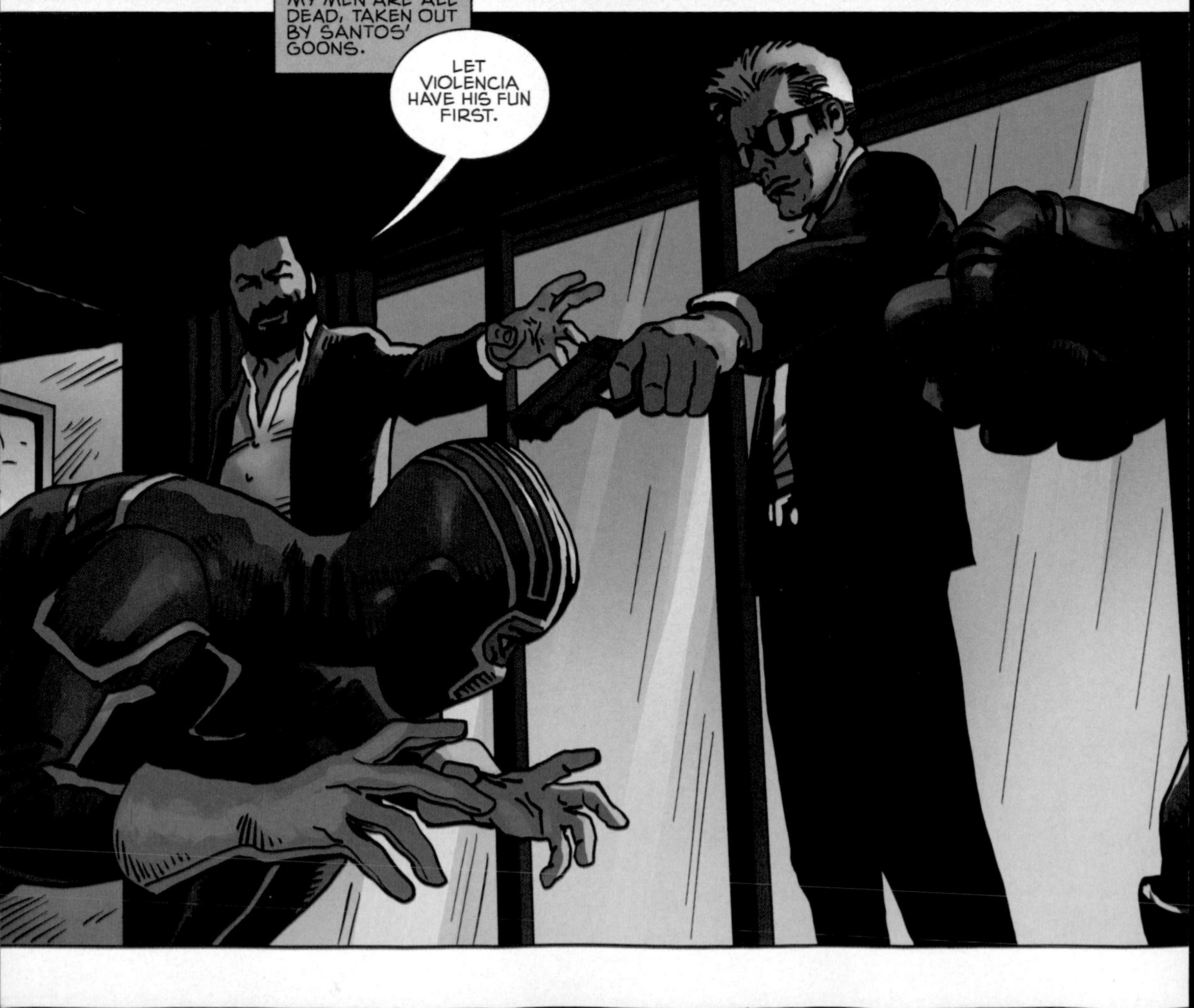
MY MEN ARE ALL DEAD, TAKEN OUT BY SANTOS' GOONS.
LET VIOLENCIA HAVE HIS FUN FIRST.

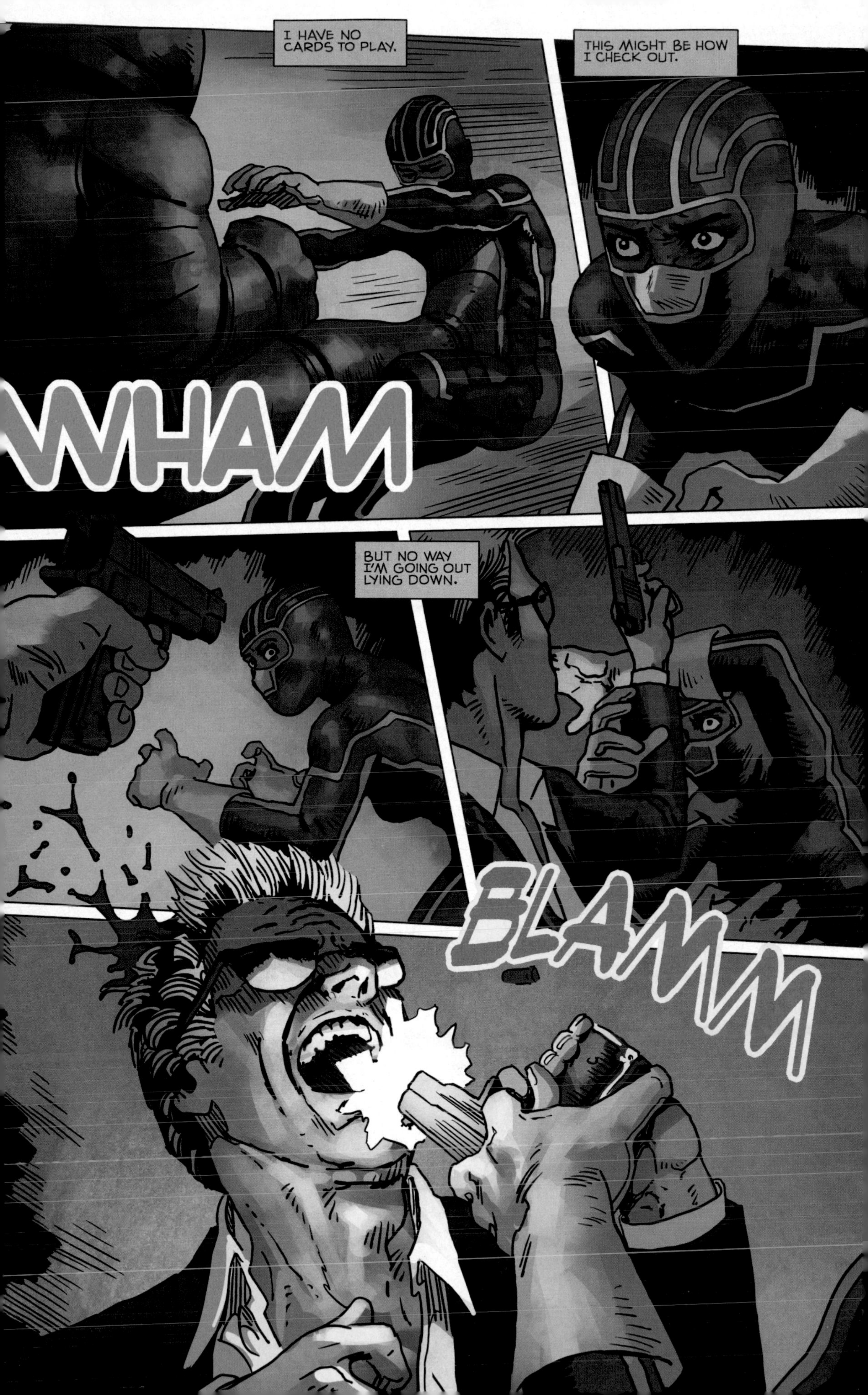
I HAVE NO CARDS TO PLAY.
THIS MIGHT BE HOW I CHECK OUT.
WHAM
BUT NO WAY I'M GOING OUT LYING DOWN.
BLAMM

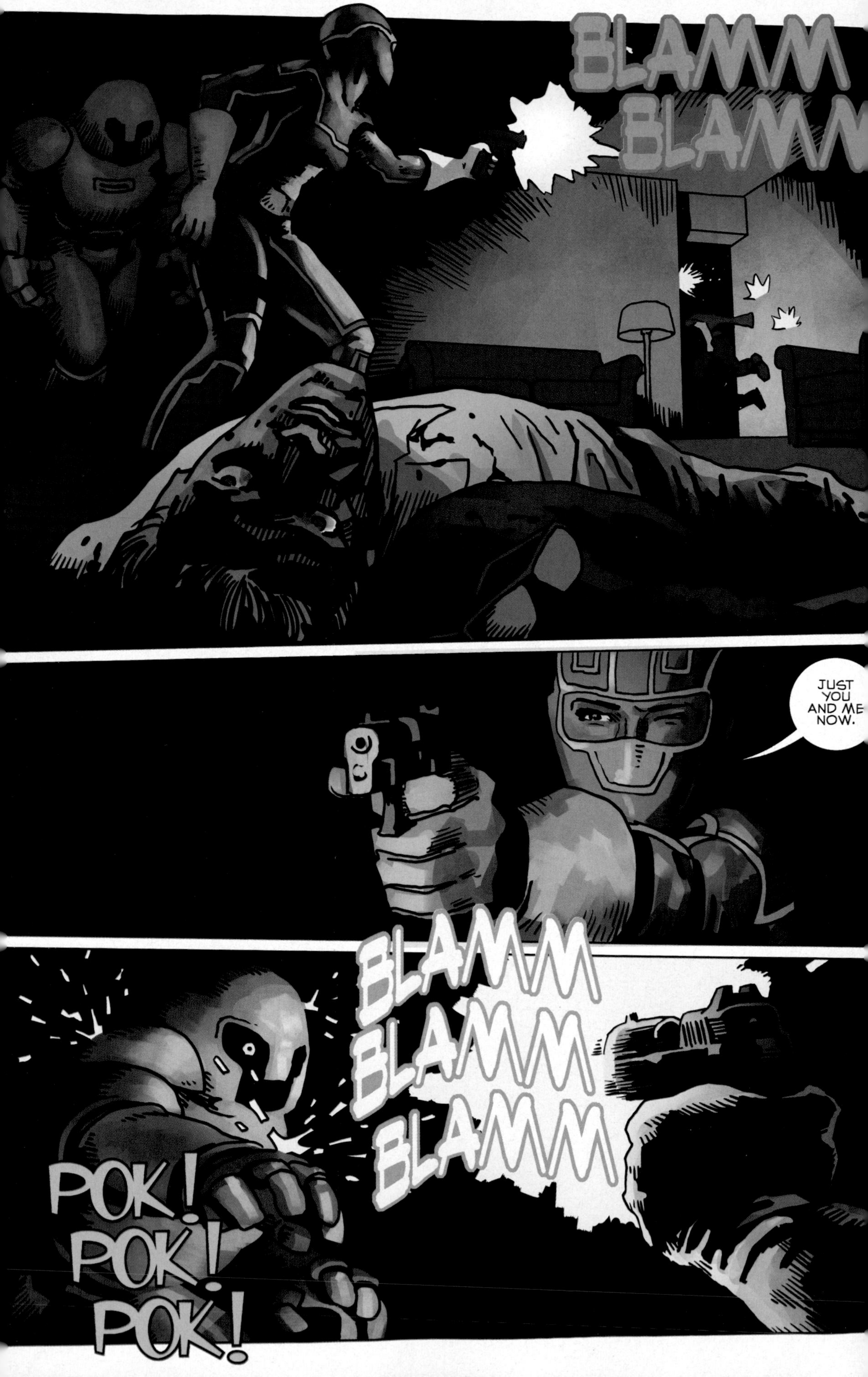
BLAMM
BLAMM
JUST YOU AND ME NOW.
BLAMM
BLAMM
BLAMM
POK!
POK!
POK!

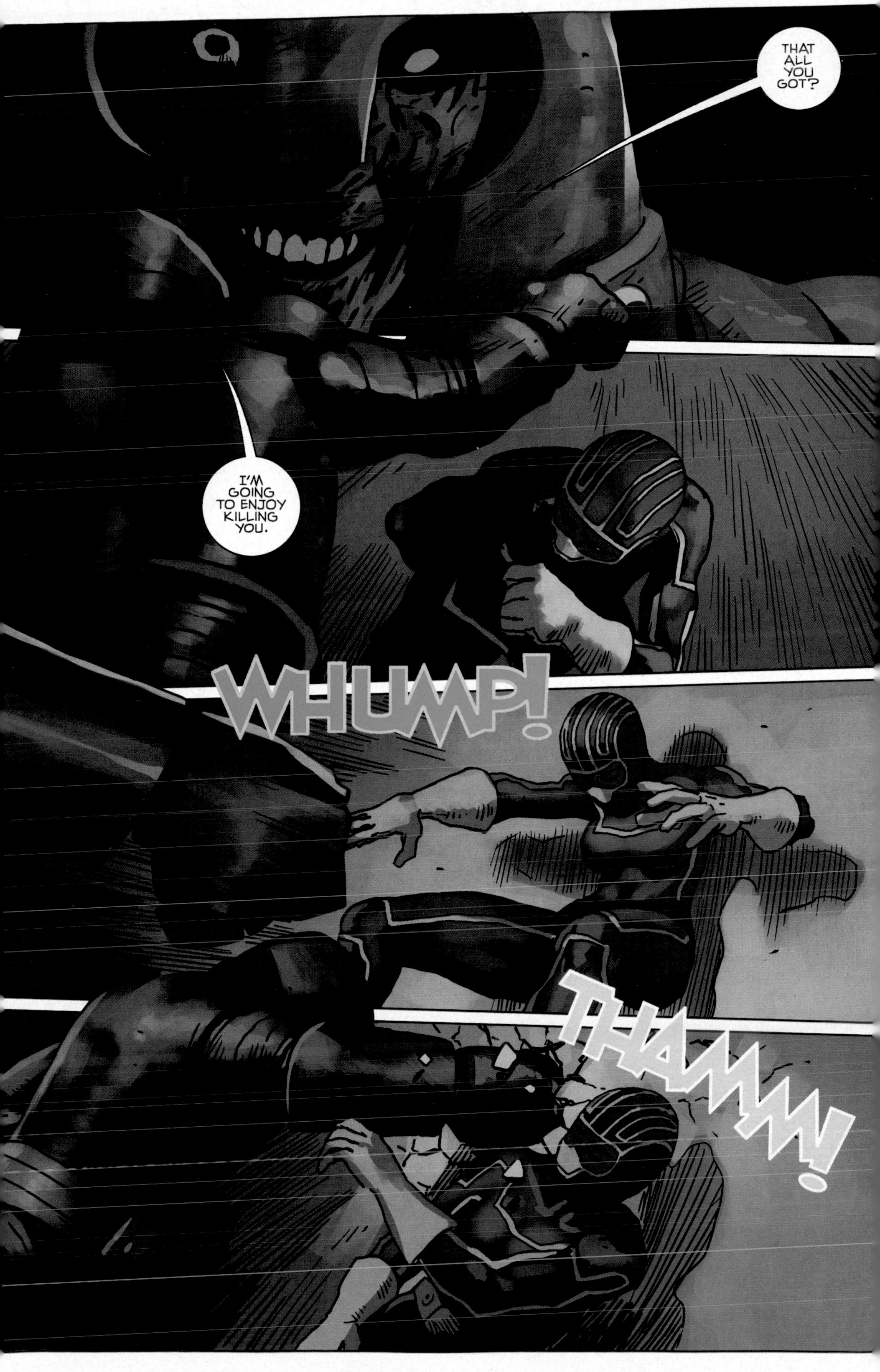
THAT ALL YOU GOT?
I'M GOING TO ENJOY KILLING YOU.
WHUMP!
THAMM!

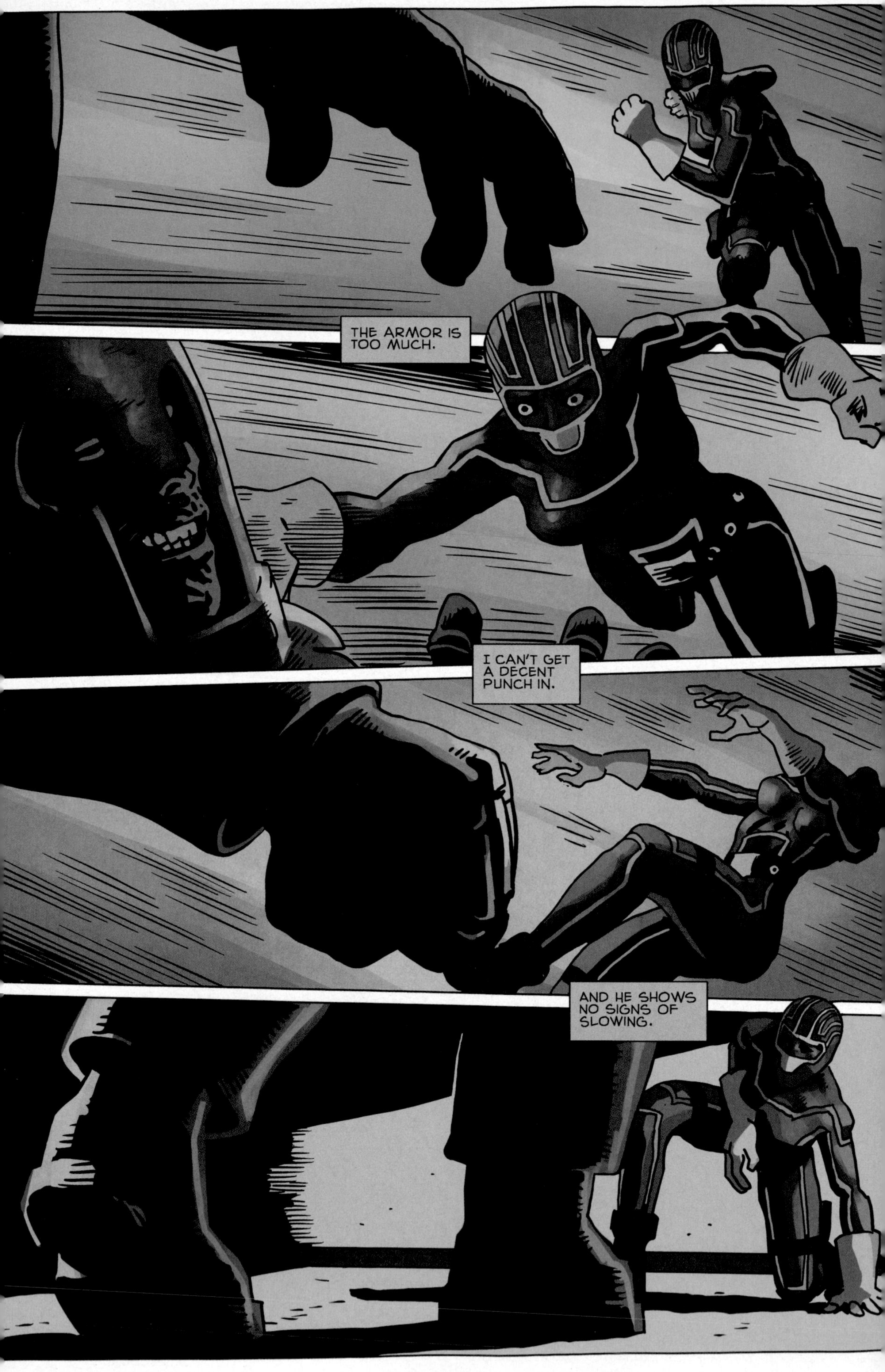
THE ARMOR IS TOO MUCH.
I CAN'T GET A DECENT PUNCH IN.
AND HE SHOWS NO SIGNS OF SLOWING.

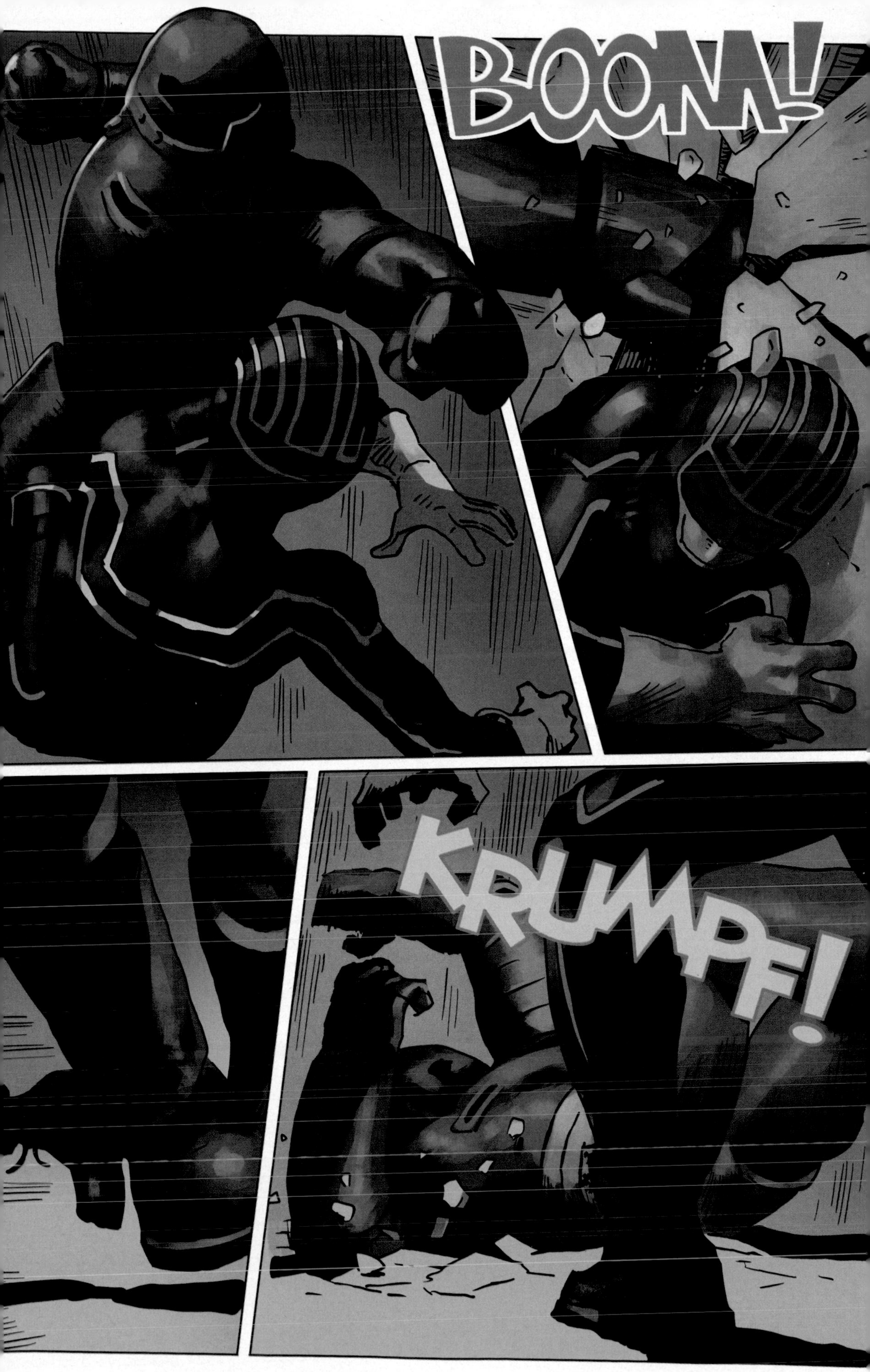
BOOM!
KRUMPF!

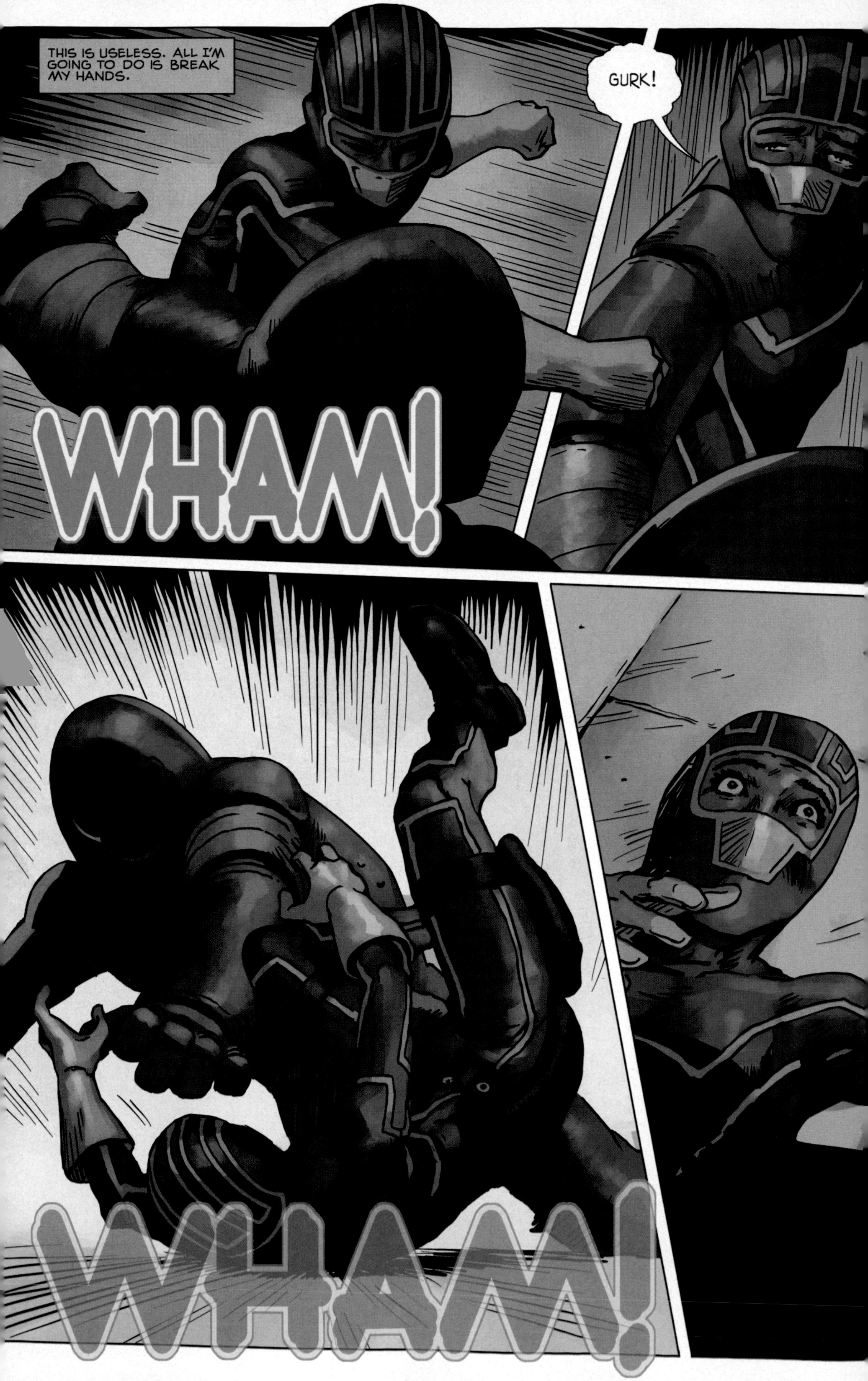
THIS IS USELESS. ALL I'M GOING TO DO IS BREAK MY HANDS.
WHAM!
GURK!
WHAM!

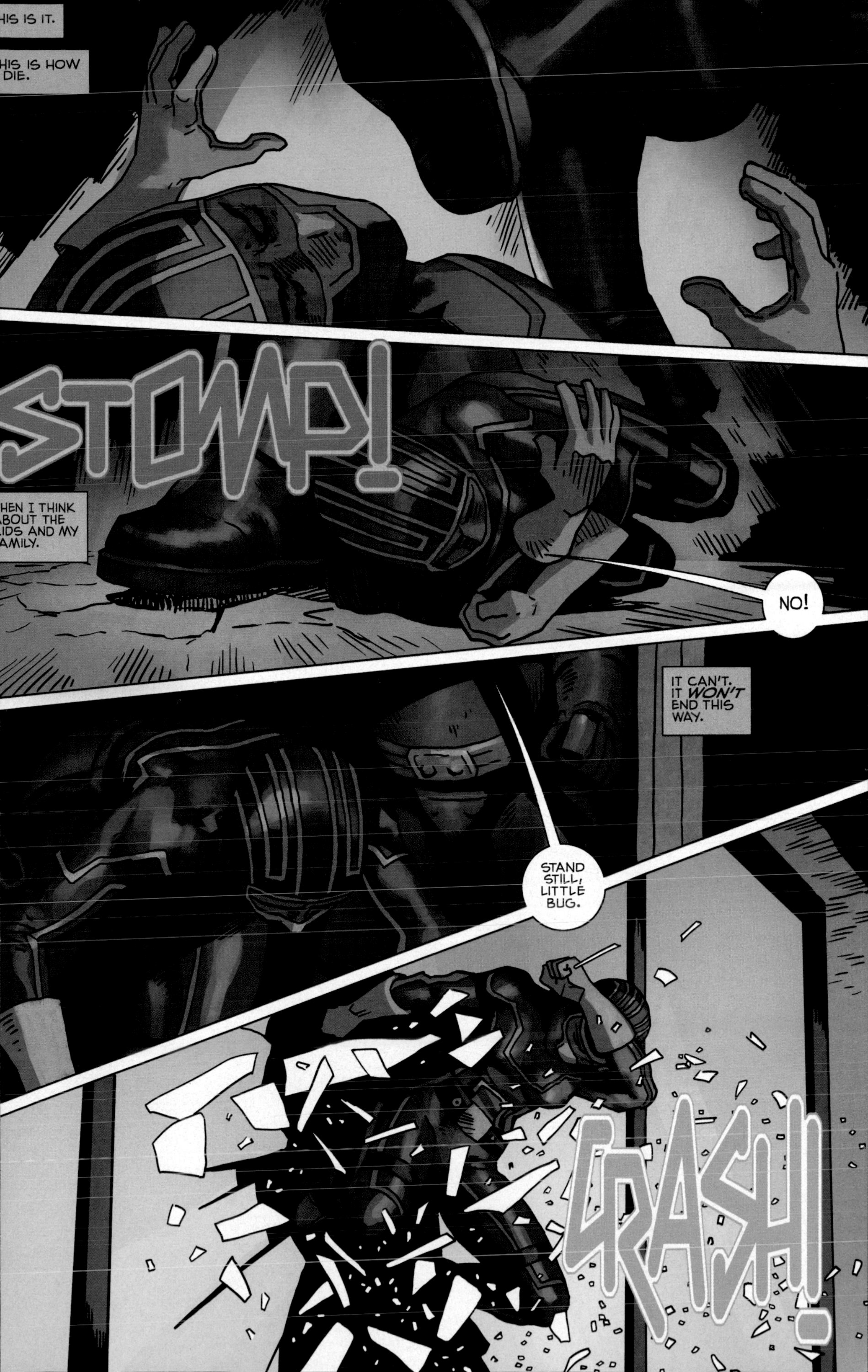
HIS IS IT.
HIS IS HOW
DIE.
STOMP!
HEN I THINK
ABOUT THE
IDS AND MY
AMILY.
NO!
IT CAN'T. IT *WON'T* END THIS WAY.
STAND STILL, LITTLE BUG.
CRASH!!

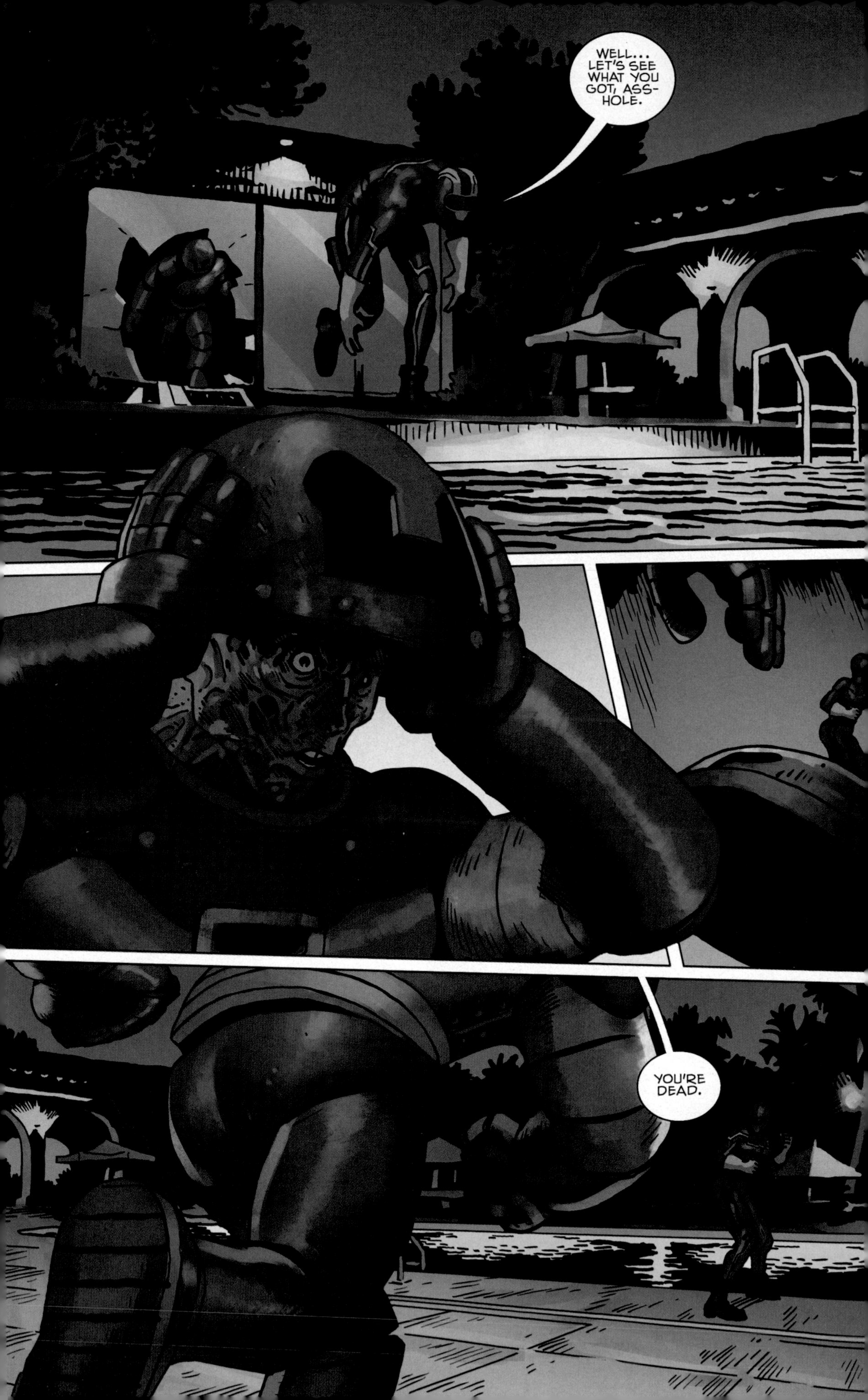
WELL... LET'S SEE WHAT YOU GOT, ASS-HOLE.
YOU'RE DEAD.

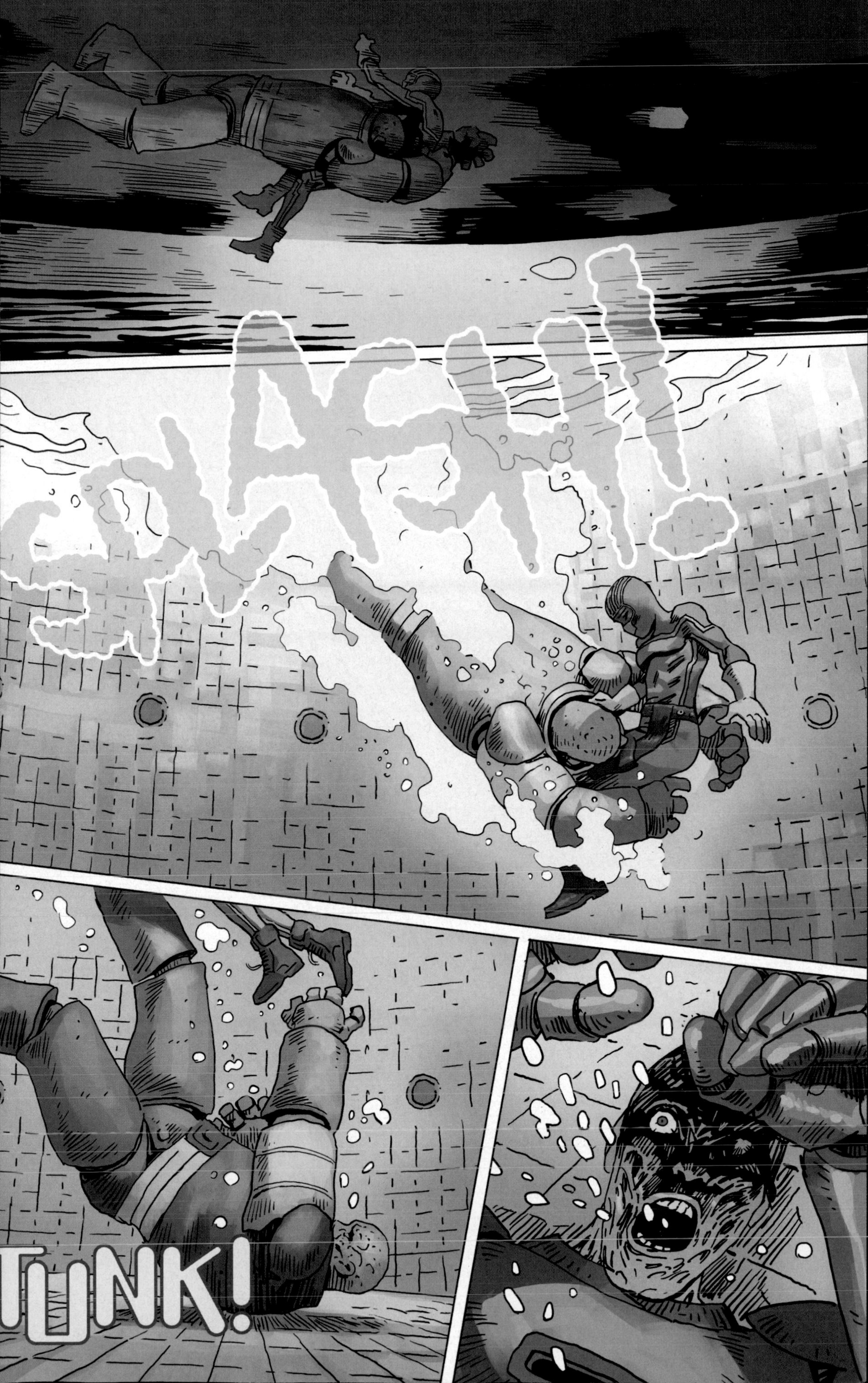
SPLASH!
TUNK!

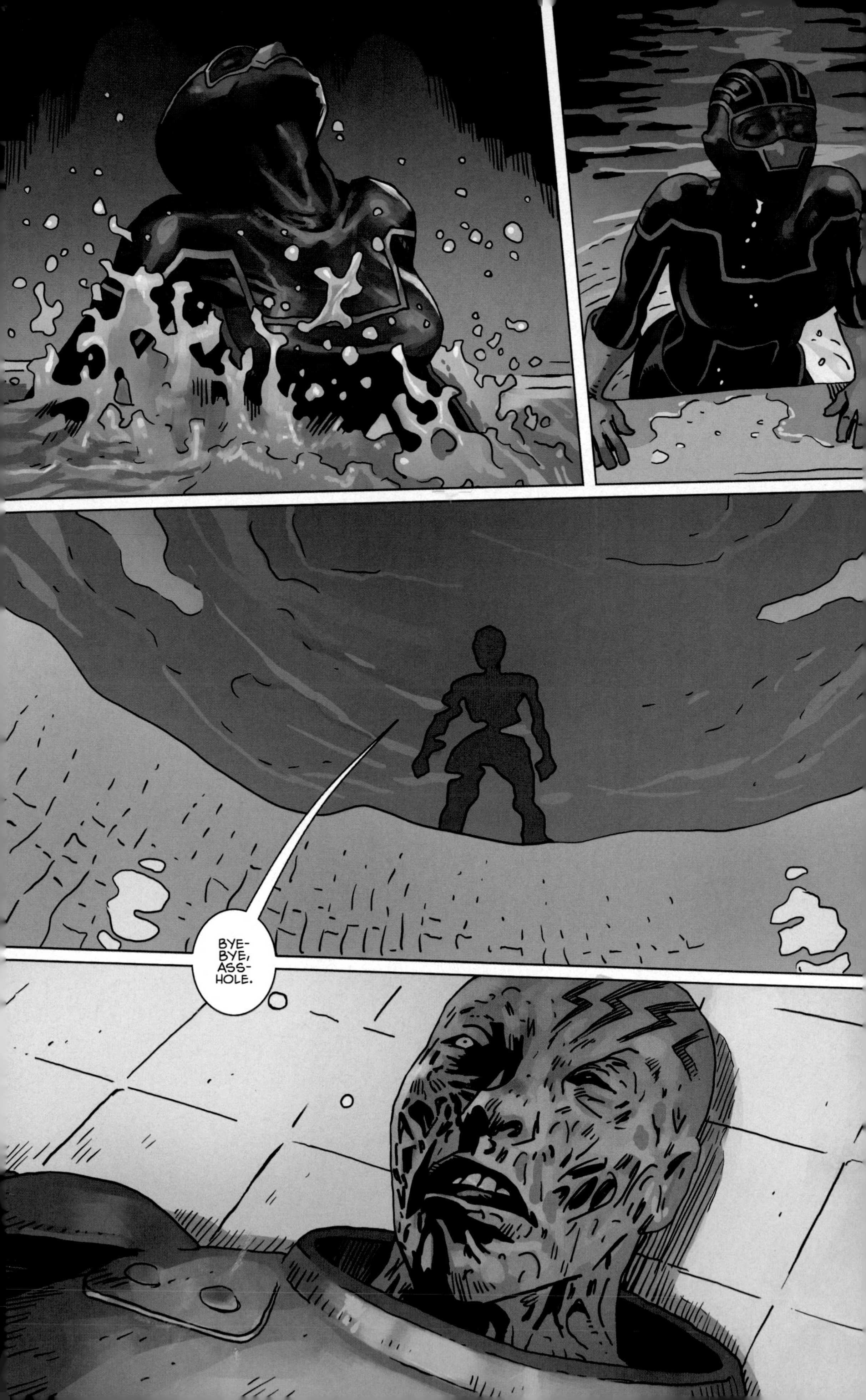
BYE-BYE, ASS-HOLE.

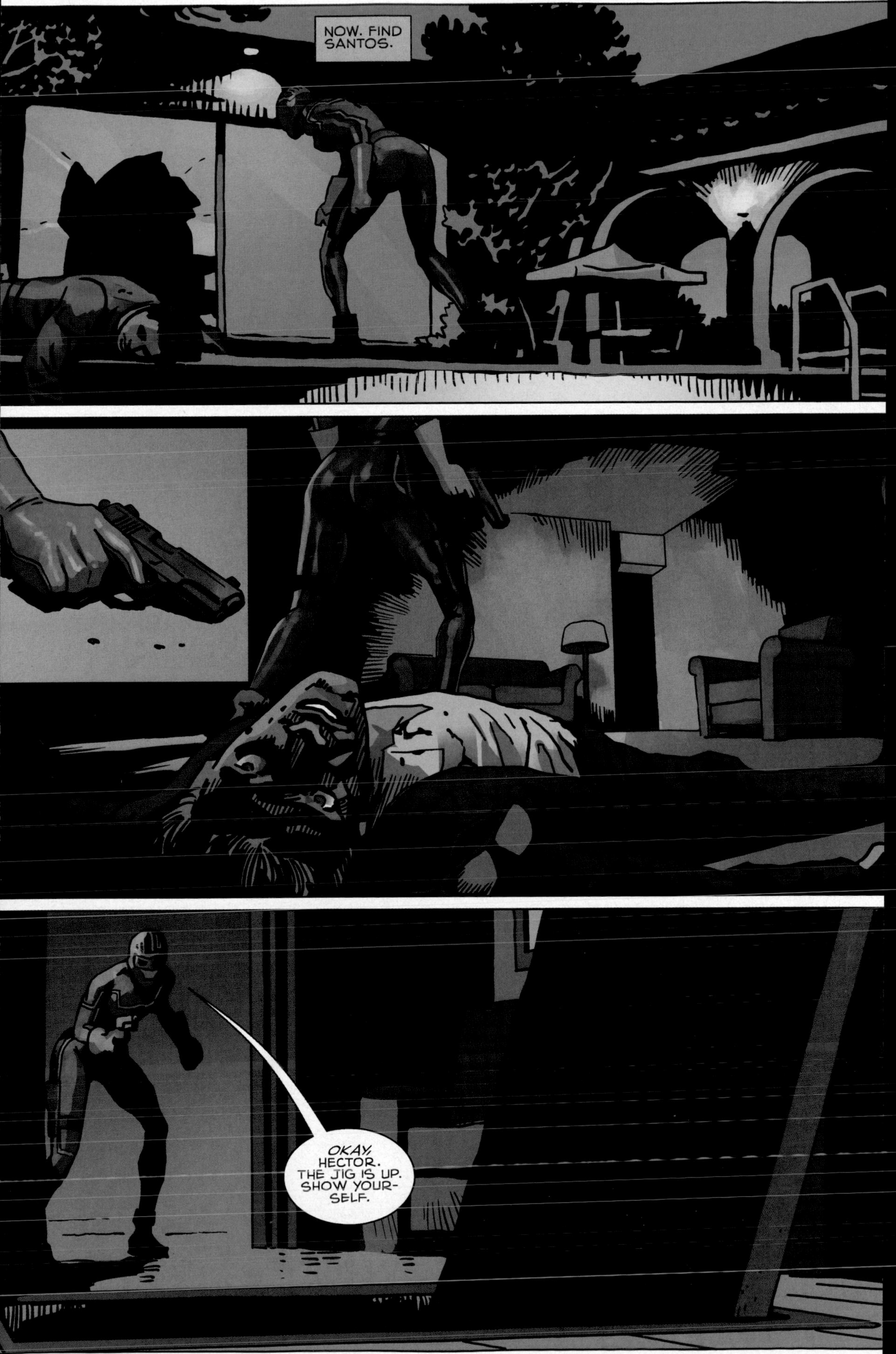
NOW. FIND SANTOS.
OKAY, HECTOR. THE JIG IS UP. SHOW YOUR-SELF.

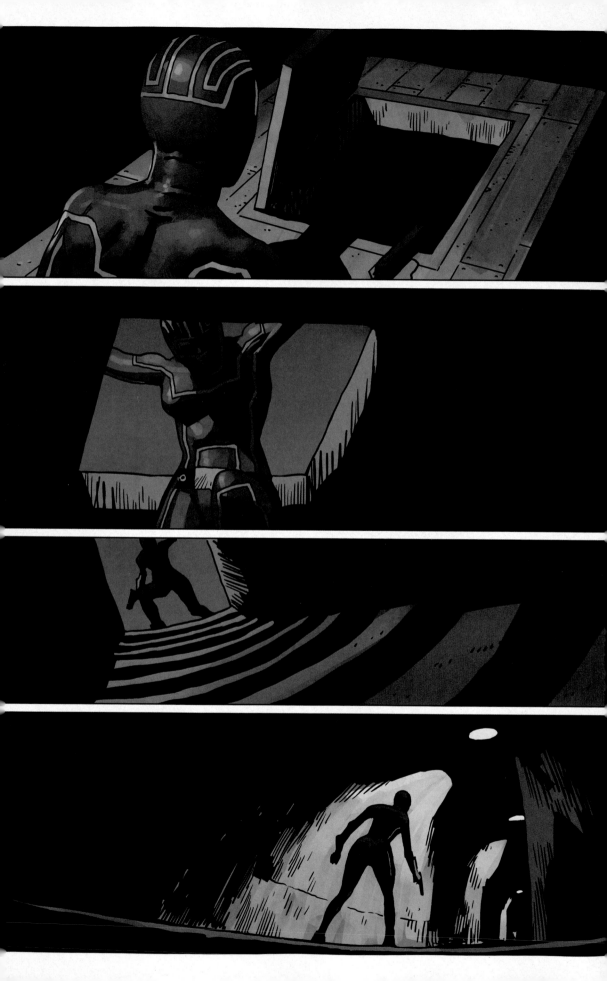

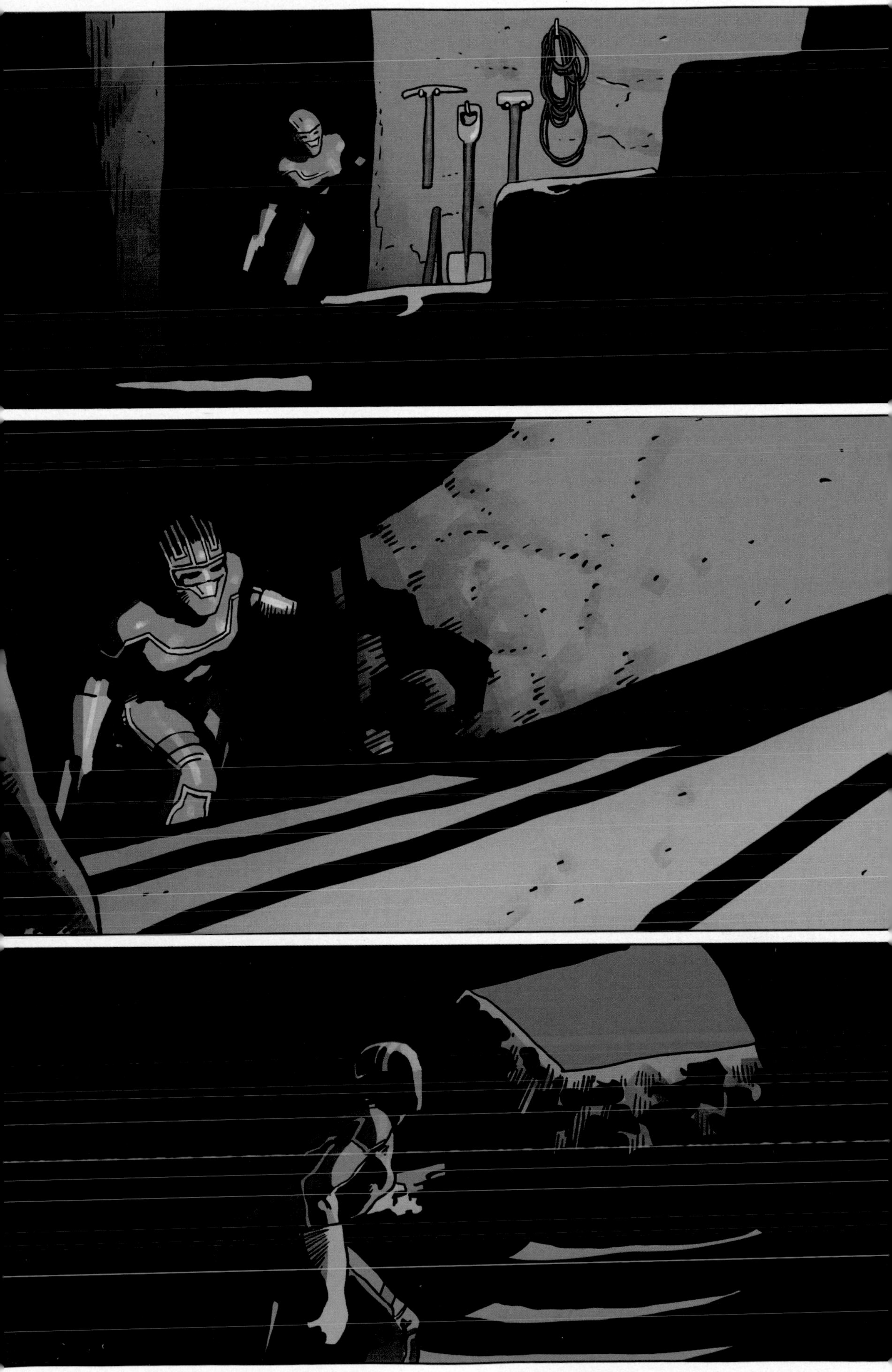

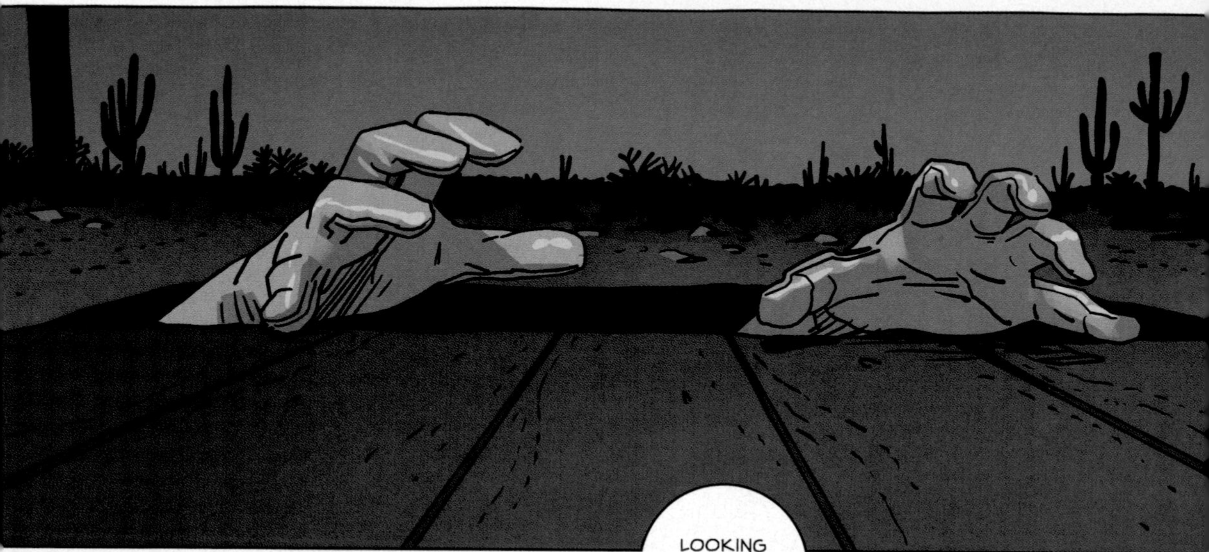

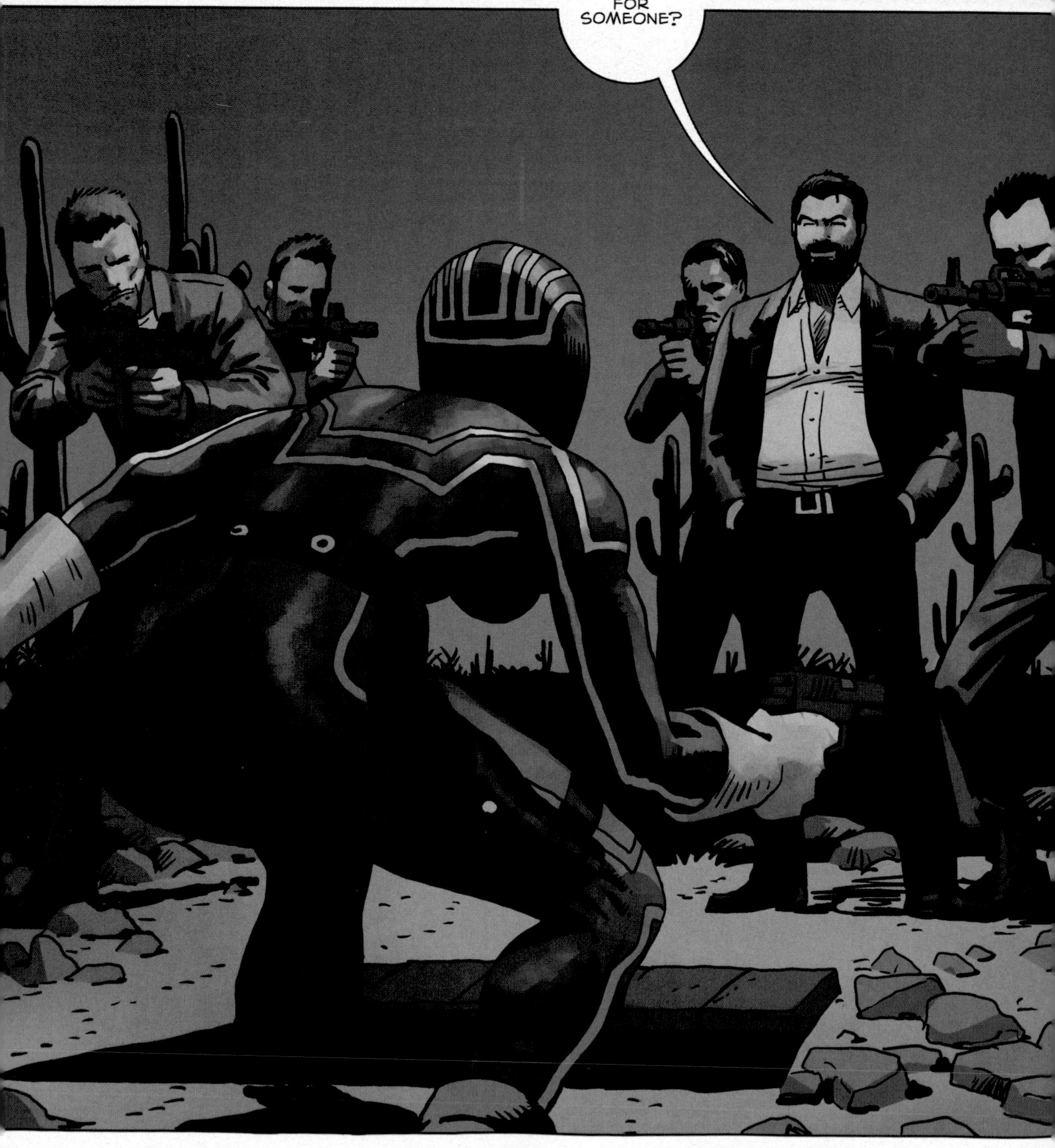
LOOKING FOR SOMEONE?

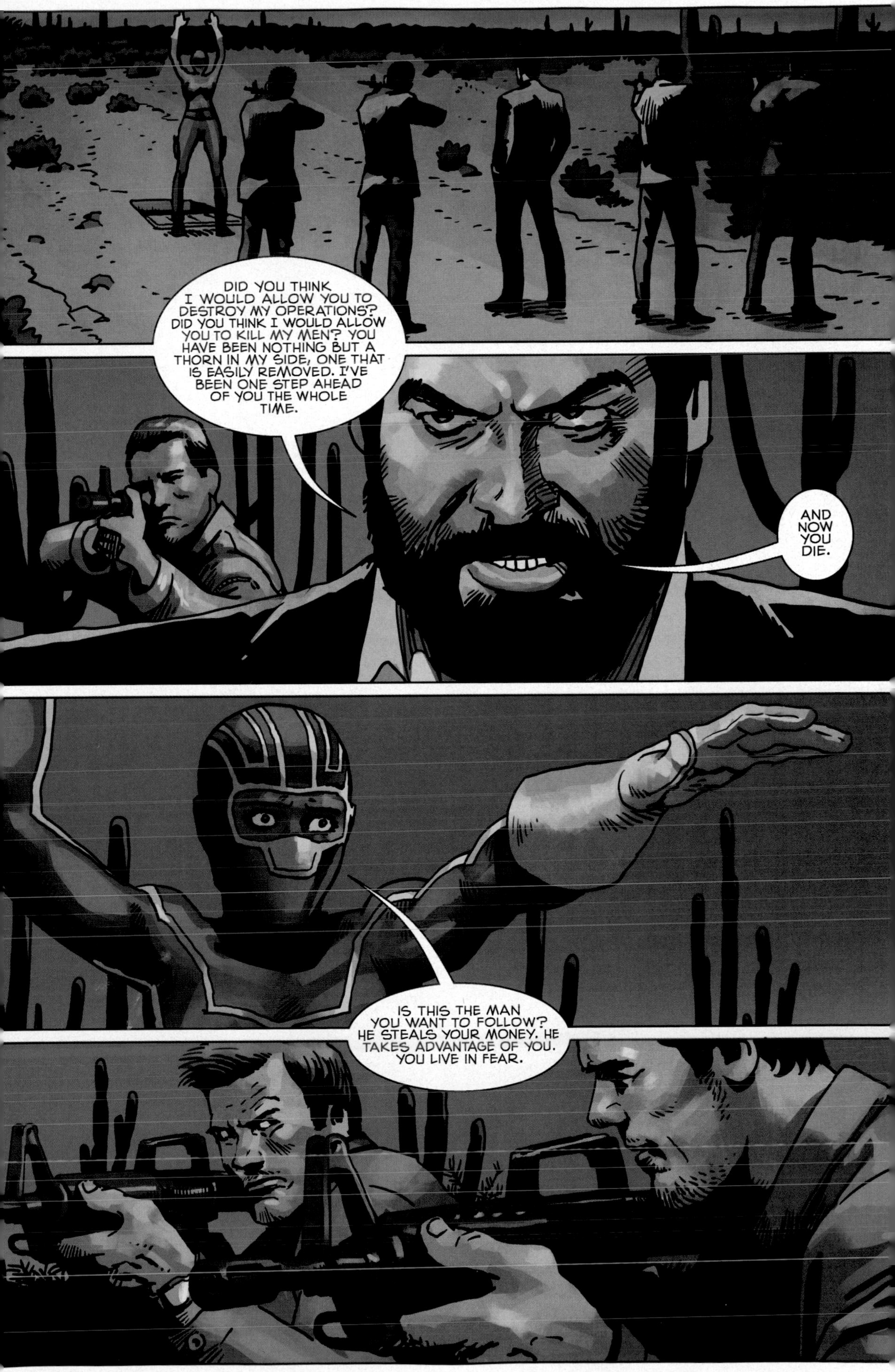
DID YOU THINK I WOULD ALLOW YOU TO DESTROY MY OPERATIONS? DID YOU THINK I WOULD ALLOW YOU TO KILL MY MEN? YOU HAVE BEEN NOTHING BUT A THORN IN MY SIDE, ONE THAT IS EASILY REMOVED. I'VE BEEN ONE STEP AHEAD OF YOU THE WHOLE TIME.
AND NOW YOU DIE.
IS THIS THE MAN YOU WANT TO FOLLOW? HE STEALS YOUR MONEY. HE TAKES ADVANTAGE OF YOU. YOU LIVE IN FEAR.

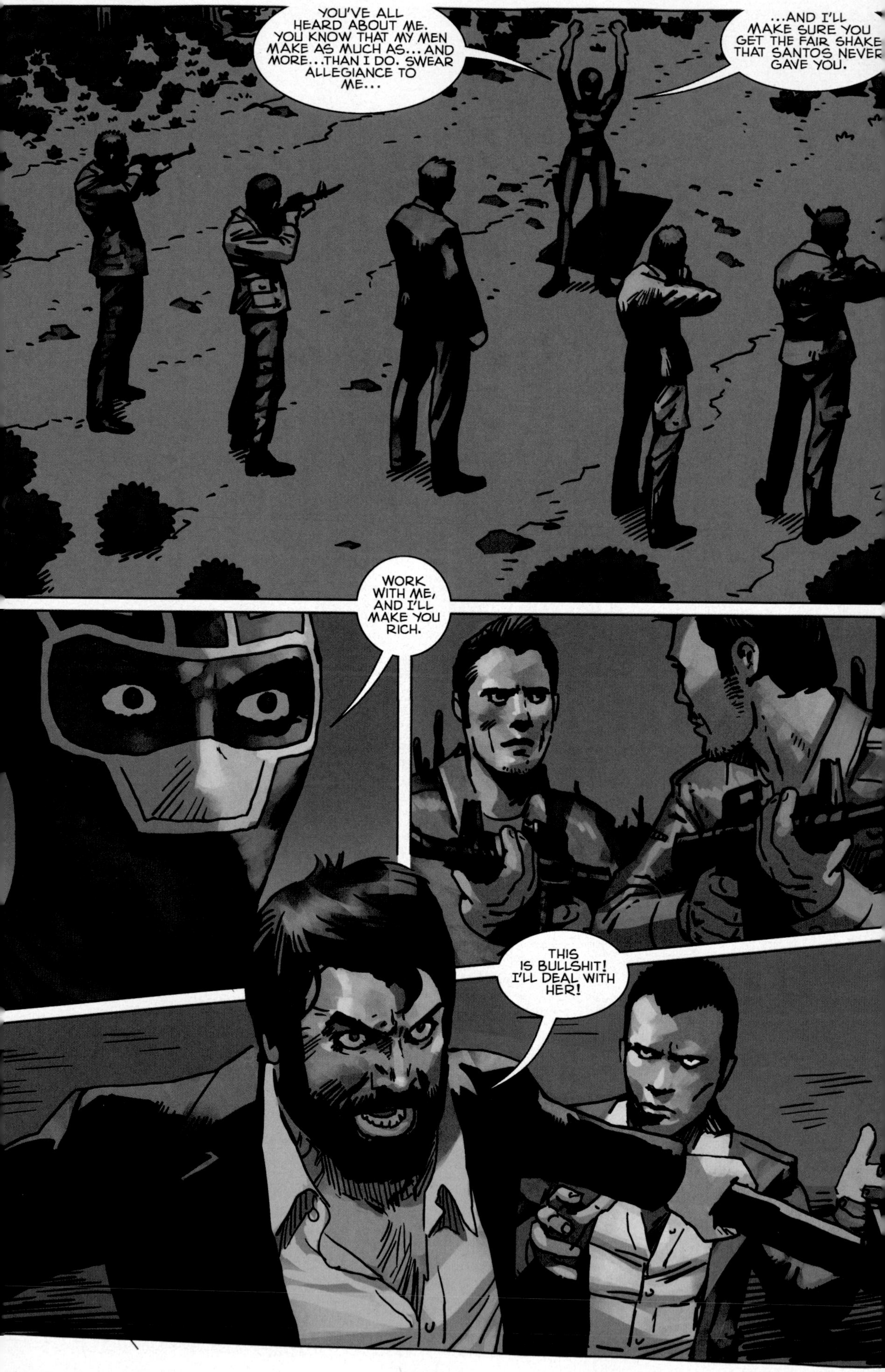
YOU'VE ALL HEARD ABOUT ME. YOU KNOW THAT MY MEN MAKE AS MUCH AS... AND MORE... THAN I DO. SWEAR ALLEGIANCE TO ME...
...AND I'LL MAKE SURE YOU GET THE FAIR SHAKE THAT SANTOS NEVER GAVE YOU.
WORK WITH ME, AND I'LL MAKE YOU RICH.
THIS IS BULLSHIT! I'LL DEAL WITH HER!

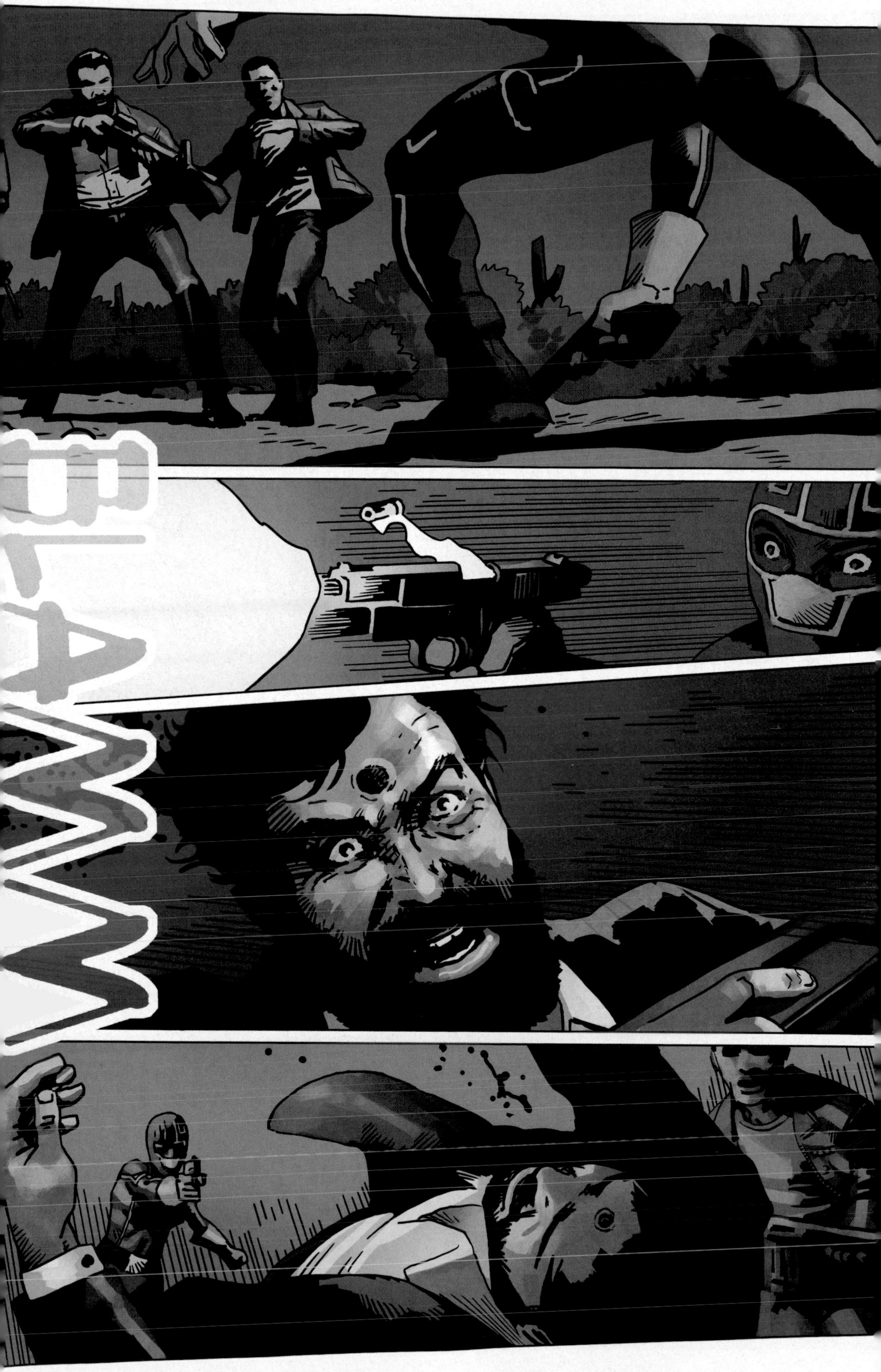
BLAM

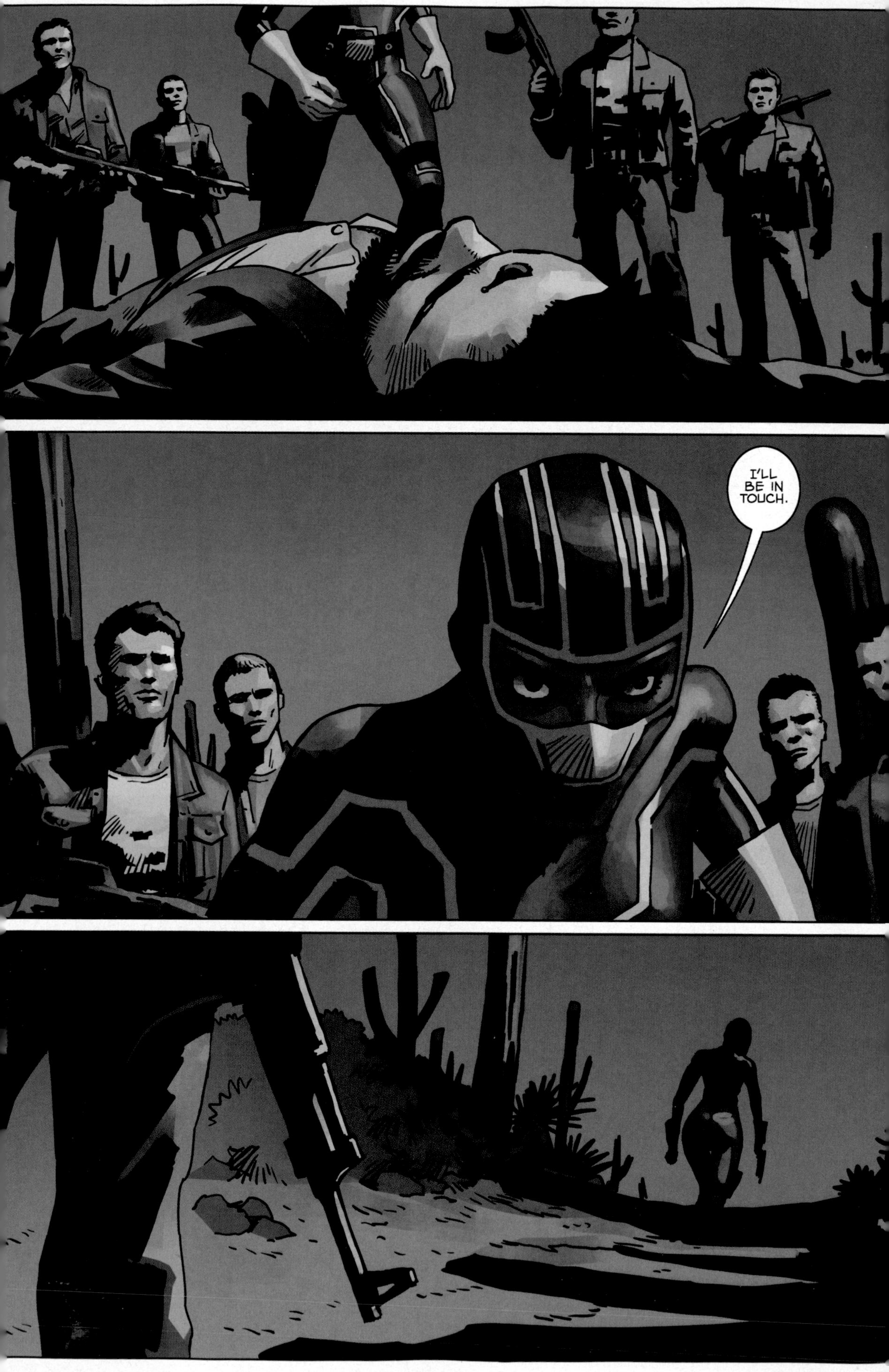
I'LL BE IN TOUCH.

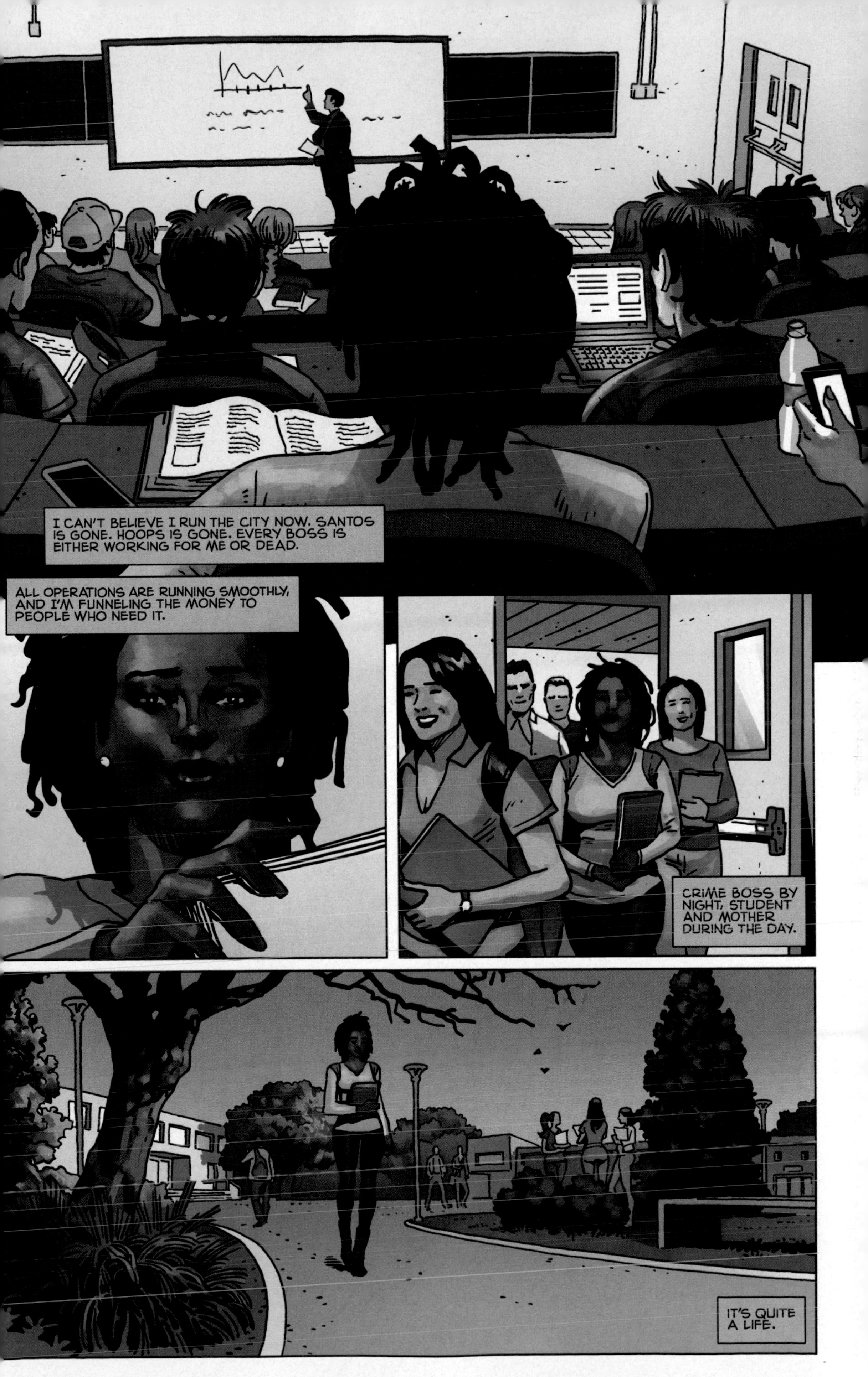
I CAN'T BELIEVE I RUN THE CITY NOW. SANTOS IS GONE. HOOPS IS GONE. EVERY BOSS IS EITHER WORKING FOR ME OR DEAD.
ALL OPERATIONS ARE RUNNING SMOOTHLY, AND I'M FUNNELING THE MONEY TO PEOPLE WHO NEED IT.
CRIME BOSS BY NIGHT, STUDENT AND MOTHER DURING THE DAY.
IT'S QUITE A LIFE.

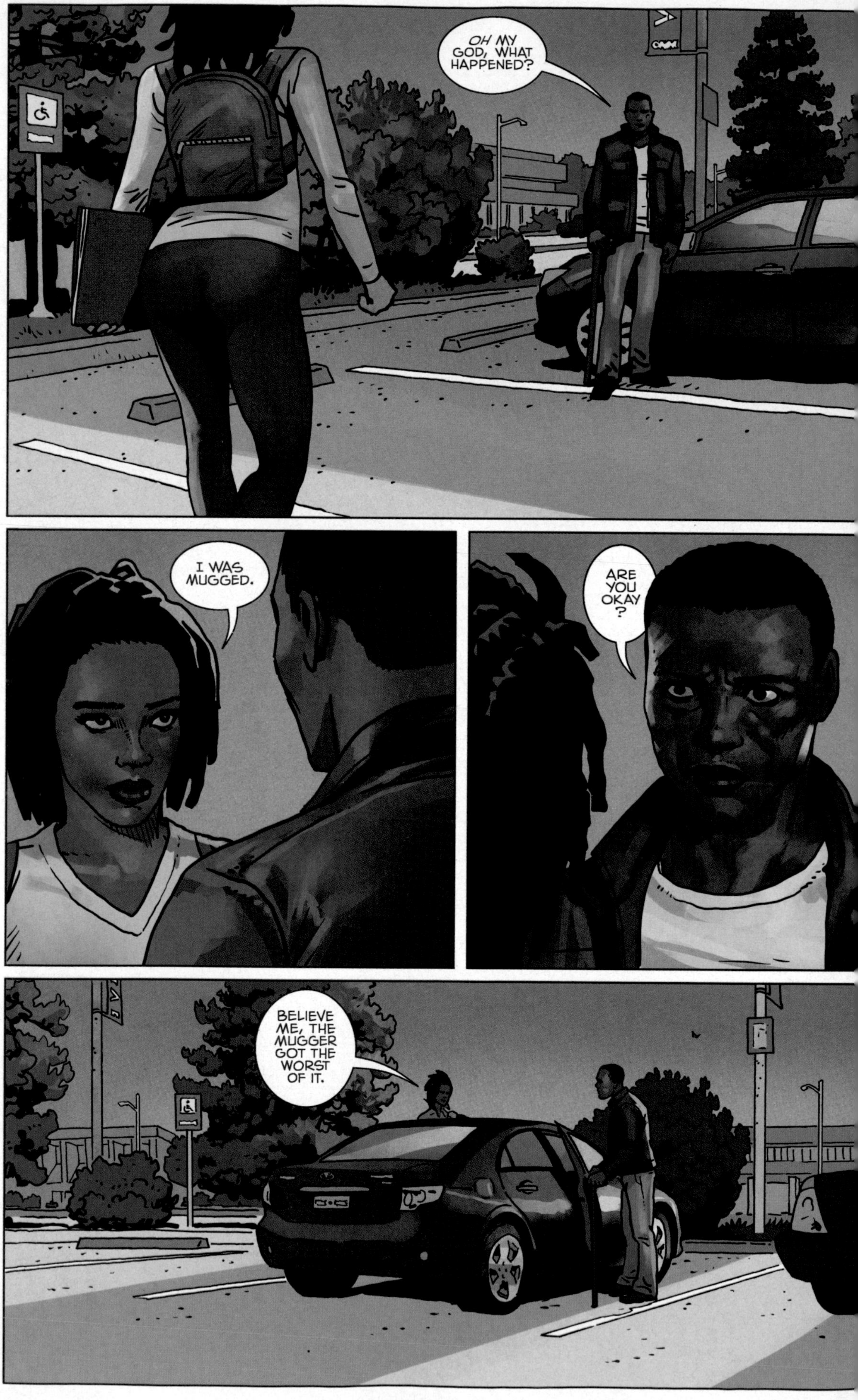
OH MY GOD, WHAT HAPPENED?
I WAS MUGGED.
ARE YOU OKAY?
BELIEVE ME, THE MUGGER GOT THE WORST OF IT.

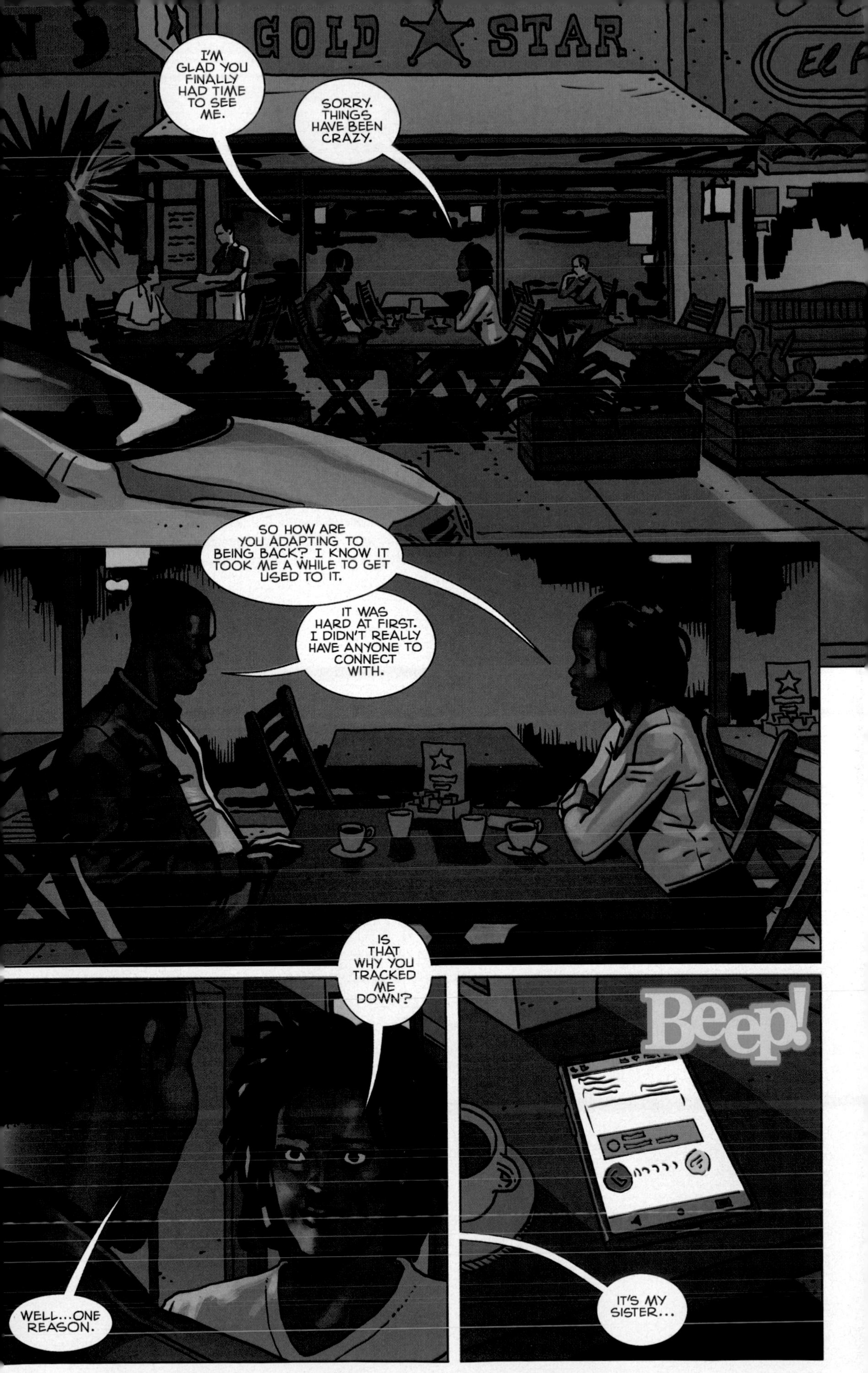
GOLD STAR
I'M GLAD YOU FINALLY HAD TIME TO SEE ME.
SORRY. THINGS HAVE BEEN CRAZY.
SO HOW ARE YOU ADAPTING TO BEING BACK? I KNOW IT TOOK ME A WHILE TO GET USED TO IT.
IT WAS HARD AT FIRST. I DIDN'T REALLY HAVE ANYONE TO CONNECT WITH.
IS THAT WHY YOU TRACKED ME DOWN?
WELL...ONE REASON.
Beep!
IT'S MY SISTER...

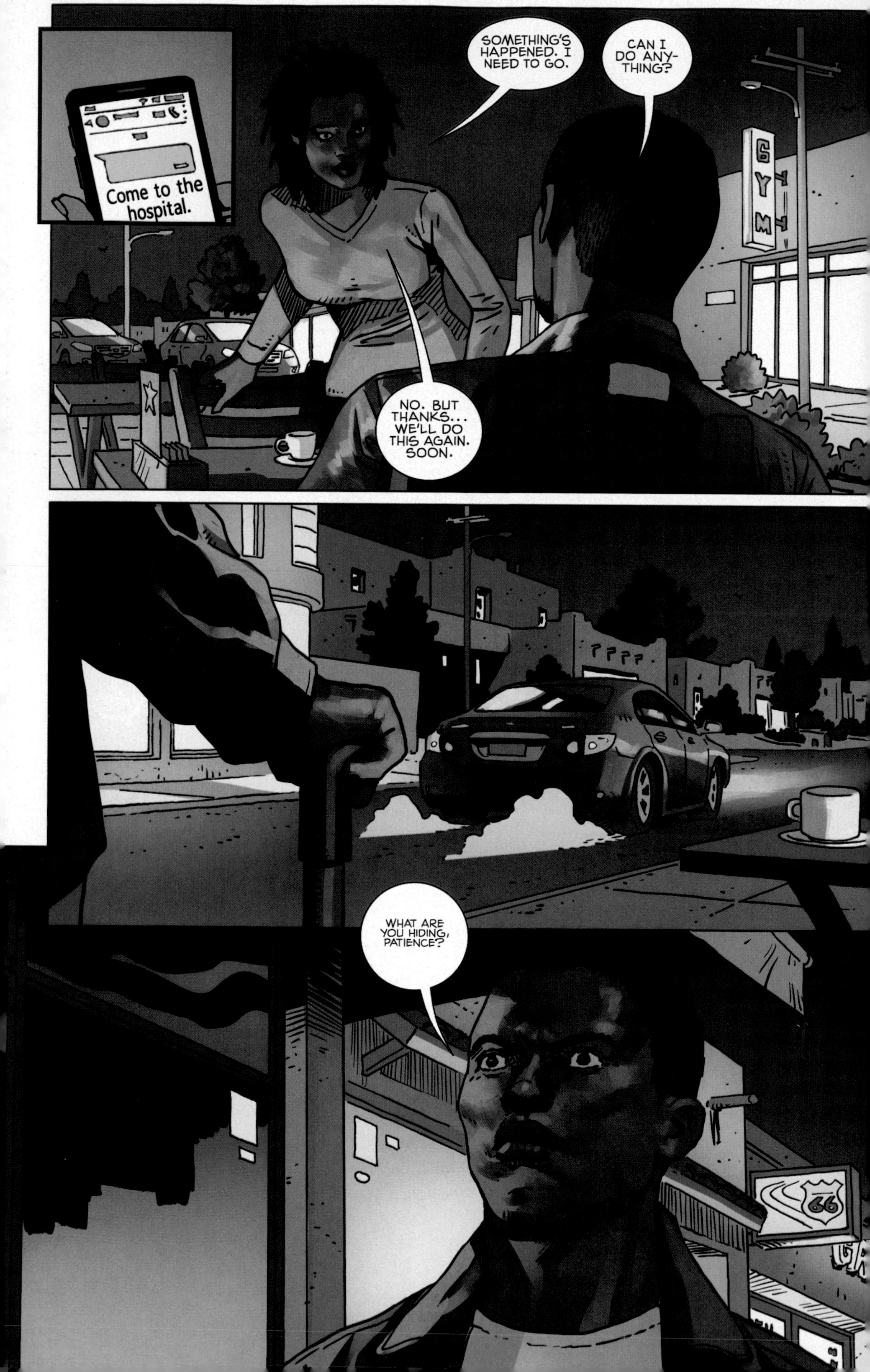
Come to the hospital.
SOMETHING'S HAPPENED. I NEED TO GO.
CAN I DO ANY-THING?
NO. BUT THANKS... WE'LL DO THIS AGAIN. SOON.
GYM
WHAT ARE YOU HIDING, PATIENCE?
66

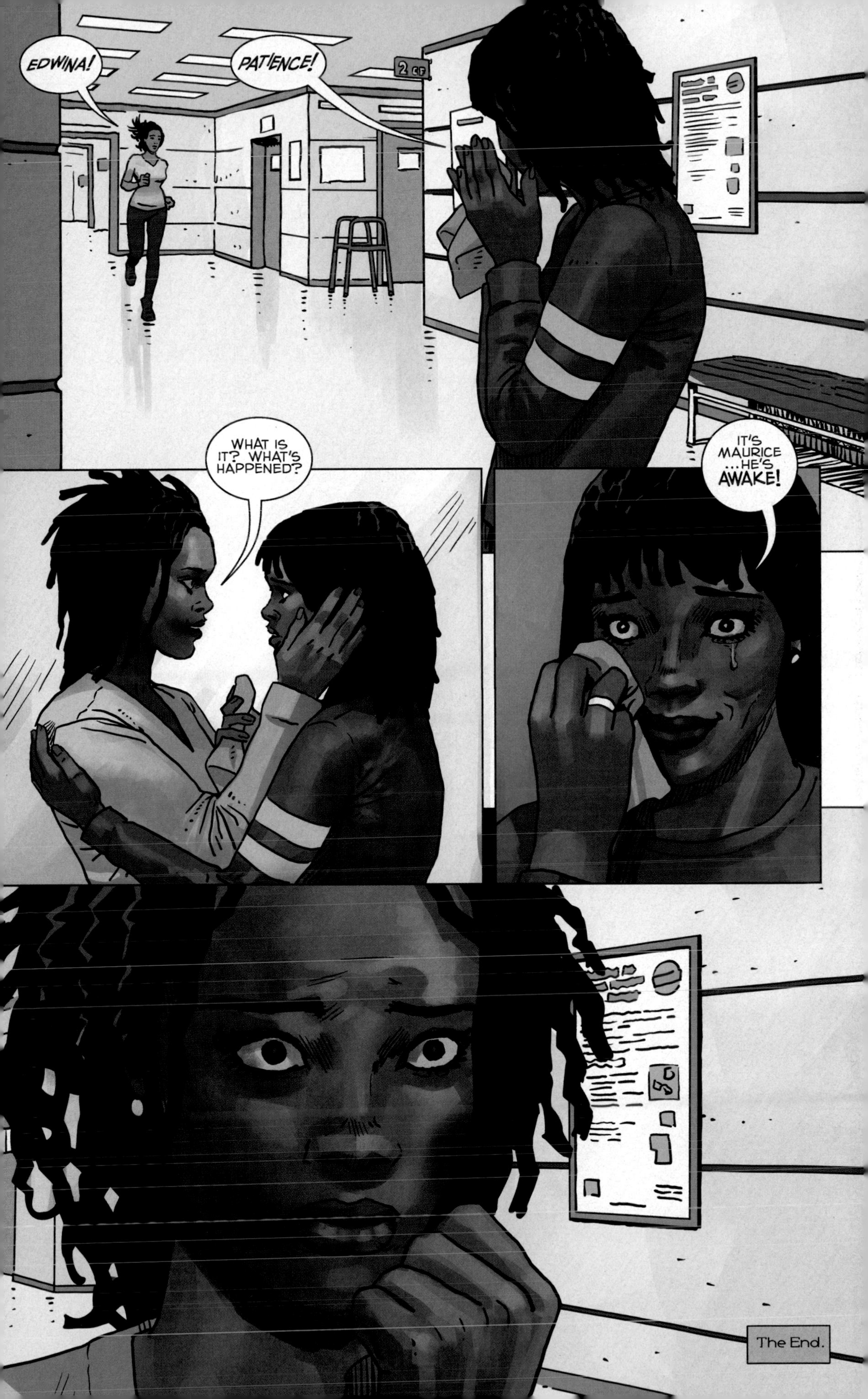
EDWINA!
PATIENCE!
2 CF
WHAT IS IT? WHAT'S HAPPENED?
IT'S MAURICE ...HE'S AWAKE!
The End.

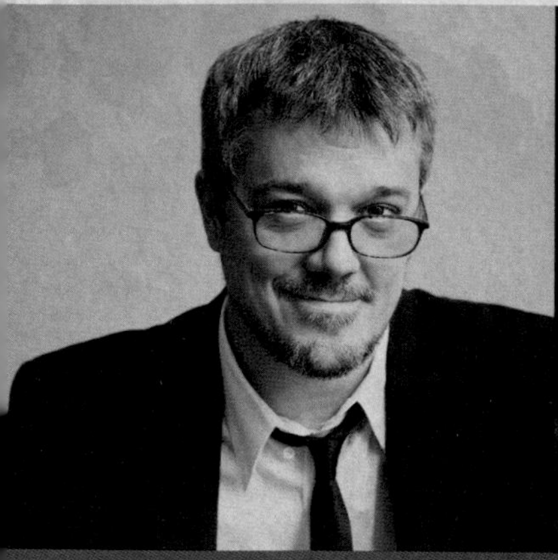

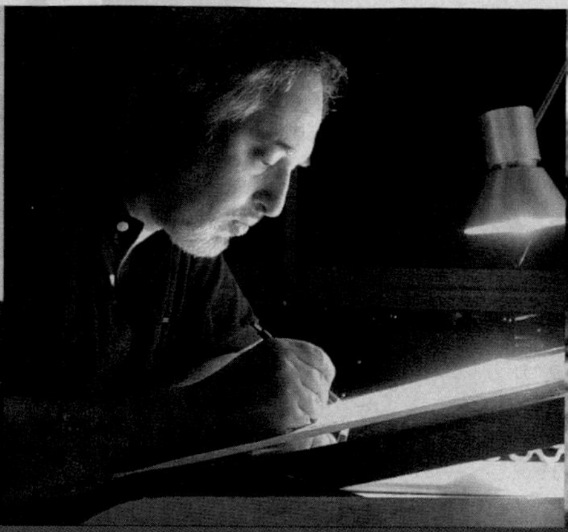

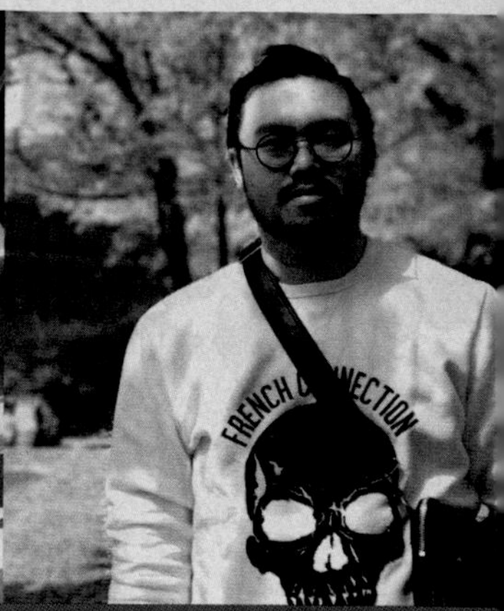

STEVE NILES

is best known for **30 DAYS OF NIGHT**, **CRIMINAL MACABRE**, **SIMON DARK**, **MYSTERY SOCIETY**, **FRANKENSTEIN ALIVE, ALIVE!**, **MONSTER & MADMAN**, **WINNEBAGO GRAVEYARD** and **BATMAN: GOTHAM COUNTY LINE.**

Niles currently works for comic publishers including Black Mask, IDW, Image and Dark Horse. Steve is currently writing **THE OCTOBER FACTION** for IDW.

30 DAYS OF NIGHT was released in 2007 as a major motion picture. Other comics by Niles, including **REMAINS**, **ALEISTER ARCANE**, and **FREAKS OF THE HEARTLAND**, have been optioned for film.

Steve lives in the desert near Los Angeles with his wife Monica and a bunch of animals.

MARCELO FRUSIN

is an Argentinian comic artist and illustrator who has published works in editorials across the US, Europe, and South America.

He is best known for his critically acclaimed run as the artist of **HELLBLAZER**, teaming with writers Warren Ellis, Brian Azzarello, and Mike Carey. With Azzarello, Frusin also illustrated and co-created the monthly western **LOVELESS**. He has also contributed to other Vertigo titles, such as **FLICH**, **WEIRD WESTERN TALES**, **WEIRD WAR TALES**, and **TRANSMETROPOLITAN**.

In addition to his work for DC Comics, he worked for Marvel illustrating specials of **X-MEN** and **WOLVERINE**. In Europe, he co-created the series **L'EXPEDITION** with the French writer Richard Marazano, published by Dargaud of France. He is currently drawing the next arc of **KICK-ASS** written by Steve Niles and published by Image Comics.

SUNNY GHO

studied Graphic Design at Trisakti University, Indonesia, before going on to work for companies such as Top Cow, Imaginary Friends Studios, and GLITCH.

He has colored an impressive array of comic book titles, including **MARVEL'S CIVIL WAR II**, **THE INDESTRUCTIBLE HULK**, and **THE AVENGERS**. For Mark Millar, he has colored **SUPERCROOKS**, **SUPERIOR**, **JUPITER'S LEGACY 2**, and **HIT-GIRL**.

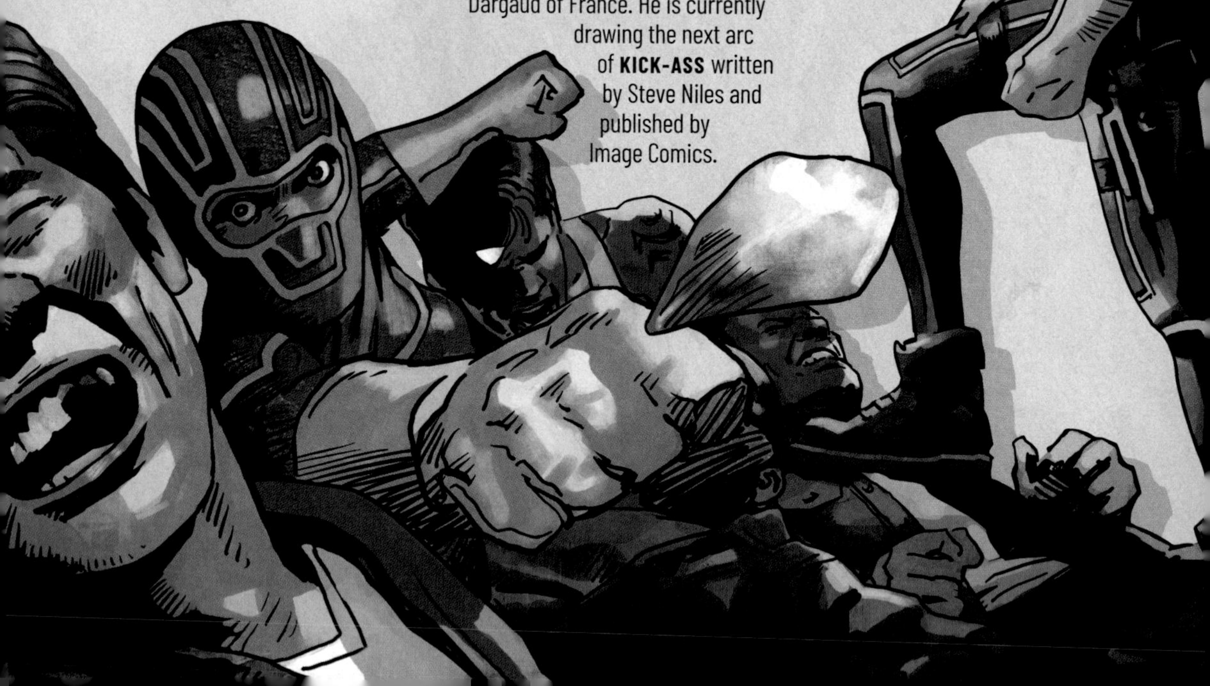

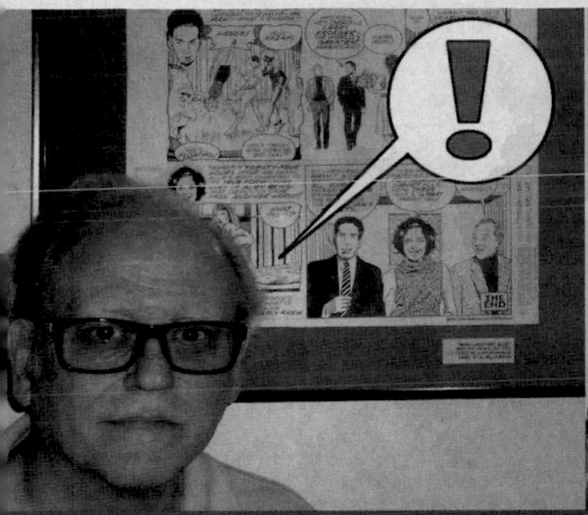

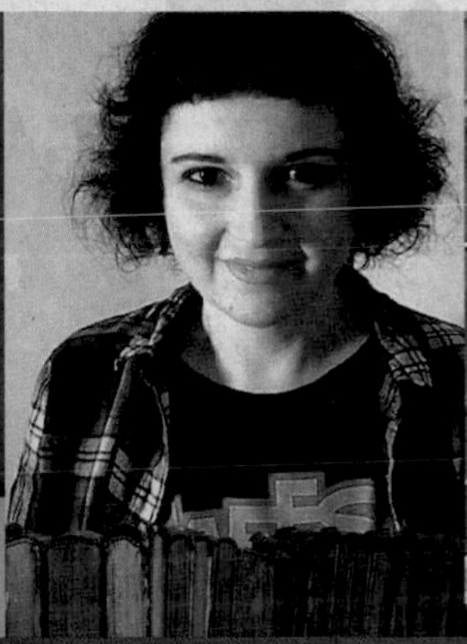

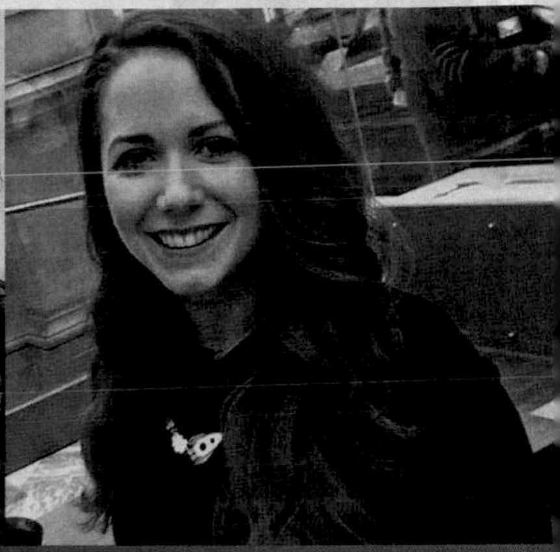

JOHN WORKMAN

managed to turn a love for the comics form into a career. During the past five decades, he has held the positions of editor, writer, art director, penciler, inker, colorist, letterer, production director, and book designer for various companies.

He created (with some help from Bhob Stewart and Bob Smith) the offbeat stories in **WILD THINGS** (with much of that material having first appeared in **STAR*REACH** and **HEAVY METAL**) and both wrote and drew the comics series **SINDY**, **FALLEN ANGELS** and **ROMA**. In 1991, he reflected on model Bettie Page in **BETTY BEING BAD** (Eros) and later produced the hardbounds **HEAVY METAL: 25 YEARS OF CLASSIC COVERS AND INNOCENT IMAGES: THE SEXY FANTASY FEMALES OF VIPER AND KISS**, as well as **THE ADVENTURES OF ROMA**, a reformatted graphic novel version of his earlier series.

He continues to write and draw — and to do a whole lot of lettering — for a number of comics companies on an international level.

MELINA MIKULIC

hasn't yet won an Eisner Award for Best Publication Design, for one simple reason: she's designed more than a thousand gorgeous comic books (including Fibra's editions of Moebius and Tezuka, and Marjane Satrapi's **PERSEPOLIS**) but all on the wrong continent. That is about to change.

She is a Master of Arts, and graduated from the Faculty of Design in Zagreb, Croatia, where she was born. As a graphic designer, she is primarily engaged in design for print, with a growing interest in illustration and interactive media. She now lives in Rijeka, where despite enjoying the Mediterranean climate, she rarely sees the sun, as she spends her time wandering through shadowy landscapes of fonts and letters.

RACHAEL FULTON

is editor of Netflix's Millarworld division, where she's currently producing **THE MAGIC ORDER**, **PRODIGY** and **SHARKEY THE BOUNTY HUNTER**.

She's also in charge of **KICK-ASS: THE NEW GIRL 1-3** and all volumes of **HIT-GIRL'S** world tour. Her past credits as editor include **EMPRESS**, **JUPITER'S LEGACY 2**, **REBORN**, and **KINGSMAN: THE RED DIAMOND**.

She is collections editor for the most recent editions of **KINGSMAN: THE SECRET SERVICE** and all volumes of **KICK-ASS: THE DAVE LIZEWSKI YEARS**.

She tweets about feminism, comics, and cats from the handle @Rachael_Fulton.

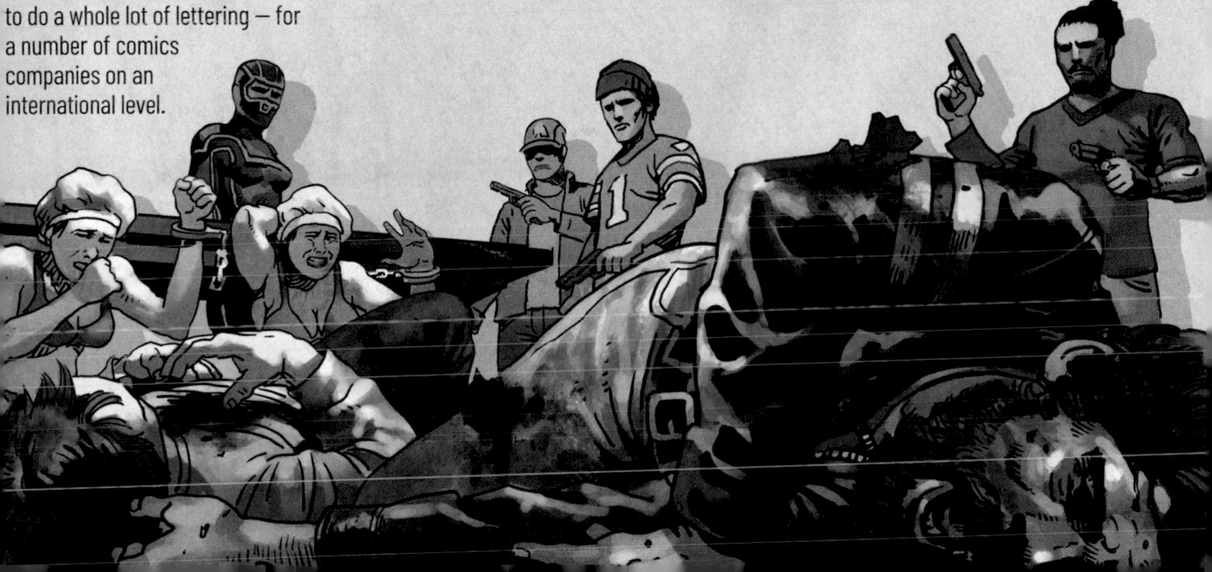

MARCELO FRUSIN
SKETCHES

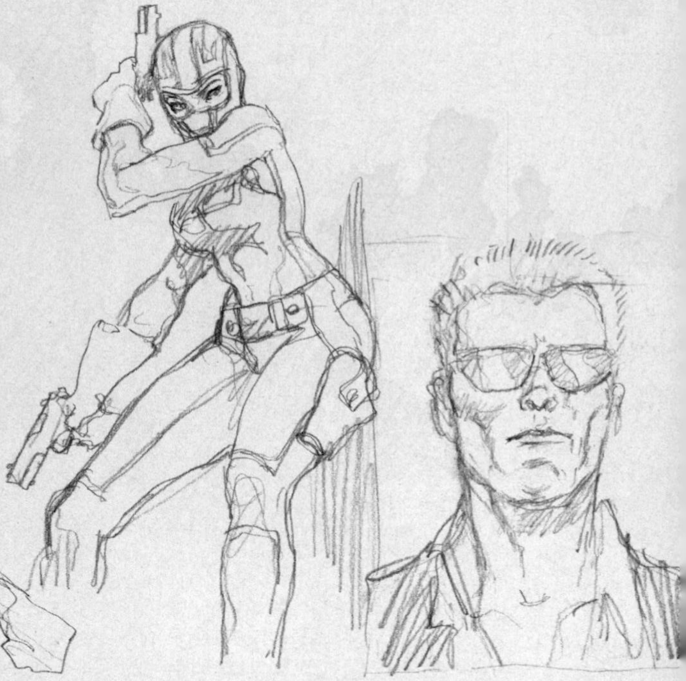

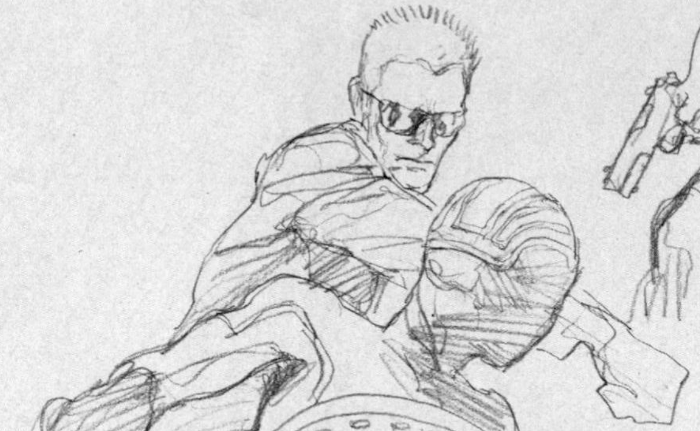

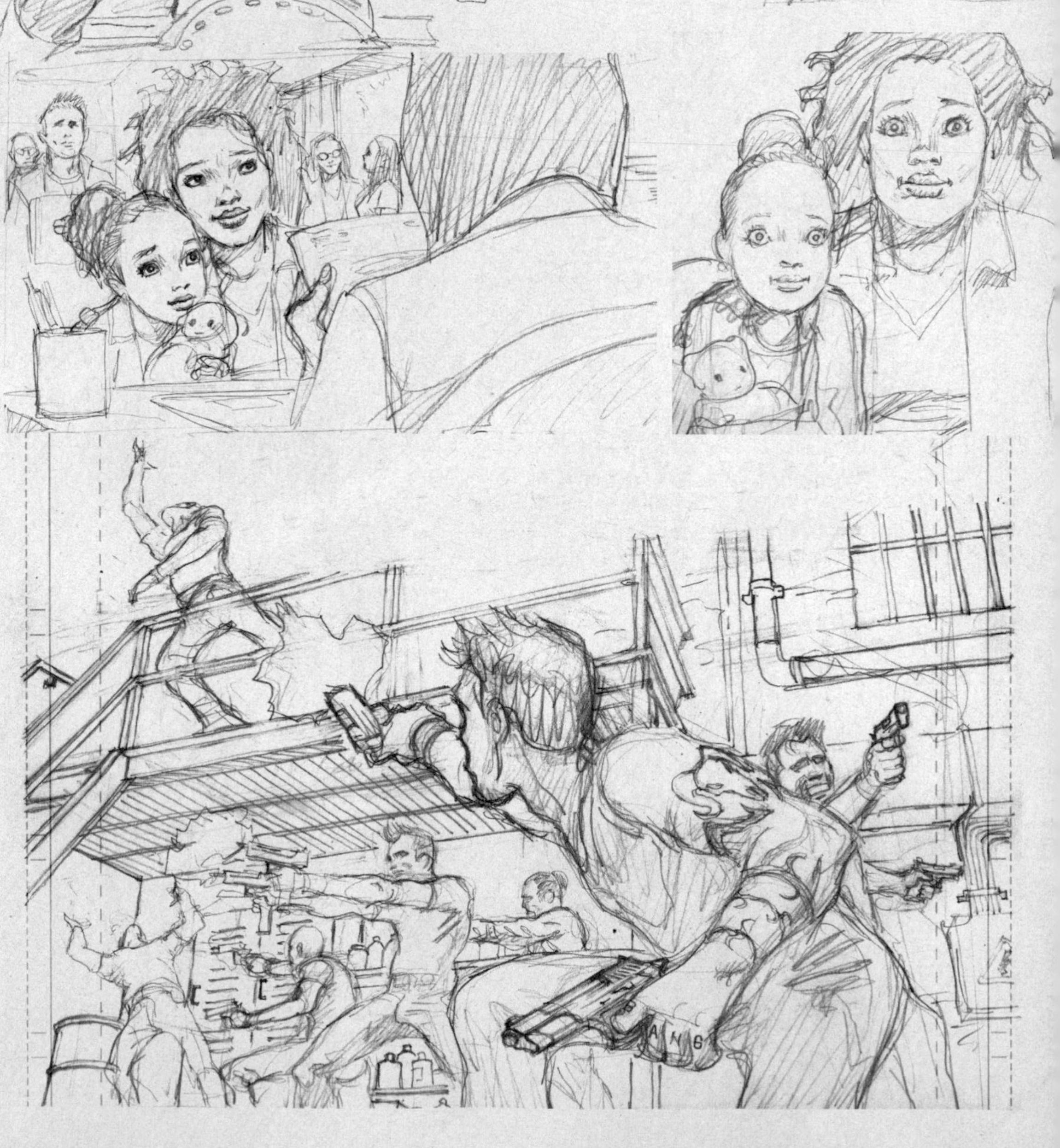

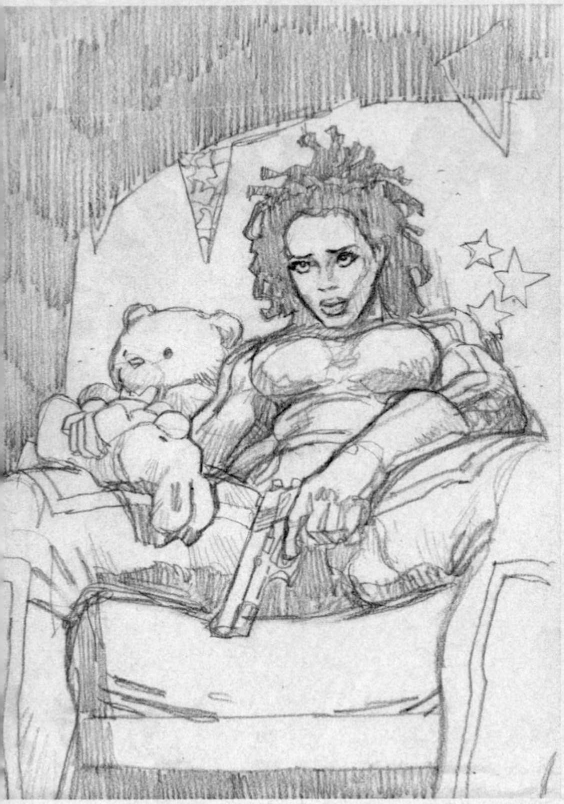

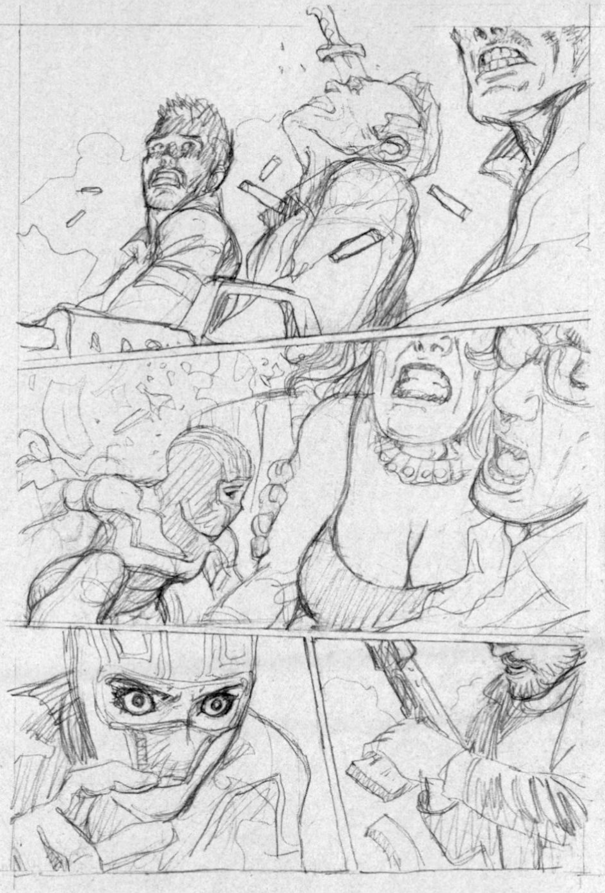

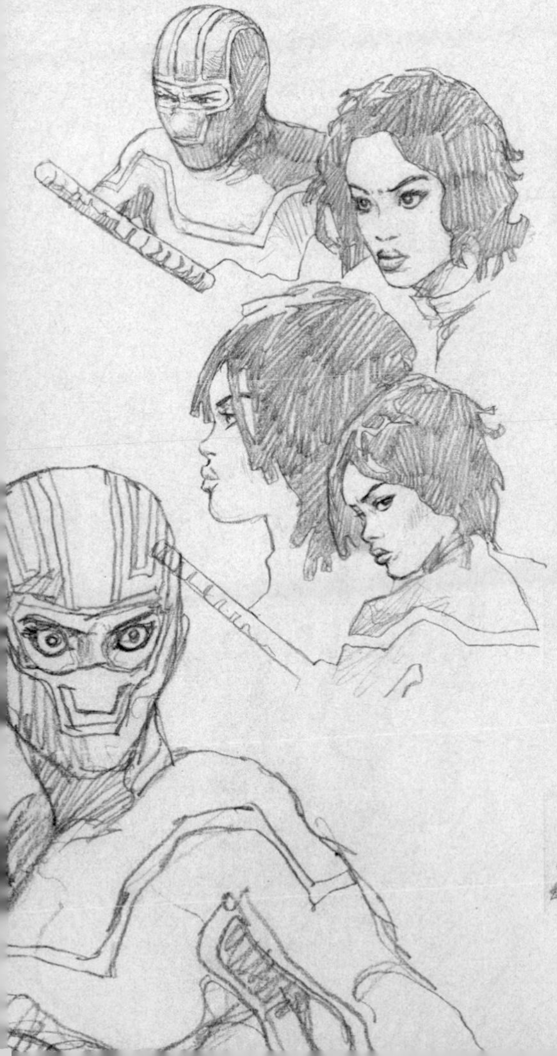

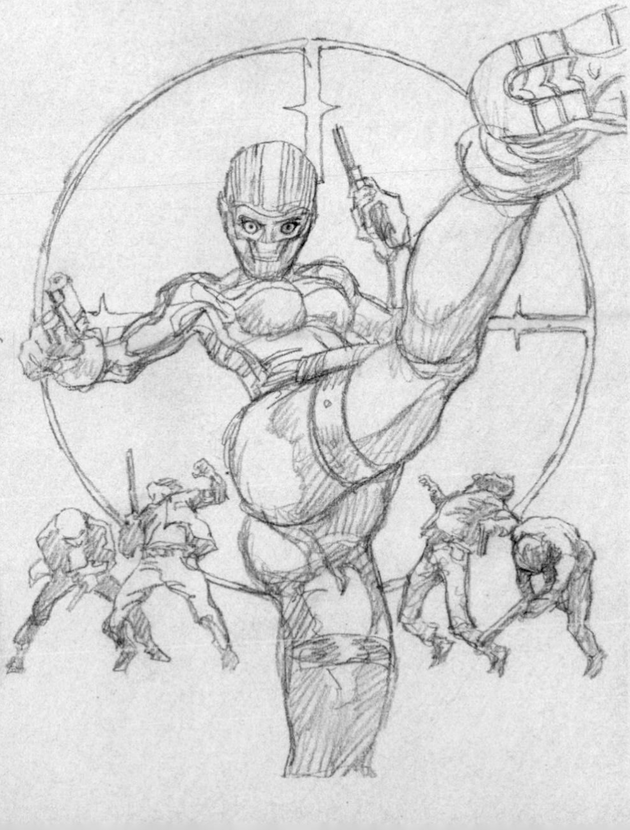

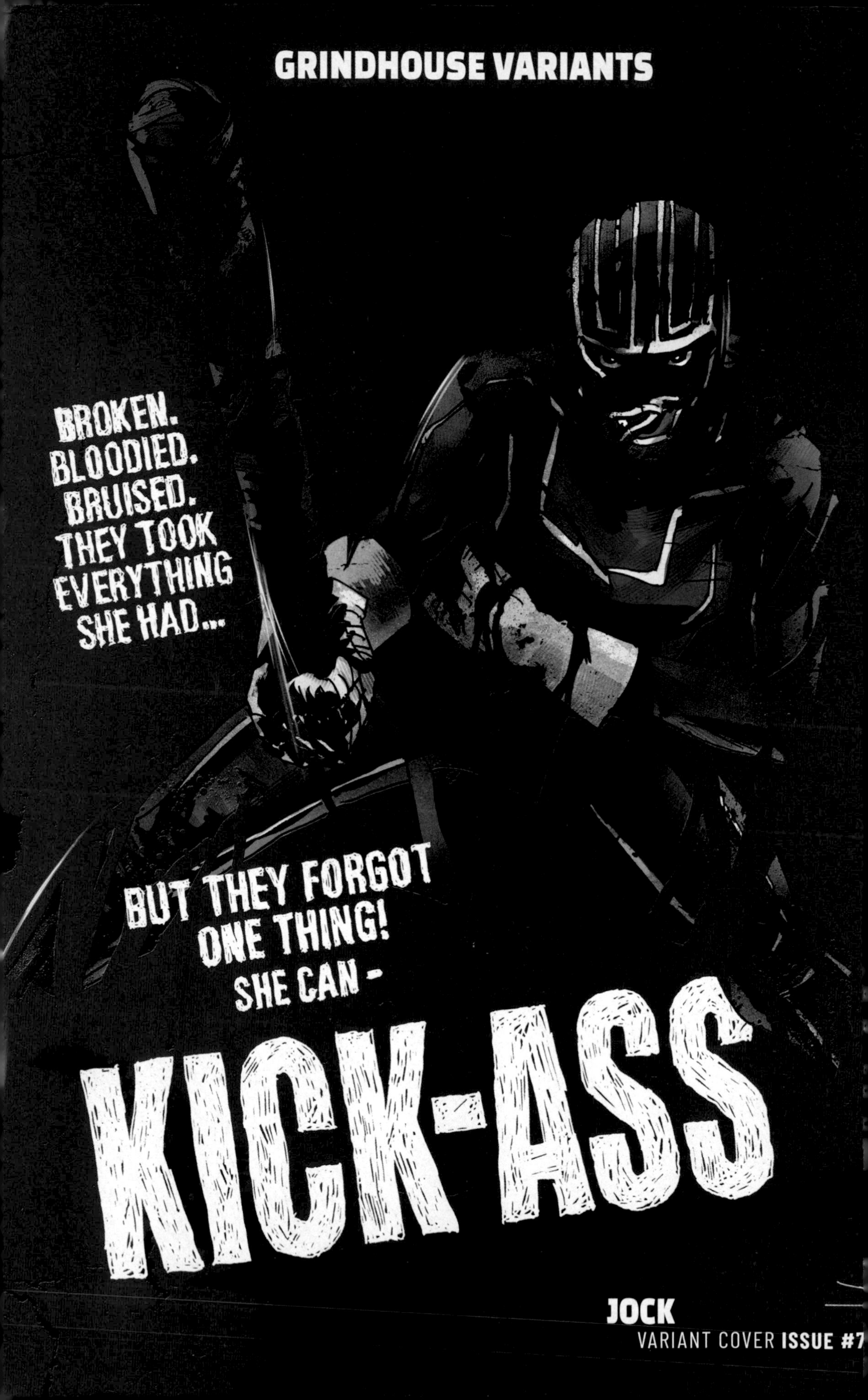
GRINDHOUSE VARIANTS
BROKEN. BLOODIED. BRUISED. THEY TOOK EVERYTHING SHE HAD...
BUT THEY FORGOT ONE THING! SHE CAN -
KICK-ASS
JOCK
VARIANT COVER ISSUE #7

RAFAEL GRAMPÁ
VARIANT COVER **ISSUE #7**

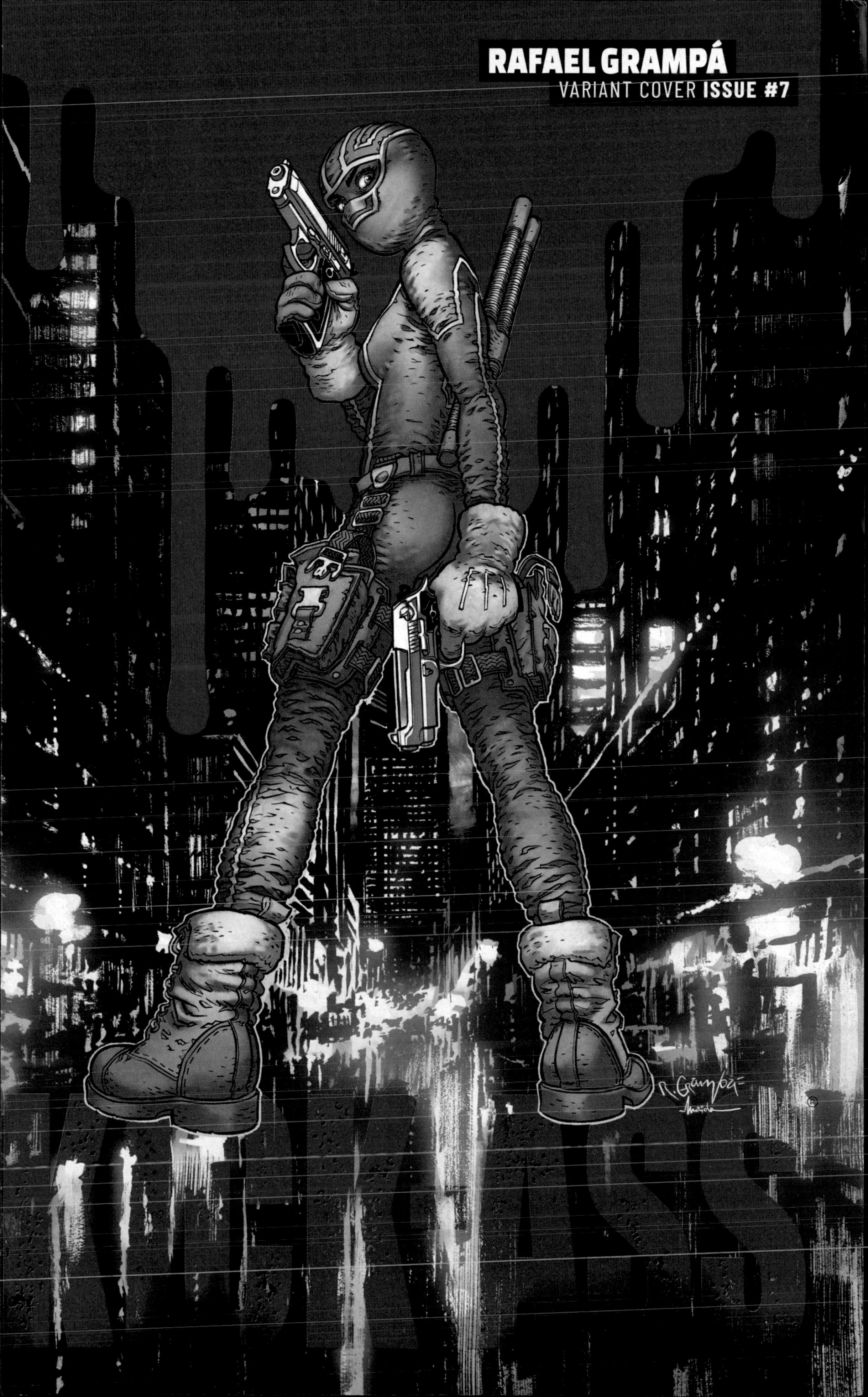

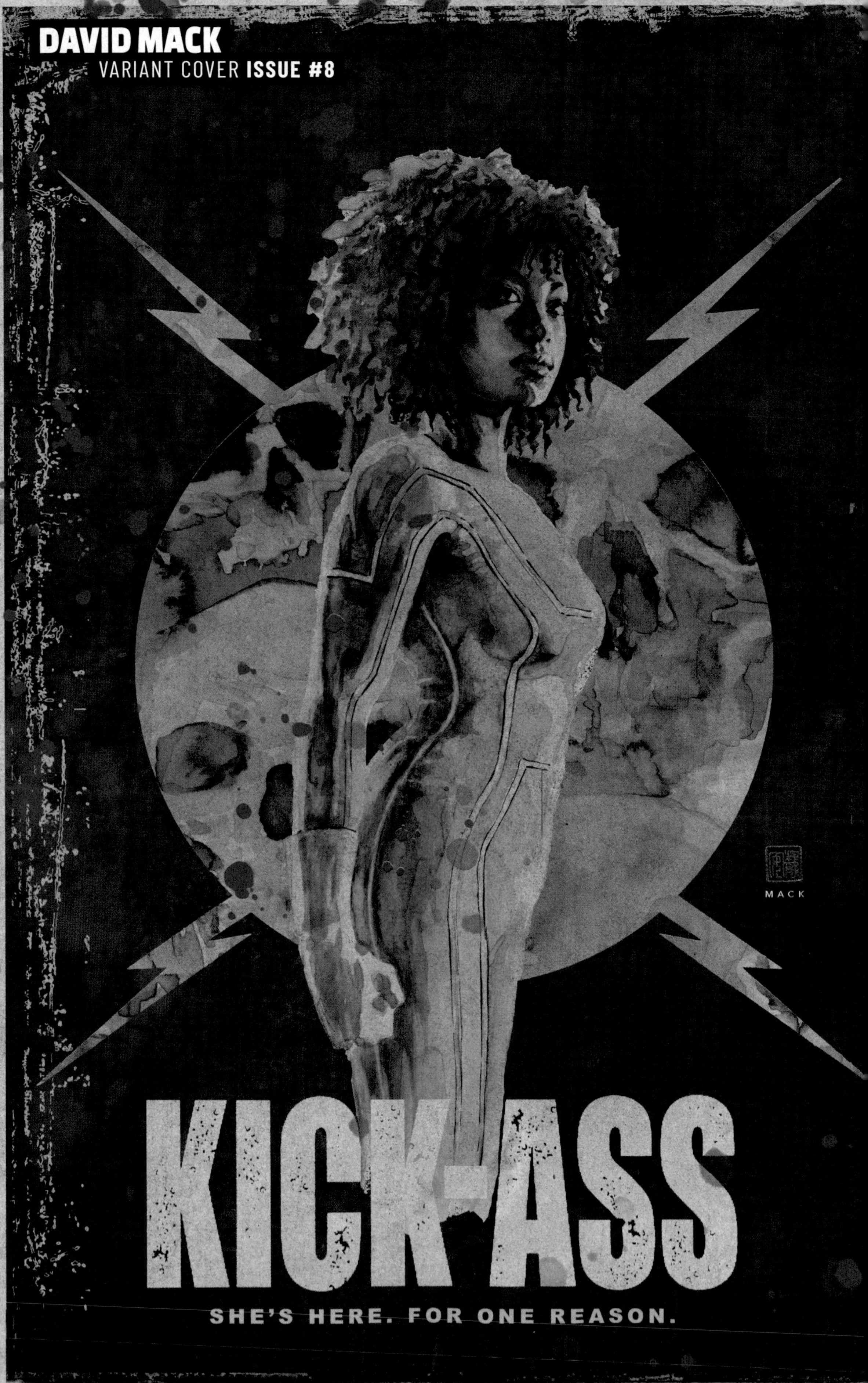
DAVID MACK
VARIANT COVER ISSUE #8
MACK
KICK-ASS
SHE'S HERE. FOR ONE REASON.

CHRISTIAN WARD
VARIANT COVER **ISSUE #9**

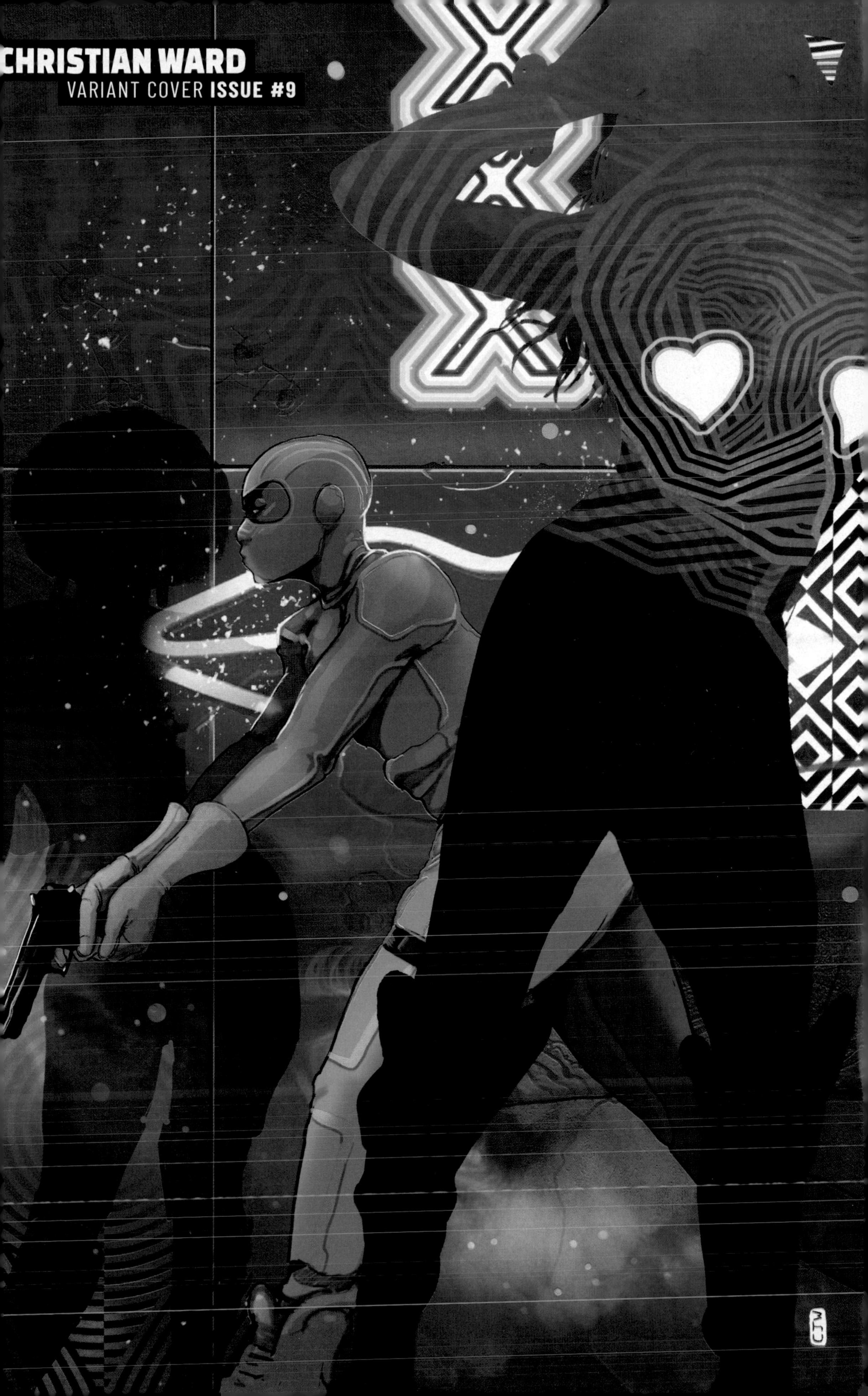

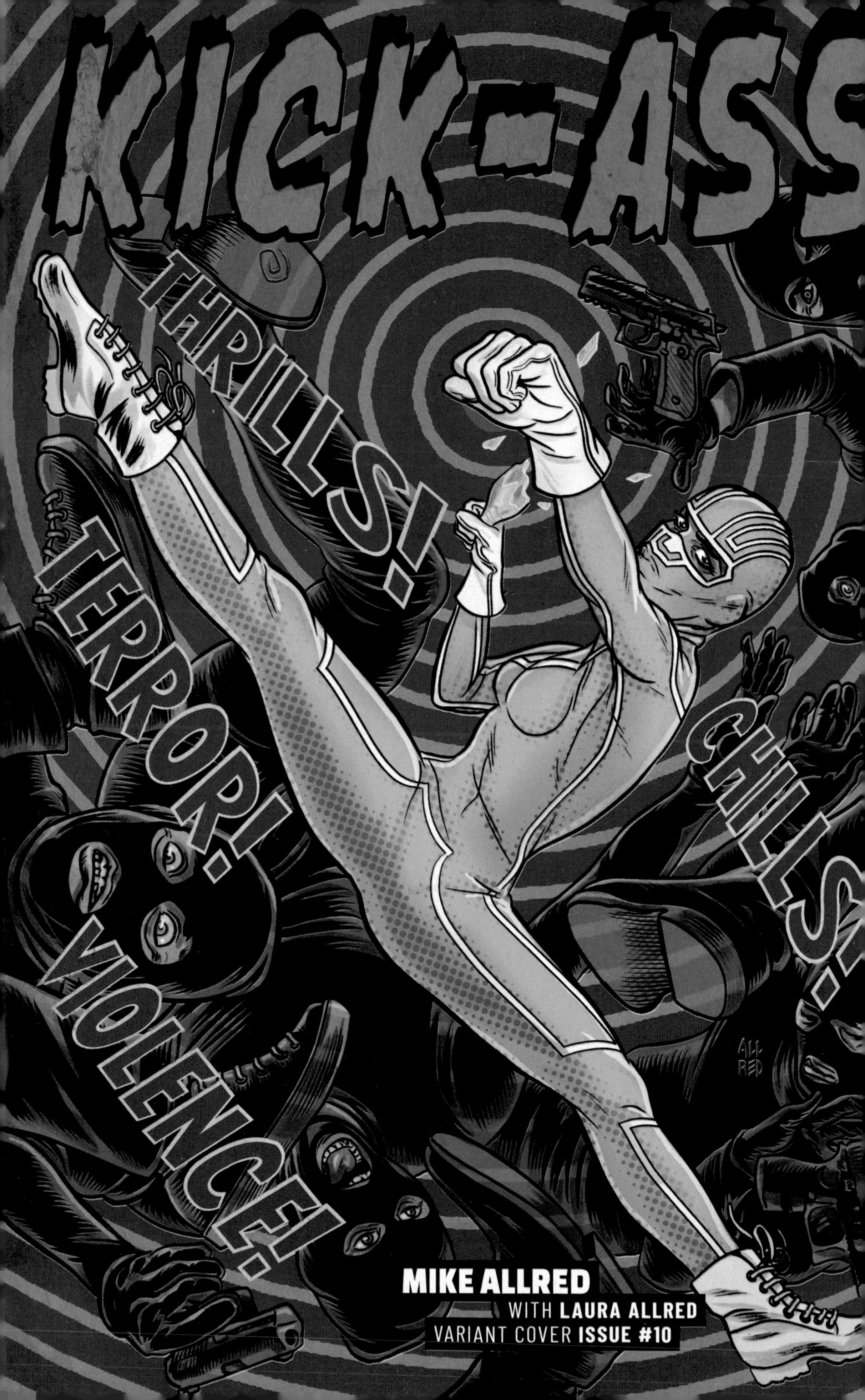
KICK-ASS
THRILLS!
TERROR!
CHILLS!
VIOLENCE!
ALLRED

MIKE ALLRED
WITH **LAURA ALLRED**
VARIANT COVER **ISSUE #10**

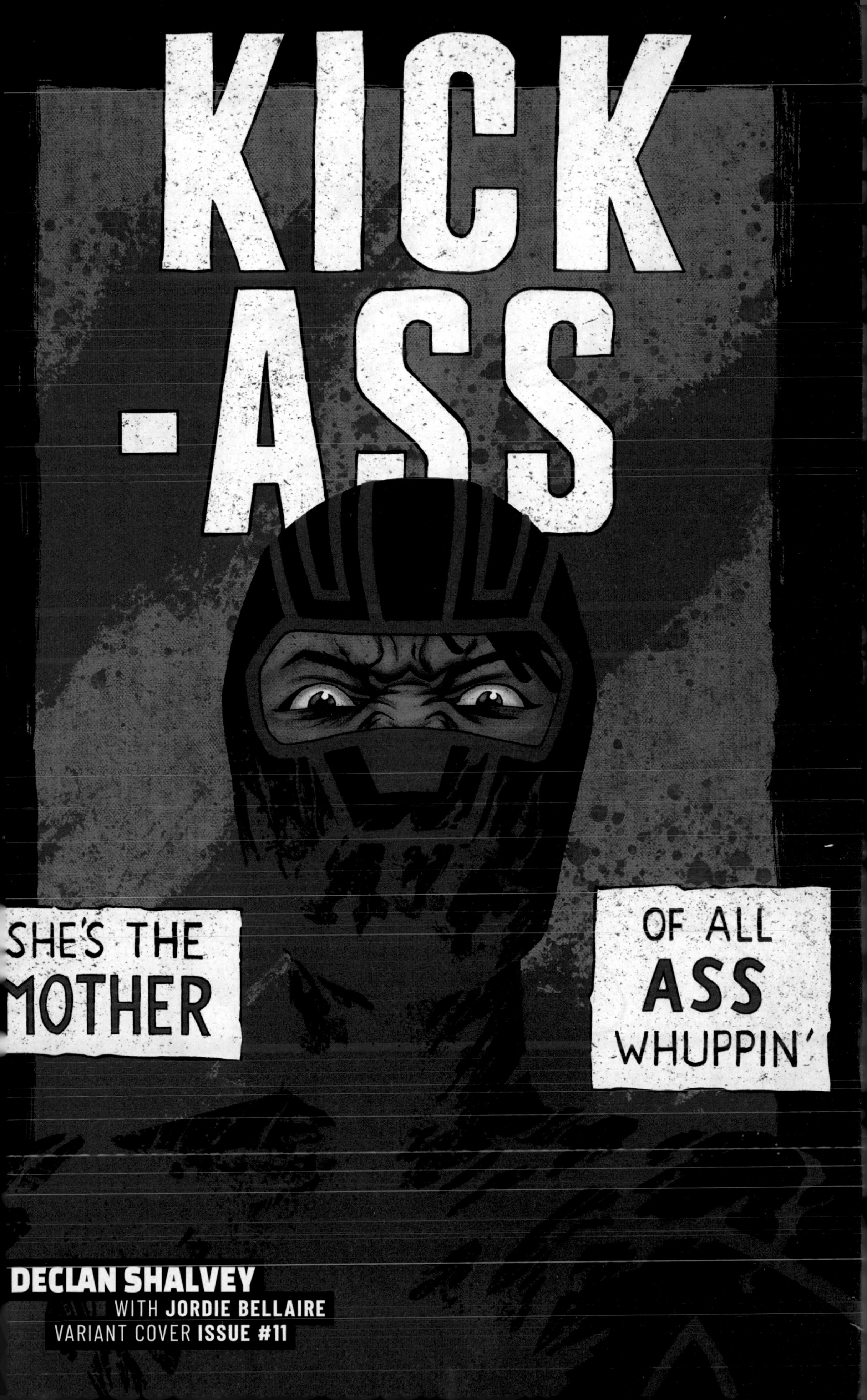
KICK-ASS
SHE'S THE MOTHER
OF ALL ASS WHUPPIN'
DECLAN SHALVEY
WITH JORDIE BELLAIRE
VARIANT COVER ISSUE #11

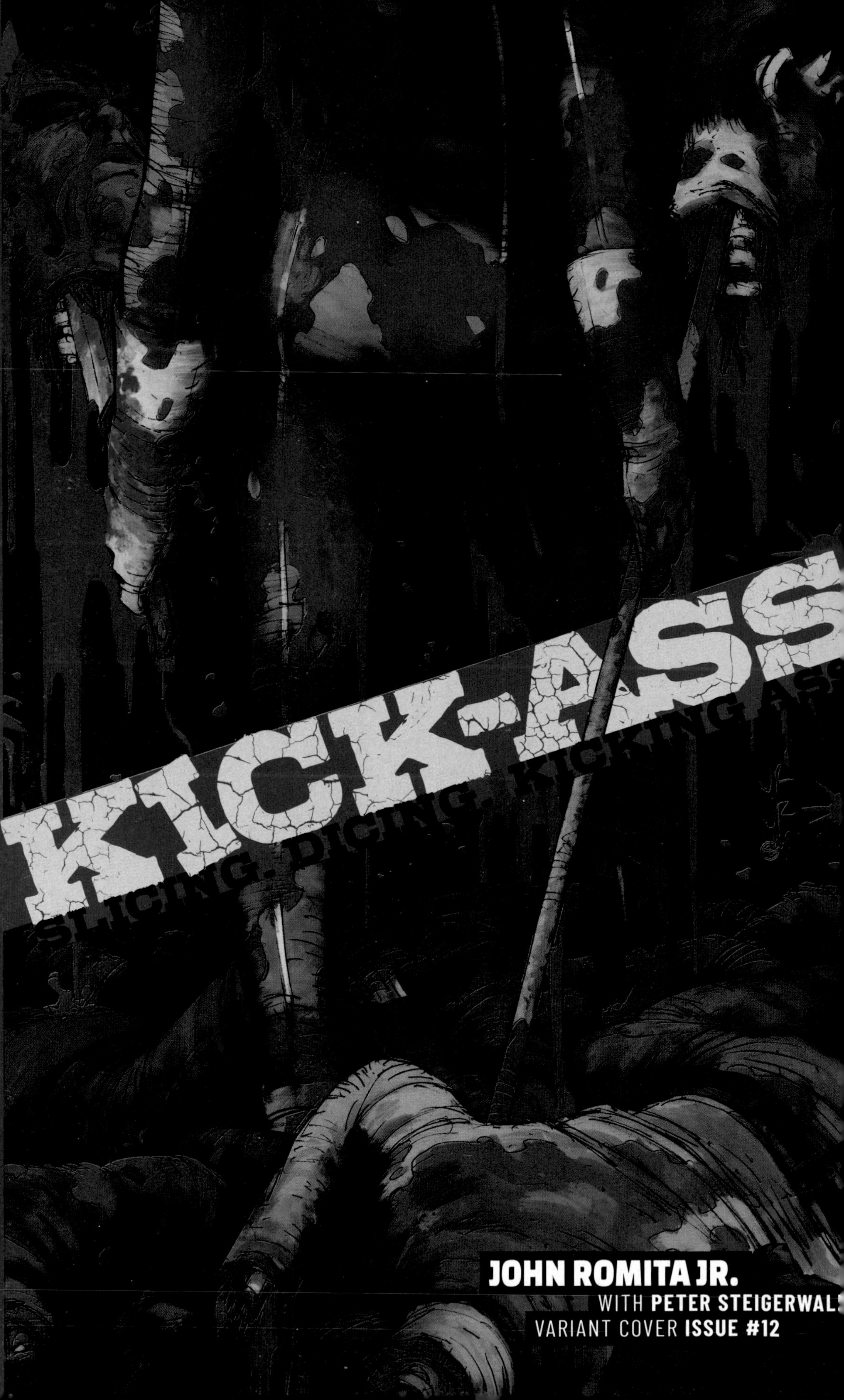
KICK-ASS
SLICING. DICING. KICKING AS
JOHN ROMITA JR.
WITH PETER STEIGERWAL
VARIANT COVER ISSUE #12